THE OTHER SIDE OF THE TRACK

It's the second year of the Great War, and eighteen-year-old Rosie Little of the Queen Alexandra's nursing service works at Charing Cross Station, helping the injured and shell-shocked troops returning from the Front. One weary soldier, Private Joe Upton, invalided out of the army after surviving a gas attack, is instantly captivated by the lovely Rosie. Falling deeply in love the young couple set up home together, but all too soon family conflicts drive a wedge between them, and their future looks uncertain. Rosie and Joe are about to face their toughest test...

THE OTHER SIDE
OF THE TRACK

THE OTHER SIDE OF THE TRACK

by

Victor Pemberton

Magna Large Print Books
Long Preston, North Yorkshire,
BD23 4ND, England.

British Library Cataloguing in Publication Data.

Pemberton, Victor
    The other side of the track.

    A catalogue record of this book is
    available from the British Library

    ISBN 0-7505-2614-9
    ISBN 978-0-7505-2614-2

First published in Great Britain in 2006 by Headline Book Publishing

Published in Large Print 2006 by arrangement with
Headline Book Publishing Ltd.

Magna Large Print is an imprint of Library Magna Books Ltd.

Printed and bound in Great Britain by
T.J. (International) Ltd., Cornwall, PL28 8RW

For Mervyn Haisman
and dedicated to the memory of
those two lovely girls,
Vina and Judy

Rosie Lee, Rosie Lee,
Oh, how I love you,
Saviour of life, weaver of dreams,
Oh, how I love you.

Dark of night, cold outside,
War, bombs and danger.
But warm and tender is your touch,
A glow of light, a ray of hope,
Oh, Rosie Lee, how I love you.

Prologue

1977

Rosie Upton looked out at the crowds of spectators gathered around the Cenotaph in Whitehall. It was a typical November morning, drab and grey, with an obstinate drizzle leaving the uncovered heads damp under the relentlessly gloomy sky. As usual, Remembrance Sunday was a day of memories for the old soldiers, sailors, airmen, land army girls, nurses, men and women of the auxiliary services, all lined up, a sea of faces. Many of them had seen the worst of at least one war, and some had lived through the hell of two or more. It was a day to look back and contemplate, to remember those who had never returned to the green shores of their homeland. As always, the Queen was there with her husband, Prince Philip, to honour those who had sacrificed their lives for the freedom of the nation. The Prime Minister, parliamentarians, diplomats and representatives from every walk of life were also in attendance.

But it would not have escaped the notice of some that it was also Rosie Upton's day, standing there with her walking stick, protected from the rain by an umbrella staunchly held over her by a young soldier from the Queen's Royal Dragoons, himself just back from a tour of duty in the troubled streets of Northern Ireland. Her once dark brown

13

hair was now a pure white, white as the snow that had so often piled high on top of the old railway carriage back in Holloway, the home that had once been a love nest for her and her Joe. But although her face was now lined, and those once deep brown eyes were more faded in the grey light of another era, the gentle smile was unmistakably that of Rosie, once Rosie Little, once Rosie Lee, the Rosie Lee of a bygone age who had captivated the only man she had ever loved.

'I bet this brings back a few mem'ries, don't it, ma'am?' asked the young East End soldier, after the Service of Remembrance had come to an end with the poignant wail of 'The Last Post'. Rosie looked at him, smiled, and gently touched that special medal that was hanging around her neck. Yes, it did bring back memories – memories that spanned a good part of the last century – and by the time she had lined up with all the other veterans for their annual march past, her foot was tapping up and down to the strains of 'Little Dolly Daydream'. And why not? After all, a long time ago it had been *her* song...

Chapter 1

A warm summer breeze flirted with the grey stone surface of Platform 2. It was such a stiflingly hot August day that the passengers thronging the fore-court of John Hawkshaw's grand rectangular-shaped railway station at Charing Cross were grateful for even this relief from the midday humidity. Today, as every day since the outbreak of war with Kaiser Wilhelm's Germany the year before, in August 1914, the place was a sea of khaki uniforms, scattered intermittently with the long white aprons of Queen Alexandra's Imperial Military Nursing Service and the Territorial Force Nursing Services. Relatives and friends waited anxiously at the ticket barrier, counting the minutes to the arrival of the first military hospital train from Folkestone, which carried their loved ones back from the ravaged battlefields of France. Ladies used their handkerchiefs to dab away the perspiration from their moist foreheads, whilst elderly, grim-faced men, too old to answer Lord Kitchener's call to join up, fanned themselves incessantly with straw boaters or workmen's flat caps, dreading what they were about to see on that first train. On two other platforms, steam engines, leading carriages crammed to capacity with more troops for the Western Front, bellowed out from their funnels palls of thick black smoke, which spiralled up to the sooty glass roofs above the platforms. War had come to Charing Cross with a vengeance. It had not ended by that first Christmas, as so many optimists had predicted.

Rosie Little waited patiently at the far end of Platform 2, struggling to keep her large-brimmed straw hat with the navy-blue ribbon under control. The hat had seemed a suitable choice to wear when she got up that morning, for the sun had been blazing through her bedroom window, but once the stiff summer breeze had started, for the past half-hour it had become a battle of wills.

15

Fortunately, the large urn of tea she had just boiled up over a Primus stove on her stall, provided by Queen Alexandra's Imperial Military Nursing Service, was now ready for the hordes of thirsty soldiers who would soon be arriving on the military hospital train. She had only recently turned eighteen and was new to the nursing service. Being as yet untrained, the only voluntary war work she was eligible for was making tea for wounded troops returning to Blighty, which meant that for the time being she had to continue wearing her civilian clothes. Today she wore a form-hugging ankle-length cream dress, her status denoted by a Red Cross armband.

During the few months that she had been doing the job, Rosie had made her mark with the returning soldiers, who had warmed to her welcoming smile and inviting cups of tea so much that they had bestowed on her the rhyming nickname of Rosie Lee.

At precisely one minute past midday, the shrill call of a train whistle echoed out across the River Thames as the hospital train made its approach across Charing Cross Bridge. At the ticket barrier on Platform 2, there was a sudden burst of excitement tinged with intense anxiety, the waiting crowds desperate to catch a glimpse of the train as it gradually slowed to a halt at the buffers, steam cascading out from beneath the engine.

At her trolley, Rosie, assisted by her trainee nurse friend Eunice Huggins, immediately started pouring cups of tea, lining them up ready for the thirsty soldiers. At the same time, nurses from both services climbed out of the carriages to help their wounded patients on to the platform, aided by a flurry of nurses who had been waiting for them. It was a poignant sight, for many of the young soldiers had their eyes bandaged, and had to wait for their wounded colleagues to line up with them for the slow move off towards ambulances waiting outside the station.

Rosie and Eunice sprang into action, taking as many cups of tea as Eunice could carry on a tray across to the injured men waiting patiently in line. As they did so, there was a huge cheer from the waiting relatives and friends at the ticket barrier, which coincided perfectly with the sound of a military brass band further along the platform, striking up a boisterous version of 'Take Me Back To Dear Old Blighty', which somehow seemed incongruous with so many wounded men being helped off the train. Rosie started handing out tea from Eunice's tray to the men queuing along the platform. Most of them were victims of poison-gas attacks on the battlefield, their eyes bandaged because of the effects of the deadly new weapon. This was not the first time Rosie had gone through the sad ritual of helping each man to take hold of a cup with both hands.

'Fanks, miss,' said one of them, a heavily bandaged youngster of no more than her own age, with a broad, cheeky grin.

'Sugar, Tommy?' Rosie asked, covering his hands gently with her own.

'Nah,' replied the young private, with a pure cockney accent. 'Sweet enuff, darlin'!' He tried a chuckle, but it was pretty hollow, and his grin soon faded.

Rosie moved down the line, handing out cups of tea one by one. But just when her hands were full, a sudden gust of wind lifted her hat right off her head, sending it flapping off along the platform towards the ticket barrier. All she could do was to gasp helplessly, and carry on with what she was doing. Then, to her astonishment, one of the soldiers in the queue suddenly broke ranks, and rushed after the hat, which seemed to have a will of its own. Stamping on the brim with his foot, he reached down, picked it up, and took it back to Rosie. It was the young private with the cheeky grin. 'Sorry it's got me boot mark on it, miss,' said the soldier, his cockney accent now betraying a hint of Yorkshire. 'At least it didn't end up on the track.'

Astonished, Rosie took the hat from him, and fixed it back on with her large hatpin. 'Thank you, Tommy,' she said with a grateful smile, aware that the private was wearing a white bandage over only one eye. 'But you shouldn't have bothered. It's only an old hat.'

'Not ter me, it's not,' replied the young soldier. 'It's *your* hat. The moment we pulled in, I saw yer from the carriage window. I took a real shine to yer. I wondered wot yer voice sounded like.'

'Not *too* disappointed, I hope?' asked Rosie, slowly moving on, handing out more cups of tea, and trying to be heard above the thumping sound of the military band.

The young soldier grinned. He had loved Rosie's posh voice. 'Oh, no,' he replied gauchely. 'I weren't disappointed. I like the way yer talk.'

Rosie thanked him with a huge smile. Whilst she

waited for Eunice to collect more cups of tea from the trolley, she found herself drawn into a brief conversation with the young soldier. He was wearing no uniform cap so she could see that he had cropped sandy hair, a fairly pallid complexion, and the one eye that was visible was pale blue.

'What happened to you, Tommy?' she asked tentatively.

'Chlorine gas,' yelled the young soldier, over the final strains of 'Take Me Back To Dear Old Blighty'. 'When we went over the top, Fritz was waitin' fer us. 'E give us a real basinful. I was lucky. Most of my mates got done over wiv mustard. Can't tell yer where it 'appened. 'Ush-'ush, an' all that.' As he spoke, he broke into a coughing fit, wheezing so violently that Rosie instinctively put her arm round his waist to support him.

'Are you all right?' she asked.

The young soldier took a moment to recover, then once the music in the background had stopped, he looked up and straight into her eyes. 'Wot's yer name, miss?' he asked.

Rosie was a bit taken aback by so sudden a question, and surprised herself by answering with a gentle smile, 'Rosie.'

'Rosie Lee,' said the young soldier.

'Rosie Little,' replied Rosie, correcting him.

'You're Rosie Lee ter me,' insisted the soldier. 'You're Rosie Lee ter all of us. I've 'ad quite a few cuppas from uvver Rosie Lees since we got back ter Blighty, but none of 'em are like you.' He grinned. 'My name's Joe,' he said, 'Joe Upton. You can call me Joe.'

'I have to get back to work, Joe,' said Rosie,

19

taking cups of tea from the replenished tray Eunice had just brought over to her. 'You'll be on your way to hospital soon.'

'I'm a Spud,' said Joe. 'That's wot my mates in the regiment call me. They call any bloke who comes from Yorkshire a Spud.'

'I know,' replied Rosie, moving along the queue of soldiers, carefully handing them cups of tea. 'Since I started doing this job, I've met a lot of Spuds. They've all been very nice.'

'Like me?' asked Joe, cheekily.

Rosie grinned back briefly. 'You're *all* very nice,' she replied tactfully. As she spoke, the rasping voice of a sergeant major bellowed out along the platform. 'Line up now, you men! Time ter move off!'

'Come on, Spud!' called one of Joe's mates. ''E'll 'ave yer knackers off!'

Joe turned and started back towards his place in the queue. He was about to call back to Rosie but the band struck up again with a song that prompted all the soldier lads to join in. It was a great current favourite, 'Little Dolly Daydream'.

'See yer soon – Rosie Lee!' called Joe, waving madly to her as he rejoined his mates in the long line-up along the platform.

Rosie smiled and waved back. What a character, she thought. After all he had been through, he was still determined to be himself.

'Right yer are, men!' bawled the sergeant major, over the lilting chorus of 'Little Dolly Daydream'. 'By the right – slow march.'

The long line of young soldiers shuffled off. It was more of a crawl than a march, but it was proud, and poignant, each of them clinging to the back of the shoulder of the man in front. As they reached the ticket barrier, the waiting crowd surged forward to greet them. It was a tearful, joyous reunion, with small children waving Union Jack flags, wives, mothers and girlfriends throwing their arms around their loved ones, and the public throwing roses as the soldiers climbed into the back of specially prepared ambulances.

Rosie watched them all go. It was a scene she had already grown used to. But for some reason, this time it was different. Her thoughts were dominated by the face of that young soldier with the bandage over one eye, that cheeky but irresistible grin that brought a smile to her face. Once again a warm breeze suddenly whistled along the rapidly deserted platform, but this time Rosie made quite sure that she held on to her hat.

Once they had finished their duties at Charing Cross Station, Rosie and Eunice had to make a quick dash to the headquarters building of Queen Alexandra's Imperial Military Nursing Service in Knightsbridge, where they would spend several hours learning how to deal with severe body wounds, respiratory diseases caused by poison-gas attacks and basic jobs such as making beds and washing severely disabled patients. It was all part of their speedy course in general nursing, for with the war up front intensifying, there was now a real urgency to train new nurses and both girls yearned to do their bit for the war effort.

Eunice was a year older than Rosie. She had left school when she was only twelve years old, having come from a pretty down-and-out family in Shoreditch. Ever since she had joined QAIMNS only a few months before, she had shown a real aptitude for the work, and in some cases caught on to things much quicker than the more educated Rosie, especially in the understanding way she talked with some of the more critically injured soldiers. But then, Eunice had a particular reason for wanting to help these desperate survivors, for her own young brother had been killed during the early days of the fighting in France.

Despite the delights of a beautiful afternoon, there was a gloomy atmosphere between the two girls as the tram wound its way along the Embankment towards the Kingsway Tunnel beneath Holborn. Even with their few months' experience dealing with military hospital trains, the sight of so many maimed young soldiers lined up on the railway platforms each day deeply depressed them.

When Rosie finally spoke, she assumed that Eunice had been sharing her thoughts. 'It's so unfair,' she said. 'It should never have been allowed.'

Eunice looked at her with a start. 'What shouldn't?' she asked.

'I mean it's obvious, isn't it?' replied Rosie, making no sense at all.

'Rosie. What're yer talkin' about?'

'The war,' replied Rosie, as if expecting her friend to have listened to everything that had been going through her mind. 'This awful war. It's a crime to have sent all those boys out to fight a war that most of them don't even understand.'

'Somebody 'as ter do it, Rosie,' said Eunice. 'Somebody 'as ter keep the flag flyin'.'

Rosie looked at her in absolute astonishment. 'Eunice!' she spluttered. 'How can you say such a thing after what happened to your brother?'

Eunice turned away, and looked out of the window. She had to shield her soft grey-green eyes from the dazzling afternoon sun, and her mass of bright red curls shimmered every time the tram swayed. 'Sid knew wot 'e was doin',' she replied wistfully. ''E was only seventeen when 'e took the King's shillin' last year. 'E never told any of us wot 'e was up to. 'E made up 'is mind, an' that's all there was to it. By the time Mum an' Dad could do anyfin' about it, 'e'd finished 'is trainin', an' was over the top.' She turned briefly back to Rosie. ''E was no diff'rent ter the rest of 'em, Rosie. They reckoned it'd all be over by Chrismas. Sid wanted ter make sure 'e did 'is bit. I'm proud of 'im. Proud of wot 'e was, an' wot he did. Sid was the best bruvver anyone could ever 'ave.'

Rosie understood what Eunice was saying, but she couldn't bring herself to agree. In her judgement those young men she saw arriving on that platform every day had been coerced into a war under the pretext that they were fighting for the survival of King and country. But was that *really* what it was all about, she asked herself, or was it just a feud between politicians of different countries, a feud that had already cost the lives of thousands?

'All I 'ope,' continued Eunice, 'is that we get a chance ter do somefin' more than servin' cups er tea on railway platforms. I 'ope they send us up front as quick as possible.'

'That won't happen yet, Eunice,' said Rosie.

'Not until we've finished our training.'

'I 'eard they've got such a shortage of nurses,' said Eunice, 'that they're goin' ter speed up our trainin' as fast as they can. It's not cups er tea they want up front, it's people like us who can save lives.'

Rosie thought about what Eunice had said, and it sent a chill down her spine. When she joined the nursing service, it had somehow not occurred to her that one day she herself might be sent to the very same battlefields as those soldiers she watched arriving off the hospital trains each morning. It was a daunting, unsettling thought, especially for a girl who had never known anything except the comfort of a middle-class home in Camden Road, and by the time she and Eunice had reached the QAIMNS headquarters in Knightsbridge, those thoughts had turned to real concern, especially when they were met on arrival by Sister Maisie MacLellan, the chief nursing officer in charge of training.

'You two lassies had better get a move on,' said Sister Maisie, in her robust Scottish voice. 'The Lady's been waiting to see you since two o'clock.'

'The Lady?' asked Rosie, bewildered that Lady Braintree, chairman of the Queen Alexandra trainee nurses' programme, should want to see them.

'Nobody told us,' added Eunice, a touch indignantly. 'We've bin on duty all mornin'.'

'Now don't get on your high horse, Eunice, dear girl,' said Sister Maisie, who was used to Eunice getting het up at the slightest thing. 'Most of the other girls from your course have been in

24

to see her. It's just a routine interview, that's all.'

After what she and Eunice had been talking about earlier, Rosie wasn't so sure. Her stomach suddenly went terribly tense.

'Now get yourselves in there,' continued Sister Maisie reassuringly. She had a pleasantly lined face, an ample figure and a soft flock of short white hair, which was pinned up beneath her white senior nurse's cap. 'You know what the Lady's like when she has to wait for her afternoon tea.' This was meant to be a joke, but as she hustled the two girls up the long wide marble staircase that led up to the first floor, it was obvious that they were not amused.

On the way up they passed hordes of girls who were hurrying in silence to catch up with their own courses, the newer recruits dressed, like Rosie and Eunice, in civilian clothes, and the more advanced trainees floating up and down the stairs in long white headscarves and uniforms, like heavenly angels moving gracefully to the afflicted soldiers who were waiting for them.

The Lady's office was at the far end of the first-floor landing, but when Rosie and Eunice got there, they had to check their instructions first with the Lady's clerk at a desk outside.

'You can go in together,' said the young woman. 'Madam's expecting you.'

Both girls had seen the Lady several times before, but had never actually been spoken to by her. Rumour had it that she was actually quite wealthy, for her husband, Sir John Braintree, was from an aristocratic family somewhere in the east of England, and an admiral serving with the

Home Fleet. However, despite her apparent affluence, the Lady insisted that she was a working nurse like all the rest of her 'gels', and dressed accordingly in the workday white headscarf and uniform.

'Well, sit you down,' she said in what could only be described as a deep bass voice. 'I've had my lunch. I'm not going to eat you!'

Rosie smiled, relieved by the Lady's lack of formality. Eunice wasn't quite so convinced, and sat stony-faced with Rosie in front of the desk without raising an eye.

'I've called you here,' said the Lady, sitting back in her chair and looking from one to the other of them over the top of her metal-rimmed spectacles, 'because I have some rather important things to say to you.'

Rosie's insides started churning again.

'But first things first,' continued the Lady, a handsome-looking woman who had the energy of someone much younger. 'I've been hearing some rather good reports about you both.'

Rosie and Eunice exchanged brief, astonished looks.

'The boys coming back on the hospital trains have been saying some very nice things about you,' said the Lady. 'They talk about your cheery, welcoming smiles, the way you comfort them.'

'We only serve them cups of tea, madam,' said Rosie, tentatively.

'You've no idea what a cup of tea served by someone with a warm smile can mean to a man who has been close to death,' the Lady said, with her own warm smile for Rosie.

She leaned forward and flicked through a file on her desk, then looked up at Eunice. 'I see you come from quite a large family, Eunice,' she said.

'Yes, madam,' Eunice replied, without looking up at the Lady.

'I'm sorry to see you lost your brother.'

Eunice remained silent.

'It's not easy to accept such a loss.'

Eunice continued to look down at her lap.

By the girl's response, the Lady knew that it would be unwise to pursue the subject any further. She had seen many young girls in those two seats who had gone through the ordeal of a family loss, either a young brother or a father. Nothing anyone could say would ever be able to make up for that loss, but it did give so many the impetus to want to do something positive for the war effort.

'I'm sure you young ladies are aware of the grave situation in France?' the Lady asked.

Both pairs of eyes flicked up at her.

The Lady leaned forward and rested both hands on her desk. 'The word from the Front is that every day the situation is getting worse. The casualties are mounting quite appallingly on both sides.' She sighed, took off her spectacles and placed them on the desk in front of her. 'The problem,' she continued, looking up at them, 'is that we don't have enough nursing strength out there to cope with those casualties. Unfortunately, the number of untrained staff back here in England far exceeds the young ladies who are working night and day out there on the front lines. There's a desperately urgent need to change

27

that situation as soon as possible.'

Rosie felt a distinct pain in her stomach.

'What I'm trying to say is that the service needs to expedite the training programmes and get as many girls out to the front-line field stations as soon as we can.' She paused, and then looked from Rosie to Eunice, then back to Rosie again. 'That's why I'm appealing to you two young ladies.'

Rosie stiffened.

'Oh, not just you two,' continued the Lady. 'I've had this identical conversation with at least half a dozen of your colleagues during the morning. There are so many problems going on up front, especially with poison gas now being used by the Allies as well as the Huns. We need to get as many of you as possible over to field stations as soon as you've completed your training programme.'

''Ow soon will that be, madam?' asked Eunice.

'That's up to you, young lady. Once your instructors are confident you're familiar with the basic groundwork, we'll review the situation. But of course a lot will depend on your own personal commitments. You're still both very young. I won't pretend that taking you out to the battlefield is going to be anything but a distressing experience for you. You'll see some terrible things. Our boys out there are suffering – suffering not only terrible wounds, but real mental trauma. You young ladies will have to learn how to be mothers to them, as well as nurses. D'you think you're up to that?'

'Yes, madam,' replied Eunice firmly, confidently. 'I'm ready ter do anyfin'.'

'Living under stress on the battlefield is not the

same as serving tea on a railway platform, Eunice.'

Eunice stiffened. 'I'm well aware of that, madam,' she replied tersely.

Considering what Eunice had gone through with the loss of her brother up front, the Lady immediately realised she had been tactless. 'I know you do, my dear,' she said with a reassuring smile. 'I know you do.'

She turned to Rosie. 'And what about you, Rosie?'

Rosie took a deep breath. 'I'll do whatever has to be done, madam,' she replied without much conviction.

'I trust neither of you is squeamish?'

Rosie looked at her with a start. 'Madam?' she asked apprehensively.

'I'm sure your tutor has told you that you'll be seeing things out there that a girl of your age might find ... difficult to cope with.'

Rosie lowered her eyes.

Despite the fact that she had interviewed several hundred girls since the start of the war, the Lady was always pained when she had to talk to them like this. Lady Braintree may have given the appearance of being a hard nut, but inside she was sensitive. She had known war at close hand herself, it wasn't pretty, it was soul-destroying. Many times she had seen young girls breaking down in tears at the bedside of a young soldier who had just died, and those memories lingered in her mind, as they would do with the two young girls sitting in front of her now. She deplored the necessity to recruit girls for such a gruelling job and in such a short time, but there was no alternative.

As she looked at Rosie's almost flawless white complexion, her summer hat tilted at a slight angle across her eyes, she could see all the terrible anxieties that were tearing the girl apart. The Lady had read Rosie's file. She knew only too well that the girl had experienced a rather sheltered upbringing and might find it more difficult than her friend Eunice to face up to some of the more extreme horrors ahead of her.

'Have either of you ever seen anyone die?' she asked.

'*I* 'ave,' Eunice answered. 'I was wiv my gran when she died. She 'ad dropsy.'

'Was it a peaceful death?' asked the Lady.

'Oh, yes,' replied Eunice. 'She just closed 'er eyes, an' went ter sleep.'

'Unfortunately,' said the Lady, 'not all the patients you lose will have that luxury.'

Eunice wished she hadn't spoken.

'Rosie?'

Rosie's eyes darted up at her.

The Lady addressed the same question to her, only more sensitively. 'Have *you* ever seen anyone ... pass away?'

For one split second, Rosie panicked. In that subliminal time, so much passed through her mind; death had never been part of her experience. Up until that moment, she had somehow imagined that it was only old people who died, like all her grandparents, and as she had not been there when it happened, she felt totally inadequate to answer such a question. 'There *was* someone,' she recalled quite suddenly. 'It was only a dog. He was very old. But I was very fond of him.' She fidgeted uneasily on her chair. 'I didn't actually *see* him die.'

The Lady smiled gently. She had a kindly face, and the more she smiled, the more she showed just how well she understood what Rosie was trying to say. 'To many of us,' she said reassuringly, 'losing a dog can be just as painful.' She sat back in her chair. 'Just one final matter,' she continued. 'From tomorrow morning, you'll both be relieved of your duties at Charing Cross Station. I want you to get some field training at the Rehabilitation Centre out at Stanmore. You'd better inform your parents that from Monday you'll be accommodated out there until further notice.'

The two girls exchanged brief looks, Eunice enthusiastically, but Rosie's reaction, although brave, was strained.

'I can't impress on you,' continued the Lady, 'how vital it is that we have you both fully operational within the month. Our field hospitals are desperately short of trained nurses. D'you both understand what I'm saying?'

'Yes, madam,' replied Eunice confidently.

'Rosie?' asked the Lady.

'I'll do everything I can, madam,' she replied.

'Thank you,' said the Lady, rising from her chair. 'But before you go, I must warn you of the dangers you face.'

Rosie and Eunice rose from their chairs.

'When we post you out to those field stations,' continued the Lady, 'just remember that you will be on active duty just as much as the soldiers themselves. We've already lost some wonderful young nurses to enemy fire, so please take care.'

When Rosie got home that evening, she was still dazed by the interview with Lady Braintree. Although she had always accepted that enrolling as a nurse during wartime might eventually involve her in some pretty gruelling and harrowing work, she had consistently put out of her mind the possibility that she herself would be called upon to put her own life at risk. She wished she could be more like Eunice; she was as tough as old nails, and came from a family who weren't afraid of roughing it and getting their hands dirty. But for Rosie, being waited on hand and foot had always been a way of life from the moment she was born. The thought of seeing men with appalling injuries, helping doctors to save lives, watching them carry out amputations – all this had never sunk in when she signed up to be a nurse. But this was reality, and at eighteen years old, she became obsessed with the horrifying thought that she might never even reach her nineteenth birthday.

Chapter 2

The Littles' grand Edwardian house in Camden Road was set on four floors, halfway between Camden Town and the Nag's Head in Holloway, and just a short distance up the hill from the grim stone façade of Holloway Women's Prison.

The Little family had lived there for over twenty years, and Rosie and her young brother, Christian, had been born there, delivered by the same two private midwives who had been paid handsomely for their services by Rosie's father, Richard Little, owner of a porcelain factory in Kentish Town. Rosie adored both her parents, especially her mother, Marian, who had been her confidante and close friend ever since she was a child. Unlike Rosie's father, Marian was the kind of person that her two children could turn to for advice, knowing that she would invariably have an answer to everything, whereas Richard Little, a popular and likeable man with both family and employees, rarely had the time to sit down and discuss domestic matters. Unfortunately, Christian, who was nearly four years younger than his sister, was a frail boy, who had been crippled by consumption since he was three years old. Confined to a wheelchair, Christian had been diagnosed as having a short life expectancy, and his family were constantly afraid for him. Rosie adored him, and had a very special relationship with her brother, the two of them sharing secrets that they could never share with anyone else, especially their own parents.

Rosie got home from her nurses' training course just as the family were about to sit down to dinner. She was glad she wasn't late, for old Mrs Winnet, their housekeeper, had cooked an oxtail stew, a favourite with all the family, and the smell of carrots, onions and rich gravy drifted seductively throughout the house.

'Make the most of it,' said Marian, as Rosie

quickly joined them at the dining table. 'The way this war's going, we shan't be able to get luxuries like this for much longer. In *The Times* this morning, it says that the Huns are going to start bombing our food supplies. Everything's badly rationed enough already.'

'I'm afraid it's inevitable, my dear,' added Richard, now in his late forties, with soft grey eyes and an abundance of dark brown hair that was greying at the temples. 'We shall all have to make sacrifices until we lick the bounders.'

'Aren't we making enough sacrifices already, Father?' asked Rosie, while being served some mashed potato by Mrs Winnet.

Richard looked up. 'What d'you mean, Rose?'

'I was at Charing Cross Station again today,' continued Rosie. 'It's heartbreaking to see the awful injuries amongst those poor young soldiers. A lot of them have been gassed. They can hardly breathe.'

'Terrible!' said Marian, who was a few years younger than her husband, with dark brown hair bunched up behind her head, and an off-centre parting, just like Rosie. In fact, though in her mid-forties, with her round, cherubic face she looked so much younger that many people often took her for Rosie's sister.

'I'm afraid that's the price we have to pay for war, Rose,' said Richard.

Rosie put down her knife and fork. 'Yes,' she said firmly. 'But why did we have to go to war in the first place, just because some old archduke had to go and get himself assassinated?'

'Come now, Rose,' returned Richard. 'You're

intelligent enough to know that's not the whole reason.'

Rosie suddenly didn't feel like eating. For one despondent moment, she sat staring at her plate, brimming with the rich stew, whilst unconsciously tidying her already tidy dark brown hair.

'If I was a soldier,' said young Christian, whose pale face was almost the colour of the white shirt he was wearing, '*I'd* want to know why I was going out to fight in a foreign country.'

'If you were a soldier, Christian,' said his father, with a sympathetic smile, 'you would have to obey orders. Otherwise there would be no army to defend us.'

Marian put down her knife and fork, and gently dabbed her lips with her table napkin. 'Well, pray God,' she said, 'you never have to *be* a soldier.' It was a curiously unguarded remark from Marian, considering the sensitive subject of her son's health.

'What about your husband, Mrs Winnet?' asked Rosie, changing the subject and catching the old lady just as she was about to disappear into the kitchen with an empty dish. 'Have you heard from Albert lately?'

'Not yet,' replied Mrs Winnet brightly. 'But I'm sure I will soon. The last letter I got 'e sounded real confident that it wouldn't be long before all the boys come back 'ome.' She quickly returned to her kitchen domain.

'I hope she's right,' said Rosie.

'Stop being so gloomy, darling,' said Marian. 'From all they're saying in the newspapers, our boys are doing a wonderful job out there.'

35

'They are doing a wonderful job, my dear,' said Richard, eating heartily. 'But in war, I'm afraid there are always casualties. That's what being a soldier is all about.'

'It's not only soldiers who suffer, Father,' said Rosie. 'There are women who've had to cope with looking after them in the most terrible conditions. All sorts of jobs – including nurses.'

Suddenly aware of what Rose was implying, both Richard and Marian looked across at her.

'Women should never be allowed to go out to the battlefields,' said Marian nervously. 'It's not natural.'

'Mother,' returned Rosie, 'somebody has to look after the injured. And there's a tremendous shortage of nurses up front.'

Marian swung a look of alarm at her husband.

Richard gently put down his knife and fork. 'Are you trying to tell us something, Rose?' he asked ominously.

Aware that everyone was looking at her, Rosie also put down her knife and fork and looked up. 'Several of us were interviewed by Lady Braintree today. She says that as soon as we've completed our training, we may have to be sent to some of the front-line field stations.'

Marian gasped and clutched her mouth in horror.

'You mean,' asked Richard grimly, 'that they really *are* taking nurses out to the battlefields?'

'Of course, Father,' replied Rosie, not too confidently. 'Somebody has to treat their wounds. Men are dying every day out there.'

'But you're not a man!' insisted Marian, devastated. 'You're only a girl. You're only just eighteen.'

'A lot of those boys up front are only eighteen, Mother,' Rosie reminded her. 'In fact there are plenty of them who are younger, who've lied about their age.'

'If I was a couple of years older *I'd* join up,' said Christian, excited by all the talk.

'Christian!' snapped Marian. 'Don't ever let me hear you say such things!'

'Well, I would!' insisted Christian, whose nose turned up slightly at the tip, just like his sister's, dark brown eyes flashing out of a sickly, pallid complexion. 'We've got to stop the Boche before they take over the whole of Europe!'

Rosie looked across and flashed him a loving smile.

Richard dabbed his lips with his napkin, then put it down beside his plate. 'Rose,' he asked seriously, 'how soon is all this going to happen?'

'I've no idea, Father,' Rosie replied. 'I have to get through my basic training first. I'm being sent to the Rehabilitation Centre out at Stanmore on Monday. But most of the girls think we might be there for only three or four weeks.'

Marian gasped.

'But basic training,' said Richard, 'is hardly going to be enough to deal with the kind of casualties you'll be up against. Surely you need more experience than that?'

Rosie paused a moment before answering. 'The experience I'm going to need,' she replied uneasily, 'is going to have to come at the field station.'

Richard exchanged a pained look with his wife.

They clearly had no more appetite for their dinner.

Ernie Appleton was clearly having a hard time. For nearly three hours he had been the guinea pig whilst the nurses of Team 2 practised on him the many first-aid techniques they had been learning during days of intensive training under the watchful eye of Sister Maisie MacLellan. Fortunately, he only had to do this twice a week, for at the end of each session his bones ached as much as if he was a real patient. Ernie was fifteen years old, and was one of the many young volunteers who were on call for the nurses' training programmes at the QAIMNS HQ in Knightsbridge. With his East End humour he was a breath of fresh air for the nursing team, who enjoyed teasing him whilst they bandaged him up, applied splints to his legs and arms, took his temperature endlessly, listened to his heart through stethoscopes, and took readings of his pulse. All this took place in a mock-up of a field hospital up front, complete with a ward equipped with oxygen cylinders and as many medical aids as were available. Despite the serious tasks they were rehearsing, there was a lot of laughter during these training sessions, which Sister Maisie allowed, only because when it was eventually going to be time for the real thing, there wouldn't be very much to laugh about.

'Come on, Ernie!' bellowed Eunice, who was at Ernie's bedside, struggling to splint one of the boy's legs. ''Ow d'yer expect me ter do this if yer don't raise yer bloomin' leg!'

'Wot d'yer take me for?' protested Ernie, who

38

was already swathed in bandages, with one leg suspended mercilessly high in a sling. 'I ain't a bleedin' contorshionist!'

'Keep still,' snapped Eunice, 'or I'll break yer leg fer real!'

'That's quite enough of that now, Eunice!' said Sister Maisie, leaving the other girls with their mock patients to come across to Eunice and Rosie.

'Just look at 'im, Sister!' protested Eunice. ''E just won't keep 'is leg still!'

'Ernie is a patient, Eunice,' scolded Sister Maisie, in her broad Scottish burr. 'He has wounds that give him great pain, that make it difficult to move his limbs. Don't you think he should be treated with a little more – tender loving care?'

'But–'

'And don't you also think,' continued Sister Maisie, 'that young lassies in Queen Alexandra's Imperial Military Nursing Service should behave like young ladies, and afford their patients the courtesy and respect they deserve?'

Eunice swung a sly look at Ernie, who was grinning at her beneath the bandages, which covered half his face.

'Rosie, my dear,' said Sister Maisie, 'why don't *you* take over?'

'Yes, Sister,' said Rosie dutifully, moving into Eunice's place.

'Remember now,' said Sister Maisie, as she watched Rosie applying the splint to Ernie's leg, 'this young soldier has just been brought in from the battlefield. He's not only in great pain, but he's also suffered extreme trauma.'

'Yes, Sister,' said Rosie, who was being as gentle as a lamb with Ernie's leg.

As she moved off, Sister Maisie threw a disapproving glance at Eunice, who put her tongue out at her the moment she had left the ward.

'Serves yer right!' said Ernie, his mocking voice muffled by the bandages. 'I don't get paid fer this bleedin' job, yer know!'

'Hush now, Ernie!' snapped Rosie, who was doing her best to take over where Eunice left off. 'Eunice was doing her best. As a matter of fact, she's far better at this job than any of us.'

'Then all I can say is,' retorted Ernie, 'Gord 'elp the poor bleedin' troops! Owwww!' He suddenly let out a loud yowl as Rosie deliberately tightened the knot on the bandage that was holding his splint together.

A few minutes later, Rosie and Eunice left Ernie to sweat it out, whilst they joined two of their friends on the opposite side of the ward, who were making up a bed for the next 'volunteer' patient. Megan Morgan, twenty-five, and from Pontypridd, was known as 'Titch' to her friends because she was barely five foot two inches tall and a bit on the tubby side. In complete contrast, her friend Binnie Osborne, thought of as the old lady of the quartet because she was in her early thirties, came from a well-to-do family in Surrey, was tall, with a pencil-thin waist, and moved very gracefully. Since the day that they had all joined the Nursing Service some weeks before, the four girls had become such good friends that they were now practically a team, which sometimes caused a little resentment from some of the other trainees who thought they were too wrapped up in themselves to care about anyone else, an accusation they all vigorously denied, although they had jokingly nicknamed themselves 'The Terrible Four'.

'So,' asked Eunice, ''as anyone 'eard when they're goin' ter shift us up front?'

'That girl, Miriam,' said Megan, whose Welsh accent was so thick you could have cut a knife through it, 'you know – the one in Admin upstairs – well, *she* told me they're going to try and push us through the course as soon as possible, maybe in the next couple of weeks.'

Rosie bit her lip anxiously. 'But they can't do that,' she said. 'Not until we've finished our basics.'

'Ha!' chortled Megan. 'Don't you believe it! They're bringing in casualties now faster than they can replace them, look you. Things must be getting pretty desperate in those trenches.'

'Well, I would have thought that quite unlikely,' said Binnie, her nurse's cap perched stylishly on top of her immaculately cut short black hair. 'If you're going to deal with critically injured men, you've got to know exactly what you're doing.'

'Especially when they've been exposed to poison gas,' added Rosie.

'Gas?' asked Binnie, with some trepidation.

'Some of the boys Eunice and I have seen coming back after being in gas attacks need specialist care. It's terrible to see them coughing their lungs out.'

'That's true,' said Eunice, who was helping Megan finish making up one of the beds. 'An' yer should just see them who've got covered with mustard gas – their faces are all burned. It's 'orrible!'

'I know,' sighed Binnie, perched on the edge of an adjoining bed. 'But I'm afraid we're going to see an awful lot of that once we get out to the field hospitals.'

'That's what my mam said,' replied Megan. 'She said she's not going to have any daughter of hers going off to such places. I told her some-one's got to do the job. My dad's out there some-where. If *he* needs help, it'd be good to know there was someone around like us to help *him*.'

'Wot about you, Rosie?' asked Eunice, knowing that Rosie had been dreading having to break the news to her parents. 'Wot did *your* mum an' dad say when yer told 'em?'

Rosie found it difficult to answer. 'My father said he'd never allow it,' she replied eventually.

'But you're over eighteen,' said Megan. 'Most women are doing war work. There's no way anyone can stop you.'

'Oh, yes there is, Titch,' said Binnie. 'If they know the right people.' She turned to Rosie. 'Does your father know the right people, Rosie?'

'Oh, yes,' Rosie replied, her lovely oval face crumpling up at the memory of the difficult scene she'd had with her parents the night before, when they'd all sat together in the conservatory, arguing about the rights and wrongs of why the war should be left to men to fight, and not young girls.

'Well, I tell yer this much,' growled Eunice, who was flicking through the notes in her exercise training book. 'If my ol' man ever tried ter tell *me* wot ter do, I'd tell 'im where ter get off. Not that

42

'e'd try, even if 'e was still at 'ome. In fact, most of my lot wouldn't even notice I'd gone!'

Binnie went to Rosie, who was staring aimlessly out of one of the ward windows into the street below. 'How did you respond to your parents, Rosie?' she asked caringly.

'I stood my ground,' she replied, with some anguish. 'I've never done such a thing in my life, and I hated it. My parents are good people. I love them. I would never do anything to hurt them. But I had to tell them that if they tried to stop me, I'd leave home and do things my own way.'

'That a gel, Rosie!' called Eunice. 'The suffragettes'd be proud of yer!'

'I wanna go ter the lav!' called poor old Ernie, who had been left on his own, suffering on the other side of the ward.

Everyone flicked him a cursory glance, then ignored him. 'Well, I think you're a very brave soul, Rosie,' said Binnie, her dark eyes flashing in her elongated features. 'My parents died young and so I don't have anyone to ask permission of to do anything now, but if I did, I doubt I'd have the courage to defy them. I don't know. I just think I have a calling for this work – oh, not only because I know my husband, Harold, is out there, but because I can't bear the thought that I'm sitting at home doing absolutely nothing to help finish this damned war.'

'Well,' said Rosie, turning to a framed photograph of Florence Nightingale on the wall, 'I only hope that when I come face to face with all these horrors, I shall be capable of coping with them.'

Binnie put a comforting arm around Rosie's

shoulder. Because of their similar family backgrounds, she felt an affinity with the girl.

'Don't worry, Rosie,' she said reassuringly. 'No matter what anyone says, we all feel the same way. None of us really knows what we're capable of doing until we're called upon to do it.'

Sister Maisie suddenly peered around the door at the end of the ward. Her voice thundered as she called, 'Come on now, ladies! Time to look at some medicines. Get yourselves down to the laboratory.'

Three of the girls immediately followed her out, leaving just Eunice to follow on behind.

'Hey!' yelled Ernie, from behind his bandages as they disappeared. 'I wanna go to the lav!'

Eunice was last to leave, and stopped just long enough to lean over him. 'Now you be a good boy, Ernie,' she joked. 'And don't yer dare wet that bed!'

Outside the gates of Holloway Women's Prison in Parkhurst Road, there was a large gathering of suffragettes, who were protesting against the imprisonment of one of their members for disorderly conduct and breaking the peace. Banners with slogans such as 'REFORM LEGISLATION' and 'GIVE US OUR RIGHTS!' were visible amongst the vast crowd, a few of whom were screaming abuse at the Prime Minister, Herbert Asquith. All in all, however, it was a good-natured meeting, with the only real threat coming from a light sprinkling of early evening rain, which had produced a flurry of umbrellas to protect the ladies' hats. Unfortunately, Rosie had no umbrella with her, for when she'd left home that morning there had been no sign of rain. When she got off the bus it took her some time to struggle her way through the mass of jeering protesters, for despite the efforts of the handful of bobbies on duty, the junction of Parkhurst and Camden Roads was completely blocked. Once she had succeeded in getting through the crowd, however, she stopped briefly to talk to a group of neighbours who were all watching the rally from a safe distance.

'If yer ask me,' grumbled Alf Jolly, who ran the small grocery provisions shop in nearby Brecknock Road, 'all these women're bleedin' loonies. I mean, one minute they say they're in favour of fightin' Kaiser Bill, then in the same breff they yell at poor ol' Asquith.'

'I agree wiv yer, Alf,' replied Josie Kinloch, a young mother of two scruffy boys, who lived on the top floor of the house next but one to Rosie. 'An' in any case, if they gave the vote ter women, I fer one wouldn't know wot ter do wiv it.'

'Yer write a cross in a box,' jibed old Monty Gubble, who lived in a basement flat too close for comfort to the prison, and who had a white beard that was longer than Father Christmas's.

Josie didn't even allow him the benefit of a glare.

'Lock 'em all up, say I!' blabbered Alf Jolly, who this evening was anything but what his name may have suggested. 'Wot der *you* fink, Rosie?'

With rainwater dripping off the brim of her hat, Rosie was in no mood to stand around talking. 'As a matter of fact, Mr Jolly,' she replied, 'I think they've got a point. In fact, they've got several points.'

'Blimey!' gasped Alf. 'Don't tell me you're one of 'em?'

'No, Mr Jolly,' Rosie retorted, 'I'm not one of them, but I do agree with a lot of the things they're trying to do. Remember, they were just as against the war as the rest of us, but after all the meetings they've held they agree that the Kaiser is a real threat to us all. As for the women's vote, well, I really don't see what's so wrong about it. After all, with respect, women have minds of their own, just the same as men. Surely we should be allowed to have an opinion, just the same as anyone else?'

'Wot does your dad say about *that?*' asked Josie Kinloch snidely.

'I'm sure my father has his own opinion, Mrs Kinloch,' returned Rosie politely.

They all turned to look back at the crowd, who were beginning to chant, 'Our girl! Our girl! Give us back *our* girl!'

Josie shouted, 'Go back an' scrub yer floors!'

Fortunately, no one heard her.

'Excuse me.' Embarrassed, Rosie started to move off. 'I need to get into some dry clothes.'

'See yer then, Rosie,' called Alf.

'Cheery-bye!' Josie's call was more tart.

'Goodbye!' Rosie hurried off.

'Well, what about *that* then?' sniffed Alf. 'Standin' up for the loonies. I never fawt Rosie Little was goin' ter turn out like that!'

'Well, what d'yer expect?' added Josie. 'Wiv a muvver and farvver like that – got their noses so

46

'igh in the air, they don't notice wot's goin' on amongst *real* people.'

'Rosie's a good gel, Josie,' insisted old Monty. 'She's doin' 'er bit fer the war effort.'

'Oh, yes,' jeered Josie. 'Regular bleedin' saint!'

'Well, fank God we've got at least *one* in 'Olloway!' chuckled the old boy, before shuffling off.

After a while, the rain stopped, leaving behind thick grey clouds, which, for most people, was worrying, for low-lying clouds would make it easy for one of the dreaded Zeppelin airships to sneak in and out unnoticed. The Zeppelins, known to people on the streets as 'gasbags', had become a formidable German weapon of destruction, causing death and mayhem ever since the raids started on the east coast of England at the beginning of the year. When the first raid on London came to the East End in May, Richard Little warned his family to be vigilant. At the first sound of the Zeppelin's engines they were to go down into the wine cellar and stay there until it was safe to return.

But when she got back home that evening, Rosie found that there was a more pressing problem to face up to.

'Father went to see someone at the Home Office about you today,' said Christian, who was sitting up in bed doing a jigsaw puzzle on a large serving tray.

Rosie, in a chair alongside, watching him, swung him a look. 'He what?' she asked, alarmed.

'I heard him and Mother talking in the sitting room,' continued Christian. 'He said this bloke –

whoever he was – he said he's promised to talk to the nursing people you're working for. He apparently told Father not to worry. He says you'll never have to go to France.' He sighed and flopped back against his pillow. 'Why is it that jigsaw puzzles are always so hard to do?'

'When did you hear this?' asked Rosie, getting up off the bed.

'Hear what?'

'What Father said to this man at the Home Office. About me.'

'Oh,' replied Christian, struggling with a piece of jigsaw that fitted somewhere in the dome of St Paul's Cathedral, 'just before you came home. He told Mother not to worry. He said he'd never let a daughter of his risk her life on a battlefield. He said war is for men, not young girls.'

Exasperated, Rosie turned and made her way to the door.

'Where are you going?' asked Christian.

'Where d'you think?' She opened the door, and was about to go when Christian called to her.

'*I* wouldn't want you to go either, Rose,' he said poignantly. 'If you didn't come back, I don't know what I'd do.'

Rosie paused at the door. For that split second, her young brother's room seemed to close in on her. Although it was an untidy room, the walls were so alive – alive with all the things that typified the life of a fourteen-year-old boy who had so much to live for. Things such as a giant poster of the great circus clown Grock, whom he had once seen perform in a big top on Islington Green, newspaper photo cuttings of his silver-

48

screen idol, Charlie Chaplin, and several shelves containing books about his passionate hobby – railway trains and automobiles. It was a room that gave no clue to the debilitating disease that she feared would one day claim the life of its young occupant.

Rosie smiled back at him, and called gently, 'I would always come back to you, Chris.'

'Got it!' exclaimed Christian, as he at last found the one missing piece of jigsaw he was searching for.

Rosie found her parents playing gin rummy at their card table in the conservatory. Rosie had always hated card games, and was hard put to join in the whist evenings her parents held every month, much preferring to prepare the refreshments for the dull collection of friends her parents had cultivated over the years. Despite the hot, muggy evening, her father kept his collar, tie and jacket on, though he looked as if he had a permanent flush. Her mother looked a little cooler in her summer dress, which was adorned at the neck by a white lace frill, but even she had to dab the perspiration from her forehead from time to time, and frequently fluttered the black lace fan her husband had bought for her in Spain during a business trip several years before.

'Father!' snapped Rosie as she approached. 'Can I have a word with you, please?'

Her parents looked up from their hands of cards with a start. 'Why?' asked Richard, somewhat taken aback by her tone. 'Is something wrong?'

'You went to see someone about me at the

Home Office today,' she said tersely. 'I want to know why.'

'I hardly think this is an opportune moment to discuss such things,' replied her father. 'We'll have a little chat later.'

'No, Father!' replied Rosie firmly. 'I have a right to know why you're trying to interfere in my life.'

This remark did not please him. Putting down his hand of cards on the table, he took off his spectacles, and glared back at her. 'As far as *I'm* concerned, Rose,' he replied calmly but firmly, 'at the age of eighteen, you *have* no rights.' Rosie started to protest, but he raised his hand to silence her, and got up from the card table. 'May I remind you that under the law of this land, until you come of age, you are still under my care and protection.'

'Father!' said Rosie, following him out of the conservatory. 'There's a war on. Millions of girls my age are volunteering for all sorts of jobs. Somebody has to take over from the men.'

'Women cannot take over from men, Rose,' he insisted. 'They can only be there to give support.'

Rosie came straight back at him. 'But don't you understand, Father, that's exactly what I'm doing. A nurse is there to help save lives.'

'But an underage girl is not equipped to go out to the battlefield,' retorted her father. 'Nor should she be expected to risk her own life.'

'Men *and* women are risking their lives every day of the week, Father!'

Whenever Richard Little had no enthusiasm to discuss something, he had the irritating habit of just walking away from the person he was talking to. This is what he did now. Rosie watched him, hands folded behind his back, strolling to the far end of the garden, which was now bathed in the deep red glow of a summer sunset, his shoulders broad and muscular from an active earlier life of rugby and cricket. The air was thick with humidity, mainly because of the low grey clouds, so that voices sounded dull and flat, as though talking in a small room. Although she loved him a great deal, she was only too aware that he had strong opinions and would rarely concede in an argument. But then Richard had worked hard to give his family the affluent way of life they were now used to. He had inherited the family's porcelain business, but over the years it was he who had built it up from its small turnover into a thriving company with a fine reputation. With all this in mind, Rosie knew only too well that she had a battle on her hands. She took a deep breath and went to pursue him.

'You know, Father,' she said as she approached him, 'I don't *want* to go out to France. I'm just as scared as any of the other girls. But they're so short of nurses out there, I have a duty to–'

'Your only duty is to your own family, Rose!' he insisted. 'Your mother and I brought you into this world, and we're not going to risk losing you in all that carnage. You also have a duty to your brother. He needs you, Rose. Don't ever forget that.'

'That's something I could *never* forget, Father,' replied Rosie, her milk-white complexion now tinged with the red glow of a fading sunset. 'I love Christian. I'll always be there when he needs me.'

'Not if you're lying dead in some muddy field in France.'

Her father's words struck a chilling note. She flicked a cursory glance over her shoulder to see her mother anxiously watching them from the door of the conservatory. Then she slowly turned back to her father. 'Father,' she said, with calm resolve, 'ever since I was a child, I've looked up to you; I've relied on you for just about everything I've ever wanted to know. To me, you've always been the most considerate and loving father a child could ever have. But I'm not a child any more. Whether I'm eighteen or twenty-one years of age, I do have a mind of my own. I now have to work things out as *I* see them. All I can say to you, Father, is that if you try to prevent me from going on in the Nursing Service, I shall never–'

'Listen!'

Rosie jumped as her father's eyes suddenly darted up towards the sky. 'What is it?'

'Quiet, Rose! Listen!'

Rosie looked up at the sky, where there gradually came the distant throbbing of an engine, encroaching out of sight above the low-lying clouds.

'Oh, God!' gasped Rosie. 'Is it?'

'Keep your voice down, Rose!' said her father. 'They can hear every little sound on the ground.'

For several moments, they stood there transfixed, hardly daring to move, eyes trying hard to pierce through the clouds. The sound, which seemed more like a motor-car engine, was getting closer and closer, louder and louder, menacing, as though it were heading straight their way.

'It's a Zeppelin!' cried Rosie, her voice strangulated in the stifling evening air. 'Father, it's a Zeppelin!'

As she spoke, her mother called out from the conservatory, 'Richard!'

'Back inside!' yelled Richard. 'Get down to the cellar as fast as you can! Hurry, Rose! I'm going in to get Christian!'

They rushed back towards the house. Only moments later, a huge sinister shape emerged from the clouds, the tip of its nose bathed in the red hues of the dying sun. Soon, the thing evolved into a long thin cigar shape, which briefly appeared before returning into the cover of the rolling clouds. The noise of its engine was now deafening, tearing apart the peace and tranquillity of a summer evening. And as it drew closer and closer over the back garden of the Littles' home, the deadened atmosphere in the air was such that those hurrying for cover could just hear the voices of the German crew in the gondola beneath the 'gasbag' high above, shouting out frenzied commands to each other, just waiting for the order to discharge their lethal cargo of bombs on to some unsuspecting target below.

In the cellar beneath the Littles' home, everyone held his or her breath as the sound of the giant airship's engines roared overhead, causing the very foundations of the entire road to vibrate as if shaking with abject terror. Marian offered a silent prayer, Rosie hugged Christian, burying his head protectively in her shoulder, and Richard gazed up at the ceiling, his expression grim and foreboding.

It was several minutes before the horrifying sound of the Zeppelin's engines faded into the distance. Although shaken, the family gradually recovered, breathing a sigh of relief that, this time at least, they had been spared a devastating tragedy. But the sound of a huge explosion in the distance was proof that not everyone had been quite so lucky.

Chapter 3

The following Monday morning, Rosie, Eunice, Binnie and Megan arrived to start their field training at the Military Rehabilitation Centre at Stanmore. Situated just a short distance from London, and set in the middle of rolling green fields, the centre was staffed by several of the voluntary nursing services, including QAIMNS. A grand seventeenth-century manor house, the building had been taken over from its aristocratic owners by the War Office for the duration, and converted into a hospital where some of the more critically wounded soldiers returning from the Front could be given the best attention the authorities could provide. In its former days, the building was pleasant enough, constructed of red brick, with tall chimney stacks. The impressive interior, from which the crystal chandeliers had been removed, had oak panelling in each room, and a magnificent staircase winding up to the first floor, where most of the spacious rooms had been converted into dormitories for the casualties of war.

'I bet this cost a bob or two in its time,' remarked Eunice, who, together with Rosie, Binnie and Megan, was standing in the Grand Hall, clutching her suitcase for what looked like the start of a long stay.

Rosie's attention, however, was focused not on the grandeur of the surroundings, but on the constant comings and goings of nursing staff from all the various agencies, some of them walking slowly alongside patients struggling on crutches, others pushing wounded soldiers in wheelchairs. Most of all she noticed the silence. No one talked, and if they did, it seemed to be in whispers. And the smell of this once grand house was no longer of fine drapes and antique furniture, but of ether and carbolic, and of all the other accoutrements of a working hospital.

They were soon joined by a thin, gaunt-looking nurse, whose perpetual frown was only accentuated by the severe way in which she had tied the ribbon of her uniform cap beneath her chin.

'Follow me, please, young ladies,' she said without ceremony and without taking the time to introduce herself. All four girls exchanged anxious looks, and duly followed her through a maze of stately rooms until they reached their dormitory accommodation at the back of the house. 'Get yourselves unpacked as soon as you can, and report back to me in the main hall again in fifteen minutes. You'll find caps and aprons in the lockers.' Before the girls had time to ask even a single question, she had scurried out of the room.

'If you ask me,' said Megan acidly, 'we're not

going to get many favours out of *that* one!'

Whilst she and the other three girls unpacked, Rosie took a cursory glance around the dormitory, which would be where she would spend whatever free time she had over the next month or so. The accommodation was pretty sparse. Five narrow iron-framed beds were lined up on either side of the room, with a slim wooden locker alongside each, only just big enough to take the few clothes the girls had been allowed to bring. There were certainly no home comforts here, and even the curtains up at the windows were faded and threadbare. A brief glimpse out of the window at the side of her bed gave Rosie an empty feeling of being totally isolated from the outside world. But when she looked down at the once beautifully landscaped gardens, she felt real anguish at the sight of so many injured soldiers being led around like children by the nurses. During those few bewildering moments, Rosie felt a real sense of loss, for despite the fact that she had openly defied her father to even come out to such a place as Stanmore, she missed her family, especially Christian. In her heart of hearts, Rosie knew that there *was* danger in what she had embarked upon. Even her narrow escape from those Zeppelin bombs a few nights before paled into insignificance against what she now faced.

A few minutes later the four girls were back in the main hall to be briefed on their duties by the gaunt-looking nurse, who was busy checking through their personal details on a clipboard. 'I'm Sister Jarrett. Matron has asked me to welcome you all,' she announced primly. 'She wants me to

56

impress upon you the importance of the work you're about to undertake.' She carefully studied the face of each of the four girls. 'During the short time you'll be here, please use me as your point of reference. If there's something you don't know, don't understand, then just ask. Mistakes here could be fatal when you transfer to a field hospital.'

Rosie felt her stomach churn.

'Follow me, please.'

They followed Sister Jarrett up the grand staircase to the first floor, where they were led into a vast room that had obviously been stripped of all its fine paintings and furniture, and was now the recreation area for those men who were able to sit up and share a cigarette with each other. It was a poignant sight, for many of the wounded soldiers were still heavily bandaged, some with leg or arm wounds, others living in a dark world behind bandaged eyes. As they passed through, the girls tried to smile at those who flicked a glance up at them, but to their surprise there was very little response. The silence in the heavily smoke-filled room was unreal, unnatural.

The girls followed Sister Jarrett through a door marked overhead 'WARD B (OPTICAL)'. Here, other nurses were attending patients who were either confined to their beds or sitting in chairs alongside. Most had their eyes bandaged, and so once again there was very little response as Rosie and her companions passed by. They came to a halt, however, when one of the nurses approached Sister Jarrett with a request.

'I'm afraid there's still a problem with Private

Battersby, Sister,' said the nurse anxiously. She could have been no more than eighteen years old, but looked even younger. 'He pulled his bandages off during the night, and I had a devil of a job to get them back on again. He just keeps telling me he wants to go home.'

Rosie and the other girls turned to look at the young soldier the nurse was referring to. He was sitting up in his bed, arms crossed, head lowered towards the bed cover. His eyes were heavily bandaged, his face badly scabbed.

Sister Jarrett left the four girls, and went across to him. 'So what's all this then, Charlie?' she said brightly, perching herself on the edge of the bed briefly, and gently taking hold of his hand. 'Want to go home – so soon?'

The young soldier raised his head. There were stains on his pyjama top where he had spilt tea. 'I don't want to stay here,' he replied, in a cultured, barely audible West London voice. 'I've got things to do.'

'What sort of things, Charlie?' asked Sister Jarrett, gently stroking his hand, her manner far removed from the brusque greeting she had given the girls.

'All sorts of things,' he replied.

Sister Jarrett leaned a little closer. 'Well, why not wait just a little bit longer?' she said. 'You'll have plenty of time to do everything you want.'

'Not everything,' replied the boy, chillingly.

Sister Jarrett was careful not to react with any emotion. 'Your mother's coming in to visit you today,' she said. 'You mustn't upset her. And I hear that lovely girlfriend of yours is coming too.'

The young soldier looked up at her without being able to see her. He hesitated, then slid back down under the bed sheets. His anguish was plain to see.

'Don't worry, Charlie,' said Sister Jarrett. 'You'll be out of here in no time now.' She gave him one last pat on the hand, then got up. She went back to the nurse who was looking after him. 'Try and get him up,' she said softly. 'A walk in the fresh air will do him good.'

Rosie and the other girls followed her into the small office at the end of the ward. Last in was Binnie, who closed the door quietly behind them. Sister Jarrett sat at her desk, and motioned to the others to sit on the wooden stools there whilst she talked to them. 'What you heard outside,' she began earnestly, 'was the kind of situation that you will have to face up to every day of the week. That boy was the only survivor of his platoon when a shell burst just ahead of them. He was thrown unconscious into a shell crater. When he woke up he found himself in a field hospital back at base. His face was pitted with shrapnel, and he had lost the sight in both his eyes.'

All four girls sat grim and silent, focusing firmly on their laps.

'Most of the patients in this ward are in very much the same position,' continued the sister. 'Full to partial blindness. It's a traumatic experience for them – *and* us.' She paused a moment, picked up a pencil and unconsciously started tapping it against the palm of her hand. 'However,' she said, 'the one thing you will have to remember is that although we are here to give all our patients unqualified support, the one thing we must *not* do is to become emotionally involved with them.' She sat back in her chair and looked at the girls lined up on the other side of her desk. 'Why d'you think that is?' she asked. She nodded towards Megan.

'Don't know, Sister,' replied Megan, awkwardly. 'Too many of them, I reckon.'

'Yes,' replied Sister Jarrett. 'And what else?' This time her eyes turned towards Rosie.

For a moment, Rosie felt uncomfortable. But after she had considered the question carefully, she answered, 'I'd say that if you became too involved, I mean if you showed too much sympathy to a patient, it might not give him the kind of strength he needs to recover.'

Sister Jarrett looked at her and smiled. 'Precisely,' she said. 'You must remember that most of the soldiers in this centre are shell-shocked. Most of them haven't even seen a female for months on end. Without their wives or girlfriends around to comfort them, a nurse takes on ... a real significance. That is something we have to be aware of at all times. None the less, we have a huge part to play in their recovery. But I say again, the golden rule must always be support – not involvement.'

A short while later, the four girls were assigned their first duties, and were informed that whilst they were at the centre they would be under the direct supervision of Sister Jarrett herself. Rosie and Eunice were to take over as relief staff in the ward treating men who had suffered the effects of poison gas, whilst Binnie and Megan were assigned to the optical ward. Once Sister Jarrett had briefed all four girls on the type of patients they would be dealing with, she then took Binnie and Megan into their ward to meet the two nurses they would be taking over from.

After taking their leave of their friends, Rosie and Eunice followed Sister Jarrett out of the optical ward, and along the first-floor landing. At the far end they reached a door marked 'RESPIR-ATORY. NO SMOKING'.

'Don't be nervous,' said Sister Jarrett, reassuringly. 'I'm sure you'll both cope perfectly – once you know what you're dealing with.' She opened the door leading into the ward.

What Rosie saw inside filled her with trepidation.

Richard Little arrived at his office soon after lunch. He had spent the morning in discussion with an official at the town hall, who had approached him about the likelihood of the porcelain factory being requisitioned by the government for war work. As business had plummeted since the beginning of the war, Little had no alternative but to go along with the suggestion that the company should help in the manufacture of gas respirators, which were now in urgent need by the military up front to protect the troops from persistent poison-gas attacks. With reluctance, Richard had agreed to consider the official's proposals, which included a date when his workforce could start training for the new scheme. It wasn't going to be easy, for most of his employees had been with him for years, and despite everyone's wish to do what they could for the war effort, closing down to make way for a completely new industry was going to upset many good workers. As he stared down with foreboding through the large interior arched window overlooking the factory floor, he tried to work out in his mind how he was going to break the news. But he was soon faced with a more worrying problem when his senior foreman, Jim Sayles, came in to see him.

'It's Hartmann, sir,' said Sayles, a man in his fifties, with a ruddy complexion that contrasted quite prominently with his long white work coat and trilby hat. 'They're not happy about him downstairs.'

'Hartmann?' asked Little, puzzled. 'D'you mean Emile Harrington?'

'Yes, sir,' replied Sayles, somewhat sheepishly.

'Why the devil are you calling him by his German name?' asked Little, quite taken aback. 'Harrington's been a naturalised British subject for years.'

'It's not me, sir,' returned Sayles, who had been with the company longer than nearly everyone, and had even worked for Little's father in the last years before he died. 'It's the others.'

'What *are* you talking about, man?' asked Little.

Sayles dug his hands deep into his coat pocket, and fidgeted nervously. 'With respect, sir,' he said, self-consciously, 'I've seen this comin' fer some time now. There've bin rumblin's down in the shops ever since the start er the war, ever since our blokes went over the top. It don't sit good on Hartmann down there, sir. It just don't sit good.'

Little stood behind his chair at the desk and stared at his foreman in near disbelief. Not only had he always had the highest personal regard for the man but, like the rest of his employees, he had always had a good working relationship with him. 'Are you telling me,' he asked, leaning forward over the back of his chair, 'that there's some kind of resentment of Harrington down there?'

'Oh, it goes further than that, sir,' sighed Sayles. 'A lot of 'em want you ter get rid of 'im.'

'What!' Little's eyes nearly popped out of his head. 'Are you joking or something?'

'I wish I was, sir,' returned Sayles despondently. 'I only wish I was.'

'But why?' Little turned the chair round and sat down. 'What's happened to bring this on?'

'I s'ppose it's 'cos of where Hartmann comes from, sir,' he replied. 'And the fact that we're fightin' the Huns.'

'This is preposterous, Jim!' exclaimed Little, running his hand in despair through his thick hair. 'Emile Harrington left Emile Hartmann behind in Germany when he was a young man. He's got absolutely nothing to do with this damned war. In fact, he's more British than you and I!'

'Once a German, always a German.'

Little did a double take. 'I don't believe I heard you say that,' he said incredulously. 'You of all people.'

'Those're not *my* words, sir,' returned Sayles, desperate to keep arm's length from the people who were clearly stirring up trouble. 'I'm just repeatin' what they're sayin' downstairs. I 'ear it all the time. I don't like it, sir, I can tell yer. I just don't like it. As a matter er fact...'

Little noticed that Sayles had lowered his voice.

'As a matter er fact,' whispered Sayles, 'I've always liked ol' Emile. Wouldn't 'urt a fly.'

Little stiffened. 'Then why the devil do you listen to such evil gossip?'

'It's not just gossip, sir,' insisted Sayles. 'This war does funny things. It turns people's minds.'

'Well, it's not going to turn *my* mind,' Little replied calmly. 'So just go back downstairs and tell those people that I have absolutely no intention at all of getting rid of Emile *Harrington*. As far as I'm concerned, he's a faithful, long-serving *British* employee of this company, and if I hear that he's being harassed in any way, whoever's responsible will have *me* to deal with.'

'Very good, sir,' sighed Sayles, not at all happy with the brief he had been given. He turned to go, but once he'd opened the door, he stopped for a moment. 'Oh, yes, sir,' he said, 'there *was* just one more fing you ought ter know.'

Little looked up from the papers he had begun to sort through on his desk. 'Yes?'

'It's...' Sayles was fumbling for words. 'Well, it's ... it's somefin' I've 'eard goin' round, somefin' ... well, it's about *Mrs* Hartmann, sir – I mean Mrs Harrington.' He now looked really uncomfortable. 'I wasn't goin' ter say anyfin', sir, but – well, yer see – there're some pretty ugly rumours goin' round ... about your daughter, Miss Rosie.'

The former bedroom of the master of Stanmore Manor was large enough to accommodate twelve beds, six each side, allowing each patient only just enough room for one small bedside locker, into which he crammed all his personal possessions. At the far end of the room, a small desk was squashed into the corner for the two duty nurses, whose awesome job it was to ensure constant observation and treatment for those men who had been caught up in some of the enemy's most deadly poison-gas attacks.

When Rosie and Eunice followed Sister Jarrett into the ward, the thing that struck Rosie most forcefully was the sound of men coughing. It was a soul-destroying sound of lungs struggling to fight off the effects of the monstrous alien chemical that had engulfed them on the battle-field, young men at various stages of their hard-fought recovery.

'You'll notice,' said Sister Jarrett, as she slowly walked Rosie and Eunice along the rows of beds, 'that this ward is one of the most well-ventilated rooms in the house. It's not hard to imagine why.'

Rosie looked at the patients in their beds: a sea of faces watching her and Eunice. All the floor-to-ceiling windows were wide open to allow as much air into the room as possible. Just as she was about to move on, however, Rosie turned with a start when a young soldier called to her from one of the beds behind.

''Ello, darlin'! You goin' ter come an' 'old my 'and while I 'ave a whiff of oxygen?'

There were ripples of croaky laughter from the other beds. Although a bit embarrassed, Rosie threw a sweet smile at the young soldier, who, like several of the other patients, was breathing through an oxygen mask.

'Behave yourself, soldier!' called Sister Jarrett, half joking. 'Any more complaints about you from my young ladies, and we'll put you all back on bully-beef ration!'

At the mention of the hated bully beef they had all endured for weeks on end in the trenches, the other men groaned and jeered.

Before leaving, Sister Jarrett introduced Rosie and Eunice to the two young nurses who were on daytime duty, and from whom they would shortly be taking over. Ruth Jarman and Helen Boswell were both London girls, who seemed to be on the move all the time, hurrying from one bed to another, adjusting oxygen cylinder levels, helping patients to sit up in bed, and generally keeping a smile on their faces as they encouraged the worst afflicted to look on the bright side.

'Whatever you do,' said Ruth, the older of the two girls, who was clearly showing the strain of working in such a traumatic atmosphere, 'never let them feel sorry for themselves. The last thing we want are any more suicides.'

'Suicides!' gasped Eunice.

'We've lost two men from this ward alone,' said Helen, who was in the middle of preparing the late afternoon tablet distribution, and who was so thin she looked as though a draught of air would blow her away. 'Some of them find it just too difficult to cope.'

'But – how?' Rosie hardly dared to ask.

'They went outside for a walk,' said Ruth softly. 'Hanged themselves from a tree with anything they could lay their hands on – ties, socks, rope.'

66

'We have to watch them all every minute of the day,' added Helen.

Rosie and Eunice followed the more experienced nurses on their rounds, stopping at each bed to have a few words with the patients. Eunice paused for a moment or so to talk to a young soldier who was sitting in a chair at the side of his bed, having just got over a severe fit of coughing.

''Ello, mate,' she said, crouching down beside him. 'You feelin' all right then?'

''Course I'm all right,' joked the boy, who could not have been more than seventeen years old, and who was fighting for breath with every word. 'Got enuff gas inside me ter keep me mum's cooker goin' fer munffs!'

Eunice laughed with him, then got up to rub his back as the coughing started again.

Meanwhile, Rosie was helping Helen to take the temperature of an older soldier, who was lying flat on his back in bed, eyes bandaged, and who had been breathing deeply through an oxygen mask.

'Got a lot of fan mail, haven't you, Herbert?' Helen said brightly. 'His wife and kids are always first in on visiting day,' she added to Rosie.

The man smiled up at her. Rosie gently felt his forehead. It was burning hot.

When they moved on, Rosie noticed that the end bed was empty.

'That's young Sandy,' Helen said with a grin. 'He hates this place; spends more time in the grounds outside than he ever does in here.'

'You mean, he goes – walking on his own?'

'Oh, yes,' replied Helen. 'But Sandy's all right.

He's not the type to do away with himself. All he wants is to get out of this place and go home. Mind you, they're all a bit like that in the Shiny Seventh. Obstinate as hell!'

'The Shiny Seventh?' Rosie asked.

'The Seventh battalion,' said Helen. 'A lot of the boys here are from the Middlesex Regiment.'

Before she had time to take it in, someone came into the ward.

'Ah – there he is!' said Helen, looking at the young soldier who was making for his bed. 'So where've you been to this time, Sandy?'

Rosie turned to look. Coming towards her was the young Tommy who had retrieved her hat for her on the platform at Charing Cross Station.

'Blimey! It's Rosie Lee!' gasped Joe Upton. 'This 'as gotta be my lucky day!'

Chapter 4

Stanmore Manor was bathed in the brilliant glow of an August sunrise. In the surrounding fields, the golden corn crops were bending gently to and fro, pulsating in a gentle breeze, preparing themselves for the great harvest that would soon be upon them. The manor house looked magnificent, its red-brick façade, stucco, stone sculptures, tiled roof and high chimney stacks standing majestically surrounded by lawns that had only just been cut, leaving behind the invigorating scent of a quintessentially English summer.

Rosie's first week at the Rehabilitation Centre had been gruelling but illuminating. Her first impressions of the patients had been one of great despair, but as she and Eunice got to know each of them in their ward, she realised that nearly all of them possessed great resilience and a determination to make as full a recovery as possible.

Rosie's main difficulty, however, had been getting used to living away from home for the first time in her life. Before she took on the job, she had always been used to relying on other people to do her chores. Eating in the nurses' canteen and doing her own washing had taken some getting used to, and as she lay awake in her dormitory bed at night, her home in Camden Road seemed so near and yet so far. Her compensation, however, was the girls she was working with. Sharing her duties with someone as positive and funny as Eunice was a real bonus, and whenever they and the other two girls in the quartet met up, they were able to talk through their problems as though they were all from the same family, which in a sense, they were. And then there was Joe, 'Sandy' to the other nurses, the boy with the sandy hair and blue eyes, whose face had lit up the moment they had met again in the respiratory ward. Remembering what Sister Jarrett had told them about not becoming emotionally involved with any of the patients, apart from the odd smile, and a few words before lights-out time, Rosie had avoided picking out Joe for special attention. But Joe was undaunted, and waited until Sunday when Rosie had her first day off.

Wandering aimlessly around the grounds of the

house, Rosie and Eunice paused briefly at the old ornamental pool with its huge stone figure of a knight in armour standing over what in better days had been a fountain with many sprays, but which because of emergency water restrictions was now reduced to no more than a few inches of rainwater.

'Just imagine actually livin' in a place like this,' said Eunice, who perched on the edge of the pool, letting her hand drift idly into the shallow water. 'I mean, yer could sleep in a diff'rent room each night for a munff.'

'I doubt the previous owner took the trouble to do that, Eunice,' said Rosie, who was looking cool in a pink ankle-length cotton dress with long filled sleeves. 'I imagine whoever he was had a large family and probably entertained quite a lot.'

'It wasn't a *he,*' said Eunice. 'It was some old duchess.'

'Who told you that?'

'One of the gels in the canteen,' replied Eunice, glancing down at her own reflection in the water. 'Apparently her ol' man had an accident an' drowned in a boat down on the lake. Or at least that's what they said it was. If yer ask me, she bumped 'im off. That's wot always 'appens in books.'

'Then we'd better keep away from the lake,' said Rosie jokily. 'There might be a ghost down there!'

Both girls giggled.

Rosie perched alongside Eunice, and added her reflection in the water. Above them a lark flew high, little wings fluttering in the breeze, and singing a song that sounded like an ode to a perfect blue sky. And in the far distance, church bells pealed, calling worshippers to the first service of the day.

'I wonder if my mum's cooked roast beef and Yorkshire pud terday,' sighed Eunice wistfully. 'We always used ter 'ave it on Sundays – when Dad was workin', that is. It's the only day we could afford it. It 'ad ter last till the following Sat'day. Then it was bangers and mash or saveloys and pease puddin'.' She turned to look at Rosie's reflection in the water. 'Wot about you, Rosie? Wot *d'you* eat on Sundays?'

'Much the same as anyone else, I suppose,' replied Rosie. 'Except we never had to cook it. That was always left to our housekeeper – Mrs Winnet.'

'Lucky ol' you,' said Eunice.

'Yes, I *have* been very lucky,' agreed Rosie.

There was a moment's silence between them as the gentle breeze sent ripples across the surface of the water, temporarily obliterating their reflections.

'Are you scared about goin' up front?' Eunice asked quite suddenly.

Rosie waited a brief moment before answering. 'Yes,' she replied.

'Me too.'

Rosie swung her a surprised look. '*You?*'

Eunice turned to her. 'I ain't made er stone, yer know.'

'I know, Eunice,' said Rosie, 'but...' As they met each other's eyes, they smiled. 'Don't worry.' She put her arm round Eunice's shoulder. 'We'll be

71

all right if we stick together.'

They leaned their heads against each other, and looked down at the water. As they did so, they saw their reflections again. But now they were joined by a third reflection.

'Watch it!' said Eunice. 'Looks like we've got company.'

Both girls swung round to find a grinning Joe Upton leaning over them. 'Can anyone join the party?' he asked.

Rosie sprang to her feet and straightened her dress. Eunice, amused, also got up.

'What are you doing here, Joe?' Rosie asked, a little flustered.

'Same as you, I reckon, Rosie,' he replied, beaming. 'Don't wanna get stuck in that 'orrible room all day.'

Eunice was grinning like the Cheshire cat, aware that the two of them couldn't take their eyes off each other. 'If you'll excuse me,' she said, 'I've got another party ter go to!'

'Eunice!' called Rosie, as Eunice made her way back to the house.

With a broad knowing grin, Eunice waved back and left them to it.

When Rosie turned back to Joe, she found him staring at her with an infectious smile.

'Any chance of a cup of Rosie?' he asked jokingly.

Rosie chuckled shyly. 'Charing Cross Station seems a long way away now.'

'Not fer me it ain't,' he replied.

Rosie fumbled for the words to say next. 'So how are you feeling now?' she asked in desperation. She had noticed straight away that the bandage he had had over one eye had been removed, to reveal a small scar.

'Did yer know I'm goin' 'ome?' he replied. Almost as he spoke, he coughed.

Before answering, Rosie waited for him to compose himself. 'I did hear one of the other girls mention it,' she said. 'I'm so pleased for you, Joe. Have the doctors told you when?'

'Not exactly,' said Joe. 'Won't be long, though. I'm much better now. A few munffs an' I'll be ready ter go back.'

She soon became mesmerised by the way his pale, smiling blue eyes seemed to be reaching right inside her. 'I hope you'll have the chance to make a full recovery,' she said.

'At least I'll get some decent grub,' he replied. 'If I know my mum, she'll feed me up no end.'

'I'd better be going,' said Rosie, about to move off.

'Mind if I walk wiv yer?' asked Joe.

'We're not supposed to fraternise with the patients.'

'You're not fraterisin',' said Joe. 'You're 'elpin' me get well again.'

Rosie chuckled, and they both moved off together.

Marian Little knew there was going to be trouble. She had anticipated it ever since her husband had told her about Rosie's involvement with Emile Harrington's wife, Clara. When Richard left the house soon after seven o'clock that morning, she had feared the worst, and there was no way she

73

was going to be able to calm her mind until he returned later in the day. This was not how Marian liked to spend her Sundays since Rosie had gone. She liked things to be the same, no hassle, no unpleasantness, just a nice breakfast with her husband and young Christian, then the regular Sunday morning visit to church, followed by the traditional lunch cooked by Mrs Winnet. Routine had been the hallmark of Marian's long marriage to Richard Little and she was finding that it meant more to her than ever nowadays. There were no secrets between Marian and her husband, and they had hardly had one disagreement about anything since the day they met. But this was different. Rosie had interfered in something that was not her business, and it was going to cause problems not only for the family firm, but also with the family's relationship with their neighbours. *Why* had Rosie done it? Marian asked herself over and over again. Didn't she realise there was a war on, and how sensitive people were about foreigners – wherever they came from? And why had Rosie become so independent that the neighbours had begun asking difficult questions about her? Why had her daughter changed?

'Will Father be back in time to take us to church?' Christian asked his mother, as she wheeled him into the sitting room from his ground-floor bedroom.

'I'm afraid not, darling,' replied Marian. 'He's got some important business to attend to. I'll read us something from the Bible instead.'

'I prefer to go to church,' said Christian rather defiantly. 'At least I get a chance to talk to people

74

there. When Rosie was here, she always took me to church.'

'I know, dear,' said Marian forlornly.

'And she always bought me an ice cream from Tony's on the way back.'

Marian had no answers to offer. She knew only too well how much Christian missed his sister, who was also his best friend. 'Well, Mrs Winnet is cooking us a lovely lunch,' was all she could say. 'The sweet today is your favourite – strawberry junket.'

'Why is father so angry with Rosie?' Christian asked bluntly, once his mother had settled his wheelchair by the window. 'Is it because of Mrs Harrington?'

Marian turned with a start. 'What do you know about that?' she asked.

'Only that she's a very nice lady,' replied Christian, who was casually opening the book he was reading on locomotives. 'Well, so Rosie says.'

Marian sat in a chair beside him. 'D'you mean Rose talks to you about Mrs Harrington?' she asked, without trying to sound too interested.

'Of course,' said Christian. 'Rosie talks to me about *everything*.'

'What kind of things?'

Christian shrugged. 'Just about what good friends they are,' he said.

Marian always did her best never to become irritated with the boy. Consumption had taken its toll on Christian over the years, and if he was ever upset or distressed, it could agitate his condition. 'You mean, they see each other?' she asked.

'Oh, yes,' replied Christian, quite matter-of-fact. 'Before Rosie went away they used to see each other lots of times.'

'Why?'

Christian refused to look up from his book. 'It's a secret.'

'A secret?'

'Between me and Rosie. I promised not to tell.'

Marian was now not only intrigued, but genuinely concerned. 'Don't you think you could tell *me?*' she asked.

Christian, puzzled by the question, flicked his eyes up to look at her for just one moment. 'Why?' he asked. 'It wouldn't be a secret if I told anyone.'

'Christian,' said Marian, trying to show restraint, 'I am not just *anyone*. I'm your mother.'

'And Rosie's my sister,' he replied. 'A secret's a secret, Mother. Isn't that what you and Father have always told me?'

The grounds of Stanmore Manor were now dotted with the white uniforms and caps of nursing staff either taking their patients for a Sunday morning stroll or gently pushing them around in wheelchairs. After the first thin summer mist at dawn that morning, it was now a glorious August day, and in contrast to the deafening constant barrage of battlefield artillery, the peace and tranquillity of the English countryside was certainly proving to be a great healer for both body and mind.

Rosie and Joe strolled down by the vast ornamental lake, where the glare from the sun's rays dappled the surface of the water between the dark cover of wild water lilies. The shores of the lake were provided with good shade by tall oak and maple trees, their leaves bristling in the gentle breeze, casting delicate shaped patterns on the old stone paths below. When they came to the ruins of the old lake house, Rosie took off her hat and ran her fingers through her soft brown hair, which had once hung over her shoulders, but was now cut short with an off-centre parting. She was relaxed and happy in Joe's company, for he was so interesting, telling stories about his mum and dad and his older brother, Paul, and about their time when he was little, living in a farm labourer's cottage in the Yorkshire Dales, where his dad worked on the land. Rosie was also fascinated to hear the way his East End accent occasionally gave way to his native Yorkshire as he revealed his extraordinary observations about people and places he knew, and told something of life in the trenches up front.

For his part, Joe loved everything about Rosie, so much so that he just couldn't take his eyes off her. It was the way she smiled when she talked, and threw her head back so that the sun could embrace her lovely clear complexion. In his mind, there was no other girl like her in the whole wide world.

'I wonder if we'll see the ghost,' she said, as they paused to look across to the far side of the lake.

Joe was puzzled. 'Ghost?'

'The master of Stanmore Manor,' she replied. 'He drowned when he was in his boat out here. Eunice swears that his wife, the duchess, had something to do with it.'

They took a moment to look all around, to take in the old lake house and the small, dark copse just beyond.

'I saw a ghost once,' said Joe.

Rosie swung a startled look at him. 'You did?'

Joe nodded. 'It was up front,' he said. 'I was on guard duty at the time, middle er the night. I could just see no man's land through a gap in the sandbags. There was this mist, then suddenly I saw it. This bloke – a young bloke in German uniform – seemed ter come from nowhere. 'E stretched out 'is 'ands as though he was tryin' ter reach out to us. I can see it now – clear as anyfin'. The look on 'is face, as though he was tryin' ter tell me somefin'. Gave me the shakes, I can tell yer.'

'But what made you think he was a ghost?' Rosie asked.

''Cos one moment 'e was there, an' the next 'e was gone – right before me very eyes.'

Rosie shivered.

'Course, none of me mates believed me when I told 'em,' continued Joe. 'They put it down ter trench fever. But I din't 'ave no fever, I can tell yer. I was as cold as a lump of ice.'

Rosie sighed, and perched down on an old tree stump. 'When you leave here, Joe,' she asked, 'will they really send you back up front?'

'I 'ope so,' he replied.

'You can't be serious?'

'Why not?' he said. 'I left a lot of me mates out there. I was lucky to get out of it all.'

'Lucky?' exclaimed Rosie. 'That poison gas

nearly killed you!'

Joe shrugged. 'Well, at least I survived. A lot of the lads didn't. They're my mates. We went fru a lot tergevver. I owe it to them ter get back out there an' do me bit.'

Rosie studied him closely as he talked. After all he'd been through, the close bond he still felt for those he had left behind astonished her.

'Yer know,' he continued, 'when you're cooped up in one of them trenches day after day, night after night, you 'ave a lot er time ter think. When it's quiet, when there ain't no guns blastin' away at yer, you 'ave time on yer 'ands. D'yer know, some of the blokes used ter read the same letter from 'ome over an' over again. Uvvers just sat an' smoked and stared up at the sky. Then a couple of the blokes wrote poems.'

'Poems?' asked Rosie.

'Oh, nuffin' much,' he continued. 'A lot er blokes in the army write poems – too many of 'em, if yer ask me. Mind you, *I* try me 'and at it from time to time. Nuffin' too fancy. Just puttin' down 'ow I feel, that's all.'

Rosie suddenly felt a surge of warmth for him. She loved the gawky, awkward way he moved around, and his ability to communicate moments that had meant so much to him. 'I'd love to read one of your poems some time,' she said.

Joe swung with a start. 'Oh, you could never do that,' he replied quickly.

'Why not?'

''Cos I only ever put down fings fer meself.'

Rosie threw him a reassuring smile. 'You know, Joe,' she said, 'sometimes it's not a bad thing to share your thoughts with people – that is, if you trust them.'

'Oh, I trust you,' Joe replied, quickly sitting beside her on the tree stump. 'Nobody can make a cup er Rosie like you.'

Rosie threw her head back and laughed, but as she did so Joe had a coughing fit. 'Are you all right, Joe?' she asked, slipping her arm round his waist. 'Just take it easy now.'

Joe recovered, and found himself looking into her eyes. He smiled. She smiled back shyly, and started to remove her arm from round his waist. 'No, don't take it away,' he pleaded. 'I like it.'

Their lips moved slowly towards each other.

'Rosie!'

They both turned with a start to see Eunice hurrying towards them.

'Hurry, Rosie!' spluttered Eunice breathlessly. 'You're wanted in Matron's office.'

'What!' gasped Rosie, leaping up in alarm from the tree stump. 'Why? What's the matter?'

'I dunno,' replied Eunice. 'But it must be some-fin' important, 'cos they've bin lookin' all over for yer.'

Matilda Buller was not an archetypal matron. Far from it. She always held herself well, creating a presence, with head up and chin tucked into her neck. She was in fact quite slight in build, and there was very little in her appearance to reveal that she had been in the nursing service for nearly thirty years. Her girls all liked her because, no matter how lowly their position, she never failed to stop to have an encouraging word with them when they passed in a hall or corridor. She also never harped on the fact that she had been widowed when she was nineteen years old.

By the time Rosie had climbed the great staircase and found her way to Mrs Buller's office at the far end of the first floor, her legs felt as though they would collapse beneath her. Why had she been summoned to Matron's office? she kept asking herself. What had she done that warranted her immediate appearance on her first day off? When she eventually reached the office door, she straightened her loose-fitting cotton dress, took off her hat, drew a deep breath, and tapped gently on the door.

'Come in!'

Rosie opened the door and went in. 'You asked to see me, ma'am,' she said falteringly. 'I'm Rose Little.'

'Ah!' said the redoubtable matron, rising from the chair at her desk. 'There you are, my dear! Come in, come in.'

Rosie closed the door, and approached the desk.

'I've heard a lot about you,' said Matron. 'Don't worry, nothing too awful. Sorry to bring you in on your day off, but I usually like to have a little introductory chat with my new girls. However...' she came from behind her desk to take a good look at Rosie, 'under the circumstances I'm afraid that will have to wait. At least until you've had a chance to talk with your visitor.'

Rosie looked puzzled. But when Matron turned her eyes towards a chair behind the door, she was shocked to see who was sitting there. 'Father!'

she gasped.

Richard Little, in Sunday best navy-blue suit, and holding a bowler hat in his hand, rose from his chair. 'Hello, Rose,' he said quietly.

'If you need anything,' said Matron, going to the door, 'you'll find me in the hall downstairs.' She opened the door, and left the room.

'Father!' exclaimed Rosie, the moment Matron had gone. 'What are you doing here?'

'Rose,' replied Richard, grim-faced, going to her, 'I have a serious situation on my hands, and I need some immediate explanations from you.'

'From me?' asked Rosie, absolutely bewildered. 'Father, what are you talking about?'

'Sit down, please, Rose,' he said.

Nervous about what was going on, Rosie hesitated, but then duly obeyed by taking over the chair her father had been sitting on.

Richard waited a moment before saying what he had to say. 'When did you start going to see Emile Harrington's wife?' he asked.

Rosie stared at him in disbelief.

'You've been going to visit Mrs Harrington on a regular basis for the past few months,' said Richard sternly. 'I want to know why.'

'Father...' She started to get up.

'Sit down, Rose!'

Taken aback by his brusque tone, Rosie did as she was told.

'You've been going to see her at her home in Leverton Street,' continued Richard. 'And you've been paying her sums of money. Don't bother to deny it, Rose, because I know for a fact that it's true.'

'I have no intention of denying it, Father,' replied Rosie, sitting back in the chair with her hat on her lap.

Richard was completely taken aback by her flagrant and unexpected response. 'Why, Rosie?' he asked.

Rosie stared at her father as though he had taken leave of his senses. Was this really the man that she had always looked up to, the man who had always been there to listen to her whenever she had a problem, the warm, loving, sensitive father who had never interfered in anything that she had wanted to do in life? In those few seconds, Matron's office seemed to blur around him as she looked into what were now deeply anxious eyes. 'Clara Harrington is my friend,' she said calmly. 'I've been giving her money – very small amounts of money – because she is the treasurer of a cause that we both belong to.'

Unable to grasp what he was hearing, Richard sat on the chair beside her. 'A cause?' he asked with incomprehension.

'For women,' replied Rosie.

'Oh my God!' gasped Richard, flopping back in his chair. 'You're mixed up with those damned suffragettes?'

'No, Father!' Rosie replied adamantly. 'This has nothing to do with politics. This is about women – young girls of my own age who've been foolish enough to get involved with...' she briefly lowered her eyes, 'certain kinds of men.' She looked up at him again. 'They need help, Father. They've been abandoned by their parents and thrown out on to the streets. Then they struggle to find enough money to go to one of these ghastly backstreet butchers who cut them open and very nearly kill them.'

'Abortion?' asked Richard, dazed by what he was hearing. 'You're talking about ... abortion?'

Rosie took a deep breath. 'Yes, Father,' she replied boldly.

'You and Mrs Harrington have been giving money to these girls to help them have abortions?'

'No, Father,' replied Rosie. 'The money is to *prevent* them from doing anything as reckless as that. It's to help them stand on their own two feet. Clara and I are not the only ones who raise funds for them; there are plenty of other women, women from all walks of life. And, in any case, it's not just about money. It's about showing these poor creatures that there *are* people who care for them.'

Richard waited a moment, then got up from his chair. He went across to the window and looked out. 'Are you aware,' he said, without turning to her, 'that what you are doing is totally illegal?' He allowed her no time to reply before looking round again at her. 'Are you also aware that your association with Mrs Harrington is not only being misinterpreted by my employees, but also causing the most bitter resentment?'

Rosie was dumbfounded. 'Father, I – I don't know what you're talking about. What do you mean, "resentment"?'

'Rose,' said Richard, coming back to her, 'are you aware that there's a war on? Are you aware that anyone with any connections to Germany is likely to be the target of intense hostility?'

84

'For God's sake, Father!' snapped Rose indignantly. 'Mrs Harrington is not a German.'

'No, but her husband is!' retorted Richard. 'He's been receiving threats from some of my own employees at the factory.'

'What!' gasped Rosie, horrified.

'They're not interested in whether Emile Harrington's wife is German or English. All they know is that you've been paying regular visits to see her, which, in their simplistic eyes is unpatriotic. You're only eighteen years old, Rose. I just don't understand this newly found independence of yours.'

'There's nothing wrong with being independent, Father,' replied Rosie defiantly. She stood up and walked past him to the other side of the room. 'You said yourself, there's a war on. That's why I'm doing this job. That's why I'm trying to do my bit. And when they send me to the front, I won't be an eighteen-year-old girl any more; I'll be just like all the others, a nurse, trying to help save the lives of the men who are out there fighting for *us*.'

'That will never happen, Rose,' insisted Richard, confronting her. 'Just let me remind you again that until you come of age, you are still under my jurisdiction, and I will make quite certain that no child of mine will ever be sent out to the battlefield.'

'If you do that, Father,' said Rosie, going to the door, 'I promise you I shall never respect anything you say again.' She opened the door, and turned back to him. 'And as far as Clara Harrington is concerned, I shall continue to see her and to be her friend, and I shall continue to work with her.' She left the room, closing the door behind her.

For several moments, Richard just stood there, dazed and shattered.

Chapter 5

On Sunday afternoon, a steady trickle of visitors passed through the tall iron gates of the manor, to make their way along the leafy main driveway to the house. Waiting patiently there to greet them were their sons and husbands, fathers and brothers, some in uniform, others in pyjamas and dressing gowns – all the patients who were well enough to stand up or move around on crutches, but also those who had to rely on nurses to support them or push them around in wheel-chairs.

Amongst the visitors were Joe's mum, Annie Upton, a woman in her late forties, who had a lovely ruddy complexion admirably set off by her Sunday best bonnet, and an ample figure shown to advantage in a simple below-the-knee-length floral cotton dress. With her was Joe's elder brother, Paul, a muscular, thick-set young man, with rugged good looks, flashing dark eyes behind thin metal-rimmed spectacles, greased brown hair, an uncomfortable stiff white collar and tie, flat cap and a grey suit that seemed much too tight for him. However, Paul's strong physical appearance disguised the fact that his poor eyesight had been responsible for him failing the army medical examination, a fact that had not entirely caused him a great deal of distress.

Joe was perched on the fountain wall, eagerly waiting to greet them before leading them off to what had once been the formal gardens behind the house, where summer visitors could sit with those they had come to see. Joe's eyes gleamed as his mum unpacked the bits and pieces of food she had brought him, including a big chunk of beef mince pie, some cold sausages and potatoes, and a packet of his favourite liquorice allsorts. Paul's contribution was a quart bottle of brown ale, which Joe and he quickly started on the moment they had settled down at one of the garden tables.

'So where's Gran?' Joe asked his mum. 'I fawt yer said she was comin' wiv yer terday?'

Annie bristled. 'She's laid up with her usual lumbago,' she said sourly in the Yorkshire accent that she had never lost over the years. 'In any case, it's just as well. She'd only've complained about sommat or other on t' way. She's becoming a right misery in 'er old age. I can't do nowt right for 'er. But, by gum, I'll tell yer this much, lad,' she said, munching on one of her own home-made biscuits. 'Did yer know they've put up t' bus fares? It cost us a penny ha'penny more to get 'ere this week!'

''Ighway bloody robbery!' growled Paul, whose accent was, like Joe's, more East End than York-shire, wiping ale foam from his lips with the back of his hand. 'They should dish out a bus pass fer visiters who 'ave ter come all the way out ter this place.'

'Oh, well,' said Joe, 'yer won't 'ave ter do it much longer, 'cos I'll soon be 'ome.'

Annie shot him a glare. 'You what?' she barked crossly.

Joe took the bottle of brown from his brother and gulped down a mouthful. 'I saw the doc last night,' he said. ''E reckons I might get out of 'ere soon. 'E says I'm much better.' Even as he spoke, he spluttered and coughed.

'Well, I wish yer'd told us that before we come!' snorted Annie. 'We could've saved the fares!'

Joe shrugged and handed the bottle of brown back to his brother. Knowing that his mum had never been the most tactful person, he usually took what she said with a pinch of salt. 'Any word from Dad?' he asked.

Annie's face crumpled. 'Not a word,' she sighed. 'I'm worried sick.'

'Oh, 'e's all right, Ma,' said Joe reassuringly. 'Yer know wot Dad's like. 'E never was much of a letter writer.'

'Some of t' lads from the Yorkshire come 'ome over two weeks ago,' said Annie impassively. 'I know 'cos I read it in t' papers. They're probably all 'ome be now. 'Cept yer dad.'

'Oh, I don't know,' said Joe, exchanging a quizzical look with his brother. 'Most of the regiments are all over the place. An' in any case, if anyfin' *ad* 'appened ter Dad, we'd've 'eard by now. Yer can bet yer life 'e'll soon be walkin' fru our front door an' wonderin' wot we're all goin' on about.'

'Yer never know,' replied Annie, munching on her biscuit, and staring aimlessly at the ground.

Paul didn't say a thing, and just looked uncomfortable. Unlike his young brother, he had never had the ability to be much of a support to anyone. 'So,' he asked, lecherously, after downing another gulp of ale, 'wos the nurses like?'

'Couldn't be better,' replied Joe, ignoring what his brother really wanted to know. 'I wouldn't do their job if they paid me a million. Emptyin' bedpans, washin' blokes with only 'alf a body, clearin' up sick, and Christ knows wot. An' yer should just see wot they 'ave ter cope wiv out in those field 'ospitals.'

Annie looked up sharply. 'Field 'ospitals?' she gasped in disbelief. 'Yer mean they send lasses up front?'

'You bet yer life they do!' replied Joe. 'I tell yer, I tip my 'at to 'em. They got real guts... Hey!' He suddenly leaped up, and called out to Rosie, whom he could just see passing in the distance. 'Rosie!'

'What's up?' asked Annie, as Joe rushed off.

'Someone I want you to meet,' Joe called back. Puzzled, Annie and Paul waited whilst Joe went across to fetch Rosie.

'Rosie,' he said proudly, 'this is me ma, and me bruvver, Paul. 'E's the ugly one er the family!'

Rosie smiled uncomfortably.

'This is Rosie,' said Joe. 'She's my nurse. Rosie looks after me.'

'Good afternoon, Mrs Upton,' said Rosie, offering her hand shyly. 'I'm very happy to meet you. Joe's told me so much about you.'

''As 'e now?' returned Annie suspiciously, with a limp handshake.

Paul's eyes were glowing as he got up to meet Rosie. 'Joe ain't mentioned nuffin' about *you*, 'he said.

'Hello, Paul,' replied Rosie, avoiding his gaze. Her hand was stinging from his hard handshake.

'Soon as we got off the train at Charing Cross,' said Joe enthusiastically, 'Rosie used ter serve all the lads wiv tea. That's why we called 'er Rosie Lee. I reckon 'all the Shiny Seventh know 'er.'

'Looks like it,' quipped Paul, with a smirk.

Rosie tried not to look embarrassed. 'You must be very pleased to see Joe looking so much better,' she said quickly.

'If 'e's "so much better",' said Annie, 'when's 'e coming home?'

Rosie shrugged. 'That's up to the doctors, Mrs Upton,' she replied. 'But you don't have to worry. We're taking good care of him.'

'I don't approve of young lasses doing war work,' said Annie, straightening her bonnet unnecessarily. 'Their place is in the 'ome, looking after t' menfolk.'

'But if the menfolk are not around, Mrs Upton,' answered Rosie politely, 'surely someone has to fill in for them?'

'Ah!' grinned Paul. 'Sounds like yer've got a mind of yer own, Rosie Lee. Just like that loony lot what want the vote.'

'I'm a nurse, Paul,' replied Rosie, correcting him. 'I'm not interested in politics.'

'But yer would like the vote?'

Rosie smiled sweetly without actually looking

90

at him. 'I imagine it will happen one day, don't you think?'

Paul grinned. He liked a girl who could answer back without needing time to work out what she was going to say.

Annie felt differently. She didn't like young girls to have minds of their own. It made her feel uncomfortable; she had spent the best part of her own life letting the breadwinner of the family make all the decisions. 'So what do *your* mam and dad reckon on you doing this job?' she asked, mischievously.

Rosie tried not to show her concerns. 'I don't really know, Mrs Upton,' she replied unconvincingly. 'That's a question you'd have to ask *them.*'

'Can't be easy for them,' Annie said, taking a huge bite from an apple, 'coming from *your* walk of life.'

'Everyone's trying to do their bit for this war, Mrs Upton,' Rosie said, 'no matter where they come from. I imagine it can't be easy for you with your husband away from home.'

Annie lowered her eyes. It wasn't very often that anyone noticed *her* feelings. 'I just wish we were still living back 'ome – I mean our *real* 'ome.'

Rosie smiled sympathetically. 'It must have been very beautiful – with all that lovely countryside. I've heard many people say what a grand place Yorkshire is.'

With a remark like that, Annie wanted to warm to the girl. But for some reason, she found it impossible to do so. 'Bethnal Green suits us fine,' was all she would say, before taking another bite out of her apple.

Rosie's face crumpled. 'I'm sure it does,' she replied tactfully. 'I'd better be getting back,' she said to Joe. 'I start my first night duty at six o'clock.'

'I'll walk yer back to the nurses' block,' said Joe.

'No,' insisted Rosie. 'You stay and have as much time as you can with your mother and Paul. I'll see you back at the ward later.' She turned to Annie. 'It was nice to meet you, Mrs Upton.'

Annie nodded. 'Tell them doctors ter send our Joe 'ome,' she said, mouth full with apple.

'I will,' said Rosie, with a polite smile. 'Goodbye, Paul. Nice to have met you.'

Paul stretched out his hand. 'You too, Rosie,' he replied, with a smile that seemed to her more like a smirk. ''Ope ter see yer again.'

Rosie smiled back. She tried not to notice how sensually he was shaking her hand. 'Goodbye,' she said gracefully, before strolling off back towards the house.

Both Joe and Paul watched her go.

'Got 'er 'ead screwed on the right way, that one,' said Paul.

'A bit too much, if yer ask me,' mumbled Annie.

'Well, yer'd better get used to it, Ma,' said Joe, eyes glued towards Rosie, who seemed to him to be floating on air as she reached the house and disappeared inside. ''Cos from now one I'm goin' ter be seein' a lot more of 'er.'

Leverton Street was little more than a stone's throw from the main shopping area of Kentish Town Road. The houses there were all Victorian

92

two-storey buildings, which at one time must have been quite pretty until they fell into disrepair during the period leading up to the start of the war. The people who lived there were a curious mix of lower-middle-class families, which included shop employees, construction workers, a candle-maker, a seamstress, a Malaysian Chinese family whose breadwinner had volunteered for Lord Kitchener's army and several Jewish money lenders. Emile Harrington and his wife, Clara, lived in a ground-floor flat in the corner house. They rarely had visitors, so when they did it took them by surprise.

'I'm sorry to call on you at home, Emile,' said Richard Little, who was standing on the front doorstep, 'but what I have to say can't be discussed at the factory.'

The startled little man who had opened the door to him was Emile Harrington, once Emile Hartmann, whose slight build, shiny cheeks and fringe of prematurely grey hair around a bald pate made him look older than he actually was.

'Mr Little!' spluttered Emile, his German accent suppressed by years of living in Kentish Town. 'What a wonderful surprise. Come in! Please come in!'

Standing behind Emile in the dimly lit front passage was Clara, who was not at all what Richard had expected. She was even shorter than her husband, and her features were only visible once she had stepped into the light. She wore her light brown hair swept into a bun behind her head, and a cameo brooch held together a high dress collar at her throat.

'This is my wife, Clara,' said Emile proudly. 'I don't think you've ever met?'

'Good evening, Mrs Harrington,' said Richard, removing his trilby hat.

'How nice to meet you at last, Mr Little,' she replied, in her own North London accent. Surprised and just a touch embarrassed that he had not responded to her greeting, Clara led him into the front parlour. Emile followed on behind.

The room was a treasure house of trinkets – everything from small porcelain figures to silver snuff boxes and little brass bells. Although the furniture and curtains were modest, the mock Persian carpet which covered the parquet floor gave the room warmth and a simple elegance.

'As you can see,' said Emile almost apologetically, 'my wife has a passion for collecting everything she can lay her hands on. I don't think we'd have had any of it if we'd had children.'

'Emile,' said his wife reproachfully, standing on a pouf to turn up the light on the two gas mantles on the wall above the mantelpiece. 'Aren't you going to offer Mr Little a drink? There's that bottle of plum brandy my mother bought us the Christmas before last.'

'Thank you, no, Mrs Harrington,' said Richard before Emile had a chance to answer. 'I've come to talk on a rather urgent matter.'

'Oh – forgive me,' said Clara, stepping down from the pouf. 'I'll leave you to talk with my husband.'

'No, please don't go,' said Richard as she made for the door. 'Actually – it's *you* I've really come to see.'

94

Clara swung a puzzled look at her husband, then turned back to her guest. '*Me?*'

'I understand you know my daughter, Mrs Harrington?' asked Richard, after an awkward hesitation.

'Rosie?' asked Clara. 'Yes, of course I know her. Such a sweet girl...'

'I've come to ask you to stop seeing her.'

Clara and Emile exchanged bewildered looks. 'I – I don't understand, Mr Little.'

'My wife and Rosie are helping young girls in distress, Mr Little,' said Emile.

'I know precisely what they're doing, Emile,' replied Richard, 'but I must ask you, Mrs Harrington, not to involve Rose.'

'But why?' asked Clara, completely taken aback. 'We're not doing anything illegal. Someone has to be there to help these poor young creatures. What we're doing is surely a very humane act.'

'It may be to you and me, Mrs Harrington,' said Richard, 'but unfortunately others may not think so. Your relationship with my daughter is attracting a certain amount of unsavoury attention at the factory.'

'Mr Little!' gasped Emile in disbelief.

Richard looked at his employee. His was a good, honest face. This was a man who had never caused a moment's trouble since he came to work at the factory many years ago. Although his was undeniably a German face, Emile's heart and soul were as British as the best of them. And his wife, Clara, looked as though she wouldn't know how to hurt anyone if she tried. They were as good, honest and cosy a couple as they were depicted in

95

the simple painting hanging on the wall over the fireplace. 'There are rumblings amongst the men, Emile,' he said. 'They don't trust you. It pains me to say it but, as far as they're concerned, once a German always a German.'

Clara clasped a hand to her mouth in horror.

'But that's absurd!' exclaimed Emile.

'*I* know that, Emile,' said Richard earnestly, 'and so do you. But the people who are stirring up trouble are small-minded men who haven't the sense to look beyond the end of their noses. They seem to have convinced themselves that your wife and my daughter are involved in some kind of propaganda campaign – to support the enemy.'

Emile recoiled. Even the idea of such a thing both disgusted and distressed him.

'May I sit down for a moment, please?'

'Oh, Mr Little – *please!*' Clara immediately straightened a cushion on one of the two arm-chairs for him to sit. Then she sat opposite him while Emile continued to stand.

'Now listen to me, both of you,' said Richard, his voice lowered as though there might have been someone eavesdropping. 'My concern for the two of you will be increased tomorrow when I tell the workforce about the emergency plans the company is about to embark upon.'

'Emergency plans?' asked Emile, his face now pale and drawn.

'As you know,' continued Richard, 'since the start of the war, the demand has dropped for what Little and Company have been producing for so many years. People no longer have money

96

to spend on new dinner services or tea sets. Austerity and uncertainty have changed all that. The need now is for factory space to produce materials that are desperately required for the war effort – especially up front. That's why I've come to an arrangement with the local authority to convert our factory. As soon as we can complete the structural work, we're going to start manufacturing gas respirators.'

Both Emile and his wife were visibly shocked.

'I'm sure you realise the immense difficulties this will cause, not least the security clearance we shall have to impose on everyone working for us.'

'Are you telling me,' said Emile, 'that someone who was born in what is now an enemy state will no longer be able to work for you?'

'Emile,' replied Richard firmly, 'I would *never* ask you to leave, *never*. Your work with my company has not only been exemplary, but you have been the most trustworthy employee anyone could ever wish to have. But there *is* a problem I have to face up to, and cannot ignore. There's the Defence of the Realm Act. Because of this war, the authorities have the power to search homes, interrogate, stop any foreign people in the street...'

'Mr Little,' agonised Emile, 'I am a British subject.'

'I *know* that, Emile,' Richard replied, with deep anguish. 'And so do those idiots at the factory. But this is war. Our boys are dying like flies out on those battlefields. People are crazed with hate, and thirsty for revenge.'

Emile found it hard to believe what he was

hearing. In a daze, he slowly rose, went to the window, and stared out aimlessly. *Crazed with hate?* Were these the same people he had lived and worked with for so many years? Were these the same people who had embraced him as one of their own when he came to work for Little and Company so long ago? Were these the same people who, knowing that Emile and his wife were childless, had brought their own children to meet them, to laugh and play with them? 'So what do you want me to do, Mr Little?'

Richard got up and went to him. 'I want you to be careful, Emile,' he said. 'Especially now. Especially at a time when things are changing in the factory. You'll be watched, not only by the authorities, but by your colleagues.'

Emile turned round to face him. 'My colleagues?' he asked. 'Colleagues who used to be my friends?'

'I tell you this for your own protection, Emile,' said Richard. 'For your protection – and mine.' He turned back to Clara. 'And I beg you not to encourage my daughter to come here to see you. Rose is young and impressionable. Her mother and I love her very much. If anything should happen to her...' He stopped when he saw that tears were rolling down Clara Harrington's cheeks. He went to her. 'I'm sorry, Mrs Harrington. I'm truly sorry. You and your husband are good people.'

'But not good enough, Mr Little,' said Emile sadly from the other side of the room. 'Just *not* good enough.'

The candle lamp flickered so much on the desk at

the end of the ward that Rosie found it difficult to write her night report. In any case, everything was so strange to her that it was hard to stop her concentration from wandering. The ward itself was in semi-darkness, but the sound of men snoring or turning restlessly in their sleep was something she had never experienced before. Nor were the human smells that mixed with the pungent hospital atmosphere of ether and other pain-killing drugs. Several times Rosie put down her pen and sat back in her chair in the semi-dark, trying to take in this new experience, trying to work out how long it would last, and if *she* would be able to last the course. It had been an eventful day, in many ways quite dreadful, especially the visit from her father whose one-sided view of her relationship with Clara Harrington had filled her with apprehension and disappointment. Why couldn't he see that the work she and Clara were doing was so important? And what would she do if he *did* carry out his threat of preventing her from pursuing her career with the nursing service? Then she thought about her brief meeting with Joe's mother and brother. What a strange woman Annie Upton was – in many ways like her own father, with her narrow view of a woman's role in life. However, she knew there was more to Annie than that. Deep beneath that veneer of in-difference was a woman who had worked hard all her life, and who loved her family. Joe's brother, Paul, however, was somewhat different. For some reason his whole manner unsettled Rosie. Perhaps it was the way he had shaken her hand and looked at her when she'd left, or perhaps it was just the way he'd seemed to talk down to his brother. It was hard to tell. She was roused from her thoughts by a rustling sound coming from Joe's bed. She got up quickly and went across to find him propped up against his pillows, wide awake.

'Joe!' she whispered, with the only light coming from the distant candle on her desk. 'Why aren't you sleeping?'

'Too much ter fink about,' he replied, his voice hushed but breathless.

'This is not the time for thinking, Joe,' she replied, perching on the edge of his bed. 'You need your sleep.'

'Not 'alf as much as I need you.'

Rosie was stopped in her tracks. 'Don't be silly now, Joe,' she said softly, but sweetly. 'You hardly know me.'

'Oh, I know yer, all right, Rosie Lee,' he replied. 'I feel as though I've known yer all my life. I only wish I had.'

Rosie started to get up, but he took hold of her hand and held on to it. 'Don't go, Rosie,' he pleaded. 'Stay and talk ter me fer a minute. Then I promise ter be a good boy.'

Rosie relented and sat down again.

'Wot did yer fink of me ma?' he asked.

For one brief moment Rosie was taken off guard by his question. 'Oh,' she stammered awkwardly, 'she's very nice, Joe. She's clearly very fond of you.'

'Yeah, I s'ppose so,' he replied dismissively. 'Though I didn't much like the way she talked to yer.'

100

'What do you mean?'

'Oh, I don't know,' he said, with a sigh. 'Ma's like that at times. She likes people ter fink she knows everythin' – but she don't. But she means well. After you'd gone, she said you was a right good-looker.'

Outside, an owl hooted.

'I have to go, Joe,' Rosie whispered. 'And you must get to sleep.'

Once again he held on to her hand. 'Can I tell yer somefin', Rosie?' he asked. 'One night when I was on guard in the trenches, this big bird come an' sit on the sandbags just in front er me. I could see 'im plain as daylight, 'cos it was a full moon, and this bird was all white colour. 'E 'ad great big eyes. Fer some reason they looked purple in that light. 'E looked straight at me – an' yer know wot? 'E wasn't a bit scared. In fact, when I put me 'and out ter touch 'im, 'e never budged an inch. 'E even let me stroke the fevvers on 'is breast. Beautiful creature – tame as they come. Amazin', i'n't it?'

'Good night, Joe,' said Rosie, finally getting up, thinking he could certainly tell a tall tale. 'Sleep well.'

'D'yer know wot 'appened to 'im?' whispered Joe. 'D'yer know wot 'appened ter that bird? 'E got done by a sniper's bullet from the uvver side. Wicked sods. They always shoot at anyfin' they set their sights on.'

One of the soldiers at the far end of the ward suddenly called out for a bedpan. Rosie went to him, calmed him down, then, after collecting her candle lamp, hurried off to the small treatment

101

room at the end of the ward. Whilst she was searching for the bedpan, she suddenly heard someone enter the room behind her, but just as she turned to look, she found her lips covered by Joe's in a warm kiss.

'Joe!' she whispered, once she'd pulled away.

'Don't be angry wiv me, Rosie,' he whispered breathlessly. 'I've wanted ter do that ever since I laid eyes on yer. I've never known a gel like you before. All the uvvers I knew seemed ter fink I was some kind er village idiot. I s'ppose they fawt that was clever. But not you. You're diff'rent, Rosie. It don't matter 'ow long yer've known someone. It's wot yer feel inside that counts.' He moved closer to her.

Rosie's first instinct was to step back out of his way. After all, he was her patient. But as she looked into his clear blue eyes in the flickering light of the candle, she felt a warm glow that ran right through her body. His lips searched for hers again, but she didn't resist. She responded by wrapping her arms around his waist, and he gently cupped her face in his hands.

It was some time before the patient at the end of the ward got his bedpan.

Chapter 6

During the following weeks, Rosie and Joe found it difficult to continue what was clearly going to be a very close relationship. After all, nurses were always expected to concentrate on their work, and warned not to have any kind of emotional involvement with the patients. This made life very difficult for Rosie, who found it almost impossible to conceal from the other girls what was going on between her and Joe. None the less, the two of them did manage to meet from time to time, mainly when Rosie was off duty, which gave her and Joe the chance to take a stroll around the extensive manor grounds. Every time they met, they were drawn more and more to each other, regardless of the fact that they came from such different backgrounds. It was not only a genuine meeting of minds, but a romantic, physical attraction that made them yearn for each other's company whenever they were apart.

Rosie's one dread, however, was that, while her romance with Joe was blooming, she and Eunice were gaining enough nursing experience in the respiratory ward to make them eligible for early service up front. Despite her growing confidence in her work, and the close bond she was forming with her friends Eunice, Titch and Binnie, Rosie found the day-to-day routine distressing, mainly because of the life-and-death struggles the soldier patients were experiencing whilst trying to recover from the deadly effects of the poison-gas attacks. Each day there was a new crisis as one patient after another cried out in pain and discomfort, with high fevers, burning sensations in their chests and frequent spasms of horrifying breathlessness. During those first few weeks, Rosie learned a great deal from the doctors about the effects of chlorine gas, which, in some patients, produced lesions and congestion in the pulmonary system, more often than not resulting in suffocation within minutes of being exposed to the deadly clouds of gas. However, the one thing that always puzzled her was the fact that none of the patients seemed willing to talk about what had happened to him, or the circumstances in which he had received his terrible life-threatening conditions. It was as if, every time she asked any of them a question about their time in the trenches, she was blocked by a wall of silence. Despite his one story about the owl, even Joe was reluctant to talk about the things that he and his mates were trying to forget. For them, it seemed as though nightmares would for a long time remain part of their day as well as the night.

By the end of September, several patients had been released from the Rehabilitation Centre, and sent back home to convalesce in the loving care of their own families. Joe's recovery, however, was still not complete, and it was clear that he would be unable to rejoin his unit for some time. None the less, his doctors agreed that a home environment would be the best way for him to regain his confidence, and so, despite the dread of being parted from Rosie, he too was finally released. Rosie herself was deeply upset that Joe wouldn't be around any more, and, despite the close relationship that now existed between them, she had an uneasy feeling that she might never see him again.

After that, events took a dramatic turn for Rosie and her friends Eunice, Titch and Binnie.

The Terrible Four sat waiting anxiously in Sister Jarrett's office. Although they had a pretty good idea why they had been summoned to see her, the reality was really quite nerve-racking, and so it came as a relief when the sister arrived and sat at her desk facing them.

'Well, young ladies,' she began, 'you have your marching orders. You're off to France next Tuesday.'

Rosie immediately tensed, whilst there was a flurry of quiet anticipation from the others.

'*All* of us, Sister?' asked Eunice. 'Are we all goin' tergevver?'

'To the same place?' asked Titch.

'You'll all be travelling together,' replied Sister Jarrett. 'At the moment I'm not sure whether you'll be posted to the same field hospital. All I can tell you is that you are to report to the sister-in-charge at St-Etienne, where several nurses have been waiting to be relieved for the past two months. I have to warn you that the Germans are dug in there, and the fighting has apparently at times been quite fierce, with loss of life, and many wounded on both sides.'

For one rare moment, The Terrible Four were

reduced to silence, trying to take in the implications of what was obviously going to be a difficult posting.

'Can you tell us please, Sister,' asked Binnie, sitting straight-backed in her chair, 'which front this field hospital is situated on?'

Sister Jarrett hesitated before replying. 'At this stage I'm not permitted to tell you,' she said evasively. 'But you'll be travelling across the Channel to Boulogne on a military transport ferry, where you'll be met by someone from GC HQ and taken to your destination.'

Rosie lowered her eyes anxiously. Her stomach felt like stone. The other girls looked nervous and apprehensive.

'Well, don't look so grim!' said Sister Jarrett, doing her best to make light of the news she had just given them. 'At least you'll all have some time with your families before then – one week to be precise. It will also give you a chance to talk things over with your parents.'

Rosie was aware that that remark was probably directed at her.

'You'll forgive my askin', ma'am,' said Titch tentatively, 'but have you any idea how long we'll be over there?'

'How long is the war going to last, my dear?' replied Sister Jarrett sympathetically. 'All I can tell you is that during the first year of the war alone there were over three hundred and fifty thousand British army service casualties. Many of those were fatal. This year alone has seen some of the fiercest battles, both in France and in Belgium. I don't have to tell you how desperately our nursing services are required out there.' She looked from one to another of the four girls. She knew exactly how they felt.

'You know,' she said, getting up from her desk and looking out of the window, 'there is a woman, a nurse I once knew, who has worked in Belgium for many years, helping to set up a training school for nurses at the medical institute there. Over the years she has worked tirelessly to modernise the treatment of so many diseases and injuries. During this war, in one way or another, she has saved the lives of many of our own soldiers. She is a remarkable, courageous woman.' She turned back slowly to the four girls, who were all staring in awe at her. 'You may have read about her in the newspapers. Her name is Edith Cavell. She is now in a German prison in Brussels awaiting trial for helping Allied soldiers escape back to their homelands.'

Rosie squeezed her hands so tightly on her lap that her knuckles turned white.

'I only tell you this,' continued Sister Jarrett, 'because Nurse Cavell is a shining example to those who believe in selfless devotion to duty. We women have an important part to play in this war. Our menfolk are dying in their thousands on those fields out there. I know I can rely on all of you to help give them all the support you possibly can.'

Later in the day, after passing on their duties to the next intake of trainee nurses, The Terrible Four packed their bags for the journey back to their homes, where they would spend one week with their families before the unnerving journey to the battlefields of France.

'This 'ole fing gives me the willies,' said Eunice, stuffing her uniform into her small suitcase. 'I mean we've done less than a munff at this place, an' 'ere we are on our way ter the Front. I just 'ope no one conks out on me out there!'

'You'll do fine, Eunice,' said Binnie reassuringly, whilst putting on her hat in front of the dormitory mirror. 'We've learned enough to take care of the basic things.'

'It's not the basic things *I'm* worried about,' added Titch, her singsong voice emphasising her anxious words. 'It's the hard parts – helping to stitch up wounds – I mean really *bad* wounds.'

'I didn't think you were squeamish, Titch,' said Binnie, teasing her.

'*Me* squeamish?' protested Titch, in a sudden burst of indignation. 'I'm not squeamish. I just don't like the sight of blood, that's all!'

Binnie grinned back at her affectionately.

Rosie packed her few things in silence. The sudden impact of what was happening was only now taking its toll on her. Eunice was right. Less than a month was far too short a time to train a nurse for the type of work they were expected to tackle. It could only mean one thing: that the situation up front was even more serious than any of those bigwigs at the top was willing to admit. So much was going through her mind. When she got out into those battle areas, would she be able to face up to all the horrors awaiting her and her three friends? Would her nerve hold? Would she be able to cope with all the discomforts of living rough, something she had never had to do in her highly sheltered life. And what about Joe? How was *he* going to feel when he knew where she was going? Would he still be there waiting for her when she returned? And how was she going to be able to break the news to her father and mother? Would her father do what he had promised, and try to hold her back from the job she had set her mind to do? The more she churned these things over, the worse she felt.

'Penny for your thoughts, Rosie?' Binnie had slipped a reassuring arm around her waist.

Rosie sighed. 'This is all so unreal, Binnie,' she said. 'As soon as we get used to this place, they ship us out. I'm not ready for this. I'm just not ready.'

Binnie gently turned her round. 'If anyone's ready, Rosie,' she said in her usual caring way, 'it's you. You know, I wish I could have been like you when I was your age. You're so level-headed about things; you have such quiet confidence.'

'Confidence! *Me?*'

'Yes, Rosie,' Binnie replied. 'You have confidence because you never do anything without thinking about it first. For someone your age, that's quite exceptional.'

'Binnie,' said Rosie. 'I'm scared out of my life!'

'You're not the only one, mate!' said Eunice.

'Nonsense, Eunice!' insisted Rosie. 'You're as tough as old Harry!'

'To 'ell wiv ol' 'Arry!' said Eunice. 'I'm dreadin' wot we're gettin' ourselves into. Wot say you, Titch?'

They were met with an unexpected silence

from Titch. But when they turned to look at the pint-sized Welsh girl, her face was crumpled up in tears.

'Titch!' exclaimed Eunice, hurrying across to her. 'Wot is it, mate?'

Titch shook her head. 'I'm not scared where I'm going,' she sniffed. 'I'm just worried that I may never get back home, that I may never see my mam again.'

As Titch started to weep, Eunice took her in her arms. 'Yer don't 'ave ter worry about that, mate,' she said, hugging Titch close to her shoulder. 'Yer ain't goin' ter be alone. We'll all be there right wiv yer, won't we, gels?'

'Of course we will!' said Rosie.

'The Terrible Four, Titch!' called Binnie proudly. 'That old Kaiser won't get *us* down!'

'Hear, hear!' agreed the others.

'Look,' said Rosie brightly. 'Let's make a vow right here and now. Let's promise that we'll never let anyone part us, we'll always stick together – right?'

'Right!' said the others.

'We may not know each other all that well,' continued Rosie, 'but there's one thing we *have* proved over these past few weeks, and that is – we've got determination.' She went amongst the other girls and held out her hand, palm upwards. 'Let's take a vow: to friendship.'

'Friendship!' declared Eunice, triumphantly slapping the palm of Rosie's hand and leaving it there.

'Friendship!' blurted Binnie, placing her hand vigorously on top of Eunice's hand.

There was a moment's hesitation as they all waited for Titch's response.

Finally Titch turned round and gently placed her own hand on top of the other three hands. 'Friendship,' she said quietly, but firmly.

'To us!' proclaimed Binnie, grinning with great admiration at Rosie. 'The Terrible Four!'

'The Terrible Four!' proclaimed all four girls, their hands locked together in a warm, united embrace.

Mrs Winnet rarely sang to herself in the kitchen when she was cooking these days. It was a very sad fact of life, but things in the Little household were not as they used to be before the war. In those days, despite Christian's illness, there was always an atmosphere of fun; people laughed and talked to each other with smiles on their faces. But not now. Now, it was all gloom and despair. Of course, she knew the reason why. No Rosie. That girl was the life and soul of the Little family, and now that she had gone there was nothing to look forward to each day. Worst of all was poor little Christian. Although everyone treated him as though he was just an ordinary fourteen-year-old boy, he wasn't ordinary at all. He was special. Soon after he was born, Mrs Winnet had wept openly as she held him in her arms, proclaiming over and over again, 'You're the livin' image of yer dad! The livin' image!' He wasn't, of course. In fact he wasn't a bit like either of his parents. If he was like anyone at all, oddly enough it was Rosie. Some people had said that if it hadn't been for the age gap, brother and sister could almost have been twins. Rosie was very proud of that. Old Mrs Winnet knew how much the girl had always loved her young brother, and had always looked after him. Sad days indeed. As far as Mrs Winnet was concerned, the best place for a cook was in her domain, her kitchen. That's where she belonged. That's where she could keep her feelings to herself. How then could she have known that today was going to be different?

'No songs today, Winnie?'

The poor woman swung round with a shocked start as the voice called to her from the door. 'Miss Rosie!' she gasped, nearly dropping the china plate she had been washing in the sink.

Rosie hurried across to throw her arms around the old housekeeper. 'I've missed you, Winnie!' she blurted. 'I can't tell you how much I've missed you!'

'You mean yer've missed me apple pie!' replied Mrs Winnet, shaking with excitement.

'You're quite right,' said Rosie, with a huge grin. 'There's no one in that hospital who knows how to cook like you.'

'Let me look at yer,' said the old lady, looking Rosie up and down. 'This ain't good, Rosie,' she pronounced. 'It just ain't good. Yer've lost weight.'

'Oh, come on now, Winnie!' said Rosie. 'I haven't been away *that* long.'

'Even so,' replied the old cook, 'you're as thin as a pencil. I can see we're goin' ter 'ave ter fatten you up.' She immediately turned away to get something from the pantry.

'I doubt you'll have much time for that, Winnie,' said Rosie.

The old lady swung back to her. 'What's that yer say?'

'I'm only home for a week,' Rosie said, adding cautiously, 'I'm being sent – to another posting.'

Mrs Winnet stared at her with some trepidation. 'Another postin'?' she asked suspiciously, 'Where to?'

'You know better than to ask questions like that, Winnie,' replied Rosie. 'There's a war on. In any case, I don't know where.'

The old lady slowly came back to her, holding a loaf of bread. 'It's nowhere ... dangerous, is it?'

'Don't be silly,' replied Rosie dismissively. 'I'm not a soldier. I'm not going to fight anyone.'

''Ave yer told yer mum an' dad about this?' asked Mrs Winnet.

'Haven't seen them yet,' replied Rosie lightly, sitting down at the kitchen table. 'Is Father at work?'

'Yes,' said the old lady. 'But 'e's been comin' 'ome early these days. If yer ask me, 'e's overdoin' fings. God knows what's goin' on at that factory now they've stopped makin' the porcelain.'

This troubled Rosie. 'So all this government stuff *is* going ahead?'

'As far as I know,' said the old lady. 'I don't ask questions. But I reckon yer dad's taken on more than 'e can cope wiv.'

'What about Mother?'

'She 'asn't been the same since yer went away,' said Mrs Winnet, slicing the loaf of bread on a board. 'It's a funny thing about your mum: when *you're* not around, she just goes ter pieces. Maybe it's 'cos she's afraid of what might happen to

113

young Chris when you're not here.'

Rosie looked up at her with a start. 'Christian?' she asked anxiously.

''E's not well, Miss Rosie. I know it's not my place ter say, but in my opinion, 'e's goin' down'ill fast.'

Rosie felt her stomach churn.

'I can't bear ter see that boy sufferin'. I can't bear ter fink that 'e does every single fing in that room of 'is – wash, sleep, read books. When 'is schoolteacher come over ter give 'im 'is lessons the uvver day I fawt ter meself 'ow he'll never 'ave the chance ter be like ordinary kids of 'is age. 'E's a prisoner in this house, that's fer sure.'

As the old lady spoke, Rosie's mother came into the room. 'Rose!' she gasped. 'Oh my God – you're home!'

She rushed to her daughter and the pair embraced.

'I saw your suitcase in the hall,' gushed Marian excitedly. 'It's wonderful, darling, absolutely wonderful!'

'Just for a week, Mother,' said Rosie.

Marian's expression collapsed. 'A week?' she asked. 'But I thought ... you mean, you're going back to that hospital?'

Rosie caught Mrs Winnet watching her. 'I'll go in and see if Christian wants anything,' said the old lady before making a discreet exit.

'It's not true, is it?' pleaded Marian, her expression bristling with anxiety. 'Tell me it's not true, Rose. You *are* home for good – aren't you?'

'Come and sit down, Mother,' replied Rosie, gently leading Marian to a seat at the kitchen table. 'Now listen to me,' she said calmly, once they had settled. 'This war is taking its toll on our boys at the Front. They need as much medical and nursing support as they can get. If we don't give it to them, they'll die.'

'But why *you*, Rose?' asked Marian desperately. 'There are plenty of women who can do that sort of work. You're only a child.'

'I am *not* a child, Mother,' protested Rosie firmly. 'I'm eighteen years old, and my country needs me.'

Marian snorted dismissively and turned her face away in disgust.

'Try to understand, Mother,' Rosie said, gently taking her mother's hand across the table. 'There's a terrible shortage of trained nurses to look after all the men who are suffering from awful injuries. I saw men close to death out at that hospital, men no older than me, no older than all the boys we used to see cycling up and down the road outside, or playing cricket or football at school. Some of them lie about their age. Some of them take the King's shilling and find themselves out in those trenches before they've even realised what they've done. Some of them never have the chance to see their loved ones again. Bravado, Mother – those boys have been recruited with such bravado, recruited for a war that they don't even understand. I've seen men coughing their lungs out because they've been caught in a deadly poison-gas attack. It's my duty to help people like that. Don't you understand, Mother? It's my duty.'

Marian slowly turned back to look at Rosie.

'And what about your duty to your family?' she asked. 'What about your duty to your mother and father, to the people who brought you into this world? What about your duty to your brother, who idolises you more than anyone else in the whole world?'

Rosie was shocked by her mother's outburst. In fact, these days she was shocked by practically everything her mother did: the way she had changed so much since Rosie was a child, when they had always been so close; how she seemed to resent Rosie's new-found independence, her insistence on doing things her way and not just to conform to how Marian wanted her to behave. Rosie found her mother's attitude towards her intolerable, aggressive and uncompromising. She was just not the same person that she used to be, a stranger to her own daughter now. To Rosie, it seemed that her mother's love for her had been replaced by anger.

'Mother,' she said calmly, 'I love Christian too. You know I do.'

'But you're prepared to let him die?'

Now Rosie was really shocked. 'Mother!' she gasped. 'What on earth are you talking about?'

Marian pulled her hand away. 'You may be interested to know,' she snapped, 'that your brother might have only a few more months to live.'

Rosie was devastated.

'Dr Jarvis came to see him only two days ago,' said Marian. 'He said that since you went away, Christian's condition has badly deteriorated.'

'Mother!' replied Rosie angrily, springing to her

feet. 'That's a wicked thing to say!'

'Wicked?' Marian asked spitefully, gently raising herself up from her chair. 'Don't you think it's wicked to put your own self-styled independence before the life of your brother?'

'Mother!' Rosie spluttered, absolutely shattered. 'How can you say such a thing?' But Rosie was given no time to respond to any more of her mother's explosion of anger, for Marian was already making her way to the door.

'I never thought I would live to see the day when my own daughter would turn out to be such a disappointment to me,' Marian called over her shoulder. She opened the door, but turned briefly to address one last biting remark to Rosie. 'Go to your German friends, Rose. They clearly give you more stimulation than your own family.' Tears streaming down her cheeks, she left the room, closing the door quietly behind her.

For a few moments, Rosie just stood there staring at the door. She couldn't believe what she had just heard. Suddenly, the kitchen walls seemed to close in on her. The saucepans hanging on the walls were reflecting light through the window from the afternoon sun outside, and the smell of sliced bread on the table, onions waiting to be peeled in the vegetable rack and the pungent aroma of the carbolic-clean floor produced a claustrophobia that Rosie had never recognised before. For the first time in her life, she felt a stranger in her own home.

Emile Harrington left the factory late that evening. It had been a busy day, and a disconcerting one, disconcerting because the workforce there, who had been his friends for so many years, were not the same as they used to be. He found it difficult to understand why they were deliberately avoiding him to the extent that, when he took his midday meal in the factory canteen, he was now forced to eat alone because none of his workmates would sit at the table with him. He found this new attitude towards him quite unsettling, and unlike anything he had experienced amongst British people before. But times had changed, and people had changed with them. Now there was a war between his former homeland and the country that had adopted him, and it was inevitable that hatred and bitterness should raise their ugly heads. The situation wasn't helped by the complete transformation of the factory into production for the government. It had been sad enough to see the dismantling of the kilns and workbenches that had produced so much beautiful porcelain work over the years, but with the arrival of new machinery and working practices that were going to mass-produce gas respirators for the soldiers at the Front, the atmosphere at Little and Company had become cold and tense.

Once he had turned into Leverton Street, Emile picked his way in the dark along the uneven paving stones, the position of each one he had come to memorise over the years. However, with the approach of autumn, the evenings were not only getting darker, but also chillier. No, it wasn't easy to see in the dark, especially with the street gaslamps turned off in case of Zeppelin attacks.

He heard the sound behind him when he was only six or seven houses away from his own. At first it sounded like someone whispering, very low, but unmistakable. Emile had always been blessed with good hearing, and he knew there was *somebody* there. A few seconds later, the whispers were replaced by footsteps, slow and methodical, and when he stopped to peer over his shoulder, the footsteps behind also came to a halt. For a brief moment, he tried to work out if he was imagining it all, and once the silence continued after he moved on, he decided that he was. It was only when he finally reached the front gate of his house that hell suddenly and violently descended upon him. A hand was clasped around his mouth, and this was accompanied by the hushed sound of a man's voice ranting into his ear: 'Bloody Hun!'

The next thing Emile knew was the feel of a sharp blow to his head. The rest was dark and silent...

Chapter 7

Rosie slept late. Still reeling from her mother's angry outburst the previous afternoon, she felt there was nothing to get up for. Her father had been no better. When he'd arrived home later that afternoon, he'd refused to listen to any of his daughter's experiences at the hospital. Worst of all, he had rejected her protests about the hurtful things her mother had said to her, especially about Emile Harrington, telling Rosie that being involved with the Harringtons at such a time was a very insensitive and dangerous thing to do.

After lying in bed, mulling all this over, Rosie got up, went to the window, and drew the curtains. It was a lovely autumn day outside, and the pavements were strewn with fallen leaves from the sycamore and chestnut trees that lined the road, creating a velvet carpet of golden brown hues, which fluttered in a stiff morning breeze. Her room overlooked the main road, and it was already very busy with dray horses and carts, open-topped omnibuses and people on pedal bicycles, all going about their business with efficient determination. For one moment she felt panic, remembering how punctual her mother always was about the family sitting down to breakfast before her father left for work. She quickly freshened up in the bathroom, put on some clothes, and went downstairs. But to her surprise, there was no one at the dining-room table except Christian, who was just finishing his bread and jam breakfast.

'Where *is* everyone?' she asked, after giving her young brother a hug.

'Father had to go out early,' said Christian, whose face lit up the moment he saw Rosie. 'Mother went with him.'

Rosie did a double take. 'To the factory?' she asked, somewhat surprised. 'They've *both* gone to the factory?'

'No,' replied Mrs Winnet as she came in from the kitchen carrying a pot of tea. 'Your mother was going to Canonbury – or so she said. To see your grandmother.'

Rosie was beginning to get worried. 'Winnie,' she pleaded, 'what's going on?'

Mrs Winnet shrugged. 'I only ever know what I'm told,' she replied, noncommittally before disappearing to the kitchen again.

'It's not true, of course,' said Christian, wiping the jam from his lips with his table napkin.

'What's not true?' pressed Rosie, sitting next to him at the table.

'They both went out at the same time,' continued Christian. 'And I know where they were going, because I heard them arguing before breakfast. Mother didn't go to see Gran in Canonbury. Father went off to the factory, but Mother went to the Great Northern.'

'What!' gasped Rosie. 'She went to the hospital?'

Christian nodded confidently.

'But why? Is she ill?'

Christian shook his head. 'She went to see the doctor about that man who works in the factory. That German bloke.'

Rosie turned quite cold. 'Are you talking about Mr Harrington?' she asked.

Christian nodded again, and drained the rest of the milk in his glass. 'Yes – Harrington,' he said. 'It's a funny old name for a German, isn't it?'

Rosie's feet wouldn't carry her fast enough down Holloway Road. She hardly noticed that it was beginning to cloud over, and the sun that had streamed through her window when she'd opened the curtains just an hour or so before was already struggling to retain its dominant position

121

in the sky. Rosie's stomach churned every inch of the way. If Christian had heard right – that Emile Harrington had been badly injured and was in hospital – then why was her mother and not her father going to the hospital? The remark from her mother about Rosie going off to see her 'German friends' had deeply hurt her, for it was so uncharacteristic of her mother, who, in the past, had always been such a loving, caring and tolerant woman.

The first drops of rain came just as Rosie was entering the side entrance of the Great Northern Hospital in Manor Gardens. As this was a civilian hospital, Rosie was quite surprised to see so many military ambulances lined up in the court-yard outside, with wounded soldiers on crutches being helped into them by nurses from the Red Cross. This suggested to Rosie that the service hospitals around the country were unable to cope with so many casualties coming back from the Front, for when she got inside the hospital she found the emergency wing bulging with outpatients, both civilian and service personnel, which made it difficult for her to reach the reception desk to find out where she might find Emile Harrington. However, during the frantic moments she spent searching around, trying to find someone from the hospital staff who could help her, she suddenly caught sight of Clara Harrington coming down the stairs from one of the emergency wards on the first floor.

'Clara!' Rosie called, hurriedly rushing across to her.

'Rosie!' Clara cried. 'My dear child! What are

you doing here?'

'Is it true?' asked Rosie, breathlessly. 'Is Emile here? What's happened to him?'

'He's going to be all right,' said Clara, nervously looking around to make sure no one was watching her. 'Let's go somewhere where we can talk.'

A few moments later they were sitting on a hard wooden bench in a secluded corner of the hospital's main entrance hall. Clara was pale and drawn, and although it wasn't a particularly warm day, she frequently dabbed her forehead with her handkerchief.

'Someone attacked Emile outside the house last night,' she said softly. 'He was just getting back from late duty at the factory.'

'But why?' asked Rosie. 'Were they trying to rob him or something?'

'No, Rosie,' Clara replied. 'They weren't trying to rob him. They attacked him because of who he is.'

Before continuing, Clara waited for a group of young men to pass by and leave through the main doors. Then she drew closer to Rosie. 'Your father must have told you about – about what's going on at the factory? About how they've turned against Emile since the war started?'

'It's nonsense!' snapped Rosie angrily. 'Emile's a good man. How dare they?'

'Oh, they dare all right,' said Clara, dabbing her forehead again. 'They have a set idea in their minds, a warped idea, and they refuse to use their brains to understand that Emile is not a threat to them or anyone else.'

'Of course he's not a threat!' protested Rosie. 'Emile's a fine man. He wouldn't hurt a fly.'

'*I* know that, Rosie, and so do you,' replied Clara, her face crumpling up with emotion. 'But ever since the Germans sank the *Lusitania* a few months ago, anyone who has even the slightest connection with Germany, now or in the past, is a target for revenge.'

'It's madness!' growled Rosie. 'Utter madness! And I'm ashamed of my father for allowing these people to get away with this.'

'Oh, but your father's doing no such thing, Rosie,' said Clara. 'In fact, he went to the factory this morning to call a meeting of the workforce. He's even angrier about what has happened to Emile than you and I are.'

Rosie was taken aback. 'But,' she stuttered, 'he told me ... my mother ... she said the most terrible things to me about...'

'Your mother came here to see us this morning,' said Clara. 'Just for a few minutes. Just to let us know that both she and your father are shocked and horrified about what happened last night.'

Rosie sprang to her feet. 'Is she here?' she asked briskly. 'Is my mother still here?'

'No,' replied Clara, getting up from the bench.

Rosie straightened herself up. This extra-ordinary, contradictory behaviour by both her parents puzzled and confused her. 'Which ward is Emile in?' she asked. 'I want to see him.'

'No, Rosie!' said Clara firmly. 'You mustn't do that. You mustn't go and see Emile. In fact, from now on, you must keep away from both him and me.' She quickly put her fingers to Rosie's lips to

124

prevent her from protesting. 'After what happened last night, after the way things are going, it's dangerous for you to mix with people like us.'

'But why, Clara?' Rosie asked, taking Clara's fingers away from her lips. 'You're my friend. The work we've been doing for the group is important.'

Clara's smile was slight, but warm, and her eyes radiated genuine love and concern for Rosie. 'Our work has nothing to do with this war, Rosie,' she said. 'When it's all over, and I pray it will be over soon, that's the time when we shall show all these people how wrong they are. You're a beautiful girl, Rosie,' she said, gently stroking Rosie's cheek with her knuckles, 'and you're a very courageous one. Your friendship has meant more to me and Emile than you'll ever know. But when I go back up those stairs, I beg you not to follow me. Just continue to do the wonderful work you're doing, and forget you ever knew us.'

Rosie felt tears welling in her eyes. But when she tried to protest, Clara leaned forward, kissed her softly on both cheeks, and left. Rosie watched her disappear into the swarm of hospital patients and visitors thronging the entrance hall. Although Clara was such a slight figure, to Rosie at that moment she somehow looked tall and strong. Clara climbed the stairs, and when she reached the first-floor landing she paused briefly, looking as though she was about to peer back over her shoulder, but she resisted the urge, and quickly disappeared along one of the long ward corridors.

Rosie remained where she was for a moment, staring up at the wide stone staircase. She felt stunned and lost. None of this made any sense to her – not only what had happened to Emile the night before, but the peculiar way in which her parents had behaved. Why? She was eighteen years old, and she knew how to take care of herself. Or did she?

This moment of uncertainty unsettled her; it made her wonder whether the whole world had gone mad. In a daze, she made for the main entrance door, oblivious to those who brushed against her.

Outside, in Holloway Road, the rain looked as if it was set in for the morning. It was all so different from a few hours before. But then, these days *everything* seemed to be changing so quickly.

It was generally accepted in the neighbourhood that Monty Gubble was older than the Tower of London. He had more lines on his face than a railway junction, white hair that was only cut on high days and holidays, a long white moustache and that famous flowing beard. But appearances often lie, and so it was with old Monty, for, despite his eighty-three years, he was as spry as a puppy, and had a mind so sharp you could cut your fingers on it. He also never missed a thing, spending, as he did, most of his time sitting on the wall in Camden Road, which was only a stone's throw away from his own basement bedsitter just round the corner from Holloway Women's Prison. During daylight hours, no one ever escaped old Monty's hawk-eyes, especially strangers. That's how he picked out the young feller who got off the bus just down the hill near the Nag's Head, and strolled up Camden Road, looking at the number over every door he passed.

'If yer want ter buy a 'ouse up 'ere, son,' he croaked to the young bloke as he approached, 'I 'ope yer've brought a good bag er spondulicks wiv yer.'

Joe Upton immediately took a shine to the old codger. When he was a kid in the Dales up in Yorkshire, he knew another bloke just like him, a right old busybody, full of mischief, artful as hell. 'Not fer me, Granddad,' he replied. 'Thrupence a week fer rent is about *my* mark. Nah, I'm looking fer me gel. She lives at number 221.'

'Camden Road?' enquired Monty. 'Sounds like yer've got yer eyes on our young Rosie.'

Joe's face lit up. 'You know 'er?' he asked eagerly.

'*Know* 'er?' retorted the old boy with a guffaw. 'I've knowd young Rosie since she come up no 'igher than my old boxer dog, Sam. An' 'er young bruvver too, young Chris.' He shook his head sadly. 'Poor lil' bugger.' He turned and nodded up the road. 'Number 221 – the one wiv the blue lace curtains. Yer can't miss it.'

'Fanks a lot, Granddad!' called Joe, as he started to make off.

'Yer won't find Rosie there, though.'

Joe stopped and looked back.

'She went out first fing. I saw 'er makin' off down terwards the Nag's 'Ead. Got the weight of the world on 'er shoulders by the looks er fings.'

'Wot d'yer mean?' asked Joe, coming back to him.

'Ah – yer don't know wot's bin goin' on round

'ere, mate.' The old codger took a dog-end from behind his ear and lit it, nearly setting fire to his whiskers. 'People ain't be'avin' the way they should since this war started. You take Rosie's mum an' dad, fer instance. Cool as cucumbers they are, got their noses up in the air and can't sniff wot's goin' on around 'em.'

Joe couldn't make out what the old boy was getting at. ''Ow d'yer mean?'

'Rosie. That's who I mean,' replied Monty, puffing out palls of smoke from his stale dog-end. 'Got a mind of 'er own, a good mind, an' they won't let 'er use it. They want 'er ter be like the rest of the lot who live round 'ere, set in their ways, against anyfin' that's diff'rent to their own opinions. Rosie's joined up as a nurse. Yer knew that, din't yer?'

Joe grinned and nodded vigorously. 'I'm one of 'er patients, mate – well, 'er *ex*-patients, that is.'

'Ah!' beamed the old boy with an artful smile. 'I fawt as much.' He turned around quickly to make sure that no one could hear him. 'Well,' he said in a low voice, ''er ol' man tried ter stop 'er. Did yer know *that?*'

'Stop 'er from wot?' asked Joe, puzzled.

'From bein' a nurse,' replied Monty. ''E reckons she's gettin' too big for 'er boots, makin' decisions wivout askin' 'im first. But I say gels've got just as much right to make up their own minds as us men. If *I* was ol' 'Erbert Asquith, *I'd* give 'em the vote termorrer – if only ter keep 'em quiet!' He chuckled away at his own joke. 'Women – Gord bless 'em! Nah, we can't do wivout 'em, can we, lad? That's the one regret I ever made in me life.

I should've found meself a decent lil' woman years ago. I mean, let's face it, everyone should have someone ter love, don't yer fink?'

'Do me a favour, Granddad?' asked Joe. 'If yer see Rosie when she comes back, will yer give 'er a message for me? That's if yer see 'er, of course.'

'Course I'll see 'er!' retorted Monty indignantly. 'I'm the eyes and ears round 'ere. Nobody gets past ol' Monty wivout my knowin' it.'

'Tell 'er,' said Joe, 'just tell 'er...' He suddenly broke into a fit of coughing.

''Ere,' said Monty. 'You all right, mate?'

Joe held up his hand, and grinned. 'I'm OK, Granddad,' he insisted, as he gradually recovered. 'Just tell Rosie I'll be back.'

'When?' asked Monty. 'Where? What time?'

'I'll find 'er, don't worry,' replied Joe. 'Just tell 'er – I'll be back.'

'Who shall I tell 'er left the message?' called Monty as Joe wandered off back down Camden Road.

'Oh, she'll know,' Joe called back casually, coughing his lungs out.

It was the middle of the afternoon when Rosie approached the front entrance of Little and Company. The façade of the building hadn't changed at all since her grandfather founded the porcelain business more than seventy years before, and now that there was a war on there was clearly very little chance of the place getting a facelift. None the less, the signboard above the main door still showed quite clearly the name of the company, even if the gold lettering and the black background were now somewhat faded. The first thing that struck her when she entered the building was the smell, so different from the aroma of hot clay ovens she had known since she was a child. It was a sickening smell of rubber. However, the welcome she got from Amy Desmond, the front-office receptionist, seemed as warm as ever, if a little strained.

'Miss Rosie! What a lovely surprise. I had no idea you were home... Your father's in the workshop. If you go up to his office, I'll tell him you're here.'

'Thank you, Amy,' said Rosie, and made her way out to the staircase in the adjoining corridor. But in a cursory glance back over her shoulder, she saw Amy and another girl staring incredulously at her. She turned away, and went on upstairs.

In the respirator workshop, Richard Little was in the middle of a discussion with Jim Sayles, his foreman. Surrounded by a group of workers, he was clearly not having an easy time.

'Well, I'm warning you,' he said firmly, addressing them all, 'once the police get here, they're going to want answers to some very awkward questions. Emile is lucky to be alive. If that attack on him has any connection with anyone here, the consequences for this company could be quite disastrous. Now, I ask you all again, were any of you responsible for what happened last night?'

'Tell me, Guv'nor,' called one of the group named Tub Smithers, a thick-set man in his fifties, with an unhealthy ruddy complexion, and

130

who, like the other male employees, was wearing a protective green rubber apron and brown trilby hat. 'Wot's all this sudden concern fer Hartmann? I mean, after all, 'e ain't one of us, is 'e?'

His question was greeted with murmurs of approval from the others, mainly the men.

'I don't want to hear any of that sort of talk, Smithers!' snapped Richard, turning angrily on the man. 'I don't want to hear it from you, or any-one else. Is that quite clear? And please remember that Emile's name is Harrington, *not* Hartmann!'

'With respect, Guv'nor,' called Ben Fizzle, better known as 'Weasel' to his workmates, for reasons that seemed perfectly obvious, 'Emile whatever yer like ter call 'im, 'e shouldn't be workin' in a place like this. Wot we're doin' 'ere's government work.'

Richard rounded on the man. 'Tell me some-thing, Fizzle,' he retorted. 'How long have *you* been working for this company?'

Weasel was quite indignant at being put on the spot. 'Can't quite remember, sir,' he replied haughtily. 'Must be over twenty years.'

'Twenty years?' repeated Richard, coldly. 'And how long during that time have you known Emile Harrington?'

As he fumbled for words, Weasel looked at the others for some help. 'All the time I've bin 'ere, I reckon,' he replied with a shrug.

'And has Emile Harrington ever given you – given *any* of you – any trouble? In fact, haven't quite a few of you become quite friendly with him?'

'Wiv respect, Guv'nor,' growled Tub Smithers, 'I don't see wot that's got ter do wiv it?'

'As a matter of fact, Smithers,' snapped Richard, doing his best to retain his dignity, 'it has a great deal to do with it. What it means is that for years Emile Harrington has worked in complete harmony with all you people, but quite suddenly, quite unjustifiably, you see him as an enemy. Now why is that?'

''Cos 'e *is* an enemy!' called one of the older women, Gert Sissons, at the back of the group. 'There's a war on now, and 'e ain't one of us no longer.'

Murmurs of agreement from everyone, except one dissenting voice.

'That's rubbish, Gert!' said a younger girl called Mickey Jarrow, who was the daughter of a railway porter up at Finsbury Park. 'Emile *is* one of us. 'E's 'elped us all out whenever we've 'ad problems wiv money or coverin' up for us when we've clocked in late – and you know it!'

'I don't know anyfin' of the sort, Mickey Jarrow!' yelled Gert from the back. 'All I know is this is no place for a Hun!'

A chorus of approval from the group.

Richard Little waited for them to quieten down before asking: 'And is that reason enough to try to kill him?'

'No one tried ter kill 'im!' called Tub Smithers. ''E 'ad an accident, an' that's all there is to it.'

The response to that from the others was silence. As he looked around at them, Richard found that nobody could look him straight in the eyes. 'I want to say something to you all,' he said, raising his voice. 'This company was formed by my father many years ago. In those days he

132

worked hard to build up a business that would give good jobs to every one of his employees. My father was a fair man. He believed in equality for every single person who worked for him. That way he knew that the benefits would provide a good standard of life for not only his own family, but for the families of everyone who worked for him. My father was one of you. He worked on the benches, just like you, and he became a friend to everyone. There was never any discrimination – everyone got along with everyone else; if ever there was a disagreement, my father would do everything in his power to sort things out.' He paused for a moment and looked around at the silent, expressionless faces. 'When Emile Hartmann came to work for us, he became one of us, because he wanted to *be* one of us. And when Emile became Emile Harrington, everyone was happy, because he was a friend to all of us. This war is a terrible thing, but we mustn't blame it on Emile Hartmann *or* Emile Harrington. This war is beyond the likes of you and me. All we can do is to do our part in helping to bring it to an end, but to do that we *have* to behave in a civilised way, because if we don't, how can we ever trust each other again?'

As he finished speaking, he was aware that everyone around him was staring up at his large arched window that overlooked the factory floor. Standing there looking down was Rosie.

A few minutes later, Richard burst into his office to find Rosie waiting there. 'What the hell d'you think you're doing here, Rose?' he barked. 'Get away from that window!'

'I'm sorry, Father,' she replied, somewhat taken aback by his outburst. 'I hadn't realised I had to have your permission to pay you a visit.'

Richard rushed across and drew the curtains at the window. 'I've told you the problems we have here. After the way these people feel about your visits to the Harringtons, this is no time for you to make matters worse.'

'I came to ask why you and Mother are behaving in the most extraordinary way,' said Rose defiantly. 'Yesterday, Mother said the most atrocious things to me about what she called my "German friends", and also about how I didn't care about Christian any more. Then the next thing I hear is that she went to the hospital to see the Harringtons. And now suddenly *you* defend Emile against that mob down there. What *is* going on, Father?'

'Sit down, Rose,' said Richard firmly.

Rosie remained standing defiantly.

'Sit down – *please*,' he asked again, this time more conciliatory.

Reluctantly, Rosie did as he asked.

'Now listen to me,' said Richard, perched on the edge of his desk close to her. 'Your mother and I have nothing against the Harringtons. To us, they are good, honest people, and I treat with contempt what they are being subjected to by people who know no better. But the fact is, a dangerous situation is developing here, and I can't afford to ignore it. The country is going mad, Rose – the whole world is going mad.' He could see by her expression that she was not convinced. 'What your mother said to you yesterday was said through anxiety, nothing more. Your mother loves you, Rose, and so do I. If anything were to happen to you because of your association with … with someone who could cause you harm, either directly or indirectly–'

'But, Father, this is absolutely absurd!' Rosie insisted. 'How can my relationship with Clara Harrington be a threat to *anyone?*'

Richard leaned down towards her. 'Rose,' he said, lowering his voice, 'Clara Harrington is married to a man who was born a German. The situation in this country has changed ever since the Germans torpedoed the *Lusitania* with all those innocent men, women and children on board. It was a cowardly, brutal, unprovoked act on an unarmed passenger ship, which had nothing to do with the war and was totally unjustified. That's why these people want revenge, Rose, and they'll go to any lengths to get it.'

'So who *are* these people who are prepared to attack a harmless man in the dark, and for no logical reason at all?'

'Cowards never identify themselves, Rose.'

'But they must be aware that they can only go so far without being caught?'

'I doubt that even enters their minds.' Richard stood up, and went to the curtained window. 'That's why I don't want these people to associate you with the Harringtons.'

'Father,' returned Rosie sharply, 'I am *not* afraid of them.'

Richard turned from the window. 'Maybe not, Rose,' he said. 'But *I* am.' He stretched down to his desk, picked up a piece of paper there, and held it up for Rose to see. 'Do you know what *this* is, Rose? It's a note. Don't ask me who it's from, because the chances are I shall never find out.'

'What is it?' asked Rosie.

'It's a threat.'

'What...?'

'A threat to burn down this building if I continue to employ Emile Harrington.'

On the way home, Rosie felt as though she was living through a nightmare. She was so absorbed with what her father had just told her that she hardly noticed the cool drizzle that moistened her coat and glistened on the paving stones. On the corner of Brecknock Road the raucous voice of a news-vendor was bellowing out the headlines of the latest bloody battle on the fields of France, which made the distant sound of a street barrel organ seem quite incongruous as it filled the late afternoon air with the poignant strains of 'I Used to Sigh for the Silvery Moon'. In Rosie's mind, the dread of the coming days sank into insignificance when she thought about the people who were turning the home front into something unjust and ugly. After all they were having to endure, how could she now tell her parents the truth about where she was being posted once her few days with them came to an end? The world seemed such an empty place, and she felt so alone within it.

As she approached home, the sight of old Monty did nothing to raise her spirits, for as much as she adored the old scoundrel, the last thing she felt like doing at that moment was to have a conversation with him. But when he actually spoke, all that changed.

'Got a message fer yer, young lady,' said the old codger, with a twinkle in his eye.

'A message?' asked Rosie, puzzled.

'From an admirer, it seems,' returned Monty.

'Monty, what are you talking about?' Rosie asked rather irritably. 'I'm really not in the mood for jokes.'

''*E* didn't seem ter fink it was a joke when I told 'im I knew yer,' replied Monty, sniffily. 'Says 'e used ter be one of your patients. Sounded like it too. It's a nasty cough 'e's got there.'

Rosie immediately perked up. 'What?' she gasped breathlessly. 'Monty, what are you saying? Who are you talking about?'

'Just this young bloke who come up ter me an' asked me where number 221 was, and when 'e tells me who 'e was lookin' for...'

'What's the message, Monty?' asked Rosie excitedly. 'Please! What did he say?'

''E din't leave no name,' said Monty, chuffed by his sudden sense of power. 'All 'e said was ter tell yer that 'e'll be back.'

'But *when*, Monty? When is he coming back?'

The old codger shrugged. ''Aven't the foggiest, gel,' he replied. 'Nice-lookin' young bloke, though. But I tell yer this much. 'E's got a funny way er talkin', ain't 'e? Yer know, I reckon 'e comes from up Norf or somefin'. Yer can always tell. They're all foreigners up there!'

Chapter 8

Rosie didn't have to wait long to see Joe. After her father had gone to the factory the next morning, old Monty managed to get a message to Mrs Winnet to tell Rosie that Joe would wait for her as long as it took at the tea stall outside the Marlborough Picture House in Holloway Road. Once she had made a suitable excuse to her mother, by ten o'clock Rosie was hurrying down Camden Road as fast as her legs would carry her. The moment she caught sight of Joe perched on a coping stone outside the picture house, all togged up in flat cap, starched collar, shirt, tie and three-piece suit, she threw all caution to the wind and practically threw herself into his arms.

'Oh, God, Joe!' she exclaimed, whilst he was smothering her lips with kisses. 'You've no idea how wonderful it is to see you!'

Joe was thrilled and overwhelmed by Rosie's greeting, for when he had set out from his home in Bethnal Green that morning, he had no idea what to expect. 'Yer didn't fink I was goin' ter let yer get away *that* easy, did yer – Rosie Lee?' he whispered, kissing her ear, totally unconcerned that the two of them were getting disapproving looks from two elderly ladies who were waiting at the tram stop nearby.

'But how did you know where to find me?'

Rosie asked.

'Yer gave me yer address before I left the 'ospital out at Stanmore, remember? I wanted ter come sooner, but, well, I didn't know 'ow yer'd feel, me just turnin' up out er the blue. I didn't know if yer'd still feel the same way about me.'

Rosie looked at him in disbelief. 'Oh, Joe,' she replied, hugging him tight. 'How could you even think such a thing? If you don't know how I feel about you by now, you *never* will.' She looked at his face, and kissed his forehead.

Joe was grinning all over. 'Wot does it matter now, Rosie?' he said. 'The main fing is – I found yer.' The two elderly ladies turned away in disgust as he again hugged and kissed her.

'But, Joe,' asked Rose with some concern, 'how are you? My neighbour who gave me your message said you were coughing badly.'

'Nah!' replied Joe dismissively. 'Don't take no notice er that silly ol' dodger. I'm dinky dink – fit as a fiddle! In fact, I'm finkin' er signin' up fer Arsenal! Come on, let's get out of 'ere.'

'Where are we going?' asked Rosie, breathlessly.

'Anywhere!' returned Joe, taking her arm and slipping it through his, then briskly leading her off to the opposite side of Holloway Road.

A few minutes later they were strolling along Seven Sisters Road, which was bustling with street traders and morning shoppers. The smell of whelks and shrimps from Fred's wet fish stall seemed to mix quite naturally with the competition coming from Meg's hot saveloy and pease pudding trolley, and the whiff of the gradually rotting cast-off vegetables that were beginning to pile up in the kerb outside Hicks the green-grocer's. As they passed the rag-and-bottle shop, Rosie reached into her purse for two pennies, which she dropped into a tobacco tin of a blind man who was playing a mouth organ on the pavement outside, whilst his black and white mongrel dog snoozed contentedly at his side. Coster-mongers all along the road were doing a roaring trade, yelling out their bargain prices, attracting crowds for everything from safety pins to second-hand shoes, and on both sides of the road pearly kings and queens were doing a fine job collecting coins for a local orphanage. The scene was as colourful as ever, and so was the language of the costermongers as they ripped into the Kaiser whenever any of their customers brought up the subject of the war.

Once they had struggled their way through to the corner of Hornsey Road, Joe stopped to buy two toffee apples from Sticky Mick's stall.

'I can't eat this,' laughed Rosie, as Joe handed one over to her. 'I've never eaten one of these things in my whole life.'

'So just see wot yer've bin missin'!' said Joe, as he teased her into taking the first lick.

Rosie gradually took a liking to the sticky toffee covering, which prompted her into taking a small bite of the apple. From that moment on she was a convert.

They continued on down Seven Sisters Road in the direction of Finsbury Park, where it was now much quieter. They stopped only briefly to watch a dray horse taking a drink from the roadside trough on the corner of Thane Villas.

'Ol' Monty says you're 'aving a rough time wiv yer mum an' dad,' said Joe. 'Wot's it all about?'

Rosie sighed. It wasn't easy for her to eat the toffee apple whilst talking, but she made the effort. 'Oh, I don't know, Joe,' she replied. 'They mean well, but they keep treating me like a child. The main trouble is they don't want me to do the things that I feel I have to do. Father tried to stop me from enrolling as a nurse.'

Joe shrugged. 'I reckon all dads are a bit like that,' he replied. 'When I joined up, my ol' man nearly did 'is nut. That's 'cos I was under age when I took the King's shillin'.'

'I'm not surprised,' said Rosie, acidly. 'Lord Kitchener has a lot to answer for.'

'I wanted ter do it,' replied Joe. 'It don't matter wot age we are, we all 'ave ter do somefin' ter stop the Huns.'

Hun. The mention of that horrible word again immediately brought back to Rosie the painful memory of what had happened to Emile Harrington the night before. 'I suppose there is good and bad in everyone,' she said. 'Even the Germans.'

'Not when they start wars,' returned Joe bitterly. 'Not when they do wot they did ter *me*.'

Rosie looked up at him forlornly, regretting what she had just said.

They moved on, wandering idly past the window of a tailor's shop, where two women in long aprons were busily spinning at their cotton wheels. On the way, Rosie told Joe about all the problems she was having with her parents, the attack on Emile Harrington and her anxieties over leaving her brother, Christian. But it was not

141

until they had reached the gates of Finsbury Park and discarded what was left of their toffee apples that Rosie dropped the real bombshell.

'You're goin' up front?' gasped Joe. '*You?* But you're a gel, Rosie. It's not a place fer gels. It's far too dangerous.'

'Now you're sounding like my father, Joe,' said Rosie, using her handkerchief to wipe the last bit of sticky toffee from her lips. 'Where d'you think the nurses come from in the field hospitals? This is war, Joe. You said yourself, we all have to do our bit.'

'But I love yer, Rosie Lee,' said Joe. 'If anyfin' was ter 'appen to you, I don't know wot I'd do.'

Rosie was quite taken aback. To be told that someone actually loved her was the most wonderful thing that had ever happened to her, and the fact that it was coming from Joe suddenly made all the awful things in her life pale into insignificance. She looked into his eyes, and saw quite clearly the love he was trying to express in such a simple but direct way.

'I love you too, Joe.'

Joe's eyes lit up. 'Yer do?'

'You'll never know how much,' replied Rosie.

They embraced again.

'Don't leave me, Rosie,' Joe pleaded. 'Don't go out to that hellhole. I couldn't cope if anyfin' should 'appen to yer. Yer can do just as good work back 'ere in Blighty.'

Rosie looked up at him. 'I can't go on being a tea girl, Joe. There are more important things for me to do in this war.'

He put his arm round her waist, and moved

142

them on. A few minutes later they came to a halt near the playing field where a platoon of young army recruits was being put through some rigorous exercise training by a somewhat aggressive sergeant major. There was now a cold nip in the air, and the men, togged only in khaki vests and shorts, were looking decidedly chilled, with blood-red faces and condensation spluttering from their mouths as they worked out their punishing routines.

'Just look at 'em,' said Joe mockingly, suddenly depressed. 'Look 'ow many of 'em 'ave grown moustaches. They all do it. Once they join up they fink it makes 'em look like a real man. I know, 'cos I did the same fing. If only they knew. If only they knew that the only time they become a man is when they see one of their mates lyin' shot up dead in a trench.'

Rosie slipped her arm round his waist, and leaned her head against his shoulder. 'Joe,' she asked dreamily, 'do you believe in love at first sight?'

He grinned and looked down at her. 'I was just about ter ask you the same question.'

'I didn't think such a thing was ever possible,' said Rosie. 'Not until that morning on the platform at Charing Cross.'

He leaned his head gently on to hers. 'I knew it long before that,' he said.

'You did?'

Joe nodded.

'When?'

'In me dreams,' replied Joe. 'I've always dreamed about meeting someone like you. And when I first saw yer on that railway platform, I knew I'd found yer.'

They hugged close. From the branch of a nearby tree, a flotilla of sparrows were chirping so loudly it seemed as though they were laughing their tiny heads off at the young army recruits who were suffering on the playing field below.

''Ow soon d'yer 'ave ter go?' asked Joe, who had gently turned Rosie's face so she was looking at him.

'I have to report for duty next Tuesday.'

Joe panicked. 'Oh, Christ!' he gasped. 'So soon?'

'It won't be for ever, Joe,' she replied. 'When I get back, I want to hear all about Bethnal Green, and your family.'

'I don't see why we 'ave ter wait ter do that,' said Joe. 'We can do that right now.'

Rosie was taken aback. 'Do what?' she asked.

'I'll take yer back 'ome ter meet me ma again, prop'ly this time.'

'What – *now?*'

'I always believe in doin' somefin' as soon yer fink about it. Yer can meet Gran too. She can be a miserable ol' git at times, but I bet you an' 'er'll get on like a 'ouse on fire.'

'Isn't it all a bit short notice?' asked Rosie. 'I mean, will your mum mind you bringing me back home?'

'Look,' insisted Joe, 'you're my gel, an' if I want ter take yer back 'ome, nobody's goin' ter stop me.'

'But, Joe–' began Rosie, anxious and bewildered.

She was interrupted when Joe suddenly burst

144

into a fit of coughing. Concerned, she held on to him, and rubbed his back in an attempt to ease the congestion in his lungs. Once he had recovered and wiped his mouth with the back of his hand, he leaned forward to kiss her.

'I taste of toffee apple,' she said, giving him a warm, affectionate smile.

'All the better,' he replied, kissing her. When their lips parted again, he asked despondently, 'Which station yer goin' from?'

Rosie hesitated before answering. 'Charing Cross,' she replied.

Joe returned her an ironic smile. 'Back ter where we started,' he said.

'Back to where we started,' said Rosie.

They kissed again. In the tree above them, the sparrows had even more to chatter about.

Annie Upton wasn't expecting a visitor, but since her son Joe had arrived home with that young nurse on his own, there wasn't much she could do about it except to put on the kettle and bring out the jam sponge she had made for tea that evening. Even if you didn't approve of something there was no need to be rude. Annie may have been brought up with hardly a farthing in her pocket, but at least her old mum and dad had taught her good manners.

'So what d'you think of Bethnal Green then?' she asked Rosie, who was sitting at the table with Joe in the back parlour of their two up two down. 'Bit different from 'oity-toity Islington, I reckon.'

'Oh, Islington's not too bad, Mrs Upton,' replied Rosie, edgily. 'On the whole, the people

145

are very nice there. We have some very nice neighbours.'

'You'd like where Rosie lives, Ma,' said Joe, trying to impress. 'They've got a lot er front gardens there.'

Annie grunted. 'Wouldn't do fer me,' she replied sourly. 'Got quite enuff ter do 'ere lookin' after me marigolds in the back yard.'

'Marigolds?' grumbled Joe's brother, Paul, who was stoking the coal in the range. 'Bloody weeds!'

'Oh, no they aren't!' snapped Gran, who was Annie's mum, still with traces of her own native Yorkshire accent. The old lady wore a long black mourning dress and shawl even after nearly thirty years of being a widow. 'In the summer I always 'ave a good show of marigolds in me window-box upstairs.' Her grumpy, parched face was crumpled up with rage. 'Everyone who sees 'em says they're a sight to be'old.'

'I bet they do!' mumbled Paul under his breath.

'Don't talk to your grandmother like that!' snapped Annie, cutting a huge piece of sponge and putting it on a plate for Rosie. 'You know 'ow sensitive she is about 'er marigolds.'

'Yes!' growled the old lady 'I'm sensitive! Youngsters 'ave no respect for old folk these days.'

'I didn't say nuffin'!' protested Paul indignantly.

Annie ignored both her mum and her elder son, and handed the slice of sponge to Rosie. 'Joe,' she said, holding up the teapot to him, 'we need some more 'ot water.'

Joe duly took the teapot and disappeared into the scullery.

'It's Rosie, in't it?' she said to Rosie, without expecting an answer.

'Rosie Lee!' called Joe buoyantly from the scullery.

Annie called out to him. "Old your tongue!' She leaned back in her chair and closed the scullery door.

Rosie chuckled. 'Take no notice of him, Mrs Upton,' she said. 'That's what Joe calls me. My real name's Little. Rosie Little.'

'Little by name,' added Paul mischievously, sitting cross-legged in front of the fire, smoking his dog-end, 'but big in every uvver way, eh, Rosie?'

At first Rosie wasn't too sure how to answer Paul's rather suggestive remark, especially as from the moment she walked through the front door he had been looking at her in a way which made her feel a touch uncomfortable. So she just smiled weakly and replied, 'Big isn't always best, Paul.'

Paul grinned.

Joe came back from the scullery with the large, chipped enamel teapot.

'So what do *your* folks do for a livin', Rosie Little?' asked Annie, pouring three cups of tea.

Prompted by Joe, Rosie had started to take a delicate bite of her jam sponge, which already seemed to be clashing with the remaining taste of the toffee apple. 'Actually,' she said, swallowing down the cake, 'my father owns a porcelain factory in Kentish Town.'

'Oh, does 'e now?' said Annie, putting milk and sugar into one of the cups of tea and handing it across to her. 'I 'ope 'e pays 'is people sufficient, does 'e?'

Rosie was a bit taken aback by that question. 'I ... presume so,' she replied falteringly. 'There don't seem to be many complaints. Most of his staff have worked for the firm since my grand-father founded it.'

'My chamber pot's made of porcelain,' said Gran Upton to Rosie. 'My 'ubbie bought it fer me on our silver weddin'. It's come in real useful, I can tell yer.'

'No one wants ter 'ear about your chamber pot, Mam!' said Annie, putting the old girl down. 'D'you want a piece of sponge, or a rock cake?'

Hurt to the core, Gran turned away. 'You know very well I can't eat *your* rock cakes,' she replied haughtily. 'Not with my delicate teeth.'

'*Wot* teef, Gran?' teased Joe. 'You ain't *got* none!'

Gran glared at him.

'Shut up, Joe!' said Annie, scolding him. 'Give this to yer gran.'

Joe took a cup of tea from his mum, and passed it across to the old lady.

'Well,' said Annie, tucking in to her own slice of jam sponge, 'my man Will 'as never done owt fancy. Before 'e joined up, 'e worked on dredging down the Regent's Canal. It was a mucky job – used to pong to 'igh 'eaven when 'e came 'ome at night, but it kept this family going, I can tell you. We've never wanted for a good meal in our stomachs. I'n't that right, boys?'

Joe nodded agreement, but Paul ignored her.

'We should all've stayed up in t' Dales,' moaned

148

Gran, blowing on her hot tea. 'It was much more 'ealthy, all the family on the land in the fresh air.'

'You could've stayed up there, Mam,' said Annie, tersely. 'No one forced you come down South.'

Gran pulled a disapproving face behind her daughter's back.

'Though I will agree,' continued Annie, 'people *are* different down 'ere.'

'In what way, Mrs Upton?' asked Rosie, who had spent a lot of her time looking at the snapshot photos on the huge rickety dresser by the door.

'Not so friendly,' replied Annie, her cheeks now flushed red with sipping hot tea. 'Took us years to get to know our neighbours next door. Talk about chalk an' cheese. It's even worse with posh folk.'

Rosie looked puzzled.

'*You* know,' explained Annie, pointedly. 'Them wi' money. They treat the likes of us more like servants than equals.' As she sipped her tea, she peered craftily at Rosie over the top of her cup. 'So what do *your* folks think of our Joe?' she asked, artfully.

It was Joe who answered the question. 'They ain't 'ad the chance to decide yet, Ma,' he said, with a mischievous look at Rosie. 'Rosie's goin' ter take me ter meet 'em.'

'I'm sure they'll love Joe,' said Rosie. '*I* do, so I don't see why *they* shouldn't.'

Joe was looking at her with a huge smug grin on his face.

Annie sat back in her chair. For the past year or

so her hair had been thinning, and when she brushed it, great tufts came out, and this was now beginning to show. But it was her eyes that told her story, her eyes that could recognise both honesty and deceit. Annie wasn't an intelligent woman, but, after years of struggling to bring up her kids, she had developed an insight that for those who didn't know her was very unsettling. And it was now those eyes and that insight that were focused on Rosie.

'Yer know, Rosie Little,' she said quietly but astutely, 'we're like two different breeds of people – your folks and mine. We don't think alike because we don't trust each other. And if we don't trust each other, I don't see 'ow we can get along.' She leaned forward, and stared Rosie straight in the eyes. 'D'you think you can love a boy who didn't 'ave a proper education, who went out to work with 'is brother in the cornfields and the cowsheds when 'e was nowt but twelve years old, who even now can only just about read and write?' She flicked a quick glance at Joe, who pretended he wasn't listening to what his ma was saying because he had heard it all before – over and over again. 'Joe knows nowt about life,' continued Annie. ''E knows nowt about 'ow other folk live.' She turned back to Rosie again. ''Ow d'you think your folks are going to take to that, Rosie Little?'

Joe made a dismissive sign to Rosie behind his ma's back.

Rosie ignored this, and calmly put down her cup of tea. 'As far as *I'm* concerned, Mrs Upton,' she replied positively, 'Joe is one of the most

150

wonderful people I've ever met. I just hope that my family will accept him because *I* love him, no matter what he does or doesn't know.'

At 221 Camden Road, Richard Little sat alone in the sitting room, reading his copy of *The Times* over and over again by the dim light of a solitary gaslamp on the wall above the mantelpiece. However, he wasn't really taking in what he was reading, for he frequently pulled out his pocket watch from his waistcoat to check the time. He was distracted by the grandfather clock sounding the hour of ten on the other side of the room, so he got up impatiently and put down his newspaper on his chair without even bothering to fold it up. Then he went to the mantelpiece and carefully turned off the gaslamp, the only light now filtering through to the sitting room from the gaslamp in the hall. He went out, turned down the solitary wall light there, then went upstairs.

As he expected, Marian was not asleep. Although the room with two single beds was in darkness, he knew only too well that she was sitting up waiting for news.

'No sign of her?' she called softly, anxiously, from her bed.

'Not yet.' Richard tried not to sound too concerned.

'D'you think something has happened to her?' asked Marian nervously 'It's after ten o'clock. Should we go to the police station?'

'For God's sake, Marian!' snapped Richard. 'Rose is eighteen years old. She's not a child.'

Marian waited for him to start undressing in

the dark before she spoke again. 'It's so unlike her,' she persisted. 'She said she was going out with her friends from the hospital, but it's very late for her.'

'Rose,' said Richard, 'is not the Rose we used to know. She's different now. She thinks differently, and she acts differently. We're just going to have to get used to it.' It was clear as he spoke that he didn't believe a word he was saying.

Marian waited for him to get into his bed. Then, after a silence, she said, 'She's still our daughter, Richard. There are so many thugs on the streets at this time of night. And what happens if there's an air raid? If anything should happen to her, we'd never forgive ourselves.'

'Go to sleep, Marian,' said Richard. He settled back in his bed, closed his eyes, and tried to relax. It was perfectly obvious, however, that until they heard that front door open downstairs, sleep was going to elude both of them.

Joe had insisted on taking Rosie all the way back home to Camden Road. It was so late when they reached the front-garden gate of number 221 that even old Monty had abandoned his usual pitch on the coping stone down the road for another day. There was a real touch of autumn now in the night air, for Rosie felt the cold chill enough to pull up her coat collar. Fortunately, all the gaslamps in the house seemed to be turned off, all except the one in the front hall, the light from which could just be seen glowing dimly through the stained-glass panels of the front door.

On the bus coming back to Camden Road, Joe had spent a great deal of the time trying to explain why his ma behaved the way she did, why she had given the impression that she disapproved of her son having a girlfriend from another walk of life.

'She don't mean it,' he had said. 'Ma says a lot er fings she don't mean. Trouble is, she lets fings get on top of 'er.'

Standing at the front gate, Joe, clearly anxious that Rosie was concerned about the way his ma had greeted her, tried to carry on explaining, but Rosie gently put her finger to his lips to pacify him.

'You mustn't trouble yourself, Joe,' she said. 'Your mother will get used to us. She has a lot to cope with, especially with your father being away from home. She must miss him very much.'

Joe suddenly went very quiet.

'What's the matter, Joe?' she asked anxiously.

He looked up at her, and could just see her eyes reflected in the yellowy light of an autumn moon that was darting in and out of dark night clouds. 'Am I *really* goin' ter meet *your* mum 'n' dad?' he asked tentatively.

Rosie hesitated for only a split second. 'Of course you are!' she replied firmly. 'When I see them in the morning, I'm going to tell them I want you to come to lunch on Sunday.'

'But wot 'appens if they take aginst me?' he asked, sounding almost childlike.

'They *won't* take against you, Joe!' she insisted.

'But 'ow d'yer know?'

'Because I *do* know,' she replied, without reveal-

153

ing what she really felt. 'And even if they did, it wouldn't make any difference to me.'

'It wouldn't?'

'Of course it wouldn't! I love you, Joe.' She pulled him close, and hugged him. 'I never believed such a thing was possible, but it is.'

'I love you too, Rosie,' he replied, holding on to her. 'But it's not goin' ter be easy for them to accept, is it? I mean, yer 'aven't even told 'em about goin' off up front next week.'

Rosie slowly pulled away. In her heart of hearts she knew only too well that what Joe was trying to say was true. There were things she was never going to be able to say to her parents, things that would certainly drive a wedge between them. Joe was right – she couldn't tell them where she was going in just a few days' time, because if she did there was no doubt in her mind that her father would try to use his contacts to stop her.

'Listen to me, Joe,' she said, looking at the outline of his face in the dark. 'I have a relationship with my family, the same as you have with *your* family. If you love me as much as I love you, then they're just going to have to get used to it, that's all. After all, my parents love each other, and so do yours.'

'It's not as simple as that, Rosie,' said Joe.

'What d'you mean?' she asked, puzzled.

'There are fings about my ma an' dad that...' He was spluttering, clearly having difficulty trying to say what he needed to. 'It's not like you fink,' he said solemnly. 'There's somefin' I've got ter tell yer...' Before he could continue, he broke into a violent fit of coughing.

154

Rosie immediately threw her arms round him again and held on to him. 'Joe!' she cried. 'Oh, my poor Joe...!'

In a first-floor window of the house, the expensive heavy bedroom curtains were gently parted to reveal Richard Little peering down into the dark street below.

Chapter 9

Rosie looked at herself in the full-length mirror in her bedroom, hoping that she had chosen the right dress for Joe's visit. She didn't want to look too 'posh' because she knew that that would make him feel uncomfortable, but then she didn't want to look drab because it might seem that she hadn't taken any trouble to please him. In the end she chose her favourite pastel-yellow ankle-length cotton dress, which was just thick enough to conceal the outline of the soft corset she wore underneath. For one minute, however, she was unsure of the neckline, which was a little lower than she remembered, but after a little tugging and pulling here and there, she managed to make it look acceptable to anyone who was waiting to disapprove. The black waistband also helped to define her waistline – not that she needed help in that direction, for, as Joe had noticed only too well, she had a lovely svelte figure. To finish, she carefully combed her hair into a neat style with its slightly off-centre part-

155

ing. In the distance she heard church bells ringing out the call to Sunday morning service.

'Rose!'

Her mother's voice calling from downstairs immediately sent her into a flap. 'Coming, Mother!' she answered. After quickly putting on her long woollen black-patterned top coat and matching wide-brimmed hat trimmed with cream ribbon, she collected her leather gloves, and hurried down, where Christian was waiting eagerly for her in his wheelchair in the hall.

A short while later, the family were seated in their usual pew at the rear of St Barnabas Church, Richard and Marian side by side, with Rosie on the end and Christian in his wheelchair in the centre aisle. The church was full, as it always was on Sundays, especially since the start of the war when the Reverend Michael Crosby had the painful duty of reading out the names of local boys and men who had fallen on the battlefields, their relatives and friends quietly sobbing amongst the grieving congregation. Despite the Reverend Michael's desperate attempts to raise the spirits of his flock, Sunday mornings had become sombre occasions, and as she listened to the latest list of casualties being read out, Rosie felt utter despair at the wanton loss of life, especially those who had barely had the time to start their lives. Time and time again her moist eyes scanned the lovely portals of the church, the high timber beams and the stone tablets around the walls commemorating notable local residents by their grateful families. The huge sprays of autumn flowers seemed particularly lovely that

156

day: carefully arranged mixtures of different coloured dahlias, Michaelmas daisies, late-flowering roses and the distinctive smell of chrysanthemums, which wafted sadly over the congregation from each side of the altar.

However, even before the vicar's address, Rosie's mind was distracted by her anxiety over Joe coming to lunch that day. She had all kinds of premonitions about how her parents would or would not take to him, how they would react to his homely background of the East End of London and the Yorkshire Dales. Her imagination was working frantically, playing out one difficult scenario after another. Why had she done it? she kept asking herself. Why had she taken the bold step of asking this boy, this wonderful, lovable boy, to meet people who would not greet him well? But then she remembered what it must have been like when Joe decided to take her to tea with his own mother, a woman who was decidedly uncomfortable about having her son mix with someone from such a different world from his own.

Only when she turned to find Chris looking at her did Rosie start to relax. His cheery, winning smile was enough to melt away any of her own doubts. Chris was an inspiration to her. He always had been, and always would be.

Surprisingly, the Reverend Michael's sermon was not a bit depressing. In fact, it turned out to be quite uplifting, for he talked about working for the future, about the time when the boys would be coming home again, and the world would once again be a good place to live in. Unfortunately – at least as far as Rosie was concerned – his pleas for the congregation to put their faith in God seemed to ring hollow with the suffering in the world. Even so, she still believed in the power of the Divine, and hoped that her nightly bedtime prayers would not go unanswered.

As soon as the church service had come to an end, Richard and Marian remained behind for a few moments to chat with the vicar. But when Rosie wheeled Chris out of the church, she got the surprise of her life. Waving madly at her from the front gates by the road outside was Joe. Using all the strength she could muster, she pushed Chris's wheelchair as fast as she could through the departing congregation, very nearly knocking down one of the elderly female parishioners.

Joe waited not a minute longer, and rushed forward to help her.

'Joe!' Rosie gasped excitedly, as they embraced. 'I thought you were coming to the house?'

'Can't wait *that* long!' insisted Joe, with his usual grin. 'I want as much time with you as I can.'

They both turned to Chris, who was beaming excitedly.

'Chris,' said Rosie, 'this is Joe. Joe, this is my brother, Christian.'

Joe took hold of Christian's hand and shook it vigorously. 'Wotcha, mate!' he said warmly. 'I'm Joe, an' I've 'eard all about *you.*'

'*Have* you?' asked Christian, pulling himself up as far as he could in his wheelchair. 'Have you *really*? Did you know I'm very sick?'

Christian's forthright greeting took the wind

out of Joe's sails. 'Oh, yeah,' he replied, as casually as he could muster.

'The doctor says I haven't got long to live,' continued Christian, without a trace of feeling sorry for himself.

'Git orf!' said Joe. 'You'll still be around when me an' Rosie are Gran'ma an' Gran'dad.'

Chris's face lit up. 'D'you think so?' he replied, champing up and down in his wheelchair like an excitable puppy dog. 'Did you hear that, Rosie? Did you hear what Joe said?'

Before she had a chance to answer, her parents approached. 'Mother, Father,' she said nervously, formally, 'I want you to meet my friend Joseph Upton.'

At such an introduction, Joe grinned like the Cheshire cat. 'Ee, Rosie,' he chuckled, reverting back mischievously to a touch of his old Yorkshire accent, 'me name's not Joseph. I'm Joe. 'Ow do, folks?' He shook hands vigorously, first with Richard, then with a completely startled Marian.

'Good morning,' said Richard.

'Good morning,' said Marian awkwardly, somewhat surprised to see this rather informal young man dressed up so smartly in a three-piece suit and straw boater.

'It's right nice to meet Rosie's folks,' said Joe brightly. 'I told me ma I was comin', an' she was real impressed, I tell you.'

Richard and Marian's smiles were quite forced. 'I think we'd better be getting home, Richard,' said Marian. 'Mrs Winnet has done roast beef. We don't want it to overcook.'

'Roast beef!' gasped Joe, enthusiastically. 'By

159

gum, I 'ope you've got Yorkshire pud wi' it?'

Rosie found it difficult to conceal a chuckle.

Sunday lunch at 221 Camden Road was turning into quite a revelation, not only for the Little family but for Joe himself. However, he took it all in his stride, quickly mastering which knife and fork to use, and also surprising Rosie by engaging in topics of conversation about the war with her father. Fortunately, he was not plagued with any coughing fits. By the time Mrs Winnet brought in the apple crumble, he realised that he was being cross-examined by Richard Little about the kind of career he intended to pursue once he was released from the army.

'Well, I wouldn't exactly call brewery work a career,' Joe replied quite honestly. 'But once you find the right place to get into, it's a good regular trade.'

'A brewery?' Richard wasn't quite sure he'd heard right.

'You mean managerial work?' asked Marian quite innocently.

'A manager? *Me?*' Joe roared with laughter.

Richard and his wife exchanged puzzled glances.

'Nah,' said Joe, who was now talking more East End than Yorkshire. 'I mean liftin'.'

Marian eyed him warily. 'Lifting?' she asked, hoping she wouldn't get the answer she dreaded.

'Yeah,' replied Joe, mouth full of apple crumble. 'You know, gettin' the barrels off the cart an' inter the pubs. Mind you, when the war's over, my ol' man wants me ter go inter the trade *'e*'s in. But it don't really appeal ter me.'

'What trade is that, Joe?' asked Richard hesitantly.

'Canal dredgin'.'

Both Richard and Marian tried not to look shocked.

'You know, cleanin' out the sludge,' continued Joe. 'Trouble is, when yer get back 'ome yer pong ter 'igh 'eaven. But the wages are good, so Dad might talk me inter it in the end.'

'I'd like to be a rat catcher,' said Christian.

Both his parents swung him an astonished look.

Christian loved both the conversation *and* his apple crumble. 'I once read about this man who killed up to a hundred rats in one night down in the sewers. He just grabbed them out of the muck as they swam by, and wrung their necks. Apparently it was all done in a matter of seconds.'

Marian shuddered.

'I don't think we want to hear about that just now, Christian,' said Richard.

Christian shrugged.

Behind them Mrs Winnet did her best to suppress a laugh, grabbed a pile of dirty plates, and quickly disappeared into the kitchen.

Rosie, who was sitting alongside Joe, reached for his hand beneath the table and squeezed it affectionately. Despite her concerns about what her parents thought of him, she loved his honesty, the way he wasn't trying to pretend to be something that he wasn't. What difference did it make whether her parents liked Joe or not? All she knew was that whether he was a beer-barrel lifter or a canal dredger, she was in love with him.

'Joe,' asked Richard, changing the subject, 'what do you think of the role of women in society?'

'Come again?' asked Joe, scratching his head.

'Do you think girls of Rose's age should be dragged into dangerous war work?'

Before answering, Joe swung a wary look at Rosie. 'Well, I look at it this way,' he replied. 'Ter *my* mind, a gel's got just as much right ter make up 'er own mind as a feller. An' in any case, someone's got ter do the jobs if blokes ain't around.' For one moment his face stiffened and he became serious. 'All I can tell yer is that where *I* come from, I saw gels doin' jobs that would've turned *my* stomach. I reckon a female's as tough as ol' nails. That's why they live longer than us blokes. Wot say you, Guv'nor?'

Before Richard Little had a chance to answer him, Joe was convulsed with a bad fit of coughing. Little waited for him to recover before asking anxiously, 'How did you get that cough, Joe?'

To her father's surprise, Rosie answered. 'Joe doesn't like to talk about what happened to him, Father. It brings back too many bad memories.'

A short silence was broken by Marian. 'Do you take coffee, young man?' she asked Joe.

Joe looked puzzled, and turned to Rosie for an explanation.

'Would you like a cup of coffee, Joe?' Rosie asked with an affectionate grin.

'Coffee?' asked Joe. 'Nah. Never tasted the stuff.'

Marian took a deep breath. 'Then why don't we leave you two men to have a glass of port,' she said, without waiting for an answer. 'Rose, shall we go out into the conservatory?'

Suddenly Rosie looked worried. But once Joe had given her a reassuring smile, she got up from the table, and took hold of Christian's wheel-chair.

'I want to stay with Joe,' protested Christian.

'No, son,' said Richard. 'Joe and I want to have a little chat together.'

Christian groaned, as Rosie, wheeling him out of the room, slowly followed her mother. As she closed the sitting-room door, however, she flicked Joe a reassuring smile.

'When will I see Joe again?' asked Christian, once Rosie had wheeled him back into his own room. He eased himself up on to the side of his bed, and stretched out for one of his train books there. 'Joe's nice. I like him,' he said.

Rosie went to the door and quietly closed it. 'Now listen to me, Chris,' she said softly, coming back and perching herself on the side of the bed alongside him. 'I've got something to tell you, but you've got to promise not to tell anyone.'

'Not even Mother or Father?'

'Especially Mother or Father.'

'So it's a secret?'

Rosie smiled affectionately. 'Just between you and me.' She leaned closer. 'Chris, I'm going away. Next week I'm being posted to somewhere up front.'

Chris looked up like a shot. 'To the Front?' he gasped. 'You mean, where all the fighting's going on?'

Rosie nodded. 'I *have* to go, Chris,' she said. 'I

163

know you're old enough and sensible enough to understand. I *have* to do my bit for the war. It's my duty.'

'But isn't it dangerous?' asked Christian. 'You may get killed.'

'Don't worry,' Rosie assured him. 'I know how to take care of myself.'

Christian thought about this for a moment. 'But what about Joe? Does *he* know you're going?'

'Yes, Chris,' replied Rosie, lowering her voice even more to prevent them from being overheard. 'He knows everything.'

'I like Joe,' he repeated. 'I hope he won't forget about me. I'd like to see him again. I'd like to talk to him.'

'What about?'

'Oh – lots of things,' replied Christian. 'About why he thinks I'm going to live to an old age when everyone else thinks I'm not.'

Rosie felt her stomach tense. 'You shouldn't be thinking about things like that, Chris,' she said. 'You should just be enjoying yourself as much as you can.'

'Are you going to marry Joe?'

Her young brother's direct question took Rosie completely by surprise. 'I don't know,' she replied evasively. 'We've only just met. However,' she added falteringly, 'Joe and I might decide to live together.'

Christian again looked up at her. 'You mean *before* you get married?'

'It's possible,' replied Rosie, watching his reactions carefully. 'Would you mind that very much?'

Christian shrugged. 'I'd only mind if I didn't see you again.'

'That will never happen, Chris. That I promise.'

'What about Mother and Father?' he asked. 'Will *they* mind?'

Rosie took a deep breath before answering. 'At the moment, Mother and Father know nothing about any of this, and you must promise me that you won't tell them. Secret?'

Christian nodded. 'Secret,' he replied.

'In any case, Joe hasn't asked me to marry him,' said Rosie.

'Oh, but he will,' replied Christian, without a second thought.

'What makes you so sure?'

Christian shrugged. 'The way he looks at you. The way you look at him.'

Rosie never failed to be astonished by her young brother's shrewd observations. It showed he had an instinct and insight, that his long illness had given him a perception that many healthy people just didn't have. But it was also his extraordinary candour that amazed her, the way he would say something – anything – that came to his mind, whether his parents approved or disapproved.

'Would you like it if Joe and I *were* to get married?' she asked.

'Yes, I would,' replied Christian, without hesitation. 'I'd like it very much.'

'Why?'

'Because he's a chap I can talk to,' replied Christian, briefly looking up at her. 'I listened to him over lunch. He says things as they come into his head. He doesn't get nervous about what people might think.' He went back to his book. 'Yes,' he said, 'chaps know how to talk to chaps, just the same way as girls know how to talk to girls. I hope you *do* marry him, Rosie. I'd really like that.'

Rosie leaned forward and kissed him gently on the forehead. She loved her brother so much that the thought of him one day not being around any more made her feel deeply despondent.

There was a knock at the door. Christian called to come in and Mrs Winnet put her head round. 'Miss Rosie,' she said softly, 'your mother wants you to join her in the conservatory.'

'Just coming,' said Rosie, going to the bedroom door.

'Rosie.'

Rosie turned to look back at her brother.

'I hope you don't get killed when you go to France.'

Rosie felt her whole body tense. She felt like crying, but mustered up a smile instead. 'Don't worry,' she said back quietly. 'You won't get rid of me *that* easily.'

The conservatory smelled of young geranium cuttings, green foliage and paraffin oil. Although it was not particularly cold outside, Marian always made sure she maintained a steady temperature in the place in order to keep her plants alive. Indoor plants and her back garden were Marian's passion in life, which made the conservatory an apt place for her to retire to when she wanted to be alone with her thoughts. And these days, she had plenty to think about.

When Rosie came in, she found her mother knitting soldiers' mittens. She had come to realise that knitting was not only Marian's way of coping with her anxieties, but also a kind of statement on the war, her way of saying that women can help the boys at the Front just as well as any other way by knitting mittens for them for the coming winter. It was significant that the mittens were always for men, never for women. Despite the fact that Marian had been a caring mother over the years, Rosie had come to know that she had turned into a very highly strung and complicated woman.

'Where did you meet this boy?' Marian asked the moment Rosie came through the door.

'He was a patient at the hospital.' Rosie's reply was immediate and firm. She was determined not to be on the defensive. 'Do you like him?'

Marian shrugged without looking up from her knitting. 'He seems charming enough,' she replied. 'But an odd choice, I would have thought.'

Rosie resisted the urge to sit down on the wicker sofa alongside her mother. She remained standing with her back to the window overlooking the garden. 'An odd choice?' she asked. 'What d'you mean?'

'Come now, dear,' said Marian, flicking a brief well-meaning smile up at her. 'You know perfectly well what I mean. He's a nice enough boy, but hardly in the same league as you.'

'I'm sorry, Mother,' said Rosie. 'I still don't know what you mean.'

Trying not to show her growing irritation, Marian stopped knitting for a moment and looked up. 'He comes from a different world from you, Rose. Don't get me wrong, I do like him, but even you must know that his field of conversation is very limited. I mean, you could hardly spend the rest of your life talking about breweries and canal dredging, now could you?'

Now Rosie was becoming irritated. 'Mother,' she retorted, 'that's a terribly condescending thing to say.'

'I'm sorry, dear,' replied Marian. 'But I have to speak as I find. But then, I'm probably being a little unfair, aren't I? I mean, I take it this boy *is* only a friend – isn't he?'

Rosie refused to answer. She crossed her arms and glared out of the window.

'I mean,' persisted Marian, returning to her knitting, 'anyone can see he's not the kind of boy you would want to take as a husband.'

'What makes you think that, Mother?'

'Well, when your father and I first met,' replied Marian quite shamelessly, 'we had both had the benefit of good education. We talked about a wide range of subjects, from classical literature to Queen Victoria and the Empire.'

'Fascinating,' mumbled Rosie under her breath.

'What was that, dear?'

'I said fascinating!'

Marian stiffened, and finally rested her knitting needles on her lap. She knew she was saying all the wrong things, that the more she spoke the more intimidating she was sounding, but somehow she just couldn't help herself. This was the first time she had had to cope with her daughter having a liaison with someone, and she was not handling the situation well. She loved Rose deeply, and the last thing she wanted to do was to stand in the way of her happiness. But her instinct automatically told her that Rose fixing her sights on a boy like this was wrong. Nice as he was, it had been proved over and over again that the mixing of classes never worked. But what could she possibly say to convince Rose of that? Without a second's thought, the solution, or what she thought would be a solution, simply tumbled from her lips: 'He's not a well person, is he, Rose?'

Rose turned from the window, and glared down at her.

'To me, that dreadful cough he has sounds quite serious. I mean, it could go on like that for years. If Christian is anything to go by, this boy could be in and out of hospital for the rest of his life.'

Now Rosie was really furious. As much as she loved her mother, she was not prepared to tolerate this brazen attempt to interfere in her life. 'This "*boy*" as you call him, Mother,' she snapped, 'is well on the road to recovery. All he needs is time and determination. Joe *has* determination – that I can promise you. And if I can help him back on that road to recovery, I shall do so. And why? Because I love him, Mother. I presume that when you met Father, it wasn't just talk about Queen Victoria and the Empire that brought you together? I mean, I'd like to think that love had something to do with it as well?'

Marian felt her stomach turn over. It was obvious that nothing she could say now was going to change Rose's mind. 'I'm sorry, darling,' she said, 'but I can only say what I feel. And I feel that by seeing this boy, you are making a big mistake.'

'Is that why you allowed me to bring him to lunch, Mother?' asked Rosie. 'So you could tell me that?'

'Let's see what your father has to say,' replied Marian stiffly. Feeling hurt and offended, she moved her knitting on to a small table at the side of the sofa, and got up. 'I think you'll find he'll feel no differently from me.'

As she spoke, Richard Little came in, followed by Joe. 'Ah, there you both are!' boomed Richard, who had a half-filled glass of port and a cigar in his hand. 'Joe and I thought it was about time we joined the ladies. We've had quite a chat, haven't we, my boy?'

Joe, beaming, nodded agreement.

'D'you know his mother works at home making matchboxes?' continued Richard. 'Fascinating! Fascinating! And so enterprising. I knew an old woman once in Clapham who did that. They say when she died she left hundreds of pounds under her bed.' He turned to Rosie. 'An interesting young man you have here, Rose,' he said, putting an arm round Joe's shoulder. 'A very interesting young man indeed!'

Joe looked across at Rosie. Like him, she was beaming.

Marian's response, however, was somewhat different. All she could do was to stare at her husband in silent disbelief.

170

Chapter 10

Charing Cross Station looked gloomy in the harsh light of a grey, windswept morning. On the way to the station, Rosie looked out through the window on the top deck of the bus and marvelled at the start of the transformation of the seasons that was now manifested in the brown and yellow hues of the roadside oaks and elms and sycamore trees, and the pavements that were just beginning to take the brunt of what would soon be an endless cascade of falling leaves. But it wasn't the gradual decline of the year that had sent her on her way with such a heavy heart; leaving her family and home, especially saying a tearful goodbye to Christian, was almost more than she could bear. This wasn't the same as going off to Stanmore Manor for a month – this was a parting, a real parting that was fraught with danger, made even more intense by the fact that she had deliberately lied to her parents about the posting that was taking her to the battlefields of France. As far as they were concerned, she was heading back to Stanmore. Of course, she realised only too well that it was only a matter of time before they would discover the truth – her father's contact at the Home Office would ensure that – but she hoped that once she had crossed the English Channel, her posting would be a *fait accompli*, and therefore difficult to reverse. None the less, her anxieties remained, and it was not until she had stepped off the bus and struggled her way with her suitcase into the station concourse that her spirits were finally lifted, for there, amongst the sea of khaki uniforms, and the bonnets and aprons of the female voluntary workers, was Joe, once again smartly togged up in his three-piece suit and flat cap.

He and Rosie practically leaped into each other's arms, hugging and tugging, smothering each other with kisses and caresses, not saying a word until they came up for breath.

'You shouldn't have come, Joe,' she said, eyes glistening with tears. 'But I'm so happy you did.'

Joe gave her the biggest smile he knew, and kissed her gently on the tip of her nose. 'Yer didn't fink I'd let yer get away that easy, did yer?'

This brought a ravishing smile from Rosie, who dropped her head on to his shoulder.

For several moments they stood there, engulfed by a tidal wave of service personnel all pushing and shoving their way towards the platform from where they would be rejoining their units, together with groups of women from different nursing organisations, who, like Rosie, wore long dark and white uniforms imprinted on the chest and cap with the emblem of the Red Cross. As the hands of the giant station clock on the concourse moved mercilessly towards the hour of eleven, Joe picked up Rosie's suitcase and, with her arm tucked round his waist, they moved slowly off through the crowds towards Platform 1, from where the departure of Rosie's train – nicknamed by the station staff *The Belles of*

Heaven because each day it carried hordes of nurses travelling back and forth to the Front – was due to leave within the next five minutes. Before they reached the platform gates, however, Rosie brought her and Joe to a brief halt.

'What happened between you and father on Sunday afternoon?' she asked eagerly. 'I didn't get a chance to talk to you privately before you went home. After you left, Father talked so enthusiastically about you.'

'As a matter er fact,' replied Joe, nonchalantly, 'me an' your dad got on like an 'ouse on fire. Look.' He reached into his coat pocket. 'See wot 'e give me.' He held out a cigar.

Rosie was dumbfounded. 'But you don't smoke,' she said incredulously. 'Especially with your condition.'

'I know,' replied Joe. 'But I didn't let 'im know that. I told 'im I'd prefer ter smoke it later. Anyway, I'll give it ter Paul. It'll make 'im fink 'e's a toff!'

They both laughed, until they were interrupted by the deafening sound of steam gushing out from the funnel of the train engine. They stared at each other thoughtfully, trying to erase from their minds the thought that they would soon be parted.

'Don't seem natural – all this,' said Joe, staring with torment into her eyes. '*I* should be the one that's getting on that train, not you.'

'You've done your bit, Joe,' Rosie replied. 'Now it's *my* turn.' She leaned forward as though to kiss him, but as she did so, the other three of The Terrible Four pushed their way through the throng to greet her.

'Rosie!' called Eunice, who looked quite ridiculous in her uniform and a black felt hat with a stuffed canary stuck on the side. Close behind her were Titch and Binnie. 'We've saved yer a seat, Rosie. Come on, we're off any minute.'

'Don't rush the poor girl,' said Binnie, giving her a reassuring smile. 'You take your time, Rosie.' She smiled then at Joe. 'You can't rush saying goodbye. Isn't that right, Joe?'

Joe nodded back gratefully at her.

'Some people 'ave all the luck,' said Titch. 'My mam didn't even come to the front door to see *me* off!'

'Come on, girls,' said Binnie to Eunice and Titch, nodding to them to leave Rosie alone with Joe.

As they went, Eunice flashed her eyes back cheekily at Joe, who laughed and blew her a teasing kiss.

Joe picked up Rosie's suitcase, and the two of them slowly followed the girls at a distance. When they reached the carriage the girls had found seats in, Joe got in and put Rosie's case up on the rack, before coming down on to the platform for the last few moments.

'I hope I don't get seasick,' said Rosie, too upset to look into his eyes.

With one hand, Joe gently raised her chin to look at her. He loved what he saw, and couldn't bear the thought that this would be the last time he would look into those eyes for maybe quite a long time. 'Yer won't get seasick,' he said, with a comforting smile. 'Yer'll be too busy finkin' about *me*.'

Despite the tears she was fighting back, this made her smile.

'But I'm warnin' yer,' he continued. 'Don't hang yer fingers over the side er the boat. Them sharks get hungry, yer know.'

'Sharks!' she replied, rising to his teasing. 'In the English Channel?'

'Full of 'em!' he said, staring longingly into her eyes. 'The time when I went over, I jumped in an' killed five of 'em wiv me bare 'ands.'

Rosie laughed, threw her arms around him and hugged him. The tears were now streaming down her cheeks. 'Oh, Joe!' she spluttered.

For his part, Joe felt a lump in his throat so big that he could hardly swallow. 'Will yer do me a favour?' he asked, whispering into her ear against the sounds of platform pandemonium all around them. 'Will yer remember that when fings get bad – I mean really bad – just remember that sooner or later, you'll be comin' back ter me?'

Rosie, eyes streaming, slowly pulled back and nodded gallantly at him.

'Promise?'

Rosie was far too full to answer, so she just nodded again.

Suddenly there was the sound of the train guard's whistle.

'Rosie!' screeched Eunice from the train compartment. ''Urry!'

Amidst the sound of train doors slamming, Rosie gave Joe one last hug and a long kiss. Then she jumped on to the train, leaving Joe to close the carriage door behind her. Rosie immediately opened the window, and peered out. 'Give my love to your mother!' she called.

'I'll do no such fing!' responded Joe. 'You save yer love fer *me* – right?'

'Right!'

The train horn fractured the air, and the wheels started to turn to the accompaniment of a military band on the station concourse playing 'Goodbye Dolly Gray'. As the train slowly moved off, Rosie reached down to take hold of Joe's hand for one last time.

'Give my love ter Madamwazelle from Armentiers!' called Joe, trying to make her laugh.

But Rosie's face was crumpled up, and all she could do was to shake her head vigorously.

'Hey – wait!'

Joe's sudden call took her by surprise. As he started to run alongside the train, which was now gathering speed, he reached into his coat pocket and took out a piece of paper. 'Rosie!' he yelled, thrusting the paper into her hand. 'Take this!'

'What is it?' she called back.

'It's fer you!' was all he had time to say, as his running came to an abrupt halt at the end of the platform.

From the train, Rosie watched him waving frantically at her with both hands and arms, just one of many friends and relatives who were seeing their girls move off into a world from which they might never return.

Only when the train turned a bend and headed off from London towards the Channel coast did Rosie sit down and join the others.

Binnie put her arm around her shoulders and

176

comforted her. 'Don't worry,' she said reassuringly. 'You'll see him again.'

After the train had gone, Joe ambled miserably out of the station, passing without noticing a news-vendor who was shouting out the latest headlines: 'Read all about it! Read all about it! Nurse Cavell sentenced ter death! Nurse Cavell sentenced ter death! Read all about it!'

In better times, before the war, the quayside at Folkestone had been buzzing with excitement as families got off the London train to find their cross-Channel ferry waiting alongside the railway track to take them on their annual holiday to the white sandy beaches of northern France. When she was very young, before Christian was born, even Rosie had found herself on this very same quayside en route with her parents to their favourite small *pension* in a tiny village by the sea just outside Boulogne. Today, however, the atmosphere was very different. In place of the bright summer dresses, coloured parasols and straw boaters, the dockside was a mass of khaki uniforms. Amongst the nurses queuing to climb the narrow gangway on to the ship was a small contingent of nuns in black habits, on their way to a front-line convent field hospital to add their own nursing skills to those of their French sisters.

The first thing The Terrible Four noticed when they approached the gangway was the towering figure of Lady Braintree, a striking, almost ethereal image set against the deceptive blue of an October sky, dressed in a long black nurse's gown, cloak and hat, watching in calm silence the arrival of her 'gels' from the far end of the quayside.

'Gives me the creeps, that one,' said Eunice, with a shudder. 'Just look at 'er. Can't wait ter get rid of us all.'

'Don't you believe it,' said Binnie, chastising her. 'I'll bet you it hurts her deeply to see every one of us getting on to this boat.'

Rosie agreed. As she and the other girls edged closer and closer to the bottom of the gangway, her eyes were glued on the redoubtable Lady, whose words had haunted Rosie's mind ever since she had first met her in the QAIMNS headquarters in Knightsbridge just a few weeks before: *I won't pretend that taking you out to the battlefield is going to be anything but a distressing experience for you. You'll see some terrible things. Our boys out there are suffering – suffering not only terrible wounds, but real mental trauma. You young ladies will have to learn how to be mothers to them, as well as nurses, D'you think you're up to that?*

Even now, especially now, Rosie still had doubts.

Emile and Clara Harrington left the Great Northern Hospital, and made their way slowly on foot down Holloway Road towards the Nag's Head. Although Emile was feeling much better after the attack on him, his head was heavily bandaged, and he was still very frail. After a short bus ride up Camden Road, the couple got off at Kentish Town, and took a slow walk to Little and Company.

In the front office, Emile received a polite but

nervous greeting from Amy Desmond. 'Hello, Mr Harrington,' she said, getting up from her seat at the counter. 'I'll take you up to Mr Little. He *is* expecting you.'

'Thank you, Amy,' replied Emile, holding up his hand to stop her from coming out from behind the counter. 'I *do* know my way up there.' He flicked a quick departing smile at Clara before starting a slow climb up the stairs.

Richard was at his desk when the knock came on his door. 'Come in!' he called, but prepared as he was for Emile's visit, he still felt unsure of himself when he actually appeared. 'Ah – there you are, my dear fellow. Please come in.'

'Good morning, sir,' said Emile, with his customary slight bow of the head.

'Sit down, Emile,' said Richard, nervously rising from his chair and going to him. 'How are you feeling now? Are you in any great pain?'

'I'm fine, sir, thank you,' returned Emile, preferring to sit on an upright chair rather than the sofa. His German accent was only just noticeable.

'I got your note,' said Richard, perching on the edge of his desk alongside Emile. 'What can I do for you?' Before Emile had a chance to answer, Richard's eyes suddenly flicked up to the great arched window overlooking the workshop. He held up his hand to delay Emile's reply, went to the window, and with a cursory glance down, drew across the white muslin curtains. Then he turned back to Emile again. 'Now?'

Emile smiled wryly. 'I've decided to leave the company, sir,' he said, with dignified calm. 'I

179

know I should be giving a week's notice, but if it's agreeable to you, I would like to go immediately.'

Richard was genuinely shocked. 'My dear fellow,' he gasped. His reaction was tinged with surprise – and relief. 'Are you sure?'

'Absolutely,' replied Emile. 'I discussed the situation with Clara last night, and she agrees it would be the most satisfactory way out of your dilemma – and mine.'

Richard was suddenly riddled with guilt. He returned to his seat at his desk and slowly sat down. He could hardly bring himself to look up at this man who had served Little and Company with such loyal devotion over the years, who could be trusted more than any person he had ever known. When he did eventually look up, for one brief moment his eyes focused on a company photograph on the wall, which showed Richard and his father seated in the back yard of the factory, with a group of employees, including Emile, standing behind.

'My dear fellow,' he said, once he had taken in the news, 'I hardly know what to say.'

Emile shrugged. 'With respect, sir,' he replied, 'there's nothing *to* say. Times have changed, so different from when I first joined the company. People have changed too.'

Richard lowered his eyes.

'Oh, I don't really blame them,' continued Emile, lightly. 'It must be easy to go blind when there are so many dark things to look at.' He paused briefly to adjust the bandage across his forehead.

Richard looked up again. 'Emile,' he said, 'I

want you to know that I am thoroughly ashamed of what happened to you the other night. I can only hope that when the police capture those who are responsible, the blackguards will be locked up for the rest of their miserable lives.'

Emile bore no grudge. For him, his time working for both Richard Little and his father had been the happiest years of his life. No. Little was an honourable man. It was those without logic, without scruples who were the real culprits. 'No, sir,' he said. 'I ask you not to blame yourself for anything that has happened to me. All I know is that as long as I am working for you, as long as this war lasts, there will never be any peace within this company.'

Richard sighed and leaned back despondently in his chair. 'What can I do for you, Emile?' he asked. 'What can I do to make up to you for what has happened? How can I repay you for all your years of loyal service?'

Emile shook his head. 'I want no repayment, sir,' he replied. 'Clara and I have enough to live on quietly in the country somewhere. Please don't worry about us. I promise you, we shall survive. However...' he paused briefly, 'I do have one request.'

Richard sat forward. 'Anything,' he said.

'Your daughter, Rosie,' said Emile, his voice as quiet and gentle as ever. 'She is a wonderful girl, a wonderful young woman. I remember the first time Clara and I met her. She came to a meeting at our house. There were several young girls there, all with problems relating to the way they had been treated by unscrupulous men. There was one of them – she wasn't much younger than Rosie herself – a sweet little thing, with golden hair and bright blue eyes, who said she felt she had nothing to live for, because her parents had thrown her out of her home, and she had nowhere to go but the streets. I can see Rosie now, taking the girl's hand, gently holding it, and giving her advice that could have come from a woman twice her age. Clara saw that same girl the other day. She said Rosie had given her some money to pay for a room to live in, and that she now had a job and was seeing a boy who truly loved her.' He smiled to himself, briefly took off his spectacles, held them up to the light, looked through the lenses, then replaced them again.

'You know, sir, that is such a remarkable quality for one so young. The last time I saw anyone like that was when I first came to this country more than twenty years ago. I remember being inter-viewed by a young man from the Home Office who wasn't much older than myself, large ears and laughing eyes. He asked me what was so special about this country, and why I wanted to come to it. I told him that when Clara and I decided to leave Germany, life for people like us was becoming tense and strained. The moment the former Chancellor of Prussia, Otto von Bismarck resigned, it was easy to see that Kaiser Wilhelm had his own agenda, a ruthless one that has eventually led to this present war. Germany was about power and expansion, and if anyone dared to challenge the regime, they were immediately silenced. Clara and I saw what was happening. We knew that freedom of speech and freedom of movement were dying a slow death.' He paused a moment. 'But do you know what that young man at the Home Office told me?' he said, with a wry smile. 'If you come to live in *this* country,' he said, 'you will never have to worry about your freedom. If you become one of us, you will never have to look over your shoulder again.' He sighed, his German accent becoming more pronounced with the memories. 'I never forget that young man,' he continued. 'I never forget your Rosie. The world is going mad, Mr Little, but as long as there are people around like her and that young man, we have nothing to fear. All I ask is that you understand Rosie, because she is someone you can be proud of.'

As the ferry left the quayside at Folkestone Harbour, a military band played a popular and appropriate song of the moment, 'Goodbye-ee'. The dull grey of the sea was broken only by the huge rolls of white foam that were split by the boat cutting through the murky waters of the English Channel. The Terrible Four watched tearfully from the upper-deck rails as their beloved Blighty gradually became no more than a thin line of coastal land fading reluctantly into the mist. Like the rest of the nurses on board, the four girls were all wearing life-jackets, a precaution in case of a sudden enemy submarine attack. Having to wear such a cumbersome thing seemed quite incongruous to both Eunice and Titch, who thought that the Germans would surely never attack a ship with so many females on board. But Binnie reminded them that if they could torpedo an unarmed passenger liner like the *Lusitania*, then they would certainly not hesitate to sink a ferry carrying troops and other personnel to the Front.

A short while later, Rosie managed to find a quiet corner of the deck where she could at last sit down and read the note Joe had thrust into her hand as the train had pulled away. Whilst she was getting the note out of her pocket she was distracted by the sound of a young nurse sobbing quietly to herself. Rosie leaned across to the poor little thing, who looked younger than most of the others.

'It's all right,' called Rosie, above the crashing of waves against the side of the boat. 'You'll be home quicker than you think.'

The girl smiled, and dabbed the tears from her eyes. Rosie returned to her note. Although it flapped a bit in the sharp sea breeze, she managed to hold it steady enough to read the words Joe had written, hearing his voice in them.

Rosie Lee, Rosie Lee,
Oh, how I love you,
Saviour of life, weaver of dreams,
Oh, how I love you.

Dark of night, cold outside,
War, bombs and danger.
But warm and tender is your touch,
A glow of light, a ray of hope,
Oh, Rosie Lee, how I love you.

Rosie rested the letter on her lap. From the bow

of the boat she could hear seagulls screeching for scraps of food as they followed behind, their pure white wings outstretched and floating along gracefully in the stiff cross-Channel breeze. With Joe's simple words ringing in her ears, her eyes told her that it was time to cry, but with the boat rolling from one side to another, she was now feeling too sick for that. But then she heard Joe's voice again: *'Yer won't get seasick. Yer'll be too busy finkin' about me.'*

'We have to go into the canteen on the lower deck,' said Binnie, appearing beside her. 'The Lady wants to talk to us.'

The ship's canteen was crowded with nurses from all the voluntary services. Most of the seats at the tables were already occupied, and the rest of the available space was jammed with girls and women, who either squatted on the floor or stood. As there was very little air in the room, the portholes and main door were left open, for the combination of the heavy spray and stiff breeze outside was causing some of the girls to feel quite seasick. Inevitably, there was a great hum of anticipation amongst them, which only increased the air of concern about why they had been called together.

Once everyone was settled, they got to their feet as the Lady entered the room, accompanied by some of the senior staff from the other services. Swathed in a long black cloak and hood, she did indeed look forbidding, and her presence immediately brought the assembly to a sudden silence. 'Please sit down,' she called out from the front of the assembly, taking down her hood as she spoke.

The nurses duly obeyed, but some girls at the back of the room wanted to get a clear view, so they remained standing.

'I have some sad and unpleasant news to pass on to you,' she began, doing her best to keep her balance as the boat swayed to and fro. 'For this purpose, my colleagues have asked me to speak on their behalf as well as my own.'

Near the back of the room, Rosie felt a sense of instant foreboding.

'A few minutes ago,' continued the Lady, 'the captain of this vessel passed a message to me which was transmitted to him from London. The message contained news from the American Legation in Brussels that at two o'clock in the early hours of this morning, our beloved Nurse Cavell...' she faltered, 'our beloved Nurse Cavell was executed by a German firing squad.'

The moment she had spoken the words, the entire room erupted into howls of horror, disgust and outrage. There were cries of 'Oh, no! Please God, no!' Some girls, overwhelmed by anguish, sobbed openly, but they were quickly brought under control by the Lady, who raised her hands and with immense compassion and under-standing called out, 'Please, young ladies! Calm yourselves. Listen to me. Please listen.'

The assembly gradually did what she asked, and apart from one distraught young nurse at a table on the side of the room, everyone returned to calm.

Despite the swaying of the boat, the Lady stood firm and erect. 'Edith Cavell,' she continued, head held high, 'Edith Cavell was, just like you and me, a nurse. But first and foremost she was a wonderful, compassionate human being. Over the years, I had the great pleasure of meeting her several times, even a long time ago when she was a nanny to a young family I knew in Essex. She had such a firm disposition, so positive about what she wanted to do, and how she would do it. Therefore, it came as no surprise to me when I heard that she had travelled around our country as a probationary nurse before embarking upon what was to be her great achievement in helping to set up a training school for nurses in Belgium. At the outbreak of the war last year, she elected to remain behind in Brussels to run the Red Cross medical institute where she was working to help not only Belgian patients but German ones too. Since then many British and Allied soldiers who were left behind in the retreat owed their lives to her when she helped them to escape from the brutal and indiscriminate treatment they had been subjected to. It is for this reason that Nurse Cavell herself has made the supreme sacrifice.'

At this point, Eunice, voice choked with tears, shouted out: 'But she was a woman! How could they kill a woman like that in cold blood?'

Calls of agreement came from other girls.

'Lady Braintree!' said another girl with more calm and reason. 'Nurse Cavell was found guilty only last night. How could they execute someone without giving them a chance to appeal?'

More agreement from the others.

Lady Braintree shook her head, and held up her hands in a plea for calm. 'I'm afraid, my dears,' she replied, 'these are questions I cannot answer. Only history can do that. But I want you to remember one thing. I want you to remember that Edith Cavell was a nurse, just like you and me. She had a mission to fulfil, and she accomplished that mission. Edith Cavell was a shining example to us all, like our glorious Florence Nightingale, an inspiration to our profession.' She took a moment to compose herself, but once again held her head up and looked straight out at the gathering of bewildered fresh young faces. 'In the name of Edith Cavell, I ask you all now to remember the light that has been extinguished, but which will always burn on in the heart of every nurse.' In a firm and resonant voice, she started to sing the words of the stirring song 'Jerusalem'.

Immediately, the entire assembly joined in. Rosie, clinging desperately to the hope that she would survive the horrifying ordeal that awaited her, reached into her pocket, and immediately felt the warmth of Joe's words in her ears: *'Oh, Rosie Lee, how I love you.'*

The small, vulnerable ferry ploughed its perilous way through the hostile waters of the English Channel, thick black smoke billowing out of its funnel, leaving a long thin trail in the wind back to the shores of dear old Blighty. And as it went, the air was filled with the sound of the unified voices of women of all ages, joined together in an act of courage and determination.

Chapter 11

The advanced dressing station at Orlais was a pretty grim place. When Rosie arrived in northern France more than a week before, she couldn't believe that everything she had been told about the Front was true, but if anything had convinced her that it was, then it was this ramshackle old farmhouse in the middle of nowhere, surrounded by muddy fields and broken ploughs. By the time the rest of The Terrible Four had got there, a major German offensive had only just been repelled, leaving the station in utter chaos. Badly mutilated casualties were being rushed in by makeshift ambulances and anything that could move, including horses and carts, and soldiers struggled through ankle-deep mud to carry their stricken comrades on stretchers made up of anything they could lay their hands on. It was a grim baptism of fire for Rosie and the other girls, especially as the dressing station was already badly understaffed and lacking the presence of experienced nurses. Things were now made worse by the news that within the past twenty-four hours German troops had buried land mines beneath the rough roads between the farmhouse and the nearby village of Orlais, which meant that food and fresh medical supplies were dwindling, and the station was virtually cut off from all help. On top of this, the nights were constantly broken by the deafening barrage of artillery gunfire, which not only lit up the sky, but scattered the entire area with lumps of white-hot shrapnel. Every hour brought new casualties, some of them with such terrible injuries that they died before there was even time for an operation by the station's one surviving medical officer. The one thing Rosie feared most of all was the possibility of a sudden enemy poison-gas attack, but even though there had been reports that a Canadian unit had suffered heavy casualties in just such a bombardment the day before, for the British troops so far this had not materialised. None the less, everyone remained on guard with gas hoods within reach at every moment.

Despite the difficult conditions, with the help of the three experienced nurses, the unit doctor and the anaesthetist, Lieutenant Wilson, Rosie and The Terrible Four coped with tremendous determination, learning minute by minute to do all the things that there was never any time for at Stanmore Manor. Although the days were long and the nights nerve-racking, the tension was occasionally relieved by the singing of Private Alfie Pickles. Badly wounded himself with shrapnel wounds and lying flat on his back on the cold stone floor, Alfie's fine tenor voice had earned him the nickname 'Caruso'. Battling against the endless artillery barrage outside, his repertoire included such current favourites as 'There's a Long, Long Trail A-Winding', 'It's a Long Way to Tipperary' and 'My Old Dutch', but the most heavily requested song amongst both patients and nurses was always the poignant 'Keep the

Home Fires Burning', which brought tears to everyone's eyes as they dreamed of their loved ones back home. From the moment she had set foot inside the farmhouse, Rosie had thought about home quite a lot, especially about Joe, about Christian and her parents, and whether her father had yet discovered that she had defied him and gone to the Front. But for the moment, as she coped with the reality of war at firsthand, she had more pressing matters on her mind.

This became only too evident one night during a fierce enemy bombardment of the advanced British lines no more than half a mile away. Ordered down into the cellar of the old farmhouse by Lieutenant Hillary, the middle-aged medical officer, The Terrible Four and the other nurses refused, opting instead to remain with their patients in the overcrowded makeshift ward, which was situated in the grounds of the farmhouse in what had once been an old cowshed. Owing to the fact that for the time being it was going to be virtually impossible to get relief doctors or nursing staff from nearby Orlais, Binnie, being the eldest nurse on duty, was appointed by Lieutenant Hillary to keep a protective watch on the other girls, and as the intense, deafening bombardment continued, Binnie made sure that everyone kept under cover. It wasn't easy, for amongst the severely injured were some men who were clearly not going to last the night, amongst them a young recruit named Tim, who had been critically injured in a hand-grenade attack two days before. In the last few minutes before he died, he made one last request to Rosie, that she

191

would allow him to touch her. Unsure of what he meant, she leaned closer to him. Slowly reaching up, his hand quivering, the boy delicately covered her breast with his hand. Rosie's immediate instinct was to pull away, but instead she took hold of his hand, and gently held it in place.

After the boy had died, Lieutenant Hillary came across to her. 'That was a very noble thing to do, young lady,' he said.

Rosie shook her head, and covered the boy's lifeless face with a grubby sheet. There were no tears. In the short time she had been there, she had learned that there was no time for things like that.

It was some days later before the enemy bombardment subsided. By then, the girls were thoroughly exhausted, and with the smell of rotting corpses desperately awaiting burial, all they wanted to do was to breathe fresh air again. But it was now cold, very cold, and when Rosie and Eunice finally managed to grab a few moments away from the frenzied activity inside the old cowshed, outside there were the first signs of frost on the abandoned wheat fields, so much so that the mud, which was everywhere, had frozen rock hard and was easier to walk on. On the outer edge of the farmyard, they stopped to perch on the remains of an old stone wall, where they could look out at the distant front line of British trenches, still now but for the sound of crows fighting with each other for whatever they could find to eat in the hard earth of the vast open spaces. However, aware that enemy snipers were probably out in the bushes just waiting for

192

any sign of movement, the two girls were careful not to make themselves sitting targets.

'So wot der we fink?' asked Eunice, gazing out at the debris left behind by endless shells.

'About what?' asked Rosie.

'All this,' replied Eunice, whose face was smudged with dirt and blood from a gruesome night's work. 'Is it like yer fawt it was goin' ter be?'

Rosie sighed. 'Oh, I imagine so. But to tell you the truth, Euny, before we came here I tried not to think what it was going to be like.'

'I know,' said Eunice. 'Me too. But every time I look out at all this, I keep finkin' about my bruvver, Sid. In a funny sort er way, it's helped me ter see what it must've bin like fer 'im when 'e got *'is* lot. Those fellers inside – every one of 'em makes me fink of 'im. I'd 'ate ter be the one who 'as ter write the letters back 'ome ter their families.'

Rosie slipped a comforting arm around her friend's shoulder.

'The only fing is,' continued Eunice, taking a deep breath, 'I wish I was like you. I wish I 'ad someone ter go back 'ome to, *if* an' *when* we ever do get 'ome.'

'Come on now, Euny,' said Rosie. 'This is not like you. Of course we'll get home. We'll get home, you'll find a nice young man, you'll get married, and you'll have dozens of children.'

This made them both rock with laughter. 'Not me!' quipped Eunice. 'I'll probably end up an ol' spinster wiv no teef an' only an 'ot-water bottle in bed at night ter keep *me* warm!'

This made Rosie laugh even more. 'Nonsense!'

she cried.

'It's true!' insisted Eunice. 'But if I *do* 'ave kids,' she added, changing the mood, 'if I 'ave a boy, I'll call 'im ... Sid.' She turned to look at Rosie. 'Don't yer fink?'

Rosie gave her a reassuring smile. 'I think that's a grand idea, Euny.'

For the next few minutes, the two girls sat there in quiet contemplation. With the distressing shouts of pain and anguish coming from the critically wounded inside, and the distant sight of more injured British Tommies struggling on foot to reach the dressing station from the advanced line of trenches, there was little time for the two girls to think of anything except the stench of war. Nearby, the crows continued their frantic search for food, until the sudden approach of a low-flying aircraft sent them flapping off in panic.

'Huns!' yelled Eunice in panic, immediately dragging herself and Rosie to the ground behind the old stone wall.

The German biplane skimmed the fields so low that the Iron Cross markings on its fuselage were clearly visible, and to the girls' horror its machine gun strafed the farmhouse with a spray of bullets, the plane only pulling up again just in time to clear the rooftop. Once the aircraft had made off in the direction of no man's land, the two girls staggered to their feet. They were covered in mud and grime.

'Yer bleedin' sod!' yelled Eunice, waving her fist angrily at the aircraft as it roared off over the British trenches. 'I'll get yer fer that!'

There was a long queue outside Alf Jolly's grocery shop in Brecknock Road. Mrs Winnet had been waiting there for nearly half an hour, irritated by the fact that it was likely to be Alf who was holding things up, chatting to every customer. Alf was well known in the neighbourhood for being an old gossip; if anyone wanted to know who was going off with someone's husband or wife, you could bet your life that Alf was the person with all the details. But Mrs Winnet was determined to persevere. A notice in Alf's window announced the rare arrival of oranges that morning, and as both young Christian and his dad loved them, she was determined to get some. Therefore, she was none too pleased when Alf suddenly appeared and took down the notice.

'Sorry about this, ladies!' he called, amidst groans from the waiting queue. 'Better luck next time.'

'If there ever *is* a next time!' sneered a very resentful young woman in the queue.

'Don't blame me, missus!' returned Alf indignantly. 'There's not much *I* can do if the Boche keep sinking our ships. Oranges don't grow in Islin'ton, yer know!'

The queue gradually dispersed.

Vowing to herself that she would stop shopping at Alf Jolly's, Mrs Winnet turned away and made off back to Camden Road. However, to her surprise, she was waylaid by Joe Upton, who was waiting for her on the corner of the main road.

''Ello, mate!' he called, catching up with her as she went.

'Good 'eavens,' Mrs Winnet said, coming to an abrupt halt. 'Wot you doin' up 'ere?'

'Come ter pay you a little visit, Mrs W,' replied Joe. 'Need a favour.'

Mrs Winnet looked at him suspiciously. Even though she and Joe had got on like a house on fire when he went to the Little house for Sunday lunch, she was a bit unsure what he was up to. 'People don't ask favours from people who ain't got no favours ter give,' she replied, moving on.

Joe grinned, took hold of her half-filled shopping bag, and carried it for her. 'This is one favour yer won't mind givin',' he assured her. 'It's about Rosie's young bruvver, Chris.'

Mrs Winnet immediately came to a halt again. 'Christian?' she asked. 'What about 'im?'

'I wanna talk to 'im, that's all,' replied Joe.

'What about?'

'I want ter get ter know 'im.'

'Why?'

''Cos 'e's my gel's bruvver,' replied Joe. 'There's nuffin' wrong wiv that, is there?'

Mrs Winnet thought about this for a moment, but was still suspicious. 'Christian's not like uvver boys. 'E's very ill.'

'That's why I wanna talk to 'im,' said Joe. 'I fink I might be able ter 'elp 'im.'

'*You?*' spluttered Mrs Winnet. '*You* 'elp Christian? You ain't no doctor.'

'Doctors don't always know everyfin',' said Joe.

'Joe,' insisted Mrs Winnet, 'that boy's going to die.'

'Let's face it,' returned Joe, quick as a flash, 'we *all* are one day – ain't we?'

196

Mrs Winnet was taken aback by Joe's home-spun philosophy. 'The poor lad's got a terrible cough.'

''E ain't the only one,' replied Joe with a shrug.

Mrs Winnet stared at him. When Rosie first introduced him to her, she liked him because he was of her own kind, from her side of the tracks, down to earth, easy to talk to and, above all, a good listener. Yet as she looked at his friendly blue eyes that were glistening out of a pale, drawn complexion, she started to ask herself what he was *really* all about. But then she remembered all the things Rosie had told her about him – how the girl had enthused about his kindness and honesty, and his utter devotion to her. As they stood there, they were distracted by the sound of the muffin and crumpet bell, tinkling on the end of Charlie Potter's barrow.

'Muffins! Crumpets!' called Charlie, ringing his bell to one side of the road then the other. 'Come on, ladies! Four a penny! Fresh made this mornin'!' He stopped briefly the moment he saw Mrs Winnet. ''Ello, gel!' he croaked, a dog-end dangling from his lips. 'Got yer purse ready?'

'Not today, Charlie, thank you,' returned Mrs Winnet. 'We'll see you next week.'

Charlie shook his head gloomily. 'The way fings're goin' in this war,' he replied, 'there won't be many more next weeks left. If the bleedin' 'Uns get over 'ere, we'll all end up like poor ol' Edif Cavell.' He moved on with his barrow calling: 'Muffins! Crumpets! Fresh made terday!'

Mrs Winnet waited for him to go, then slowly started to walk on, Joe at her side. 'What exactly do yer want me ter do, Joe?' she asked.

'Rosie said in the afternoons you take Chris out in his wheelchair. Is that right?'

'When the weather's fine,' answered Mrs Winnet. 'Why?'

'Just tell me when and where yer go,' asked Joe. 'I'll meet yer.'

Mrs Winnet came to a halt again. 'I'm not sure I can do that, Joe,' she replied. 'If Master or Madam found out, I'd be in trouble.'

'Why?' asked Joe. 'I ain't an outcast or somefin'. Why should they mind if I just wanna talk ter Chris?'

'Then why not come to the house and ask them?'

This stopped Joe in his tracks. After a moment's thought, he replied: ''Cos they don't know me that well, Mrs W – not yet, anyway. In fact, there's a lot er fings they don't know about me an' Rosie. When I talk ter Chris, I want it ter be just between 'im an' me, kind er man ter man, like. I don't want ter interfere or nuffink, but – well, yer see, I love Rosie, an' I want ter do somefin' fer the person who means a lot to 'er.' He looked at her with pleading eyes. 'Will yer 'elp me do that, Mrs W? Will yer?'

Caruso was singing his heart out. Against a background of nurses hurrying from one patient to another, desperately trying to ease their pain without drugs, his repertoire tonight included old favourites such as 'I Used to Sigh for the Silvery Moon', 'There's a Long, Long Trail A-Winding' and the perennial 'Nellie Dean', and he was accompanied on a mouth organ by his mate stretched out flat on his back on the cold stone floor next to him. For a few short moments, the patients in the makeshift ward forgot their life-threatening injuries, and did their best to put to the back of their minds the danger they were in. Everyone knew it might be days, even weeks, before an attempt would be made by British troops to forge a way along the mined road to bring relief and help to the beleaguered and isolated dressing station. Despite their fears, everyone was robustly joining in the chorus of every song as loud as they possibly could, a kind of act of defiance to the Boche, who had so far failed to breach the British front-line trenches. Although she didn't know the words of all the songs, Rosie and the other girls joined in too. The Terrible Four, since taking over from the previous nursing team, were working endless shifts, not only to tend their patients' terrible wounds, but also to keep up their own morale. If there was work to do they would rather not be idle; rather not have time to think and to be frightened.

With emergency medical supplies practically exhausted, Lieutenant Hillary was now in the impossible situation of being unable to carry out any more operations, which left the more critically injured patients at high risk. To make matters worse, his anaesthetist, Lieutenant Wilson, was himself now seriously ill with shrapnel wounds incurred during a previous enemy artillery bombardment on the farmhouse several days before. Now utterly exhausted and demoralised, Hillary was persuaded by his nurses to take a break. He was a popular man amongst those who worked alongside him, for he was quiet, unassuming, but calmly efficient at all times, a man who had proved over and over again his ability to cope with any crisis. Married, with three children, whatever rare moments he had off were spent endlessly reading letters from home, and looking at snapshots of the family sent by his wife. Rosie had liked and respected him from the moment she'd first met him, and once the singsong had come to an end, she followed him outside to see if she could glean any information from him about the chances of an early end to the dreadful predicament they were all caught up in.

'If I could tell you that, young lady,' said Hillary, puffing on his pipe for his first smoke that day, 'General Haig would take me on to his private staff!' He and Rosie ambled along idly together across the cobblestones of the mucky old farmyard. 'No,' sighed Hillary. 'I fear we're going to be stuck out here until our chaps can clear a path through those damned land mines. But it's going to take time.'

'But how long can we wait, sir?' asked Rosie anxiously. 'These men are so terribly ill. You said yourself they're all going to die if we don't get them to hospital as soon as possible.'

'To do that we need ambulances,' replied Hillary. 'And there's no way they're going to get through until those mines are cleared.'

Rosie felt a surge of desperation. 'What happens, sir,' she asked apprehensively, 'if the Germans start another offensive? What happens if they break through our lines?'

Hillary brought them both to a halt, then turned to look at the distant front-line trenches, now quiet and almost invisible after days of constant bombardment. 'Then we get the hell out of here as fast as we can,' he answered, clenching the stem of his pipe between his teeth.

'With all these casualties?'

'Only those who can get up and walk,' replied Hillary, grimly. 'The others would have to stay behind and take their chances with the Boche.'

'You mean become prisoners?'

Hillary shrugged. 'That's about it,' he replied. 'Though how we get out of this place with the roads blocked, God only knows.'

The implication of his remark chilled Rosie. As it was, the night was cold, and the cape covering her uniform not really adequate.

For a few moments they stood there together, side by side, staring up at the October moon, which was casting a luminous white glow across the farmyard. There were so many stars crowding the sky that it seemed as though they were all jostling for places of their own. In the far distance, an owl hooted, and was immediately answered by his lady love from the bough of a far-off tree.

'Tell me something, young lady,' said Hillary, his eyes still turned towards the sky. 'What's a nice girl like you doing in a hellhole like this?'

'Somebody has to do the job, sir,' she replied, her eyes still scanning the sky. 'There's so much to do out here.'

'I don't approve of it, you know,' said Hillary.

Rosie swung a look at him. His full moustache

and short sideburns were a dazzling white in the moonlight. 'Sir?' she asked, puzzled.

'Young girls like you being sent out to conditions like this without training, without hardly any experience of life. Oh, this is not a criticism, Rose,' he said. 'More an observation. I have a daughter of my own. I couldn't bear the thought of her coming out to all this. It would be so unfair.' He turned his gaze back towards the sky again. 'What do *your* parents think about you doing this job?'

Rosie was cautious in her reply. 'I suppose they have to accept it, sir,' she said. 'If soldiers have to go off to fight wars, then the least we can do is to give them all the support they need.'

Hillary smiled to himself. 'Do you have a boyfriend?' he asked, puffing on his pipe.

Rosie hesitated just one moment. 'Yes, sir,' she replied confidently. 'I do.'

'Splendid!' he replied. 'What does he do?'

'He's in the army, sir,' replied Rosie. 'Well, he *was* – until he was caught up in a gas attack.'

'Ah!' sighed Hillary. 'Poor fellow. Which regiment?'

'The Middlesex, sir. The Seventh.'

'The *Shiny* Seventh!'

'Yes, sir.'

'Only a private, sir,' replied Rosie.

'There's no such thing as *only a private*, Rose,' insisted Hillary. 'Our Tommies are the salt of the earth. Most of them were dragged into all this without really knowing what it was all about, and yet we couldn't fight this ruddy war without them. As a matter of fact, I'm very proud to be serving alongside them.' He paused. 'Are you going to marry him?'

'A bit too early to say, sir,' Rosie replied. 'He hasn't asked me yet.'

'Oh, but he will.'

Rosie turned to look at him. She remembered that her brother Christian had said the same thing. 'What makes you say that, sir?'

'Because he'd be very foolish not to,' replied Hillary with a warm smile. 'I hope he'll ask you sooner rather than later. These days we never know if and when we're going to see our loved ones again. Everyone must grab the moment while they can. Who knows?' He looked up at the sky again. 'There may never be a tomorrow.'

Quite suddenly, a bat screeched out and, to Rosie's horror, zoomed down low over their heads before flapping off noisily to join more of its kind inside what was left of the old farmhouse roof.

'If you'll excuse me, please, sir,' she said, 'I'd better get back.'

Hillary didn't answer. His eyes were still transfixed on the sky.

Rosie started to make her way back to the cowshed ward.

'Rose!'

Hillary's voice brought her to a halt. 'Sir?' she asked.

'I just want you to know,' he said, 'that I admire you a great deal. You *and* all the other girls. I admire you all a great deal indeed.' He started relighting his pipe with a match.

'Thank you, sir,' Rosie replied. She continued

to make her way back to the ward, her mind brimming with the things he had said to her. He was not just an officer. He was a gentleman.

She reached the door of the cowshed. But just as she did so, a single rifleshot suddenly rang out, echoing across the fields. She swung round in horror just in time to see Hillary crumpling down on to the ground at the very spot where they had just been talking.

'Sir!' she yelled out in horror, rushing across to him. 'Oh, God!'

Joe was having one of his coughing fits. His lungs felt as though they were still clogged up with chlorine gas, and it only made things worse when he tried to take deep breaths. However, the attack, as usual, passed in a few moments, and once he had recovered himself he was able to continue on his way on foot up Camden Road for his pre-arranged meeting in Hilldrop Crescent with Mrs Winnet and Rosie's young brother, Christian. However, he had to make a slight detour when he discovered the road outside Holloway Women's Prison blocked by the crowd of suffragettes who each day caused as much disruption as they possibly could to try to secure the release of their sister member who had been incarcerated inside for causing a breach of the peace.

Nearby, old Monty Gubble was enjoying all the rumpus. In recent weeks it had become the highlight of his day to watch the angry women, both young and old, hammering with the handles of their umbrellas on the massive iron doors of the prison, shouting abusive slogans at any unfortunate members of the prison staff who dared to show their faces. A few days before, however, Monty's enjoyment of the proceedings had been somewhat marred when some of the ladies turned their wrath on to him, pulling off his faithful old trilby hat, and using it like a cricket ball with their rolled-up brollies.

'Sounds like they're in good voice terday, mate,' said Joe as he approached the old rascal, who, as usual, was perched on a coping stone. 'You better watch out or they'll cut off your whiskers an' use 'em ter polish the floor!'

Monty's whole body shook with laughter when he heard that. He had no real gripe against the ladies, and in any case, they *did* reshape and brush his battered hat before they gave it back to him. 'They ain't so bad,' he said. 'At least they stick ter their guns.' When he saw Joe moving on, he got up from the coping stone, and walked with him. The old joints weren't working too well that morning, so he leaned heavily on his walking stick, the handle of which was shaped like a snake's head. 'The way you're goin',' he said, 'yer'll soon be takin' up residence this end. So wot yer up to this time?'

'Nuffin' much,' replied Joe. 'Just goin' up ter spend a bit er time wiv Rosie's bruvver, Chris. I reckon 'e can do wiv a bit er cheerin' up.'

'Ah – well said!' croaked Monty, using the back of his hand to wipe away a dewdrop from the tip of his nose, only to have it immediately replaced with another one. 'I've known that poor little mite since 'e was only a twinkle in 'is dad's eye. When I see ol' Ma Winnet pushin' 'im in 'is wheelchair every mornin', I still can't take it in that 'e won't be around fer much longer.'

'That's a matter of opinion, old man,' said Joe.

Monty pulled a face. 'Matter of opinion?' He came to a halt. 'It's a matter er fact. From wot *I've* bin told, the boy's only got a few more munffs ter live.'

'Maybe,' replied Joe. 'Maybe not.'

'Wot yer talkin' about?'

'Well, let's face it, mate,' said Joe. 'You ain't dead till yer lie down, are yer?' Without another word, he walked off, quickening his pace as he went.

Monty, watching Joe until he was halfway up the hill, shook his head, convinced that Rosie's boyfriend was a likely contender for the loony bin.

A few minutes later, Joe found his way to Hilldrop Crescent, where he went straight to the bench seat nearest the summerhouse in the small public garden there. He didn't have long to wait, for Mrs Winnet soon appeared at the garden gates, pushing young Christian in his wheelchair.

The moment the boy caught sight of Joe, he was quite ecstatic. 'Joe!' he bellowed as Joe got up from the bench to greet them. 'This is wonderful! I didn't know you were going to be here! This is wonderful, wonderful!'

'Wotcha, mate!' called Joe, going straight up to the boy, and ruffling his hair. 'Fancy meetin' *you* 'ere!' He flicked a quick, grateful look at Mrs Winnet, then sitting down on the bench, turned the wheelchair round to face him.

'Please don't be too long,' said Mrs Winnet

sternly, 'Madam is due back from the hairdresser any minute.' She strode off, leaving Christian alone with Joe.

'So,' began Joe, with his usual broad grin. ''Ow's it goin', mate?'

Christian was beaming. He couldn't take his eyes off Joe. 'I can't get over seeing you,' he replied excitedly, his pure voice younger than his years. 'When Rosie went away, I thought I'd never see you again.'

'Now whatever gave yer *that* idea?' asked Joe. 'You're my mate now. Mates don't just bugger off an' not come back.'

'Bugger off?' asked Christian, quizzically. 'What does that mean?'

Joe took a quick, guilty look over his shoulder. 'Yer'd better ferget I said that. Slip er the tongue.' He moved closer to the boy. 'I wanna ask yer somefin', Chris. Why d'yer spend all yer time in this chair?'

Christian shrugged. 'I can't walk.'

'Since when?'

'Since as long as I can remember. Since the doctor first told me I've got consumption.'

Joe pulled a face. 'Yer don't believe everyfin' the doc tells yer, do yer? I mean, wot's consumption got ter do wiv not bein' able ter walk?'

Once again Christian shrugged. 'Don't know,' he replied innocently. 'Mother said if I tried to walk, I'd start coughing even more.'

Hearing this, Joe shook his head in despair. 'Well, I'll tell yer,' he continued, '*I've* always bin told that consumption is ter do wiv 'avin a lousy set er lungs. Is that wot *you* reckon?'

207

Christian looked blank. 'I suppose so,' he replied.

'Well, in that case,' continued Joe, '*I* must 'ave consumption too, 'cos I've got worse lungs than Kaiser Bill. An' yer know wot 'appened ter '*im*, don't yer?'

Christian shook his head.

Joe took another quick glance all around, and lowered his voice even more. 'One day when 'e was sittin' on the lav, 'e swallered 'is pipe!'

Christian roared with laughter.

'It's true!' insisted Joe. 'Smoke kept comin' out of 'is ears fer munffs after!'

Christian rocked back and forth with laughter, which quite suddenly broke into a deep, hacking cough.

Joe quickly put his around the boy's shoulders. 'Don't worry mate,' he said, comforting him. 'Ol' Kaiser Bill 'ad a lousy cough, just like you. So do I. But it comes an' goes.' When Christian had recovered from his coughing fit, Joe noticed that the boy had a small dribble of blood on his lips. Joe quickly reached into his pocket for a handkerchief, and without comment, dabbed it. 'Still,' he said, 'on the whole, I reckon you an' me are pretty lucky, don't yer fink?'

Christian looked up at him. 'Why?' he asked, his eyes glistening with the strain of coughing.

'We've got the same gelfriend, ain't we?' said Joe, cheerily 'Well, she's *my* gelfriend, an' *your* sister. But we boaf fink the world of 'er, don't we?'

Christian nodded vigorously.

'So I'll tell yer somefin',' continued Joe. 'Before

Rosie went away, she and I talked a lot about you. I told 'er I don't fink you're nearly as ill as yer fink. Yer see, when you're not feelin' so speshul, uvver people always fink they know better – they're always tellin' yer wot *they* fink is good for yer. But yer know, mate, sometimes yer 'ave ter work fings out fer yerself. Sometimes yer 'ave ter say to yerself, "I want ter try this on me own. I want ter see if I can do it. If I can't, well, OK, but if I don't try, if I keep finkin' it's only a matter er time, then wot's the point of goin' on?" Yer know, I don't often talk about wot 'appened ter me when I was shut up wiv my mates in those dugouts, knee-deep in mud, rats runnin' all over the place, but I wanna tell *you*. I wanna tell you just one fing. We never gave up, Chris. No matter wot we saw, no matter wot anyone said, we never gave up.'

They were interrupted by a fat old pigeon cooing from the branch of a tree just above them.

'All right, mate!' called Joe, following it with a pigeon sound of his own.

Christian was amused by this. 'What are you doing?' he asked.

'Wot d'yer fink I'm doin'?' asked Joe. 'I'm talkin' ter ol' Percy Pigeon.'

'*Who?*'

''Im up there,' replied Joe, nodding up towards the pigeon. ''E just asked me if I've got any scraps. I told 'im 'e's out of luck terday.'

Christian was fascinated. 'You can talk – to *pigeons?*'

'Course I can!' boasted Joe. 'It's easy. Yer should try it yerself some time. After all, they speak the same lingo as us. All yer 'ave ter do is ter listen. We fink we know a lot, but birds an' animals know an 'eck of a lot more than any of us.' He looked up at the pigeon, and made another cooing sound. 'And they know 'ow ter do fings fer themselves,' he added. 'Just like our Rosie. She don't need anyone ter tell *er* wot ter do.' He turned to the boy and gave him a beaming, reassuring smile. 'An' neivver do you, Chris. Neivver do you.'

Lieutenant Hillary was in a critical condition. Cut down by a single sniper's shot the night before, he was now lying on a mattress on the floor of the old cowshed, unconscious and bleeding profusely. The situation was desperate, because neither The Terrible Four nor the other nurses were experienced enough to know how to deal with the more gravely ill casualties without Hillary's guidance. Nor was Lieutenant Wilson, the anaesthetist, any help; he was running a high fever from his own wounds, rambling, and unable to give any coherent instructions about how the girls should cope. The situation was now out of control. With the lines down between the farmhouse and the British field headquarters in Orlais, there was not even communication with doctors there.

Titch and Eunice were beside themselves with worry. 'If he dies,' asked Titch, her Welsh accent more pronounced than ever in her anxiety, 'what are we going to do? The field telephones are not working, and with those mines in the road there's no way we can get anyone to come out from headquarters.'

'The lieutenant is not *going* to die, Titch,' insisted Binnie, who as the eldest member of the team was doing her best to keep them all from panicking. 'We'll keep the wound as clean as we can until someone gets here.'

'But that's just the point!' spluttered Eunice, working herself up. 'Nobody *knows* wot's 'appened 'ere. We might not get 'elp for days!'

'That's right,' added Titch, lowering her voice. 'An' what're we going to do about all this lot? They need attention twenty-four hours a day!'

'Now don't be silly, you two!' snapped Binnie, who was helping one of the more experienced nurses to change the cotton-wool dressing on Lieutenant Hillary's bleeding wound. 'Of course headquarters knows what's happening here. If they can't get ambulances through they must be working all out to clear those mines. We've just got to keep our heads, use our common sense, and be patient.'

'Common sense ain't goin' ter keep people alive!' snapped Eunice, who was trying unsuccessfully to steady her nerves. 'Wot we need is some help, medical supplies, food, somefin' ter 'elp save these poor blokes' lives! 'Eadquarters needs ter know 'ow desperate it is out 'ere!'

'Don't worry, gels!'

They all turned to find one of the wounded patients painfully easing himself out of bed.

'Jacko!' yelled Eunice, rushing across to him. 'Wot the 'eck d'yer fink you're doing?'

'I'll get some 'elp for yer!' called the middle-aged soldier, who had a heavily bandaged bayonet wound in the side of his neck. 'I know a

211

way to get ter 'eadquarters wivout usin' the roads. I'll go fru the woods. Jerry wouldn't 'ave buried mines there 'cos 'e wouldn't be able to get be'ind our boys up in the field trenches. Let me do it!' He struggled to get up. 'I know the way!'

'Don't be so stupid, Jacko!' called Binnie, whose hands were smothered in Lieutenant Hillary's blood. 'Get back into bed immediately!'

'I tell yer I do know the way!' insisted Jacko. 'I *can* do it!'

'You're doin' nuffin', mate!' growled Eunice, gently easing him back on to his place on the stone floor. 'The state *you're* in yer won't even get as far as the front door!'

'*I'll* do it.'

Everyone turned to see Rosie busily putting on her cape. 'What are you doing, Rosie?' asked Binnie, eyes wide in astonishment.

'I'm going back to headquarters to get help,' replied Rosie firmly. 'If Jacko knows the way through the woods, I'll find it.'

'Don't be ridiculous!' growled Binnie. 'There are enemy snipers out there. It's far too dangerous. You're not a soldier.'

Rosie swung her an astonished look. 'I never thought I'd hear you of all people say that to me, Binnie,' she said. 'In this fight, there's no such thing as male and female. We're all soldiers.' She immediately hurried across to talk to Jacko.

Binnie watched her with incredulity. None the less, what Rosie had said was true. In their short term of training back in London, they had been taught to be prepared to rise to any occasion, and if ever there *was* one, this was it right now.

'All right,' Binnie said, going across to where Rosie was listening to the directions Jacko was giving her, 'but wait until it's dark. You'll be far too much of a sitting target during daylight. If the moon is out, wait for it to go behind clouds before you move on.'

Jacko agreed. Behind them, Titch was sobbing.

Rosie got up and went to her. 'Now don't be so silly, Titch,' she said, putting her arms around her. 'For God's sake, it can't be more than five miles or so. I've walked more than that around Hyde Park many a time.'

'This isn't Hyde Park!' cried Titch, hugging her.

Eunice did the same, and for several moments, with the other nurses and patients looking on, all three stood there in a deep, tearful embrace.

'Don't worry,' Rosie called to those watching. 'You won't get rid of me that easily.'

A short while later, the old cowshed door opened. Rosie and Binnie came out quietly, and quickly closed the door behind them. As predicted by Binnie, the moon was indeed popping in and out of slow-moving night clouds, and a chilly night breeze was whistling across the farmyard.

'Remember what I said,' whispered Binnie. 'Wait until the moon goes behind the clouds before you move. And for God's sake, tread carefully. If the Boche *have* laid any mines in those woods...'

'Don't worry,' replied Rosie. 'I promise I won't let you down.'

'You know,' said Binnie, 'I don't think you

213

could ever let *anyone* down. I say that because somehow I feel as though I've known you all my life. And I only wish I had.'

They embraced, remaining in quiet contemplation for several moments.

'Binnie,' said Rosie. 'If anything *should* happen to me...'

Binnie held her out at arm's length. 'Nothing *is* going to happen to you,' she said softly. 'I'm quite sure of that. Just be careful, that's all.'

'No, but if it does,' pleaded Rosie calmly, 'please write to Joe for me. And my parents, of course. *And* Christian.'

After one last embrace, not another word was spoken. At Rosie's request, Binnie went back inside. From this moment on, all Rosie wanted was to be alone.

Chapter 12

When she was a little girl, Rosie had been afraid of the dark. At night she would lie awake in her bed and imagine that there were faces all over the ceiling, staring down at her, waiting to carry her off to some far distant place called Monsterland. The countryside around Orlais reminded her of those sleepless nights, for the late autumn moon was dipping in and out of dark clouds, the trees and foliage of the woods throwing sinister, threatening shadows that quivered menacingly in the cold, early morning breeze. In the far distance, the rumble of artillery gunfire was sending shock waves across the wide open landscape, lighting up the sky with intermittent bursts of yellow and white, whilst the smell of cordite and smoke and rotting human and animal corpses soured what would have otherwise been crisp, sweetly fresh air.

Rosie knew she had been wise to take Binnie's advice about only moving when the moon was behind the clouds, for although she had made slow progress, she calculated that, thanks to Jacko's careful directions, she had avoided the area that had been land-mined by the Boche, and had now covered almost half the journey to the field headquarters of military command. Every so often when the moon did escape from behind the clouds, it lit up the rooftops of the tiny village of Orlais, turning it into what looked like a community of Lilliputians. By now, however, she felt very much alone, and only Joe's poem, which she clutched in her pocket all the way, gave her the strength and support she needed to keep going. Lieutenant Hillary's chest wound from that single sniper shot had been a terrible shock to her, especially as she had been with him just moments before, and she knew that if it hadn't already claimed his life, his survival now depended on her, and her alone. However, her incident-free journey came to an abrupt end just as she was within striking distance of the outskirts of the village itself.

'Halt!'

The man's staccato voice that barked out of nowhere scared her stiff. A tall figure was blocking her way in the dark, but as the moon once again emerged from behind the clouds, she could see the man's German military uniform and unshaved face quite clearly, and also the rifle and bayonet he was pointing at her. In fact, he was hardly a man, merely a teenage boy in a man's uniform, doing his best to terrify Rosie.

'I am a nurse,' she said hurriedly, but refusing to panic.

The German boy soldier remained silent.

'I – I'm looking after wounded soldiers.'

The boy soldier was clearly unimpressed, for as the dark night clouds overwhelmed the moon again, she watched him move closer towards her, the tip of his bayonet only a few inches away from her stomach. During those few seconds that she waited for him to lunge at her, her mind was suddenly consumed with thoughts of home, of her parents, of Christian and of Joe's poem, which she was clutching tightly in her hand in the pocket of her cape. In a flash she decided to make a run for it, but just as she was about to do so, a shot rang out, and as she threw herself to the ground, for one terrifying moment she was convinced that she had suffered the same fate as Nurse Edith Cavell. But before she could catch her breath, she heard a slumping sound, and when the moon emerged once more, she found herself looking into the glazed, lifeless eyes of the boy soldier stretched out on the ground in front of her. She got up quickly. The boy had a bullet hole in the middle of his back.

'*Cochon!*'

Rosie turned with a start, and in the full light of

the moon found a middle-aged peasant woman with rifle in hand, staring down at the young boy soldier's corpse.

'He was just a boy,' said Rosie, who understood some French from her school days.

'Old enough to kill my father and mother,' replied the French woman in heavily accented English. She wore a man's long dark overcoat with a scarf around her head. Stretching her hand down to Rosie, she helped her to get up. 'The Boche are always sending boys behind Allied lines. They think a cowardly sniper's bullet will help undermine us.' She took a close, hard look at Rosie. *Vous êtes infirmière, n'est-ce pas?*

'Yes,' replied Rosie, understanding what the woman had asked her. 'I'm a nurse from the advanced dressing station. Our medical officer out there has been shot by a sniper. The roads have been mined and we need urgent help to save his life and all our other badly injured patients.'

'You – walked – all the way from the dressing station?' asked the woman incredulously.

'Yes,' replied Rosie.

'In the dark? With land mines on the road?'

'The moon helped,' replied Rosie, looking up at the sky, her face now a luminous white. 'Someone had to do it. Everyone is going to die out there unless we get help very quickly.'

Just as the moon disappeared behind fast-moving clouds again, the woman drew closer. There was the smell of wine as she spoke. 'What is your name?' she asked.

'Rose. Rose Little.'

'It is not wise to walk out here alone after dark,

217

Rose Little,' said the woman. 'There are Boche *cochons* everywhere. *C'est très dangereux.*'

'I am not afraid,' replied Rosie defiantly, pulling up the hood of her cape.

Once again the moon illuminated the woman's face. She had strong Gallic features, and Rosie thought how feminine she would look if she didn't have to do a man's job. Her dark, piercing eyes showed the strain of having to deal with a war that had killed so many of her own people. 'You're so young,' she said despondently, as she caught a brief glimpse of Rosie standing there in the moonlight. 'This war won't even give our children the time to grow up.'

'*Please,*' begged Rosie with great urgency, 'help me to get to headquarters. It really *is* a matter of life and death.'

'Follow me!' said the woman, leading the way.

'What about the boy?' called Rosie, taking one last look down at the young corpse who seemed to be not much older than her brother, Christian.

'Leave him for the birds!' replied the woman coldly, without looking back.

Christian was awake early. Light was only just beginning to filer through a chink in the heavy embroidered curtains at his bedroom window. Usually, he didn't wake up quite so early, but this morning he could hear a sound coming from outside, which immediately aroused his curiosity. Throwing back the bed sheets and eiderdown, with some effort he managed to ease himself out of bed and lower himself into his wheelchair alongside. Encouraged by the persistent sound outside, he wheeled himself across to the window, and pulled back the curtains just enough to look out. What he was greeted with were two sparrows, perched side by side on the branch of the chestnut tree immediately outside his window, chirping busily at the slowly rising sun. This brought a great smile to his face, and his first inclination was to try to raise the window. However, when this proved too much for him, he settled for just pressing his face against the glass, and, remembering how Joe had talked to the pigeon, he made some sounds that he hoped would be recognised by the two sparrows. To his astonishment, once the birds realised the face at the window was not going to harm them, one of them responded with a loud twittering sound. Jumping up and down with excitement, this at once prompted Christian to try to lever himself up from the wheelchair. With tremendous effort and strain, he continued making the sounds through the glass, joining in what to him was a clear conversation between himself and the two sparrows, proof that what Joe had told him was true.

'Christian!'

The boy swung with a start to find his mother at the bedroom door.

'What on earth do you think you're doing?' Leaving the door wide open, Marian rushed straight across to him, and eased him down into his wheelchair again. 'D'you want to kill yourself, you foolish boy?'

'I was only talking to those birds,' explained Christian, whose whole expression changed when the two sparrows fluttered away in panic at the sudden movement behind the window.

'Don't be ridiculous, Christian!' said Marian, quietly but firmly, wheeling his chair back to the bed. 'Birds don't talk. Not in our language anyway.'

'That's not what Joe says.'

Marian brought the wheelchair to an abrupt halt.

'Who?' she asked, without trying to show too much interest.

'Joe,' replied Christian. 'Rosie's boyfriend. He says birds can understand what we say to them. He says they can speak the same lingo as us.'

'When did he tell you this?' asked Marian.

'When I saw him out in the square,' replied Christian quite innocently – and forgetfully. 'When I was with Mrs Winnet.'

Marian tensed. She felt betrayed – not only by Mrs Winnet, but also by Christian himself. She felt the blood drain from her face. Sooner or later Christian was going to die, and other people – people with no knowledge of the adverse effect they could have – would be responsible. Her boy, her dear boy, was clearly in danger, and she had to do something about it. 'What else did this Joe have to say?' she asked tersely.

'He said sometimes I'm not as ill as I think,' replied Christian, 'that sometimes I should try and work things out for myself.'

'And what do you think he means by that, Christian?' she asked.

'I'm not *really* sure,' said Christian. 'But I think he meant that if I want to get up and walk, I should try.'

220

Marian tingled all over. It was as though she had suddenly felt all control slipping away from her grasp. 'Get back into bed, Christian,' she said with some urgency, using her arms to help him out of the wheelchair.

'Why?'

Marian abruptly stopped what she was doing. The boy was resisting. For the first time in his life he was resisting, refusing to do what *she* wanted him to do. 'It is much too early for you to get up, darling. You're not well. Look how pale you are.'

'I don't *feel* pale,' said Christian firmly. 'I don't feel not well. I feel strong.'

'Get back into bed, darling, please,' said his mother, with a sickly smile. 'For Mother?'

Christian looked at her, and saw what he had seen all his life. Determination. Gradually, he didn't feel nearly as well as he had thought. Almost without thinking, he let her ease him up from the wheelchair and on to the side of the bed. As he did so, he began to cough, lightly at first, then vigorously.

'You see what I mean, darling,' said Marian, as she helped him to slip back under the bedclothes. 'Birds can't talk. There's no such word as "lingo".'

She waited for the boy's coughing to subside, then leaned down and gently kissed him on his forehead. 'Don't worry, Mother's here,' she said, pleased that his eyes had closed. She got up, and went quietly to the door.

'Mother?'

Marian was startled to hear him call to her. She stopped and turned.

221

'When's Rosie coming home from the Front?'

Lady Braintree sipped tea from a chipped enamel cup. It wasn't exactly what she had been used to, even back at QAIMNS headquarters in London, but none the less, on these cold early winter mornings in France a cup of hot tea tasted better than a glass of champagne. Rosie was also enjoying her cup of tea. It tasted good, and in addition she could clasp it between her hands to try to get some warmth back into them. The French peasant woman who had shot the young German boy soldier was also there, but she preferred *café noir* to the tasteless tea the English insisted on drinking, and as there was no *café* available, she was content to go without. Rosie and she had reached the British field head-quarters in Orlais during the early hours of the morning, and Rosie only agreed to relax once she had been assured that the road to the advanced dressing station was at that moment being cleared of land mines, and that two replacement medical officers would soon be on their way to attend to the critically wounded Lieutenant Hillary, his anaesthetist and all the other desperately injured patients.

The field headquarters as such was a grim place, set up in what used to be the mayor's office, but now little more than a shell after heavy bombardment of the village by Boche artillery several weeks before. Rosie wanted to get back to her duties as quickly as possible, and therefore was irritated when she was asked first to go and see the redoubtable Lady Braintree.

'I'm very proud of you,' said the Lady, looking more like a mother superior, dressed to keep warm from head to foot in her nurse's cape and hood. 'Antoinette here told me that you had taken a great risk by walking all that way from the dressing station. I think you went well beyond the call of duty.'

Rosie flicked a quick look up at the peasant woman, and saw that beneath all her grubby exterior, she was really quite beautiful, with dark flashing green eyes and curly red hair that was cut short, almost like a soldier's, which was, after all, what she had become.

'However,' continued the Lady, 'I'm afraid that we have a problem on our hands, and at the present time I have no way of solving it. Unfortunately, my dear, the problem is you.'

Rosie was shocked. '*Me*, madam?' she asked, dumbfounded.

The Lady sat back in her chair. 'I've just received an urgent communication from headquarters to say that you are to be sent back immediately.'

'Back where?' asked Rosie, with incredulity.

'Back home to London,' said the Lady with a sigh. 'I'm afraid I have no alternative but to obey orders. They come from a somewhat superior position to my own.'

Rosie immediately understood what had happened; she was thunderstruck. 'I – I can't believe it,' she spluttered. 'I don't want to go back. My place is here – with my friends. I want to go back and join them at the dressing station. Who's responsible for this? Please, madam, I don't want to sound impertinent, but I do have a right to know.'

223

The Lady flicked Antoinette a brief, knowing look.

It was enough for the French woman to acknowledge that she should leave the room. As she left she gave Rosie a reassuring smile. 'I'll see you outside,' she said.

'Please sit down, my dear,' said the Lady to Rosie, once they were alone.

Rosie sat tentatively on a stool by the crackling wood fire in the grate of what had once been a rather grand ornamental fireplace. Even so, the large barren room was still freezing cold for there was a large shell hole in the ceiling, which stretched right up to the roof of the building.

The Lady came across and joined her, warming her hands in front of the fire. 'I'm afraid the directive came from the War Office,' she began solemnly. 'But I have no doubt it could have originated in any one of those obscure government ministries. None the less, wherever it came from they seem to be quite determined that you should not remain on active duty out here.'

There and then, Rosie knew *exactly* who was really responsible for that directive. Ever since she had left home to come out to the Front, she had been subconsciously expecting it. 'My father,' she said half to herself.

The Lady avoided her look.

'It *was* my father, wasn't it?' asked Rosie, without really expecting an answer. 'I knew he would do something like this sooner or later. But I won't let him. *Please*, madam,' she begged. 'Don't let him do this. I'm not a child.'

'*I* know that, my dear,' replied the Lady. 'We *all*

know it – especially after the heroic thing you did last night. However,' she sighed, 'unfortunately you are of an age when your parents still have a right to say what you can or cannot do.'

'But there's a war on,' protested Rosie. 'Our soldiers are being maimed and killed every day out here. Many of them are no older than me, some of them even younger.'

'I know that also, my dear,' said the Lady with great understanding. 'I know that.'

'My parents have done everything in their power to stop me,' said Rosie. 'They seem to think that everyone else can do their bit in this war except me. That's why I didn't want them to know that I was being posted out here. I guessed my father would do this. I knew he would use every contact he could to keep me at home.'

'I must say,' said the Lady, 'it really is most extraordinary that you've managed to keep it from him. I knew when you first joined the voluntary nursing service that there was some opposition from your parents; that happens all the time with so many of the young ladies who join us. But are you telling me that he never knew you were being posted out here to the Front?'

Rosie hesitated a moment, and looked down. 'Yes,' she replied.

'Then what did you tell him?'

'I told him…' she faltered, 'I told him I was going back to Stanmore Manor.'

For what seemed like an eternity to Rosie, the Lady remained silent. A thin shaft of ice-cold air forced its way down through the shell hole in the roof, and made the flames in the grate spit and crackle. But Rosie had no time even to notice it, for she was taken aback by the sound of the Lady suddenly breaking into laughter. Rosie couldn't believe what she was hearing. As the Lady moved back to the old kitchen table she was using as a desk, it seemed incredible to Rosie to see this brave, distinguished woman breaking the atmosphere in such a way

'You're quite a character, aren't you, young lady?' said the Lady. 'Something tells me you could teach that illustrious actress Ellen Terry a thing or two!'

Rosie was baffled.

'To have fooled your own father with a cock-and-bull story like that is quite an achievement, you know!' The Lady's laugh turned into a chuckle, which in turn was replaced by a worried expression. 'But then, our own people should have known better. I'd say we're going to get into hot water with the powers that be for putting you on the active service list without informing your parents.'

Rosie immediately looked concerned.

'Oh, don't be upset, my dear,' said the Lady reassuringly. 'It happens all the time – authority versus reality. Sometimes I wonder what they'd do if we just let the Kaiser walk in and do things *his* way.' She strolled back to the fire, picked up a lump of timber and dropped it gently on to the flames. Rosie watched her, in awe of the Lady's soft, elegant features now showing the strain of extreme responsibility, her eyes reflecting the leaping flames in the grate. 'You know, Rose,' she said, warming her hands again, 'there's no one in this world who doesn't hate bringing young girls like you into a place like this. It's unnatural, unhealthy and in so many ways just plain immoral. I can't tell you how much I hate it. I can't tell you how much I hate the thought of throwing young minds like yours into this cauldron, without training, without time to even think about what you're being asked to do. A nurse is someone quite special. God knows, our dear departed Edith Cavell has taught us all that. A nurse is not only expected to know all the rudimentary things of looking after a patient, to know about the medicines she is administering, to know exactly what she is doing when she is carrying out a doctor's instructions, but she must also give comfort to those who survive, and to those who do not. How dare we expect a young girl to be trained as a nurse in just a matter of a few months? It's ludicrous, impossible and totally irresponsible. And yet,' she sighed deeply, 'it has to be done.' She looked directly at Rosie and her smile was warm and affectionate. 'Don't blame your father or your mother, Rose,' she said. 'Blame those who start these insane wars.'

Richard Little arrived home for lunch to find his wife waiting anxiously for him. Before he had left for his office early that morning, she had told him what she had heard from Christian about Rose being posted to the Front, insisting that he should do something about it immediately.

'What happened?' she demanded, before he had even taken off his overcoat. 'Did you get hold of that fellow at the Home Office? Are they bringing Rose home?'

'Yes, Marian,' he replied, as she followed him briskly into the sitting room. 'He promised to contact the War Office and have her shipped back home at the earliest opportunity.'

'And when will that be?' pressed Marian, who was in such a high state of emotion that, unlike her husband, she couldn't relax enough to sit down.

'I have no idea,' replied Richard, who was just as upset as his wife, but for different reasons. 'They're going to notify me as soon as possible. There should be a message at any moment.'

'It's utterly indefensible!' ranted Marian. 'To think that Rose could do such a thing! To think that she could deceive her own mother and father, and in such a sly and cunning manner!'

'Rose is *not* sly, Marian,' insisted Richard. 'Nor is she cunning. However, I *will* admit that what she has done is a petulant error of judgement.'

'Error of judgement be damned!' bellowed Marian. 'How long have I told you that Rose is getting out of hand?'

'Now don't let's go through all that again, Marian,' returned Richard, sitting forward in his usual armchair by the fireplace, clutching his forehead in despair.

Refusing to be fobbed off, Marian came straight back to stand over him. 'She *is* out of hand, Richard,' she insisted. 'All this nonsense about independence, and mixing with all those lunatic women outside the prison gates each day.'

'We have no proof of that, Marian,' protested Richard. 'Yes, she *is* sympathetic to the suffragette cause, but so are many other women.'

'*I* am a woman too, Richard,' replied Marian in frustration. 'And *I* don't care for their silly politics. A woman's place is in the home. Men are there to take care of running the country.'

Richard wanted to respond with his own views on the mess men had made of the country, but he thought his opinion on *that* subject would be lost on his wife. Marian had changed so much over the years. When they first married, she was the sweetest little thing in the world – and the prettiest. But what Richard liked most of all about her in those early days was the fact they were so close, and always used to talk things over calmly, and share their opinions. These days they had drifted so much apart that he just didn't recognise her any more. So why did he still love her? That was a question he had often asked himself, which made him wonder whether their relationship would ever be the same again.

'Oh, Richard,' Marian sighed, sitting in an armchair facing him. 'Don't you realise what could have happened to Rose if we had let her stay out there in that terrible place? Our Rose, our own daughter.' She was close to tears. 'We could have lost her, Richard. We could have lost her, and then when Christian goes, we'd have lost *both* our babies.'

As she broke down, Richard got up to go to comfort her. But just as he did so, there was a tap on the door.

'A messenger brought this for you, sir,' said Mrs Winnet as she entered, carrying an envelope.

Marian immediately sprang up from her chair.

'Oh, Richard!' she gasped.

'Thank you, Mrs Winnet,' said Richard, eagerly taking the envelope from her. He waited for her to go, then quickly tore it open and read the contents. 'She's coming home,' he announced.

Marian gasped, and wept with relief.

'They're putting her on the night ferry that should get her in to Charing Cross Station at eleven o'clock tomorrow morning.'

Marian was now sobbing, so Richard went to her and put his arms around her. 'There's nothing to worry about now, darling,' he said. 'She's coming home.'

Marian slowly looked up at him, her face streaked with tears. But her expression had changed. It was hard and really quite ugly. 'I'll never forgive her for this,' she said. 'I'll never forgive her – *or* you.'

In the hall outside, Mrs Winnet had her ear to the door. She had heard all she wanted to hear, and now had urgent things to do.

When Rosie came out of Lady Braintree's ramshackle office, it was pouring with rain, and the narrow main street through the village was ankle-deep in mud. But Antoinette was there to take her into the small bar café next door, where they could wait until transport arrived to take Rosie back to the dressing station to collect her personal belongings. The bar was empty, dark, cold and dingy, and reeked of the stale smoke of the cigarettes of the soldiers who had been drowning their sorrows the evening before. 'It's so typical of us French,' said Antoinette. 'Here we are living on scraps of any food we can find, but when it comes to wine, there never seems to be any shortage!'

They sat at a table near the fireplace, which had no more than one log of wood burning there to keep the entire place warm. As Antoinette went to the counter to order some drinks, a barrage of distant artillery fire was enough to shake the already badly damaged roof of the old building. At the counter, Antoinette laughed and joked with the elderly bar owner about the German boy soldier she had killed during the night. Rosie was astonished to see how the French peasant woman still managed to look so elegant in men's trousers and overcoat, and even a black beret that was worn with just that touch of style, which had always been the hallmark of the way a French woman dressed.

Rosie was very unsure when Antoinette brought back two small glasses of cognac. 'I've never drunk alcohol in my life,' she said.

Antoinette roared with laughter. 'Then you're the first English person I've ever met who hasn't!' she jibed. 'Drink up, *ma petite*. It will warm your stomach as well as your heart.' She watched Rosie carefully as she sipped the cognac as if it was medicine. 'So you're going home, *n'est-ce pas?*' she asked.

Rosie nodded. The cognac was certainly doing what Antoinette had told her it would do, for she could immediately feel the warmth seeping through her blood. 'I'm so ashamed of what my father has done,' she said bitterly.

'Ah!' said Antoinette, taking more than a sip

231

from her own glass. *'Toujours le père!* We all have such problems with our fathers – and our mothers too.' There was a pained expression on her face. 'I don't have that problem any more.'

Rosie felt deeply for this troubled woman. As she watched her taking a delicate sniff of her cognac each time before actually sipping it, she could see that the rough exterior disguised a highly vulnerable and sensitive nature.

'But you know,' continued Antoinette, 'I don't blame your father. I don't blame him at all. You're his daughter. You are very precious to him. Why shouldn't he do everything in his power to protect the one he loves?'

'Because we're at war,' replied Rosie, catching sight, in the mirror behind the bar, of her face and cape still smudged with mud from her encounter with the German boy soldier in the early hours of the morning. 'Because if we want to stop our country being invaded, every parent's son *and* daughter has to do their duty.'

Antoinette smiled. 'Yes,' she replied with just a suggestion of irony. 'The English would not take easily to invasion by foreigners. They say you are a nation of garden lovers. I like that. I used to have a little garden of my own at my house just outside the village – until the Boche blew it to pieces, before that boy, that stupid boy, broke in to steal what little food we had, and killed my mother and father because they wouldn't give it to him.' To Rosie's surprise, Antoinette lit a cigarette, sat back in her chair and inhaled deeply, surprised because the only other woman she had actually ever seen smoking a cigarette was a guest at one of her mother's bridge parties. 'No,' continued Antoinette, 'we French have also not taken easily to having foreign intruders on our land. It's like having someone break into your house. Once they have gone, you feel – unclean.'

'What about your husband, Antoinette?' asked Rosie. 'Is he in the army?'

Antoinette grinned, again with irony. 'No, my dear child,' she replied. 'There is no husband. I could never marry a man, because I don't respect them. Don't ask me why; there are too many reasons.' She looked across at Rosie, who was once again struggling to sip her cognac. 'But what about you? Who is the lucky man in *your* life?'

'His name is Joe,' replied Rosie. 'And I love him very much.'

'That's good,' said Antoinette. 'Every woman should have a Joe she can love.'

Rosie found that an odd remark from someone who clearly found it difficult to love *anyone*. 'Perhaps one day,' she said, 'when all this is over, I can bring him here to meet you. I'd like him to meet you.'

'Why?' asked Antoinette, surprised. 'You don't know me.'

'And you don't know *me*,' replied Rosie. 'And yet, I feel as though I've known you all my life.'

Antoinette's guard was briefly lowered. She sat back in her chair, and swallowed the last of her cognac, a faint suggestion of tears welling in her eyes. For one fleeting moment she was no longer the partisan. She was a woman.

They were suddenly interrupted by a continuous burst of thunderous gunfire right over-head. 'Zeppelin! Zeppelin!' yelled the bar owner, as Rosie and Antoinette rushed out of the place with him.

Outside, the rain had stopped. The sky was pitted with small puffs of white smoke from hundreds of exploding shells. Throughout the village, soldiers and civilians were looking and pointing up excitedly at the great spectacle that was unfolding before their very eyes. A giant German Zeppelin airship, which had been trying to slip in and out of the dark grey clouds, had been hit by a team of ground artillery, and had burst into flames. Rosie watched in horror as the great ball of fire fluttered down towards the ground, scattering both debris and crew on to the surrounding fields.

Overjoyed, Antoinette shook her fist up at the falling monster, shouting, *'Vive la France!'*

Unable to join in the general euphoria, Rosie turned away to go back inside the bar again, but Antoinette quickly caught up with her and, slip-ping a comforting arm around her waist, brought her to a halt.

'Go home, Rose Little,' she said warmly, staring deep into Rosie's eyes. 'Go home and love your Joe. Oh, God, how I envy you!'

Chapter 13

From the train window, the English countryside looked so different from the muddy, bloodstained fields of France. Rosie noticed that the moment she left the troop-carrying ferry boat at Folkestone Harbour and stepped on to the military train bound for London. But her thoughts were very firmly back in France, and especially at the advanced dressing station, where just a few hours before she had bid a very sad and tearful farewell to her dear friends of The Terrible Four. She still couldn't believe what had happened to her, the speed with which she had been dispatched from the Front because of her father's intervention. When she said goodbye to Binnie, Eunice and Titch, she felt thoroughly ashamed that she had been given such preferential treatment to swap the squalor of the old cowshed for the luxury of a sitting room in Camden Road.

The compartment she was travelling in was jammed with soldiers lucky enough to get a spot of home leave after a gruelling period in the trenches, but it seemed as though every one of them was smoking a fag, and Rosie could hardly breathe in the suffocating atmosphere. Occasionally, one or other of the soldiers had tried to open a conversation with her, but she was too dispirited to talk much, and spent most of the journey gazing out wistfully at the gradually disappearing autumn colours, and the thick trail of black smoke rushing past the carriage window from the funnel of the train engine.

Ever since she had left Boulogne Rosie's thoughts had been overwhelmed with images of war, of death and destruction, of mud everywhere, of dirt and grime, of men groaning with pain from their wounds, and of Tim, the young soldier whom she had selflessly granted the dying wish of letting him place his hand intimately on her breast. She thought also of Lieutenant Hillary, whose life had been saved just in the nick of time, thanks to her own long walk in the dark to get help at the village of Orlais. And then there was Antoinette, that strange, rough, but beautiful creature, whose cruel experience of men had forced her to exclude them from her life, a woman of great courage but immense complication. Rosie closed her eyes, and leaned her head back against the well-used leather seat. In her mind's eye she could see Antoinette quite clearly, a strong, firm figure in black, in her man's trousers, overcoat and beret, waving slowly, relentlessly from the harbour wall as the boat pulled away from the quayside, arms outstretched, waving both hands until she became no more than a mirage on the horizon to be finally engulfed by the harsh grey sea.

By the time the train reached the South London suburbs and gradually eased its way towards the platform at Charing Cross Station, Rosie felt battered by all the images, and she smouldered with hate and disgust for what her father had done. However, when she climbed out of the carriage, her mood changed instantly.

'Rosie! Rosie Lee!'

The voice calling to her brought her back to reality with a thump, for, over the sounds of carriage doors opening and closing, and crowds of passengers being met by their families, it was the voice of Joe, very unmistakably *her* Joe. And then she saw him, waving frantically at her, pushing and shoving the crowds aside as he weaved his way towards her.

'Joe!' she called breathlessly, ecstatically, dropping her luggage to the ground as soon as he reached her. She immediately threw herself into his arms, and amidst the cat-calls and wolf-whistles from the soldiers easing past them, they smothered each other with kisses. 'Oh Joe!' she gasped, half laughing, half crying.

'"Rosie Lee, Rosie Lee",' recited Joe from his own poem, '"How I love my Rosie Lee"...!'

Rosie hugged him tight. 'Oh, Joe, oh, Joe!' she rambled over and over again. 'How did you know? How did you know?'

'Don't you worry, mate,' he replied. 'I've got me contacts!'

He picked up her luggage, and with what seemed to be the resident military band playing 'Little Dolly Daydream' in the background, they slowly moved off, staring into each other's eyes, oblivious to the crowds who were swerving impatiently past them.

'Miss Little?'

They looked up to find a young trainee nurse from QAIMNS hurrying towards them.

'Miss *Rose* Little?'

'Yes,' replied Rosie.

237

'Hello,' said the fresh-faced young girl with a beaming smile. 'I've got a message for you from Sister Maisie. You're to report to headquarters at ten o'clock tomorrow morning. She's expecting you.'

'Thank you,' said Rosie gloomily, fearing the worst.

'I bet you're glad to be back home, aren't you? It must be awful out there?'

Rosie smiled without comment.

'I'll probably be out there myself any minute,' said the girl. 'At the moment they've put me on temporary tea duty. How about a nice cuppa before you go?'

'No, fanks, mate,' said Joe, answering for both of them. 'I've got all the Rosie Lee *I* want.'

The young nurse left them, and for a moment or so they stood where they were, waiting for the crowds to disperse. Rosie felt a strange feeling in her stomach as she watched the young girl return to her tea trolley at the far end of the platform. It was as though she still ought to be doing the job herself, as though it was the only job she was fit for.

'I hate Father for what he's done,' she said.

'*I* don't,' replied Joe. 'I ain't 'ad a decent night's sleep since yer went. In any case, from wot *I* 'ear, it ain't just yer dad that's done 'is nut 'cos yer didn't tell 'im about you goin' off ter the Front. From wot ol' Ma Winnet told me, your mum weren't too pleased neivver.'

'I know that, Joe,' said Rosie pointedly. 'I know that.'

'So wot yer goin' ter do, mate?' he asked.

'Do?' asked Rosie. 'About what?'

'About *them*,' he replied. 'Yer mum an' dad. After this they ain't goin' ter let you off the 'ook so light. Yer know that, don't yer?'

'Yes, Joe,' she replied. 'I do know that. But I won't let *them* off the hook lightly either.'

'So,' repeated Joe, taking her hand and slowly leading her off again. 'Wot yer goin' ter do?'

'I don't know, Joe,' sighed Rosie. 'Honest to God, I just don't know.'

'I do,' said Joe. 'Yer can marry me.'

This immediately brought Rosie to a halt. 'Joe!' she gasped.

'Unless, er course, yer don't want to?'

'Oh, Joe,' said Rosie. 'You're not proposing to me, right here in the middle of a railway platform, are you?'

'Why not?' asked Joe, indignantly. 'Let's face it, this is where we met, din't we?'

Rosie still couldn't take it in, so much so that she hadn't even noticed that the crowds had now dispersed and that they were virtually the only two people left on the platform. 'Oh, Joe,' she said wistfully, 'there's nothing I'd like more in this whole wide world. But there's no way it could ever happen. I'm under age. Father would never allow it.'

'Get orff!' said Joe. 'Yer said yerself, yer ol' man finks the world er me.'

'He did then,' said Rosie. 'After you came to lunch that day, he said wonderful things about you. But after this, after what I've done, I'm not so sure. Especially with the way Mother's been behaving.'

'OK,' said Joe, resolutely, leading them off again along the platform, 'if *they* wanna dig *their* 'eels in, we'll do the same.'

Rosie followed him with some bewilderment. 'Joe?' she called. 'What *do* you mean?'

Before Joe could answer, the train driver released a deafening gush of steam from the engine. Joe and Rosie covered their ears. But by the time the sound had subsided, they had reached the platform barrier, and when they did, Rosie had a shock for she suddenly caught a glimpse of the solitary figure left waiting there, a middle-aged man replete in bowler hat, overcoat, pin-striped suit and rolled umbrella.

'Rose,' said the grim-faced Richard Little. 'How could you do such a thing?'

The moment he saw Richard Little and Rosie getting out of the taxi outside number 221 Camden Road, old Monty Gubble just wished he could be a mouse in the corner of the Little's dining room. He more or less knew, however, what would be going on in there, for his old pal Elsie Winnet always told him most things that went on inside the place. And why not? After all, Monty had known her and her husband, Albert, for years. In fact he knew something was up when Elsie had come out of number 221 and told him she was taking a bus up to Bethnal Green to let young Rosie's boyfriend know what was going on. Even so, he would still have liked to be that mouse.

Inside the Littles' sitting room, Rosie sat straight-backed on the sofa, listening to her father's quiet admonition for the underhand way in which she had managed to take up a posting up front without his knowledge.

'What you have done is indefensible, Rose,' he said, pacing up and down the room, hands folded behind his back. 'You will remember that when I came out to see you at Stanmore Manor I had to remind you that until you come of age, you are still under my jurisdiction? Do you remember that, Rose? Do you?'

'Yes, Father,' replied Rose coldly. 'I do.'

'And do you remember how I warned you that I would make quite certain no child of mine would ever be sent out to the battlefield?'

Again Rosie replied without so much as a glance up at him. 'Yes, Father, I do,' she said.

'And yet you chose to defy me,' said Richard, stopping directly in front of her. 'Why, Rose?' he asked, more in sadness than in anger. 'Why?'

After a moment Rosie looked up at him. 'For many reasons, Father,' she replied defiantly.

'You see, Richard!' snapped Marian, who was perched on a window seat on the other side of the room. 'What did I tell you?'

'Please be quiet, Marian,' replied Richard, with irritation. 'I asked you to leave this to me.'

'But you heard what she said,' insisted Marian. 'This girl is out of hand!'

'Marian – *please!*'

Her husband's angry rebuke forced Marian to make no further comment.

Richard turned once again to Rosie. '*What* reasons, Rose?' he asked in a quiet, civilised way.

241

'First and foremost, Father,' said Rosie, 'is the fact that I am no longer the child you and Mother take me for.'

Marian snorted with frustration.

'Secondly,' continued Rosie, 'as *I* have to remind you and Mother repeatedly, we are at war, Father, and every person, whether man or woman, has to do their bit.'

'I know that, Rosie,' Richard assured her. 'Believe me, I do know what you're saying. But girls of your age should not be expected to go out to places of conflict where soldiers are engaged in bloody battle. I've often said the same thing to people in authority. There have to be limitations.'

'There are *no* limitations in war, Father,' replied Rosie, firmly. 'The vocation I have chosen during this emergency is to be a nurse. When men are taken from the battlefield, maimed and dying, they need nurses like me to look after them. In the short time I spent in France, I came to realise that only too well.'

'You are *not* a nurse, Rose,' called Marian.

'*Please*, Marian,' sighed Richard, losing his patience with her.

This time, however, Marian refused to be silenced, and came across to confront Rosie. 'You spend a few weeks as a tea girl on a railway platform,' she said, 'and a few weeks in a military convalescence home in Middlesex. It takes years of training to become a nurse, Rose – *not* just a few weeks putting on bandages.'

Rosie was angered by her mother's disparaging remark. 'You may be interested to know, Mother,' she replied tersely, 'that a tea girl meeting wounded soldiers off a troop train is to them the first real sign that they are home. I don't think that's such a terrible thing to do, do *you?*'

Being put down by her own daughter did not suit Marian. Exasperated, she turned away in frustration.

'Rose,' said Richard, trying to be conciliatory, 'I think you're being a little unfair to your mother and me. Our only concern throughout all this has been your welfare and, above all, your safety. You're our daughter, Rose. If anything were to have happened to you, we could not live with the fact that we never tried to stop you putting yourself in such danger. That's why I used my contact to prevent you from going to France. It wasn't a selfish act on my part; it was only what any father would try to do. But what hurt us both deeply was that you chose to do all these things behind our backs. That's not what parents are for, Rose. We're here to protect you.'

'Father,' said Rosie, responding to her father's attempts to explain his position, 'if I had told you that I was being posted up front, would you have tried to stop me?'

'You know what the answer to that is!' called Marian.

Richard swung a glare at her.

'Precisely,' said Rosie, directing her reply to her father. 'That's why I wasn't prepared to jeopardise my chance to go with other girls, girls just like myself, who were prepared to take chances at a time when there is such a desperate shortage of nurses. Don't you understand? I didn't deceive you. I would never deceive people I love so much.

243

But when you're wrong about something – and I do know that you're wrong – I have to do what *I* think is best. If you try to chain me down, I will always break loose.'

Richard didn't know how to respond. He just turned with a sigh, and went to his armchair.

Rosie watched him with some guilt. Then she got up and went to him. 'Father,' she said softly, and with compassion, 'please don't blame me. I'm just growing up faster than you expected, that's all.'

Richard nodded. It was as though he was trying hard to understand. Rosie then looked across at her mother, who was staring out of the window, arms crossed, her back turned towards her. 'Mother,' she said, 'please don't hate me. We used to be such good friends. I wouldn't ever want that to change.'

'It seems to me you have *other* friends now,' replied Marian, refusing to look at her. 'I'm sure the son of a canal dredger can offer you better advice than your own parents.'

Rosie felt as though her mother had turned to stone. This remark had hurt her deeply. 'I hope you won't resent that, Mother,' she said. 'Because that son of a canal dredger has asked me to marry him.'

'Marry? You and that smart-talking lass from Islington?' Annie Upton roared with laughter, her massive frame in danger of popping one of the buttons on her dress. 'And what're you going to feed 'er on, son? You're still in the army. You don't even make enough to give *me* some rent.'

When Joe got home from meeting Rosie at Charing Cross Station, his mum was in the middle of stuffing a large double mattress with straw. With that, and her part-time job assembling matchboxes, each week she managed to bring in the princely sum of two shillings and threepence, which, with the few bob her eldest son, Paul, earned in a fish-curing warehouse in Limehouse, was at least enough to keep the wolf from the door until Annie's husband, Will Upton, got home from the army and went back to being the main breadwinner of the family.

'Yer don't 'ave ter worry about me, Mum,' replied Joe, as he sat down opposite her in the back parlour, idly handing her clumps of straw from the pile on the floor. 'I've got plans.'

'We've *all* got plans,' said Annie. 'What we've not got is cash.'

'Not now, maybe,' Joe assured her, 'but once the war's over, you mark my words, fings'll be diff'rent.' As he spoke, he broke into a violent fit of coughing.

'Things'll be different, will they?' asked Annie sceptically. 'I dare say.' She waited for him to recover before speaking again. 'You can't live on nowt, son. I should know. I've been trying it for years. A lass like you've got won't want to live like that. She comes from folk who never know what it's like to go to bed on an empty stomach.'

'It won't always be like that,' said Joe, trying to get his breathing under control. 'I won't always 'ave this condition. The doctor up at the manor told me it's just a question er time. I've just got ter be patient, that's all.'

'And what about your lady love?' asked Annie, snidely. 'Is *she* going to be patient too?'

Joe stopped handing straw to his mother, and flopped back exhausted in his chair at the table. 'Rosie's a special person, Ma,' he said. 'All she wants to do is to look after me.'

Annie looked up briefly from what she was doing. 'Fine marriage that'd be,' she said. 'You don't get wed just to 'ave someone to look after you, you know.'

'That's not wot I mean,' replied Joe, whose face was blood red from his coughing fit. 'All I'm sayin' is that me an' Rosie would look after each uvver. We'd make a good team. An' wot's more, we luv each uvver.'

'Love?' Annie snorted dismissively. How many times had she heard that word mentioned since she got together with Will Upton nearly twenty-five years ago? How many times had she *thought* about that word when she lay awake in her bed at night waiting for her man to come back home after a night out with some other woman? For Annie, bringing up two kids hadn't been about love. It had been about a labour of love. 'Well, you can call it what you like,' she said, putting on her specs that were so old they had been stuck together with sticking plaster, 'but love won't pay the rent. And in any case, what do your prospective in-laws think about all this? 'Ave *they* given their blessing to the son of a canal dredger getting 'ooked up to their lass?'

'It won't make no diff'rence ter them who I am or where I come from,' replied Joe with only a slight suggestion of confidence.

'Is that so?' asked Annie, who was now straining her eyes to thread twine through the eye of a mattress needle. 'So 'appens you've asked their permission?'

Joe shrugged dismissively. 'No,' he replied. 'Not yet.'

'And what if they say no?'

'They won't.'

'You're sure about that, are you?'

Joe was getting irritated with this conversation. 'Look, Ma,' he snapped, getting up from the table, 'it don't matter a monkey's ter me if they say yes or no. Wotever 'appens, me an' Rosie are goin' ter get tergevver.'

'I'm only trying to warn you of the pitfalls,' said Annie, putting down her needle and twine, and carefully taking off her specs to look up at him. 'If you want to bring up a family of your own, first of all think what it's going to mean. 'Ow are you going to get a job wi' your condition? Where are you going to live? 'Ow are you going to pay the rent?'

'Bleedin' 'ell, Ma!' ranted Joe. 'Rosie ain't 'elpless. She can get a job too, yer know.'

'Ah!' said Annie, almost smugly. 'Now we get to it. So you want *your* wife to be the same as me, do you? You want 'er to be the breadwinner of your family?'

'That's a disgustin' fing ter say, Ma,' snapped Joe. 'An' it's just not true.'

Annie now realised that she had gone too far. She had hurt him, and the one thing she had never wanted to do was to hurt her favourite boy. Paul may have been the brainy one of the family, but Joe was the most loving. The trouble was, Joe had always been a bit of a hothead; he acted before he thought things out, and critical though Annie was of him, the last thing she wanted was for the boy to get his fingers burned. 'Come and sit down, lad,' she said, with as much affection as she was capable.

Joe stood with his back to her, looking down obstinately into the oven grate.

'Come on, you dope!' cried Annie. 'I'm your mam. Stop feeling bloody sorry for yourself!'

Reluctantly, Joe turned, went back to the table and sat down.

'Now listen to me, son,' said Annie. 'I've never wanted owt for you or your brother but t' best. Right?'

Joe nodded.

'Now I know you love this lass, but all I'm asking you to do is to go careful, like. She comes from folk that 'ave money and position. Everything comes easy to them. They can do owt they want to make your life 'ell.'

'Ma...'

'No, lad,' said Annie, stretching across the table to put her fingers to his lips. 'Hear me out first. If you don't agree, then I'll shut up.' She took her fingers away, and rested her hands on the stuffed mattress in front of her. 'I've made so many mistakes in *my* life that I wouldn't be much of a mother if I didn't try to stop you doing the same. All I want to know is, if Rosie's old man doesn't give you permission to marry 'er, what're you going to do?'

Joe thought about this only briefly. 'We go off

somewhere, an' live tergevver.'

Annie sighed. 'And you know what *that* could mean, don't you?' she warned.

Joe shrugged.

'She's under age, lad,' said Annie. ''Appen they could get in touch wi' your commanding officer and get you locked up. Are you prepared to take that risk?'

'Yes, I am,' replied Joe firmly.

Annie sighed again, and sat back in her chair. 'All right, lad,' she said sternly. 'If that's what you want, then I'll back you up all I can. But just remember one thing. Remember what 'appened wi' me an' your dad. I'm tellin' yer, son, before you do owt rash, tell Rosie about it. She's got a right to know.'

Chapter 14

Sister Maisie MacLellan was feeling very harassed. The new intake of trainee volunteer nurses had only arrived at the QAIMNS head-quarters a few days before, but in her words: 'There's not a bright head amongst the lot of 'em!' The sight of Rosie coming into her tiny office on the second floor did nothing to raise her spirits either, for the news she had to give her was clearly going to upset the poor girl.

'I'm sorry, Rosie, my dear,' she said, her broad Glaswegian accent thicker than ever, 'but I'm afraid you've been suspended from nursing duties until further notice.'

Although Rosie was angered by this news, she was not altogether surprised. In fact, since being called back from France, she had come to expect anything and everything. 'Would it be too much to ask the reason for this decision?' she asked.

Sister Maisie was now utterly flustered, so much so that a lock of her pure white hair had somehow escaped from beneath her senior nurse's cap and was bobbing up and down her forehead. 'If I could tell you that, lassie,' she replied, 'I'd have a mind like some of those at the top who make such decisions – and that's the last thing I'd want, I can tell you. But if you want to know what *I* think,' she said, leaning towards Rosie over her desk and lowering her voice, 'I'd say our people upstairs have been hauled over the coals for sending you up front without consulting the orders we received the moment you joined the service.'

Rosie also sat forward in her chair, facing Sister Maisie. '*What* orders, Sister?' she asked.

'That under no circumstances whatever were you to be allowed to be sent overseas on active duty. Even I didn't know about that.'

'And you have no idea who issued those orders?'

'None at all,' Sister Maisie replied. 'But Lady Braintree knew. I have no doubt about that.'

'Lady Braintree?' Rosie was puzzled. 'But if *she* knew, then why did she allow me to go up front?'

Sister Maisie shrugged. 'You know as much as I do, lassie,' she replied. 'But I imagine a directive like this came from someone high up the scale, probably one of those fusty old men at the War

Office. However, to add insult to injury, I've been told that, as a temporary measure, I can relocate you back to your old job – at Charing Cross Station.'

Rosie's first reaction was to fly into a rage, but then she thought better of it. After all, it was no fault of poor old Sister Maisie, who was clearly having enough problems of her own with her new trainees. 'Tea girl?' she asked, with some irony.

Embarrassed, Sister Maisie lowered her eyes. 'That's about it, I'm afraid, lassie,' she said. 'But if you don't want to do it–'

'Oh, but I do,' replied Rosie. 'I'll be very proud to take over my old job again.'

Sister Maisie's eyes flicked up in astonishment. Was she hearing right? Rosie was worth so much more than a menial duty like that. Could she really mean what she was saying?

Rosie, of course, had her own reasons for taking on the job. After all, not only was that where she first met Joe, but it also meant that after the way her mother had referred to her as 'a tea girl on a railway platform', Marian would be none too pleased to know that Rosie would soon be back at Charing Cross serving cups of 'Rosie Lee' to the troops. 'How soon can I start?' she asked brightly.

Sister Maisie was bewildered by Rosie's response. 'Whenever you like, dear,' she replied with a shrug.

'Tomorrow morning?'

'Certainly,' she replied. 'If that's what you wish.'

'I do,' said Rosie, getting up from her chair.

'As a matter of fact,' said Sister Maisie, getting up at the same time, 'the timing couldn't be better. The young lassie on the trolley down there at the moment is straining at the leash to go up front. It seems to be a kind of desperation to get her own back for her father. He was killed by a land mine a few weeks ago.'

Rosie felt her stomach shrivel up inside. That fresh-faced young girl, the girl with that lovely, beaming smile. *I bet you're glad to be home, aren't you? It must be awful out there?* Rosie could still hear the girl's voice, so young, so pure and innocent, showing no emotion, taking life in her stride. *I'll probably be out there myself any minute.*

Joe was waiting for Rosie when she came out of the QAIMNS building. She was reluctant to talk about the reasons why she had been summoned there, but did perk up a little when telling Joe that she would be going back to her old job on the platform at Charing Cross Station. But after what Sister Maisie had told her about the people in high places who had been responsible for bringing her back from France, her mind was now brimming with determination to get away from home. This became her main topic of conversation as she and Joe strolled through Hyde Park on their way to Marble Arch to catch an omnibus home to Islington. On their way, they passed an army recruiting centre in a marquee fronted by bizarre posters such as those of Lord Kitchener pointing his finger ominously at the reader telling him that 'YOUR COUNTRY NEEDS YOU – NOW!', another showing John Bull asking the question

252

'WHO'S ABSENT? IS IT YOU?' and another directed at the female members of the family proclaiming loyally, 'WOMEN OF BRITAIN SAY – GO!'

Rosie turned her eyes away from all the razzmatazz, and was really quite cross when a sergeant major came out of the marquee entrance with a silly provocative call to arms: 'Come on now, young man! Is your young lady worth fighting for, or isn't she?' Considering all Joe had been through, Rosie was furious. She held on tightly to his arm, and angrily led him off without comment. To get away from all the irritating bravado, they made a diversion down towards the Serpentine lake, but it took a long time before they lost the wailing sound of a gramophone record playing incessantly in the marquee, a nauseating rendition of 'I'll Make a Man of You' by that well-known music-hall artiste, Miss Gwendoline Brogden.

Despite the cold weather, the chestnut, oak and maple trees around the lake created a wonderful picture as the last of their different coloured leaves fluttered down in the chilly midday breeze. The whole lakeside was deserted, so Rosie and Joe quickly found a bench to sit on, and were gradually approached by a posse of water birds such as graceful white swans and Muscovy and Aylesbury ducks. Rosie quickly snuggled up to Joe, leaning her head against his chest. For several minutes, they sat there in silence, watching the birds waddle back and forth along the water's edge, and listening to their chatter as they searched for food. It was Rosie who finally

253

broke the silence.

'Joe,' she asked, 'when you met me at Charing Cross Station, what did you mean when you said that if my parents want to dig their heels in about us getting married, we'll do the same?'

Joe took a moment to answer. 'I meant that no one was going to stop you an' me being tergevver.'

'But if my father won't give his permission for me to get married,' said Rosie, 'I don't see what we could do about it, unless of course...' she hesitated, 'unless we went off and lived together.'

Joe sat up with a start. 'Blimey, Rosie!' he gasped. 'D'yer know what you're sayin'?'

'Yes, I do,' she replied without the blink of an eye. 'I'd be game, if you would.'

'B-but we could never do that, Rosie,' said Joe, completely taken aback. 'Your dad'd 'ave the law down on us in a flash. We're boaf under age. The flatfoots'd chuck me in the cooler and frow away the key. And Gord knows wot they'd do ter you.'

'I'm not so sure you're right, Joe,' she replied confidently. 'We could find a place somewhere, and not tell them where it was.'

'Yer've got ter be kiddin', Rosie,' said Joe. 'If you carry on doin' the teas on Charing Cross Station, your dad could get you any time he wanted. And in any case, what would we do fer money? I'm still in the army, remember. I'm only on indefinite compassionate leave. I'm an invalid, Rosie. There's no way I can earn enuff ter keep us till I get on me feet again.'

'No,' replied Rosie. 'But *I* can.'

Joe was thunderstruck, and pulled away from

her. 'Don't say fings like that ter me, Rosie,' he said, in a sudden fit of anger. 'Don't you ever say fings like that. No woman is ever goin' ter be a breadwinner in my family.'

'Your mother is,' Rosie reminded him. The moment she said it, however, she wished she hadn't.

'My ma's diff'rent,' he said. 'She's used ter roughin' it.'

'Oh, don't be so stupid, Joe!' snapped Rosie. It was the first time she had had a cross word with him. 'That's a terribly old-fashioned thing to say!'

Joe didn't like that, and immediately stood up, scattering all the birds around them. 'Well, I'm very sorry,' he snapped back. 'I din't know yer only went wiv fellers who ain't ol'-fashioned.'

Rosie got up quickly, just in time to stop him wandering off. 'Joe!' she called, rushing after him. 'Joe dearest.' She brought him to a halt. 'All I meant was that I'm perfectly capable of getting a job, just until you can take over. The work I'll be doing for the nursing service is only part-time now, and I could easily get something to help bring in enough money to pay the rent. In any case, I have a small monthly allowance from my father.'

'Oh, yeah,' said Joe dismissively. 'An' yer fink that'll go on once you an' me get tergevver?'

Rosie stopped trying to pacify him. Quite suddenly she felt as though he didn't mean all he said he had meant. Quite suddenly she felt as though he didn't care enough for her, care enough at least to set up home with her.

And for Joe, after the conversation he'd had with his mum, things *did* seem to be different. Perhaps he *was* rushing into things without realising the consequences. What was it Annie had said? *'I've made so many mistakes in* my *life that I wouldn't be much of a mother if I didn't try to stop you doing the same... Remember what 'appened wi' me an' your dad. I'm tellin' yer son, before you do owt rash, tell Rosie about it. She's got a right to know.'*

'I'm sorry, Joe,' said Rosie. 'I have no right to expect you to take on board someone who has so many problems. Forgive me.' She turned, and started to stroll off.

'Rosie.'

She stopped and turned to look back at him.

'I've got somefin' I want ter tell yer,' he said. 'Somefin' I *'ave* ter tell yer.' He went to her, took hold of her hands and held them. But then his courage failed him. 'I want yer ter know that I love you more than anyfin' else in the 'ole wide world, an' there's nuffin' I'd like better than fer you an' me ter live tergevver. So if that's wot *you* want, it's wot *I* want too.'

For one brief moment, Rosie stood quite still, just staring into his eyes. Then she took hold of his hands, and kissed both palms. 'I'm so happy, Joe,' she said, drawing him to her. 'I just know everything is going to turn out all right.'

As she spoke, Joe burst into a violent fit of coughing so bad that Rosie had to help him back to the bench seat.

From the recruitment marquee on the other side of the park, the poignant strains of another gramophone record drifted eerily across the autumn foliage. This time it was of a military band playing 'It's a Long Way to Tipperary'. However, the sounds were not appreciated by the Serpentine birds, so they gradually withdrew into the peace and calm of their own waterside sanctuary.

At Charing Cross Station, Platform 1 was crowded with the usual relatives and friends all waiting for the arrival of the morning hospital train. Rosie was now into her third day back on the tea trolley, and with only ten minutes to go until the platform would be the scene of more emotional reunions, she already had a large urn of tea boiled up for the thirsty patients who would soon be needing it. It had been a trying few days for her. After her first disagreement with Joe about whether or not they should live together, she had felt very unsettled about what the future would bring. Even so, she still loved Joe and, despite his misgivings, he had made it abundantly clear that he still loved her. In one way their little tiff had been a good thing, for it gave them both the chance to see another side to each other. Rosie's one great anxiety now was the meeting she had arranged with Joe and her father, a desperate last attempt to see if he would change his entrenched ideas about Joe's class and background, and allow the two of them to get married. All this was weighing heavily on Rosie's mind as the hands of the huge station clock moved closer to the time of the train's arrival. But what she didn't expect was to see Joe's brother,

Paul, ambling along the platform towards her from the ticket barrier.

''Ello, Rosie,' he called as he approached. 'So this is where it all goes on, does it?'

'Hello, Paul,' replied Rosie, with little enthusiasm. Being in Paul's company always made her feel uneasy, although she still hadn't quite worked out why. 'What are you doing here? I thought you worked over at Limehouse?'

''Alf-day terday, Rosie,' Paul replied. 'We 'ave ter wait fer the new batch er fish ter come in.'

'All the way from the North Sea,' said Rosie. 'I must say I tip my hat to the fisherman, never knowing when those German submarines are going to suddenly appear. They're such brave souls.'

'All part of the job, Rosie,' replied Paul. 'All part of the job.'

Rosie carried on preparing her tea trolley, doing her best not to show too much interest in why Paul was there. None the less she couldn't fail to notice what a good-looking boy he was. Behind his metal spectacles, he had fine, rugged features, with short dark hair that was a totally different colour from both his mother and his brother's.

'So 'ow much longer yer goin' ter be doin' *this* job, Rosie Lee?' he asked.

Rosie felt quite resentful that he had used Joe's way of addressing her. 'As long as I'm needed,' replied Rosie, busily, but unnecessarily, rearranging the cups on her trolley.

'But I fawt you was s'pposed ter be a nurse.'

'Someone has to do the job, Paul,' she replied,

doing her best to disguise her irritation.

'So then wot 'appens?'

'What do you mean?' Rosie asked casually.

'Yer know wot I mean, Rosie,' replied Paul, with one of his sickly smiles. 'You an' Joe.'

Rosie shrugged. 'It's up to him really. We'll just have to wait and see.'

'You're goin' ter live tergevver,' he said. 'That right?'

Rosie tensed. 'As I said, Paul,' she replied, 'we'll just have to wait and see.'

'Yer don't 'ave ter worry, Rosie,' said Paul. 'I 'eard Joe talkin' ter Mum about it the uvver night. In fact, 'e's bin out lookin' fer a place fer the two of yer.'

'Oh, really?' replied Rosie, as though she didn't know what he was talking about, though, of course, she did.

'Not much luck so far, though,' said Paul. 'Everyfin's so pricey. Yer 'ave ter 'ave loads er dosh ter get a decent place these days.' He lit up a fag. 'Still,' he continued, 'I'll 'elp 'im ter find somefin'.'

Rosie did her best not to react to what Paul had said. The last thing in the world she wanted was for him to get involved in her relationship with Joe. 'I'm sure Joe knows what he's doing,' she replied.

''E would do, if 'e din't 'ave that cough.'

This remark prompted Rosie to look up with a start. 'Joe's going to get better, Paul,' she said. 'I remember the medical officer out at Stanmore telling me that in time there's no doubt that Joe will fully recover.'

'Course 'e will,' said Paul, confidently. 'Joe's got guts. 'E won't let no cough get 'im down.' He paused just long enough to take a puff of his fag. 'I'm very fond er my bruvver, yer know.'

Rosie looked at him and smiled. It was the first thing he had said to her that she liked; it prompted her to give him a warm, grateful smile. What she hadn't expected was the smile she got in return. It unsettled her, because for the first time she noticed just how handsome Paul really was. For a few seconds she held the look he was giving her, and then quickly continued what she was doing.

'Oh, yes,' continued Paul. 'Joe an' me 'ave always bin mates. Not that 'e likes the same fings as me – oh, no. Bleedin' lousy at football. Whenever 'e played at school 'e nearly always scored a goal for the uvver side!' He chuckled at his own remark.

Rosie smiled, without responding.

'Mind you,' continued Paul, 'Joe's more like Mum than me. I take after Dad. 'Im an' me 'ave always bin very close.' He paused just long enough to see if Rosie was going to offer any response. 'Dad's comin' 'ome,' he said suddenly.

Rosie looked up with a start.

'Did Joe tell yer?' asked Paul. 'No, probably not. We only got the card this mornin'. Sounds like 'e's comin' 'ome any minute. Just fer a coupla weeks, though.'

'Oh, Paul,' said Rosie. 'That's wonderful!'

''Ope so,' said Paul.

'Why d'you say that?'

'Well,' said Paul, 'we 'aven't seen 'im since 'e

went an' joined up. Stupid ol' bugger. 'E 'ad no need ter do it. 'E's over forty. 'E wasn't goin' ter be called up 'cos it ain't compulsory fer a man 'is age. Well – not yet, anyway'

'I shall look forward to meeting him,' said Rosie.

'I'll bet 'e'll look forward ter meetin' you too,' replied Paul. ''E won't make no complaints about 'avin' such a good-looker in the family.'

Embarrassed, Rosie continued with her work. As she did so, the sound of a train whistle heralded the approach of the hospital train. There was an immediate scurry forward from the crowd waiting on the platform, and a flock of pigeons that had been scouring for scraps of food suddenly panicked and fluttered up towards the glass station roof. As the train slowly pulled alongside the platform, thick black smoke billowed out from the funnel, and the moment the driver pulled the train to a halt at the buffers, he released a deafening gush of steam.

''Ow about comin' round the boozer wiv me one night?'

Rosie swung round to find Paul standing close behind her. 'I'm sorry,' she said, pretending that she hadn't heard what he had said. 'What did you say?'

'I said,' called Paul, shouting out above the noise of carriage doors opening and closing along the platform, 'come an' 'ave a drink wiv me some time. If you're goin' ter join our 'appy family, I fink it's about time we got ter know each uvver, don't you, Rosie Lee?'

Joe had polished his shoes so much that you could see your face in them. In his short period of square bashing when he had first joined up, he spent every day from morning to night doing chores that seemed to him and his mates to be a complete waste of time, but now, for his meeting with Rosie's dad, he wanted to look his best. He had togged himself up in his Sunday best three-piece navy-blue suit and flat cap. 'Fit to meet a bloody duke,' said his mum as she looked him over before he left home. He only wished it *was* a duke he was going to meet, because that would be far less of an ordeal than asking Rosie's dad if he could marry her – not made any easier by the fact that Richard Little had only agreed to meet Joe if he came to see him in his office at the factory, which was clearly a way of Mr Little excluding his wife from interfering too much in the discussion. Fortunately, Rosie was there, sitting beside Joe on the sofa, ready to give him an encouraging smile whenever she felt he was getting tongue-tied.

'You know, young man,' said Richard, as though he was revealing to Joe something the boy didn't already know, 'marriage is an important moment in one's life. There are so many things to consider, such as compatibility, and the necessity to make quite sure there is always enough money in the bank to pay your creditors. Incidentally...' he leaned forward across his desk and addressed himself directly to Joe, 'who do *you* bank with?'

'Come again?' asked Joe, after flicking a puzzled look at Rosie.

'Joe doesn't have a bank account, Father,' said

Rosie. 'You know very well he wouldn't be allowed to open one until he officially comes of age. And, in any case, he's still in the army.'

'No bank account?' asked Richard, half to himself. 'Then if you don't have money in the bank, how would you manage to support a wife and family?'

Rosie wanted to answer that question too, but knowing how sensitive Joe felt about such things, she refrained from doing so.

'I can assure you, Mr Little,' replied Joe very firmly, 'no wife er mine would ever go wivout.'

'Without?' asked Richard, puzzled. 'Without what?'

'Wivout anyfin',' replied Joe. 'My dad may not earn much, but 'e's always looked after 'is family. An' I intend ter do the same.'

'Money doesn't grow on trees, Joe,' replied Richard. 'It has to be worked for, and the only way to do that is to get a good job. Could *you* get a good job to support your wife, Joe?'

'Er course I would, sir,' replied Joe without a moment's thought. 'If I could find one.'

'And what sort of work would that be?'

After a moment's hesitation Joe replied: 'I'm a jack of all trades, sir. I could turn me 'and ter most fings.'

'Provided, of course, you are well enough,' said Richard.

Rosie took exception to this remark. 'Father,' she retorted, 'I've told you before, Joe is getting better every day. The medical officer at Stanmore said–'

'What school did you go to, Joe?' said Richard,

263

without allowing her to finish what she was going to say.

'After we moved 'ere from Yorkshire, I went to Befnal Green Juniors,' replied Joe instantly. 'But I left when I was twelve. Got a job down the market at Petticoat Lane. Peelin' spuds at old Fred's fish 'n' chip stall.'

Rosie watched her father's reaction carefully.

Richard got up from his chair, folded his hands behind his back and stood by the great arched window overlooking the factory floor below. 'Joe,' he asked, not without sensitivity, 'don't you think education is a very important part of one's life?'

'Oh, definitely, sir,' replied Joe confidently. 'I couldn't agree more.'

'And yet your parents allowed you to leave school when you were only twelve years old?'

'That's right, sir.'

'Don't you think that was a mistake?'

'Not really, sir,' replied Joe. 'Ma an' Dad was pretty 'ard up at the time an' they needed all the cash they could get. Up Norf where I come from, when we was kids, me an' my bruvver used ter work on the land diggin' up carrots fer just a penny a day. It weren't much, but it 'elped out. In any case, I reckon there're some fings in life that yer can't learn at school.'

'Oh, really?' asked Richard. 'Such as?'

Joe shrugged. ''Ow ter stay alive when yer ain't got much ter eat. 'Ow ter look after yer ma when she ain't feelin' well. 'Ow ter know wot's goin' on in the world.'

'Don't you think reading and writing and knowing how to add up has something to do with

264

that?' asked Richard, somewhat pompously.

'Not in *my* neck er the woods, it don't, sir,' replied Joe. 'Ma always says that knowin' 'ow ter survive is the most important fing in life. An' let's face it, school don't teach yer 'ow ter smoke cigars, do they?'

The irony of Joe's answer was not lost on Richard. For one brief moment, turning to look down at the factory floor, he seemed to be in deep thought. 'You know, Joe,' he said, 'I have people working down there who work hard for their living, people who have families of their own to support; some of them have been here for the best part of their lives. During these terrible times we're living in, I'm lucky to have them working for me. On the other hand, *they* are lucky to have a job. Good jobs are not easy to come by, Joe, and when this war's over, it's going to be even more difficult. If you can't find a job with prospects, you will have real problems.' He returned to his desk and sat down again. 'What I have to say to you, Joe, is that Rose's mother and I love our daughter too much to allow her to take such a risk.'

Rosie stiffened.

'Risk?' asked Joe, baffled.

'Look,' replied Richard, 'I want you to know that I have nothing personal against you. In fact, I happen to think that you're quite a decent sort of young chap, and I enjoyed the afternoon we all spent together. But the fact is, Rose comes from ... well, let's say ... from a different kind of environment to your own. She's been brought up differently, hasn't had to rough it like you. You must try to understand that I don't want her to have to have that sort of life. Rose is precious to us. I have a duty to protect her.'

'Protect 'er?' asked Joe, who knew exactly what Little was getting at. 'Protect 'er from wot?'

Rosie stood up. 'Come, Joe,' she said, going to the door.

'Now, Rosie,' said Richard, getting up from his chair. 'Be reasonable.'

'Oh, I shall be reasonable, Father,' Rosie replied ominously, opening the door for Joe. 'Joe and I are going to be reasonable for the rest of our lives. Or at least, we shall try.'

Joe took one last long look at Richard, then left the room. Rosie quickly followed him out.

After they had gone, Richard's eyes were transfixed on the door. He now knew that whatever he said, whatever he tried to do, he had lost Rosie for ever.

Chapter 15

After her father's absolute refusal to allow her to get married, it was several days before the real implication of what he had said began to cause anxiety, not only to Rosie but also to Joe. Yes, they had talked about going off and living together somewhere, but exactly where and how were becoming serious problems. It had been over a week now since Joe had started his search for a place in which he and Rosie could live, but so far his attempts had proved impossible. Everywhere he went he found himself up against greedy landlords, out to exploit the housing shortage by asking for rents that in better times would have been over double the market value. At one place in Plaistow he had looked over, the owner was asking three shillings for a one-bedroom basement flat that was really an old cellar, with no windows, and daylight only available through a grille in the pavement outside.

'Don't worry about the rain comin' in,' said the tight-fisted little man who owned the place. 'My previous tenant said it was no problem at all ter put a bucket under the grille when it rained.'

In Shoreditch, Joe was even offered what was virtually an old corrugated-iron shed in the back yard of someone's garden. The owner, an Italian woman, reckoned that at two bob a week, her 'property' was a bargain, despite the fact that it comprised very little more than a single space for living in, with a bucket outside in the garden for slops, a single-ring paraffin cooker, which also served as a heater, a double bedstead screened off by curtains and a rickety old table and two chairs that, like the landlady herself, had seen better days.

Joe thought that he had finally found the place of his dreams when he went to see a perfect two-bedroom flat in West Ham, above what was advertised on a card in a newsagent's shop window as 'a high-class ladies' lingerie boutique', but in fact it turned out to be a disguise for a house of ill repute, in which the tenants would be expected to help run the business. However, there

was eventually a gleam of opportunity when Joe
started talking to old Monty Gubble about his
predicament.

'Well, why din't yer tell this ter me before?' said
the old codger, whose jaw was aching after losing
his penultimate yellow front tooth. 'I know just
the place for yer. I'll get on ter Cuthbert right
away.'

'Who on earth is Cuffbert?' said Joe, nearly
choking with laughter.

'Don't you mock my best mate!' growled
Monty. 'Me an' Cuthbert fought side by side wiv
Lord Raglan against the Ruskies in the Crimean
War. We went fru 'ell an' 'igh water tergevver, I
can tell yer.'

'Blimey, Monty!' gasped Joe, teasing him. 'I
knew yer was old, but I din't fink yer was *that*
old!'

'Age is only a word,' replied Monty indignantly.
'It's experience wot counts.'

'Only jokin', mate,' said Joe, putting his arm
around the old man's shoulders as they strolled
slowly along Camden Road together. 'So – this
Cuffbert. 'E knows somewhere ter kip, does 'e?'

'That 'e does,' replied Monty. 'In fact, if yer talk
nice to 'im, nicer than yer talk ter me, 'e might
even give yer a discount.'

Joe stopped dead in his tracks. 'Yer mean – 'e
owns the place?'

'That 'e does,' replied Monty, repeating himself. ''E made 'imself a bit er cash on the dogs
years ago, stashed it away, then bought a nice
little place fer 'im an' 'is missus ter live in down
near Forest Gate. Sad ter say, she died just a few

years after that, an' Cuthbert's bin livin' on 'is own there ever since.'

'Poor ol' Cuffbert,' said Joe. He felt guilty that he had teased Monty about his age, because he had always admired and respected the old timers who had fought in both the Crimean and Boer Wars. To him, they were the salt of the earth, and he just hoped that in future years people would feel the same about the young blokes like himself who had slogged it out in the front-line dugouts of France.

'So where *is* this place?' he asked. 'When can me and Rosie take a look?'

'I'll drop a note ter Cuthbert,' replied Monty, who was puffing a bit, and had to stop for a moment to perch on a coping stone. ''E'll be glad of a bit er company. But I'm warnin' yer,' he added, with a mischievous twinkle in his eye, 'Cuthbert ain't always everyone's cuppa tea. Some people fink 'e's a bit of an eccentric.'

'Not like you then, eh, Monty?' said Joe, ribbing him.

'See fer yerself,' replied Monty. 'Just let me know when yer want ter go.' He chuckled to himself. 'I'm lookin' forward ter this!'

Ever since her father had spoken to her and Joe about getting married, Rosie had hardly said a word to her parents. She still went down to meals with the family, not only for Christian's sake, but also because she didn't want to arouse their suspicions too much about what she intended to do about her future relationship with Joe. Her father, of course, knew that Rosie's feelings would never be the same towards him again, but her mother behaved as though the problem with her daughter was settled, and that from now on the family could behave as though nothing had ever happened. However, that was not the case.

The only person Rosie now felt that she could confide in at the house was Mrs Winnet, who over the years had proved to be more than a housekeeper to the family, a dear and trusted friend as well – especially to Rosie and Christian. Nowadays in their eyes she was more of a mother to them than Marian, and whenever they had a problem to sort out, it was usually to her that they turned. Although only middle-aged, Elsie Winnet was a treasure chest of wisdom, and she was psychic too, for she was always forecasting events before they happened, including the start of the war itself. But she missed her husband, Albert, very much, and when he rushed off to become one of Lord Kitchener's early recruits, she had left their little ground-floor flat in Tufnell Park, and moved in to an attic room on the top floor of the Little family house in Camden Road. Therefore, when Rosie decided once and for all to leave home to go and live with Joe, because Christian was too young to hear about this sort of thing, the one person she needed to talk to was Mrs Winnet. To her surprise, however, the family's housekeeper was not as sympathetic to Rosie's plans as she had expected.

'You're goin' ter live wiv that boy?' asked Mrs Winnet, more in shock than in delight, as they went shopping together along the busy Seven Sisters Road. 'Really, Miss Rosie. Surely that's not a very nice thing ter do, is it?'

'Why d'you say that, Winnie?' asked Rosie.

'Well, I don't hold with folk livin' in sin,' she replied prudishly. 'It don't take long ter make an 'onest woman of yer in front of a vicar.'

'If I could do that,' replied Rosie, 'I'd do it. But my father is so absolutely determined not to let me, I have no alternative.'

'It's not your farvver,' said Mrs Winnet, joining a queue of women that had formed at the back of a horse-drawn cart from which the driver was selling dried figs and dates. 'I'm afraid it's yer muvver.'

'Yes, I know,' sighed Rosie.

'Honest ter God, I don't know wot's come over 'er these days. She's always gettin' worked up about everyfin'. Not only you but young Christian too. I just wish she'd leave the poor little soul alone. 'E don't need all that namby-pamby stuff. Leave 'im alone, say I, an' 'e'll live a lot longer.' As she reached the front of the queue she lowered her voice. 'If yer ask me, it's all ter do wiv that terrible man from up Canonbury.'

Rosie did a double take. 'What man, Winnie?' she asked with intense curiosity.

Before Rosie could get an answer, however, she had to wait until Mrs Winnet had bought the dried fruit. This being a Friday afternoon, there were plenty of customers milling around the stalls, stocking up for the weekend, and at the same time seeing if they could pick up any bargains amongst the bundles of second-hand clothes on sale everywhere. Whilst she waited, Rosie's attention strayed briefly to one of the stalls

271

where several cages with tiny budgerigars were huddled up together in the cold, waiting to be bought. She hated the thought of any creatures being caged up. To her way of thinking, everyone and everything was entitled to its freedom, including herself. By the time Mrs Winnet had purchased her dried fruit at the cart, it was coming on to rain – just a light sprinkle of late autumn mist, but enough to see a flurry of umbrellas spurred into action, so that within minutes the sea of ladies' hats, long frock coats and shopping bags was completely hidden beneath the ceiling of coloured brollies.

'*What* man, Winnie?' asked Rosie impatiently, the moment Mrs Winnet emerged from the queue, and whilst both women struggled to put up their own umbrellas.

'Some preacher or somefin' who comes ter visit 'er a couple er times a week,' said Mrs Winnet. 'Only when yer dad's not there, that is. Mind you, he does know this man. They went ter one of 'is lectures up West about a year or so ago. Awful-lookin' man, big dark eyes, pointed chin, wears a long black jacket, and trousers tucked into 'is boots. Gives me the creeps just ter look at 'im.' She shivered. 'I think yer mum's got it into 'er mind that 'e can 'elp or somefin', a bit like that terrible man in Russia – Ras somefin' or uvver.'

Rosie's stomach turned over. As they continued to make slow progress through the sea of umbrellas, she did recall her parents going to the lecture this man gave. The thought that her mother was seeing him on a regular basis unsettled her deeply, for as she remembered, the lecture had turned out to be about spiritualism.

'Still,' continued Mrs Winnet as they struggled through the damp crowds of shoppers, 'two wrongs don't make a right. Are you absolutely sure you wanna go off and live wiv this boy?'

'You think I'm making a mistake, Winnie?'

'I'm not sayin' yer are, an' I'm not sayin' yer not. All I'm sayin' is yer should be careful.'

'But I thought you liked Joe?' asked Rosie. 'You and he seem to get on so well together.'

'Whevver I get on well wiv 'im or not 'as got nuffin' ter do wiv it,' said Mrs Winnet, pulling her coat collar up snugly around her neck. 'The point is, can yer trust 'im ter look after yer, not only in bad times but good as well?'

'I *have* to get away from home, Winnie,' said Rosie. 'If I don't, I think I'll go stark raving mad.'

Mrs Winnet brought them to a halt outside a baker's shop where the sweet smell of freshly baked bread was drifting up from the ovens in the cellars below. 'Is that a good enough reason fer jumpin' out of the fryin' pan inter the fire?' she asked.

'You think that's what I'm doing?' asked Rosie anxiously.

The rain was now dripping down from the spokes of Mrs Winnet's umbrella. 'All I'm sayin' is that yer shouldn't blame yer dad *too* much,' she replied. 'I 'appen ter know 'e's only finkin' about you, Miss Rosie. 'E's a good man, your dad. There's nuffin' selfish about *'im.*' She sighed. 'I only wish I could say the same about yer mum.'

When Joe got back home, he was surprised but over the moon to find his dad in the back parlour, tucking into one of Annie's scrag end of mutton stews. Friday evening was usually the family's fish and chip night, but since Will Upton had spent the past few months in the trenches in Belgium, Annie was determined to make his dreams come true. What Paul had told Rosie about his dad was only partially true. There was certainly a similarity in their personalities. Both of them had an eye for the girls, and when they were together they often exchanged stories about who they had both fancied. But physically, Will was, unlike either of his sons, brawny, with a boxer's nose, square jaw and dark grey eyes. When he had joined up at the beginning of the war, Annie knew only too well that he had done so to get away from her, and have a good time on his own, even if that time in the trenches had not proved to be quite as good as he might have expected.

'So who's the little lass I've bin 'earing so much about, Joe?' asked Will, mouth full of stew, his Yorkshire accent more pronounced than either of his two boys, mainly because he was serving in a Yorkshire regiment. 'She sounds quite a catch.'

'She's more than that, Dad,' replied Joe, warming his hands in front of the oven grate. 'She's special.'

'All lasses are special, lad,' said Will, shiftily. 'As long as you treat 'em right.'

'Well, *I* fink she's lovely,' said Gran, who was having great difficulty, with arthritic fingers, trying to knit a scarf for herself. 'A real lady.'

'That's grand,' said Will, with a grin. 'Makes a

274

'nice change.'

Annie, who was in the scullery, ironing, did not react to his remark.

'Mind you,' said Will, 'she can't be that much of a lady if you two intend moving in wi' each other.'

'But yer don't mind,' asked Joe, 'do yer, Dad?'

'*Me?*' replied Will. 'Why should *I* mind? If it's all right wiv yer mam, it's all right wi' me. Right, Annie?'

'Nowt to do wi' me,' called Annie from the scullery. 'Kids of today do as they want.'

'But what about her ol' man?' asked Will, pouring himself a glass of brown ale at the parlour table. 'What's 'e say about all this – about you kipping down wi' 'is daughter?'

Joe shrugged.

'You *'ave* talked it over wi' 'im, 'aven't you?'

'I asked 'im if I could marry Rosie,' replied Joe. 'He said no.'

Will roared with laughter. 'So that's why you and this lass are moving in together? Sounds to me like you're asking for trouble, lad!'

'I don't see wot else I can do,' replied Joe, irritated by his dad's insensitivity. 'I love Rosie, and I want us ter be tergevver.'

'What you're doing's got nowt to do wi' love, my lad!' said Will, lecherously.

Gran looked up with a start. 'Don't you be so coarse, William Upton,' she said. 'Joe's not like that, an' you know it!'

The moment the old girl had returned to her knitting, Will pulled a face at her. Then he nodded to Joe to follow him into the front

275

parlour. The room was bitterly cold, for there was no fire in there, but Will didn't seem to care. He immediately flopped down on to the old thread-worn sofa and lit up a fag.

'Don't look so fed up wi' t' world, lad,' he said to Joe, who remained standing with his back to the unlit fire in the grate. 'Worse things can 'appen, believe me. Much worse.' He looked up at Joe, and he suddenly felt a wave of affection for the boy. Their relationship had always been much different from that between Paul and his dad, and Will was aware that if he ever said the wrong thing to Joe, the boy would take it to heart. 'You an' me've 'ad a pretty rough time of it, lad?' he said. 'You in France, me in Belgium. If only I'd known what I know now, yer'd never've got me anywhere near that recruiting centre. We was conned, you know that, don't you? Conned inter owt that we never knew nowt about, and still know nowt about. When I 'eard about you getting caught up in that poison-gas attack, I wanted to go out and kill every bloody general I could lay me 'ands on. The thought of a lad of mine coughing 'is lungs out cut me up, I can tell yer.' He took a deep puff of his fag, and filled the small room with smoke. The tattoos of snakes on both his arms seemed to take on a living form as he moved, but the pain he was suffering inside had nothing to do with snakes, it was to do with the horrors of all he had left behind in the front-line dugouts.

'You mind, Joe,' he continued, 'I can put up wi' most things meself, but when it's one of me own...' He looked away. 'What I'm trying to say

276

is – and I'm not much good at this sort of thing – that after all you and me've bin through, the idea that some old gasbag won't let you marry 'is daughter is the least of your problems. You know about me and your mam. You know what 'appened all them years ago. But we still survive. Despite that, in a funny sort of way we still think sommat of each other. So if you want to go off and kip down wi' this lass, then you go ahead an' do it, lad, 'cos I for one won't stop you.'

Joe was taken aback by the frankness and unusual understanding his dad was showing. It was something he had not experienced before, for Will Upton had never been the kind of dad who would take time out to give his boys advice.

'Unfortunately,' Joe said awkwardly, 'it's not as easy as that. The fact is, wiv my condition, I don't see 'ow I'm goin' ter find a job. An' wivout a job, 'ow am I goin' ter find the money ter keep a wife?'

'Is that what 'e told you?' asked Will. 'The old gasbag?'

'More or less,' replied Joe. 'But it's true.'

'You want some brass?'

Joe swung a startled look at him.

'*I'll* give you some,' said Will, getting up and digging his hand into his pocket. ''Ere you go. It's not much, but it'll give you a lift up for the time being.'

Joe was staggered. He couldn't believe his eyes as his dad held out two one-pound notes for him.

'Go on – take it!' said Will. 'I don't need it. You don't 'ave to fret, I've not nicked it!'

Joe stretched out slowly, and tentatively took

the two notes.

'You know where that come from?' asked Will with a mischievous grin. 'I won it in a bet. These mates of mine, soon after we fought our way into this town in Belgium, they bet me that I'd never find a lass who'd sleep wi' me. Well, I did. She was the daughter of the local butcher. An' I tell yer sommat, she was out of this world: slim, blonde frizzy hair, clear skin, green eyes, an' legs that ... well, I'll leave the rest to yer imagination.'

Joe handed the notes back to him. 'I'm sorry, Dad,' he said, with anguish. 'I can't take this. It wouldn't be right.'

Will looked at him in absolute astonishment. 'Why not? 'Cos I gambled on sommat an' won? Or is it 'cos of yer mam?'

Joe turned away and looked into the empty fireplace.

For one moment, Will held on to the two one-pound notes, until his attention gradually wandered up to the two sepia photographs of his boys, one on each side of the fireplace on the walls of the two alcoves. It showed them when they were young kids years before, pulling up carrots in the fields in Yorkshire. Looking at them and remembering those days brought a smile to Will's face. His two boys were so different then, and even more so now. Paul, the cheeky one, out for a good time whatever the cost, a real girl-getter, just like his dad. On the other hand, Joe was the quiet, shy, sensitive one, always nervous about getting involved with things that were not straightforward. 'No-risk Joe' his dad used to call him. That's what his youngest son was like even now.

'Let me tell you sommat, Joe,' he said, speaking quietly to the boy over his shoulder. 'You're not a kid no more. You and me, we've both bin in the trenches. You're a man now. You 'ave to realise that people do wot they 'ave to do, 'cos when we die, we're dead for a 'eck of a long time.' He took hold of Joe's arm, and gently eased him round to face him. 'Know what I mean?'

Joe was glum. After thinking about what his father had said for a moment, he slowly shook his head.

Will smiled. 'Well, you will, lad,' he said, pressng the two one-pound notes back into the palm of Joe's hand. 'Believe me, sooner or later – you will.'

Forest Gate was a suburb of East London in the borough of West Ham, little more than five miles from Islington, a spit and a cough from West Ham Park to the south and Wanstead Flats to the north. It also wasn't all that far from Epping Forest, where, when they first came to London, Joe, Paul and their dad often used to go newt hunting with their home-made fishing nets in the large natural pond. Although Forest Gate wasn't famous for anything in particular, it was a pleasant enough place. The people who lived there were, on the whole, working class, and lived in little backstreet houses built during Victorian times, families invariably sharing with other tenants. There was also a railway station nearby, which, during the summer months, was crowded with holidaymakers and day-trippers bound for the ever popular seaside resort of Southend, known to North Londoners and East Enders as 'London by the Sea'.

When Rosie and Joe got off the tram at Forest Gate, it took them some time to find Cuthbert Jiggles' place. This was mainly due to old Monty Gubble's directions, which were, somewhat vague and muddled, to say the least. After making enquiries on the way, they did eventually find the place, which turned out to be more of a cottage, standing all on its own at the end of a cul-de-sac almost directly beneath a railway arch. The cottage's appearance was quite a shock to Rosie and Joe, for, despite Monty's assurances that they wouldn't be disappointed, they couldn't actually see how there could be much room for them. However, when Cuthbert himself appeared at the door, they soon discovered things weren't all they seemed.

'Monty Gubble?' asked the old man at the front door. 'Course I know 'im! Me an' Private Monty were Raglan's boys down the Crimea. We've bin like bruvvers ever since. Don't worry, 'e wrote me you was comin', so wot yer standin' on the doorstep for? I don't stand on ceremony in *my* 'ouse, yer know!'

Despite the fact that he was not at all what Rosie had expected, she adored him on sight. If Monty was older than the Tower of London, she thought, then Cuthbert was surely a survivor of the Stone Age, for his long white beard reached almost to his waist, and his head was completely hairless and so shiny that it looked like a billiard ball. In fact, Cuthbert and Monty were so alike Rosie reckoned they could almost be brothers.

But what fascinated Rosie and Joe about Cuthbert was the old army tunic he wore – bright scarlet, with gold cuffs and buttons, as smart as if he were just marching off to the Crimea. And the cottage itself was little short of a revelation, decked out patriotically with flags and bunting, faded old pictures and cuttings from newspapers and magazines showing scenes from the Crimean War, a soldier's bayonet mounted on the wall, together with an effigy of Tsar Nicholas I, who was responsible for the aggressive policy of trying to form a Russian empire throughout the whole of South-East Europe, and the avowed enemy of the British and Allied troops who were sent there to thwart him.

'Right!' said Cuthbert. 'Sit yerself down – no, not you, young gel! Go an' put the kettle on. I could do with a nice cuppa tea. Two sugars, please.'

Rosie threw a grin at Joe, and found her way into the kitchen, which, to say the least, was like a junk shop, full of pots and pans that clearly hadn't been washed for weeks, half-eaten chicken legs and vegetables, and a gas stove that would clearly soon be on exhibition in a museum. But once she had found a teapot and cups, her biggest shock came when she turned on the tap at the old stone sink and the whole place shook as the water pipes rumbled and grumbled and complained bitterly about being neglected.

'Take no notice er that!' yelled Cuthbert from the next room. 'That fing ain't worked proper since me an' Gladys moved in!'

A few minutes later, Rosie achieved the near-impossible, and brought in a tray with three cups of tea without saucers.

'Coals to Newcastle, eh, gel?' said Cuthbert, with a chuckle.

Rosie looked puzzled.

'Monty said in his note you serve tea ter the boys up at Charing Cross Station,' he explained. 'Is that right?'

Rosie nodded. 'Yes,' she replied. 'For the time being, anyway.'

'Well done!' said Cuthbert. 'We 'ad a gel like you out in Sebastopol. Name er Kitty. Always forget ter give me sugar. 'Ave *you* put sugar in mine?'

Rosie assured him that she had, and gave him his cup of tea.

'So you two want ter come an' live wiv ol' Cuffbert, do yer?' said the old rogue.

Rosie exchanged an anxious look with Joe, and allowed him to answer the question.

'Well, not exactly, Mr Jiggles,' replied Joe.

'Wot d'yer mean, "not exactly"?' snapped Cuthbert irritably. 'Eivver yer do or yer don't!'

'No,' stuttered Joe, 'wot I mean is – well, it don't look as though yer've got much room ter put people up. 'Ow many rooms do yer 'ave 'ere?'

'I've got this room, I've got me kitchen, I've got me bedroom, and I've got me lav in the back yard. That's quite enuff!' As he hadn't a tooth in his head, he was so animated he repeatedly sprayed Joe with spittle. 'In any case, it's none of yer business 'ow many rooms I 'ave.'

'But if we're goin' ter rent a room 'ere,' replied Joe, wiping his face with the back of his hand, 'where is it?'

At once, Cuthbert, discarding the tea Rosie had just made for him, led the two of them out into the back yard. For this expedition, he had put on his army cap, and once they had passed through a door at the far end of the yard, he used his walking stick to beat a path for them through the undergrowth full of weeds, dead Michaelmas daisies and fallen leaves. 'Follow me, men!' he called as he led his troops.

They eventually reached a clearing, which opened out on to what looked like a disused railway track, evidently not used for years, and which lay at the top of a steep bank. Joe helped the old boy to climb up the bank, leaving Rosie, at her own request, to make her own way. Once they had reached the top, behind them in the distance on one side they could see a clutch of houses and shacks that seemed to be the boundary of Forest Gate, but on the other side of the track Joe was first to see something that virtually took his breath away.

''Ere we are then!' announced Cuthbert breathlessly, proudly. ''Ome from 'ome! All mod cons, an' a bargain at twice the price.'

'Blimey!' gasped Joe as he stretched out his hand to help Rosie reach the top of the bank. 'Take a look at this!'

Down below, nestling imperiously in the middle of a muddy field, was a battered old railway carriage, inscribed on the side with faded gold letters: 'GREAT EASTERN'.

'That's my ol' gel,' said Cuthbert affectionately. 'That's my ol' Bess. She's done a few miles in 'er time, I can tell yer – just like me!'

Rosie suddenly roared with laughter, so much so that it echoed around the field and across the track.

'Rosie!' spluttered Joe. 'What're yer laughin' at? This is no good. We can't live 'ere. That's not an 'ome. That's not an 'ouse. We can't live in a place like that!'

This only made Rosie laugh even more. 'Why not?' she replied.

''Cos,' spluttered Joe, ''cos – well, we just can't, that's all!'

'Oh, Joe!' gushed Rosie excitedly, throwing her arms around him. 'Of course we can live there. I love the place. I absolutely love it!'

Old Cuthbert watched the couple in total bewilderment, and wondered what the hell he was letting himself in for.

Chapter 16

The moment Rosie climbed the two steps up to the old railway carriage, the door handle came away in her hand.

'Yer can fix that in a jiffy,' said Cuthbert with total confidence. He took the door handle from her and shoved it straight back in where it came from. 'Just needs a coupla screws an' Dad's yer farvver!'

Joe clutched his head in despair, and followed Rosie up into the carriage. What they saw was astonishing, for nearly all the interior fittings had been removed, and the whole thing had been converted into what looked like really comfortable living quarters – narrow and shabby, but definitely comfortable. On the carriage window was a sticker showing: 'THIRD CLASS'.

'It's a nice kitchen, Joe,' said Rosie, as all three of them came in through the main carriage door. 'Just needs a bit of a clean-up.'

'Yer can say that again,' grumbled Joe, wiping his finger along the hotplate of the antiquated gas cooker. 'Yer'd be lucky ter get a kettle of water ter boil on 'ere.'

'Yer may like ter know that me an' Gladys 'ad many a meal in 'ere, young feller-me-lad,' said Cuthbert. 'It was like goin' on 'oliday.' He sighed. ''Appy days!'

They moved on through a set of curtains that led into the next section, which was a dining-cum-living room, with a table and two chairs, a small sofa and a narrow dresser set into a recess by the window on one side of the carriage. Rosie had a perpetual smile on her face as they looked around the place, quickly working out in her mind how she could make use of what was on offer.

'But this is the real piece of resistance,' said Cuthbert, glowing with pride as he showed them through the next curtain into a vacant area that contained a door, marked 'LADIES ONLY', which he opened. 'Yer don't see many indoor lavs like this,' he bragged. 'No rushin' outside in the cold durin' the night!'

Joe peered in. The tiny compartment contained

nothing more than a slops bin.

'Of course,' said Cuthbert, 'yer 'ave ter do a bit of emptyin' every so often.'

Joe sighed. He was used to a proper outside lav in the back yard at Bethnal Green.

Rosie peered in over his shoulder. 'We'll manage,' she whispered in his ear reassuringly.

'I'm not going any furvver,' said Cuthbert. 'That next room is where me an' Gladys slept when we come out 'ere. It brings back too many memories fer me.' He left them, and went back to wait for them in the living room.

Rosie took hold of the door handle, but suddenly got nervous, so she sent Joe in. For a moment or so, she waited anxiously for his reaction. But when she didn't hear anything coming from the room, she called quietly: 'Joe?' With no reply, she gently pushed open the door, and peered in. Joe was stretched out on the bare mattress of a brass double bedstead. Embarrassed at first, Rosie gradually entered, then suddenly leaped on the mattress at the side of him. 'Oh, Joe!' she babbled excitedly. 'This is so wonderful! I feel like an old married woman already.'

'Now don't you get any funny ideas, miss!' he joked.

Rosie giggled like a naughty schoolgirl. She was in heaven.

They looked around at the bare walls. There had clearly once been some photos hanging there, which had been taken away, leaving clean white spaces, but the only thing that *had* remained was a lady's feather hat, which was hanging on a hook behind the door. For a moment, Rosie lay there deep in thought, thinking about old Cuthbert and his wife, Gladys, sleeping on the bed where she and Joe were lying now. For Rosie, that hat behind the door told quite a story – the story of two people who loved each other a great deal. It prompted her to turn to face Joe, who was himself miles away, staring at the ceiling as though it was as far and as infinite as a night sky full of stars.

She slipped her hand under his jacket to keep warm. '"Rosie Lee, Rosie Lee, How I love my Rosie Lee..." Joe, it's lovely.'

Joe was embarrassed. 'Oh, that ol' fing,' he muttered. 'We all did fings like that when we was down the dugout. It kept us goin' while we waited ter go over the top. But I never wrote anyfin' down. I used ter get this mate er mine ter do it for me.'

'But this one you *must* have written down yourself,' Rosie reminded him.

'Yeah, that's right,' replied Joe awkwardly, clearly covering up. 'I'm a poet an' don't know it!' He chuckled at his own pun.

'*I* think it's the most beautiful poem I've ever read,' she said wistfully. 'I know it all by heart, word for word.' To prove it, she started to recite:

'Rosie Lee, Rosie Lee,
Oh, how I love you,
Saviour of life, weaver of dreams,
Oh, how I love you.'

At this point, Joe started to recite with her.

'Dark of night, cold outside,
War, bombs and danger.

287

But warm and tender is your touch,
A glow of light, a ray of hope...'

Joe completed the last line himself.

'Oh, Rosie Lee, how I love you.'

Their lips moved close together, and they kissed.
'Oy! You two in there!'
Old Cuthbert's voice calling to them from outside, and his banging on the window with his walking stick, sent them leaping off the bed.
''Ow much longer?' yelled Cuthbert. 'It's perishin' out here. Yer must've made yer mind up by now!'
Adjusting their clothes quickly, Rosie and Joe rushed out to meet him.
'Sorry about that, Mr Jiggles,' Rosie said. 'We just wanted to get a proper feel of the place.'
'Oh, yes?' sniffed the old boy sceptically. 'I've 'eard all that before. Now are yer goin' ter take the place, or ain't yer?'
Rosie exchanged one quick glance with Joe, before she let him answer. ''Ow much?' Joe asked.
''Ow much?' replied Cuthbert. 'What yer talkin' about? I don't want no money.'
Joe's eyes nearly popped out of his head. 'No money? Yer mean, buckshee?'
'That's right,' replied Cuthbert. 'On one condition, that is.'
Joe exchanged a sceptical look with Rosie. 'Oh, yeah,' he replied. 'Wos that?'
'In exchange for this beautiful 'ome that I am so generously off'rin',' said Cuthbert with a

288

twinkle in his eye, 'I get my place cleaned up once a week, plus a tidy-up every day. There's two of yer, so once yer've got fings organised, it shouldn't take yer long. Wot d'yer say?'

Rosie was so excited she could hardly breathe. 'Oh, Mr Jiggles!' she gushed, throwing her arms around him and hugging him tight. 'We'll be happy to clean for you, won't we, Joe?'

Cuthbert was taken aback and embarrassed by Rosie's outburst, so before Joe had a chance to answer, he broke loose. 'I ain't finished yet, young gel!' he said irascibly. 'There's one more fing.'

Rosie's excitement suddenly waned. 'What's that?' she asked apprehensively.

'I want one good meal cooked fer me each day,' answered the old codger. 'Yes, an' a decent cuppa tea brought ter me every mornin'. An' when yer make it, don't ferget me sugar!'

Marian Little always looked forward to her Saturdays. Not only was it the one day of the week that Richard took sole charge of being with Christian, but it was also the time when she could do anything, or go out anywhere she wanted. Today, she had something special she wanted to do, so she made quite sure that she chose the right dress, hat and veil, gloves and topcoat, but also a neat and tidy head of hair, for which she spent a great deal of time at her dressing-table mirror. Marian was a beautiful woman, and when she dressed up she turned many an eye. But just of late, she was showing the strain of all the problems that were besetting the family, and, in particular, Rosie's wild relationship with a boy from such an alien environment to her own. After Richard had refused his permission for Rosie to get married to the boy, Marian had hoped that the matter had been settled once and for all. However, that did not seem to be the case, for Rosie was spending far too much time away from home, which Marian thought inappropriate for a girl of her age. Therefore, something had to be done, and done quickly, and the only person who could give her some firm advice was her dear friend Mr Willoughby.

The houses in Canonbury Square were tall and elegant, homes for the rich and famous, with a sixteenth-century tower in adjoining Canonbury Place, an unusual and fascinating building which locals seemed to take for granted. Marian loved coming to such a place because it reminded her of her maiden days when she'd attended a finishing school in a house just like one of these, in Kensington.

When she reached the house she was looking for, Mr Willoughby greeted her with his customary good manners, and once they had settled down to talk in his tastefully furnished drawing room, his housekeeper brought in tea on a silver engraved tray, and served it from a classic silver teapot into a fine bone-china Royal Albert tea set.

'It really is good of you to see me, Mr Willoughby,' said Marian, sitting opposite him on the chaise longue, raising her veil to reveal her slightly powdered features. 'I know how busy you are, but the fact is, I have such a problem on my hands that I really do need your advice.'

Mr Willoughby was not a bit like the portrait painted of him to Joe by Mrs Winnet. He was, in fact, quite a pleasant-looking man, in no way resembling the infamous Rasputin in Tsarist Russia. Admittedly Mr Willoughby was tall and thin, but he had a kind face and welcoming eyes, and a wonderful flock of dark hair that just reached the collar of his jacket.

'I presume it's that young daughter of yours again?' he asked, using his teeth to hold on to his pipe that seemed to need relighting a great many times.

'I'm afraid so,' replied Marian. 'She now wants to get married to this boy from the East End.'

'Ah!' replied Mr Willoughby, sitting back in his armchair, watching his visitor with intense concentration.

'Needless to say, my husband is quite adamant that nothing of the sort will happen.' Marian nervously crossed her ankles and uncrossed them again almost immediately.

'Oh, really?' asked Mr Willoughby.

'Indeed, yes,' replied Marian firmly. 'He was quite forceful with her, made it very clear that he would not tolerate her disobeying his orders.'

'And what was her response?'

Marian sighed, and picked up her teacup and saucer. 'Unfortunately, Rose has become such a self-willed young creature,' she said. 'I just don't understand it. She was such a loving child when she was young.'

Mr Willoughby sat back in his chair and eyed her with some scepticism. 'I'm afraid the world is moving on fast, Mrs Little. This war has turned the heads of quite a lot of people.'

Marian sipped her tea with very little pleasure. She had hoped – indeed, expected – a more positive reply from her host. After all, she had admired his work ever since she and her husband had listened to one of his lectures about life after death more than a year before. In fact, Joshua Willoughby was renowned for his insight into the living *and* the dead. His lecture, which had been called 'The Other Side', had been rich in information about how the dead can influence the living by warning them of the disasters that might befall them if they didn't listen to the teachings of philosophers like himself. That is why Marian had gone to visit him in the first place. After all, Mr Willoughby *was* a spiritualist, and she was sure that he was the one person with whose help she could enlist the aid of past members of her family to put Rose back on to the straight and narrow path of common sense.

'I don't mean to sound discourteous, Mr Willoughby,' she said, peering at him over the top of her teacup, 'but I really am quite tired of listening to that excuse.'

'Excuse?' Mr Willoughby was a bit stung by her remark.

'The war is an excuse for everything and everybody,' she replied. 'In my opinion, people rely too much on that premise to disguise their own weaknesses.'

Mr Willoughby was quite taken aback by her acid remark. 'Mrs Little,' he asked, sitting forward in his chair and fixing her with eyes that seemed to look right through her, 'what exactly do you want me to do to help you in your predicament?'

Marian put her cup and saucer down on the polished coffee table in front of her, and dabbed her lips with her handkerchief. 'Let me talk to those whom I have loved in the past. Let me see if there is some way they can offer me the advice I so desperately need.'

Again Mr Willoughby was taken aback. 'Mrs Little,' he said, sucking on his pipe and exhaling a thin river of rich tobacco smoke, 'the only way you could do that is if I were to hold a seance in your house.'

Marian nodded slightly, but graciously.

'You're prepared to undertake such a thing?'

'I am prepared to undertake anything that would give me back my daughter.'

Even with all his worldly knowledge and wisdom, Mr Willoughby was shocked. At the same time, he was intrigued by this woman's bold approach. After a moment's thought, he got up from his chair and went to sit nearby on the stool at his Steinway grand piano. 'Mrs Little,' he said, 'Sir Arthur Conan Doyle once said that spiritualism is a religion for those who find themselves outside all religions. Do you consider *yourself* to be a religious woman?'

'Of course,' replied Marian, unflinchingly.

'Then I fail to see how my practice can help you.'

Feeling herself to be in a tight corner, Marian thought carefully before replying, and when she finally did, she turned to face the fire in the magnificent grate with its fine grey marble surround.

'Mr Willoughby,' she said slowly, as though recalling something that had clearly preyed on her mind for some time, 'I heard recently of a mother who had lost her son in one of the early battles of the war – at Mons, a small Belgian town near the French border. It was, as you can imagine, a bitter, terrible blow for the poor woman, so much so that she herself had contemplated taking her own life, despite the loving support from her husband at a time of such grief. But, by chance, she met someone who offered to help her, a modest enough woman who works in the same field as yourself, who I'm sure you know but whom, for obvious reasons, I'm not inclined to name. However, distraught though the grieving mother was, she agreed to take part in a seance in a desperate attempt to make contact with the spirit of her dearly departed son. The only reason for doing this was to say goodbye to him, something that had been denied her by the brutality of battle. Suffice to say, contact *was* made, and through the medium her son sent her reassuring words that convinced her that she should go on living and wait until the allocated time before they met again.' She stared into the fire, mesmerised by what she had just recounted. Then she turned to look across at Mr Willoughby, whose head was bowed reverently, pipe smouldering away in an ashtray on a small table beside the piano.

'Fortunately, my woes are nothing to do with grief,' she continued, 'nothing to do with the type of anguish suffered by that poor lost soul. But they *are* to do with love, Mr Willoughby. I love my daughter, and I love my son and, as long as I live,

I have to do for them what I think, what I *know*, is right. Will you help me to do that, Mr Willoughby? Will you?'

On the top deck of the tram going home from Forest Gate, Rosie was brimming with ideas about how she and Joe were going to adapt to living in an old railway carriage.

'Cuthbert said it's mounted on a length of track that was once used as a siding for storing railway stock. He also said the main line goes straight to Southend. Gosh, Joe! Just think of it. Once we've moved in we could go on a day trip to the sea. I haven't seen the sea since my parents used to take Christian and me on our annual holidays to Hayling Island down in Hampshire. Would you like to do that, Joe? Would you?'

Joe was very sullen, and for most of the journey he had stared out of the tram window, not participating in Rosie's intense enthusiasm. 'Rosie, tell me somefin' quite honest,' he asked eventually. 'Are yer sure about all this?'

Rosie did a double take. 'Sure?' she asked in astonishment. 'Sure about what?'

'About leavin' 'ome,' he said. 'About movin' in to a place like that?'

'Joe! What are you trying to say? I thought you wanted us to move in together?'

'Er course I do!' he insisted defensively. 'It's just that I'm worried about what's goin' ter 'appen between you an' yer mum 'n' dad.'

It took Rosie a moment to take this in. 'Frankly, Joe,' she said, 'I don't care a fig about what *they* think. If my mother had her way, she'd incar-

295

cerate me in that house for the rest of my life. That's not what I want, Joe. I want my freedom.'

'Depends on 'ow much yer 'ave ter pay fer it.'

Joe's remark suddenly depressed her. 'You know, Joe,' she said, 'sometimes you baffle me. One minute you say you want to marry me, and the next you worry about what my parents will think. Well, you *know* what they think, and if we listen to them, there'll be no future for us.'

'Look, Rosie,' said Joe, slipping his arm around her shoulders, 'I want ter marry you all right, but livin' tergevver is a big step, somefin' we 'ave ter work out before we actually do it.'

'So what do you want to work out, Joe?' asked Rosie, who was beginning to get a little huffy with him. 'Will a ring on my finger make you love me any more?'

Joe didn't like that. 'Stop gettin' on your 'igh 'orse, Rosie!' he snapped.

'I am *not* getting on my high horse!' she snapped back, pulling his arm away from her shoulders. 'I am merely trying to point out that we've talked about this over and over again. I mean, I don't see why we went all the way to look at that railway carriage if you're undecided about everything.'

Now Joe was getting depressed by what she was saying. But he found it impossible to tell her that the reason he was expressing doubts now was because of what his mum had said to him: *'She's under age, son... Are you prepared to take that risk?'* Taking a risk in life, *any* risk, wasn't something that came easily to Joe. His dad knew what he was like. He had practically told him so when they talked together. Joe may have bragged about standing up to people, but he couldn't. He never had, and he never could. 'Look, Rosie,' he started to say, but even as he spoke, his mum's voice overwhelmed his words: *'Remember what 'appened to me and your dad ... tell Rosie about it, tell 'er ... tell 'er...'*

'What, Joe?' asked Rosie. 'What are you trying to tell me?'

Before he could speak again, Joe suddenly broke out into a violent fit of coughing. This time it was really quite nasty, and he struggled over and over again to get his breath. 'Sod it!' he shouted out in frustration, prompting the other passengers to look round to see what was going on.

Rosie held on to him tightly until the cough gradually showed signs of abating. 'It's all right, Joe,' she said, trying to comfort and reassure him. 'It's going to be all right. Just remember what the MO said. When you get an attack like this, don't panic.'

'I'm *not* panicking!' he growled through clenched teeth, flopping back exhausted against the seat. 'I'm just bleedin' fed up with all this!'

Rosie held on to him, wiped his face with her handkerchief, then kissed him gently on the forehead. 'I love you, Joe,' she said. 'I won't let any harm come to you.'

'I've got no guts,' he replied breathlessly. 'That's my trouble. I've got no guts.'

'Don't be silly,' she replied. 'I think you're coping with all this wonderfully. Everyone thinks you've got plenty of guts – even your brother, Paul. As a matter of fact, he says he's very fond of you.'

Weak as he was, Joe looked up at her with a start. 'Paul?' he asked.

'Yes,' replied Rosie. 'He said you would never let a cough get *you* down. He was very funny about when you played football at school. He said you nearly always scored a goal for the other side.'

Joe's eyes were bulging wide at her. 'When did you see Paul?' he asked her grimly.

Rosie was suddenly aware that he was cold and tense. 'He – he came to the station,' she stuttered awkwardly. 'To Charing Cross.'

'Wot for?'

Rosie shrugged. 'No particular reason. Just to see the work I was doing.'

'Servin' cups er tea?' His reply was tinged with anger and sarcasm.

'*You've* never complained about that, Joe,' she replied, stung by the thoughtlessness of his remark.

'Keep away from 'im, Rosie,' said Joe, intensely. 'Just keep away from 'im. I don't want yer ter see my bruvver on yer own. Do I make myself clear? I don't want yer ever ter see my bruvver.'

Rosie stared at him in disbelief.

''Cos if yer do,' warned Joe, staring her out, 'yer can ferget about me. Yer can ferget about livin' in a bleedin' railway carriage.'

Chapter 17

On Monday morning, the midday military hospital train from Folkestone arrived on time at Platform 1, Charing Cross Station, to be met as usual by a crowd of relatives and friends. Rosie was there too, handing out as many hot cuppas as she could, together with her own special words of comfort and reassurance to the most seriously injured patients. As she had no assistant to help her, it was tough and exhausting work pouring tea and collecting the empty cups from all parts of the platform. By the time the final casualties had left the train, filed off the platform and out of the station concourse, she had been whistled at by practically every male who had laid eyes on her, not only because she was like a breath of fresh air to men who had been starved of female company since they had left home, but because her reputation as 'Rosie Lee' had rapidly spread to the troops still serving out on the battlefields.

'You're their sweetheart,' one of the VAD nurses told her as she wheeled a seriously injured patient out to one of the ambulances. 'They were all talking about you on the way over.'

Rosie acknowledged with a smile the sweet remark, but was still feeling too upset to take much notice after her terrible row with Joe the day before. She wondered whether things would ever be the same between them again. She was also deeply concerned about the safety of her three friends in The Terrible Four. With a heavy heart, she quickly collected the last of the empty cups, packed them on to her trolley, and made her way to the station canteen kitchen to prepare for the arrival of the next hospital train that afternoon. But just as she reached the barrier, she saw Joe hurrying towards her.

'Rosie!'

Despite the distressing things he had said to her as they were coming back from seeing old Cuthbert's railway carriage at Forest Gate, her face lit up.

'Joe!' she called, as they hugged. 'What are you doing here?'

'I come ter say sorry,' he said awkwardly. 'I don't know wot come over me on that tram. It's just that Paul – well, 'e's me bruvver and I know 'im so well. 'E's got a fing about gels. 'E'll do anyfin' ter chat 'em up – 'e don't care who it is. Oh, don't get me wrong, Rosie. I do love 'im. 'Im an' me've always bin mates. Mind you, if we ever 'ad a scrap, *e'd* be the one that wins. It's just that – well, you're my gel – ain't yer?'

Rosie took a moment to look at him. What she saw was someone who knew so little about life, knew so little about who he could or couldn't trust. 'Of course I'm your girl, Joe,' she answered. 'Your brother means nothing to me, so *please* don't ever think otherwise.'

He hugged her tight. 'If I was ter lose yer now, Rosie Lee,' he said softly into her ear, 'I don't know wot I'd do. Will yer fergive me?'

Before she could answer, a man approached

300

them. 'I 'ope I'm not barging in,' he said.

Rosie was taken by surprise.

'Rosie,' said Joe, eagerly, 'I want yer ter meet my dad. Dad, this is Rosie.'

'Pleased to meet you, Rosie,' said Will Upton, who gave her the kind of look that she had come to expect from Paul.

Rosie shook hands with him. 'How nice to meet you, Mr Upton,' she replied. 'Joe's told me so much about you.'

'All the right things, I 'ope?'

Their laughter seemed a little hollow.

'Is there somewhere we can talk?' asked Joe. 'Dad's home on leave and he wants ter 'ave a quick word wiv us.'

'Well, I've got to get the tea ready for the next train,' she said, 'but we can go over to the station canteen for a few minutes. I'll meet you there once I've got rid of the trolley.'

A few minutes later, the three of them managed to find a table to sit at in the station canteen. The place was crowded to suffocation with soldiers, sailors, their relatives and friends, and the cigarette smoke was so thick you could cut it with a knife. For the first few minutes, Rosie felt a bit uncomfortable to be in the company of Joe's father, feeling much the same as she did when Paul was around. Will Upton was a handsome man, who seemed to have a perpetual smile on his face, which, after a while, Rosie found quite unsettling.

'I just wanted to make sure you two know what you're taking on,' said Will, directing his words mainly to Rosie, whilst sipping from a pint glass of brown ale. 'Me and Joe's mam've bin talking

301

things over, and although we've got no objections to you personally, Rosie, we're worried about what 'appens if Joe's regiment finds out that you two're living together without being married.'

Rosie threw a puzzled look first at Joe, then at his dad. 'Does Joe *have* to tell them?' she asked.

'No,' replied Will. 'But I dare say, it wouldn't be long before they found out.'

'And what could they do about it if they did?' asked Rosie rather grandly.

'To tell you the truth, lass,' replied Will, 'I 'aven't the foggiest. All I know is that the brass caps've got a real bee in their bonnets about the so-called morals of the men serving under 'em. It doesn't matter what they get up to themselves as long as Tommy Private don't do t' same. Oh, they don't mind if we go out and get our 'eads blown off fer King an' country, as long as we don't give the regiment a bad name.'

'Surely this is a free country, Mr Upton?' asked Rosie. 'And in any case, with a war going on, the military would hardly have enough time to keep a check on the home life of every single soldier.'

'Don't you believe it, Rosie,' Will assured her. 'An' the way people be'ave these days, I'm not so sure this *is* a free country. I mean, did yer know what ol' Asquith and 'is lot've got up their sleeves now?'

Rosie shook her head and feared the worst.

'Can you believe they're talking about cutting down the drinking hours in t'pubs?' he lamented. 'A couple of hours in the middle of the day, and only opening from six or so to about nine in t'evenings. And it's even less on Sundays. I mean,

I ask yer, Rosie, what sort of a life is it if a working man can't 'ave a pint whenever 'e wants it? I tell you...' he paused only for a brief moment whilst he gulped down quite a lot of his brown ale, 'this country's going to t'dogs!'

Rosie looked confused. She didn't really understand what pub licensing hours had to do with her and Joe moving in together. 'Mr Upton,' she asked point-blank, 'do you object to what Joe and I want to do?'

'Object?' asked Will, looking first at her, then at Joe. 'No, I don't object, but I can't say I approve.'

'Why not?' Rosie asked, again rather grandly. 'I've heard that since the war started, there are lots of unmarried couples living together. I mean, we have to be realistic about things. For many young people, there might never be a tomorrow. I can't believe that you and Mrs Upton wouldn't have done the same thing if you were in the same position as Joe and me?'

Will exchanged a sudden look of alarm with his son. Rosie's question had clearly taken them both off guard. 'All I can say, Rosie,' he said, loosening the button of his tunic collar, 'is that people aren't ready for this sort of thing. One day mebbe, but not now.'

'Soldier!'

All three of them turned to see a regimental sergeant major standing over them.

'Wot d'yer fink this is?' barked the middle-aged man with a clipped moustache, who was in army uniform and cap, his eyes blazing with anger. 'Stand up when you're in the presence of an RSM.'

Will immediately stood up.

'Stand to attention!'

Watched by all the other soldiers around, Will immediately did as he was told.

The sergeant major was now standing so close to Will that he was practically spitting at him. 'You disgustin' little man!' he snapped, eyeball to eyeball, his moustache twitching as he talked. 'Don't you know you're wearin' the King's uniform?'

'Yes, I do,' replied Will, standing stiffly to attention.

'Yes, you do – *wot?*' barked the man, his voice cracking with indignation.

'Yes, I do, Sergeant Major!' Will replied parrot-fashion.

'An' wot did they teach you in trainin' on the first day you wore the King's uniform?'

'They taught us to respect it, Sergeant Major.'

The man drew even closer to Will. 'Then *do* it, soldier!' shouted the man, to the intense amusement of the other ranks around. 'Do up that button!'

Will immediately did what he was told.

'An' if ever I see you improperly dressed in public again,' yelled the man, 'I'll 'ave yer up before your CO quicker than you can drink 'alf a bitter. Do I make myself clear, soldier? Do I?'

'Yes, Sergeant Major!' snapped Will, his eyes fixed and glazed.

'Right! Carry on!' He turned to Rosie, and touching the brim of his cap with his baton, actually smiled courteously at her. 'Sorry for the intrusion, miss,' he said, ignoring Joe completely.

With that, he strode off.

Will waited for him to go, then gradually sat down again. 'See what I mean?' he said to Rosie. 'But you can't blame '*im*. 'E's only doing what 'e's told to do, what they'd expect everyone else to do. You ask me if I object to the two of you movin' in together. Well, as far as *I'm* concerned, I don't. Go ahead and take the risk, by all means. After all...' he unbuttoned his tunic collar again, 'if you *do* decide to toe the line, you could end up like one of them. An' I wouldn't wish that on *anyone!*'

Joshua Willoughby got out of a taxi immediately in front of the Little residence in Camden Road. It was the first time he had visited the place, and he was not at all impressed – not because of the house itself, which was pleasant enough, but because of the loud chanting of women outside Holloway Prison just down the road, which had held up his taxi in a traffic jam for nearly ten minutes. Although he was pretty much a mild-mannered man, Mr Willoughby was not in the best of moods, for despite doing his best to persuade Mrs Little that using a seance would in no way solve the problems that were besetting her, she was determined to explore every means at her disposal, and that included trying to make contact with her dear departed mother, who would most certainly give her the advice she needed to prevent Rosie from doing something that she would undoubtedly regret for the rest of her life. So, the thought of what he was letting himself in for had been plaguing him ever since the redoubtable Mrs Little had first approached him. He was therefore somewhat surprised to be greeted at the front door by Richard Little.

'Mr Willoughby,' said Richard, showing him in. 'How very kind of you to come.'

'A pleasure, sir,' said Willoughby, not meaning a word of it. 'A pleasure.' He took off his bowler hat and gave it to Richard to hang up for him.

'My wife and her friends are waiting in the drawing room,' said Richard. 'But before we join them, I wonder if I might have a few moments of your time alone?'

'By all means,' replied Willoughby. He followed Richard into his study at the back of the ground floor. It was a small, cosy room, with a fire burning in the grate, which Mr Willoughby made for immediately to warm his freezing-cold hands. 'I trust you have no objections?' he asked, holding up his pipe for Richard to see.

'Not at all,' replied Richard. 'I use one myself from time to time, but I have to be in a more relaxed mood. Please sit down.'

Both men sat facing each other by the fire. The space was rather cramped.

'Mr Willoughby,' began Richard, 'I feel that we've brought you here under false pretences.'

'Oh, yes?' asked Willoughby, lighting up his pipe.

'As you know, I admire enormously the work you're doing,' said Richard. 'That paper on the scientific research into life after death you wrote for the Royal Society was a fascinating piece of work, and well received, I understand?'

Willoughby chuckled. 'Not by *everyone*, Mr

Little,' he replied with an ironic grin. 'Not by everyone.'

'My wife thought it was a revelation.'

Willoughby nodded without comment.

'But I have to say,' continued Richard solemnly, 'that, in my opinion, she's been carried away by the achievements being made in your field, so much so that I feel she doesn't really understand the true nature of your work. You'll forgive my saying, but there *has* been quite a lot of coverage in the national press about spiritualism just lately. It seems that every woman in the land wants to get in touch with a husband, or a son, or a relative killed in this dreadful war. And, present company excepted, of course, there are so many mediums around who are – well, what shall we say...?'

'Fakes?' asked Willoughby, puffing on the stem of his pipe.

Richard shrugged. 'I'm sure you understand what I mean?'

'Yes, Mr Little,' replied Willoughby with an ironic little grin. 'I do.'

'In which case,' said Richard, 'may I ask you a very frank question?'

'My dear fellow, please fire away.'

Richard hesitated. 'My wife,' he said, 'seems to think that by making contact with her late departed mother, she can somehow find a way to get our daughter to do the things that the girl clearly doesn't want to do. Marian doesn't want Rose to get married to someone that she doesn't approve of.' He turned briefly to look into the fire, then back again. 'Mr Willoughby, do we have the right to oppose two people who are so very much in love?'

'Mr Little,' replied Willoughby, sitting forward in his chair, 'I *know* what your wife is trying to do, and I must say that I have the very same misgivings myself. However, you have my asked my opinion, and so I'll tell you. Everyone has the right to do what they think is best for their own children, and in many ways I understand your wife's concerns. But spiritualism is not a philosophy to help solve the problems of the living, it is a belief that the spirits of the dead can help those whom they have left behind by communicating with them through people like me, people who understand what grief is, and how it can affect the lives of those who live on. The problems of the living should *not* be the problems of the dead.'

Richard sat back in his chair. Willoughby had confirmed to him what he already knew. 'Then,' he asked, 'am I correct in thinking that you can't really help my wife at all?'

'Yes, Mr Little,' replied Willoughby. 'You *are* correct. The only person who can do that is you.'

The Biograph Cinema just behind Victoria Station was packed to capacity. A new Charlie Chaplin moving picture was always a great draw, and tonight's evening performances of *The Property Man* and *His Favorite Pastime* were not only a sell-out, but were drawing gales of laughter from most of the soldiers and their girlfriends in the audience. Amongst them were Rosie and Joe, who sat snuggled up together all the way through, laughing uproariously with the rest of them at the inimitable Charlie, but also spending a lot of the time staring into each other's eyes in the flickering light from the picture screen. Even so, Rosie was still relieved when the picture was over, for during the performance Joe had had several nasty coughing fits, brought on by the thick blue haze of cigarette smoke coming from what seemed to be every soldier in the tiny auditorium.

When the picture ended, Rosie and Joe strolled hand in hand back towards the station. They bought some chips from the fish and chip stall in the station forecourt and, before boarding their bus for Holloway, they went to a bench on the concourse to eat them. Eating chips out of a newspaper was a new experience for Rosie.

'You know,' she said, taking a small bite of a hot chip, 'my father once called fish and chips "poor man's food". If this is what poor people eat, then I'm looking forward to being one of them!'

Joe slid one arm around her shoulders whilst eating from the newspaper spread out on his lap. 'So Dad din't put yer off then?' he asked. 'Wot 'e said about takin' the risk?'

'Not at all,' replied Rosie, chewing her hot chip. 'Actually I liked him. I like him a lot. I like the way he says what he thinks. A person should always do that. But he's an odd chap, though.'

'Why d'yer say that?' asked Joe.

'Oh, I don't know,' said Rosie. 'It's the way he looks at one – kind of inquisitive.'

This disturbed Joe. He knew what she was trying to say. He knew only too well.

'He's a very handsome man, isn't he?' continued Rosie. 'I bet he was quite a chap with the girls when he was young – before he was married, of course.'

''E still is.'

Rosie swung a surprised look at him. 'What d'you mean?'

'I mean that Dad still likes the girls,' replied Joe with some difficulty. ''E's just like Paul. They're two of a kind.'

Rosie was a bit taken aback, but tried to make light of what Joe was saying. 'Well,' she said, rolling up her newspaper, 'I suppose there's no harm in a married man liking girls, as long as it goes no further than that.'

Joe turned to look at her. 'Oh, Rosie,' he sighed, 'I only wish it *could* be like that.'

Rosie went quite silent. Somehow, this was something that did not really come as a surprise to her; that wandering eye of Joe's father had definitely disturbed her when she'd met him that morning. At first she thought she was imagining things, but what Joe now said had confirmed her worst fears. 'Oh dear, Joe,' she said anxiously. 'Your poor mother.'

'Yer don't 'ave ter pity 'er eivver!' snapped Joe, suddenly rolling up his newspaper without finishing his chips. '*She* ain't much better!' He got up and took both their newspapers to the nearby rubbish bin.

'Joe!' said Rosie, hurrying across to join him. 'What d'you mean?'

'I don't want ter talk about it!' he said.

'But you *must*,' she insisted. 'If we're going to spend the rest of our lives together we shouldn't keep things from each other.'

'Not now, Rosie,' he begged. 'I don't want ter talk about it now.'

'When?'

'When the time's right.'

'When will that be, Joe? *When?*'

Joe turned to look at her. As he stared into those bright shining eyes, he was afraid his whole world would collapse around him. He loved her so much, and he knew that she loved him. But would she still love him after he had told her what he would sooner or later *have* to tell her? 'Oh, Rosie,' he sighed. 'I just don't know.'

Rosie gave him one of her great big smiles, and hugged him tight. 'You silly old thing,' she said, trying to comfort him.

'Come on now, you two!'

They turned with a start to find a police constable approaching them.

'This is a public thoroughfare,' warned the policeman. 'There's a time an' a place fer all that. On yer way now!'

Rosie and Joe quickly moved on. But they had only gone a few steps when Rosie suddenly brought them to a halt. 'Joe!' she announced with a flourish. 'I've got an idea. Let's go to the railway carriage.'

'Rosie!' gasped Joe. 'You loony or somefin'? This time er night?'

'Why not?' asked Rosie eagerly. 'We've only seen it in daylight so far. I'd love to know what it's like in the dark.'

'Yer wouldn't see a fing!'

'Oh, come on, Joe,' she persisted. 'Stop being

311

such an old fuddy-duddy. There's a candle there. That's all the light we need.'

'It'll be freezin' cold.'

'We can snuggle up, can't we?'

Joe didn't quite know how to answer that one.

'Look,' said Rosie, suddenly excited by the idea, 'I'm pretty sure that if we walk up to Westminster Bridge, we can get a tram straight through there to Forest Gate.'

Joe was now thrown into a real quandary. 'But 'ow we goin' ter get in wivout a key?'

'When I was talking to Cuthbert he told me that the carriage is never locked.'

''E'll do 'is nut if he finds out.'

'Why should he?' asked Rosie. 'I bet you he'll be fast asleep when we get there, and we'll be gone in the morning before he even knows. Oh, come on, Joe! We can test the place out. It'll be fun!'

Joe was anxious, and much undecided.

'Of course,' said Rosie, suddenly aware that she was pushing him too far, 'if you really don't want to...'

Joe hesitated just one more moment. Then he looked up at her and smiled. 'Come on!' he said, grabbing hold of her hand, and leading them off out of the station.

After she had said good night to her three friends, Marian Little stormed back into the drawing room where her husband was stoking up the dying embers in the grate.

'How dare you, Richard?' she growled. 'How dare you humiliate me like that, and in front of my friends too?'

'I'm sorry, Marian,' he replied. He had dreaded this moment ever since he had told her about the conversation he had had earlier that evening with Joshua Willoughby. 'I just didn't want you to make a fool of yourself. It was wrong what you were trying to do, futile.'

'Who are you to tell me what is or isn't futile?' she replied, pacing the room angrily. 'Don't you care about your daughter? Don't you care what is happening to her?'

'Yes, Marian,' he said. 'I *do* care about my daughter. I care about my son too. But I also care about you, and what you were trying to do was extremely dangerous. And I have to say that Willoughby agreed with me.'

'Dangerous?' she asked, shaking with anger. 'What *are* you talking about?'

'Using the dead to help the living *is* dangerous, Marian,' he warned. 'You have no idea *what* forces you could unleash in this house. Don't forget there are evil forces out there as well as good.'

'Rubbish!' insisted Marian. 'All *you* want to do is to close your eyes to the whole thing.'

Now Richard was beginning to get angry with her. 'There is nothing to close my eyes *to*, Marian!' he snapped back. 'We cannot use your dead mother to persuade our daughter to do something she cannot and will not do!'

'That's offensive, Richard!' replied Marian, lowering her voice.

'Offensive or not,' he said, 'we have to realise that Rose is no longer a child.'

'She is only eighteen years of age!' insisted Marian. 'In the eyes of the law–'

'To hell with the eyes of the law!' returned Richard. 'This is our daughter we're talking about, not some seedy criminal from the underworld!'

'So,' said Marian, 'not content with not allowing Mr Willoughby to go ahead with his seance here, you now tell me that, as far as our daughter is concerned, we have absolutely nothing to worry about?' Slowly, she walked right up to him. 'Oh, God, Richard,' she said, her voice croaking with constrained emotion. 'You've changed so much. I don't know you any more.' She left him, and went to the door. As she did so, the grandfather clock sounded ten o'clock. This prompted her to pause and turn back to him. 'Oh, by the way,' she called, 'you may or may not be interested to know that our daughter is not yet home. But I shouldn't worry too much, if I was you. I'm sure it won't disturb your sleep too much.'

The sound of an owl hooting from a tree nearby was soon overtaken by the distant rumble of the night mail train to the Essex coast. Otherwise most of Forest Gate was bathing in the heavenly mist of slumber, helped considerably by the blackout of a cloudy night sky. Rosie and Joe were as quiet as mice, stealing their way through the undergrowth after climbing over the fence at the side of old Cuthbert's back yard. As they had only just made the last tram of the evening, there was now no turning back, and as they struggled to find their way in the dark, Rosie gradually had misgivings about the daring venture she had

314

thrust upon Joe.

By the time they had reached the old railway carriage, they were both frozen to the core, for a night frost was already forming on the damp, sodden weeds, and a thin layer of mist was bringing with it a miserable fine shower of rain.

'What 'appens if 'e's locked the door?' whispered Joe. 'I don't fancy spendin' the night out 'ere, fanks very much.'

Even as he spoke, Rosie turned the door handle, and the door opened. Her heart thumping with excitement, she stepped inside. 'Mind how you go,' she called softly. 'It's a bit dark in here.'

That was an understatement. In fact, it was pitch-black, and as Joe entered, he cursed as he tripped on an old rug by the door, and only just stopped himself from falling to the floor.

Rosie laughed. 'Ssh!' she whispered as he cursed again. 'You're so clumsy, Joe. Be careful you don't wake Cuthbert. If only you smoked,' said Rosie, 'you'd have a box of matches with you.' She quickly corrected herself. 'No, I'm glad you don't smoke. Not with *your* cough.'

What with the place being so dark, and their not being able to see anything, Rosie suddenly became nervous. 'Joe,' she whispered, 'I can't see you. Where are you?' Her anxiety grew when Joe didn't reply. 'Joe? Did you hear me? Where are you?' With still no reply, she was beginning to panic. 'Joe. Please, dear. Don't play games. I've never liked being alone in the dark, even when I was a little girl.'

As she spoke Joe struck a match, and lit a candle.

With great relief, she went to him, and threw her arms round his waist. 'You clever thing!' she said.

He hugged her to him. 'We can't stay 'ere all night, though, Rosie.'

'Why not?' she asked boldly.

'Well,' he said, dithering like mad, 'fer one fing, it's freezin' cold. An' also – well, we shouldn't be doin' this. Not yet. Not till we move in. It don't seem right.'

Rosie began to feel guilty. 'D'you really think so?' she asked. 'I mean, I don't know what difference it makes if we're going to move in together in a few days' time.' When he didn't reply, she leaned her head against his shoulder. 'I'm sorry, Joe,' she said softly.

'Wot for?' he asked.

'For bullying you into this.' She hugged him tighter. 'You know, sometimes I only think about the things that *I* want. I forget that there are two of us, each with a mind of our own. The trouble is, I've fallen head over heels in love with you, and I want to be with you all the time.'

He leaned down and kissed her. The light from the flickering candle was casting dancing shadows across their faces, and their eyes reflected the dingy, unpainted walls of the tiny kitchen they were standing in.

'Shall I tell yer somefin', Rosie Lee?' asked Joe. 'I'd sooner be in 'ere wiv you than anyone else in the 'ole wide world.'

'And so I should hope!' replied Rosie.

She picked up the lighted candle in its holder, then, taking Joe's hand, gently led him through the curtain towards the bedroom at the end of the carriage. He followed her meekly, and without protest. They went in.

'My God!' gasped Rosie. 'Look at this.'

'Wot?' asked Joe, peering in. 'Wot is it?' He also gasped at what he saw. 'Blimey!'

To their astonishment, the bed was already made up, complete with sheets, four pillows, two blankets and a heavyweight eiderdown.

'That cunnin' ol'–'

'No, Joe,' insisted Rosie, correcting him. 'Cuthbert's a *lovely* old man. He must have known. Come on. Let's get into bed.' She pulled back the bedclothes, took off her hat and kicked off her shoes, then with all her clothes on, she leaped in. 'Oh my God!' she squealed. 'It's freezing! Come on, Joe. Come and warm me!'

With some trepidation, Joe did as he was asked. Putting the candle down on a stool at the side of the bed, and kicking off his own shoes, he jumped in beside her, causing the bedsprings to make a terrible pinging sound as he did so. Then he quickly pulled the bedclothes over both of them.

They immediately snuggled up together.

'My nose is freezing!' she grumbled.

He immediately blew hot breath into his hand and covered her nose with it.

'Not so rough!' she said, shivering with the cold.

'My feet are like ice,' said Joe, rubbing them together to try to massage some life back into them.

Rosie used her own feet to help, and they

317

tangled them together in a frantic rush to get warm.

After that, they lay back in absolute silence. It was several minutes before either of them spoke. They just lay there, listening to the owl hooting messages to his lady love outside, allowing time for their own thoughts to sink in.

Joe was first to speak. 'I must say,' he whispered, eyes closed in the dark, 'I never expected it ter be like this.'

'Like what?' asked Rosie.

'Snuggled up in a freezin'-cold bed in a railway carriage in the middle of a field,' he grumbled. 'I'd always 'oped I'd be able ter give my gel somefin' better than *this!*'

She turned to face him. 'I promise you, Joe,' she whispered lovingly, 'this is my idea of heaven.'

She leaned forward and kissed him. He responded, in a way that pleasantly surprised and excited her. With their lips pressed close together, they moved their bodies so that they were touching. After a few moments of lying in that position, Rosie searched for one of Joe's hands and gently placed it on her breast. Encouraged by his sighs, she undid the buttons on the top of her dress, and led his hand inside, under her brassiere, allowing it to rest on her naked breast. Joe was clearly so aroused he felt free to take Rosie's hand, and place it on the bulge in the crutch of his trousers. Rosie groaned, and started to explore. In those few moments, they both forgot all about the cold, and started a slow, rhythmical rolling around and around in the bed. Everything seemed so right, so natural to Rosie.

Just being with the boy she had come to love so much was for her all the proof she needed to start a life of her own. With their lips still pressed tight together, both of them rubbed, caressed and hugged each other's bodies until they were quite breathless. Rosie now knew that the time had come for her to prove her love to him; with his help, she slowly, carefully started to remove first her coat, then her dress. For a moment they lay back just like that, she in only her petticoat; he, bare-chested, wearing only his trousers.

Joe blew out the candle, then turned back to her. 'Rosie?' he asked uncertainly 'Are yer sure about this?'

Rosie didn't reply immediately, but when she did it was with absolute sincerity. 'Oh, yes, my dearest one,' she murmured softly. 'I love you so very much.'

She moved on to her back to allow him to ease himself over her. But the moment he had done so, he suddenly changed his mind and rolled away from her.

'No!' he spluttered in deep anguish. 'I'm sorry, I can't! I just can't!'

Rosie sat up with a horrified start, covering her breasts with the bedclothes. 'Joe!' she cried. 'What is it? What have I done?'

Although she couldn't see him in the dark, she knew he was distressed because his breathing had become fast and erratic.

There was a long silence before Joe finally spoke. 'It's not you, Rosie,' he said. 'It's me. I can't do this. I can't do it till – till yer know what I should've told yer long ago.'

'Oh, God, Joe,' replied Rosie, fearing the worst, imagining some terrible admission. 'What is it? Tell me!'

In the dark, Joe sounded close to tears. 'I'm not,' he began with immense difficulty, 'I'm not – all I seem ter be. My family – me ma an' dad – they did fings – they did fings that – they was wrong, Rosie. They was so wrong. They should never've done it, Rosie. They should never've done it...'

Chapter 18

Rosie held Joe in her arms in bed whilst he told her about the things that had haunted him ever since he was a young boy.

'When she was up in Yorkshire,' he said, his voice barely audible in the dark of the old railway carriage, 'Ma wasn't like she is now. She was a real good-looker – I could show yer pictures. She was thin, wiv a beautiful face, an' eyes that used ter drive the fellers mad. That's the trouble. Ma loved men. She only came alive when she was bunkin' down wiv 'em. Before she'd even met Dad, in just two or three years, she'd 'ad three kids – all boys.' He hesitated, finding it difficult to go on. 'She got rid er the lot of 'em.'

'Got *rid* of them?' asked Rosie, horrified.

'She left each one on the doorstep at the work-house orphanage in Sheffield.'

'Oh God, Joe,' sighed Rosie. 'How terrible.'

'Oh, you ain't 'eard the 'alf of it,' said Joe, sitting up, telling his tale in absolute anguish. 'When Dad came along, she 'ad two more. Paul was one of 'em. I don't know who the uvver one was 'cos I've never seen 'im.'

Rosie was finding all this hard to take in. 'Then – what about *you?*' she hardly dared to ask. 'Who–'

'The feller you met this mornin', Rosie,' replied Joe, ''e ain't my real dad. I 'aven't the foggiest idea where I come from, but it ain't from 'im. An' they 'ave the cheek ter call me the baby er the family!'

Rosie pulled him close, and leaned her head on his shoulder. 'Oh, Joe,' she whispered. 'My poor, poor Joe.'

'It's funny, in't it?' he said reflectively. 'I've often thought, I've got five 'alf bruvvers out there somewhere, and apart from Paul, I don't know any of 'em. I don't know where they are, what they look like, or whevver they feel as bitter about their mum an' dads as I do. All I know is, I've 'ad ter live wiv all this ever since boaf Ma 'n' Dad told me about it.'

'They actually told you all this?' asked Rosie incredulously.

'Oh, yes,' replied Joe. 'Me *an'* Paul. They reckoned it was our right ter know wot kind er parents we 'ave. They disgust me, Rosie.' He lay back on his pillow. 'Yer know, I once went to a fortune-teller at a funfair up at Victoria Park. She was a silly ol' bag – told me more about me past than me future. But she did tell me that this kind er fing 'appens all the time – especially in the workin' classes – people breedin' masses er kids like

321

rabbits. I've never understood why. Maybe it's got somefin' ter do wiv tryin' ter keep warm at night.'

Rosie refused to accept the implication of his remark, and squeezed his hand hard. 'Why didn't you tell me all this before, Joe?' she asked. 'Don't you know that it wouldn't have made any difference to me at all?'

'Of course it makes a diff'rence!' he said, pulling his hand away. 'Don't yer realise, I ain't no one's boy? My farvver, my so-called *real* farvver – I don't who 'e is or where 'e is. I'm a bastard kid, Rosie. You fink you 'ave problems wiv *your* parents, but *my* ma 'n' dad ain't even married!'

Rosie was so taken aback she didn't know what to say.

'Yer see!' said Joe. 'It don't get better. It just gets worse. Everyfin' gets worse an' worse an' worse...' He suddenly broke into a violent fit of coughing. 'Sod it!' he yelled, fighting for breath. 'Sod it! Sod it! Sod it!'

Rosie threw her arms around him, and eased him forward. 'It's all right, Joe,' she said, rubbing his back to try to get the lungs cleared. 'You're not to worry Everything's going to be all right. I'm going to look after you, d'you hear? I'm going to make sure you're going to get strong and healthy again.'

After a few moments, still breathless, Joe gradually recovered.

'Now listen to me, my dear one,' whispered Rosie. 'It makes no difference to me where you come from or from whom. It's not true that you're no one's boy. You're *my* boy, and I'm *your* girl. And I tell you what, we're going to make

322

something of this silly old railway carriage. By the time we're finished with it, it'll be the envy of everyone who lives on the other side of the track. It doesn't matter about the past. We're together, Joe – that's all that counts. You and me – together.'

In the dark, Joe slowly turned towards her. His Rosie Lee was there all right, and as far as *he* was concerned, she always would be.

When Rosie got back home, the welcome light of dawn was gradually flooding the grey rooftops of Camden Road. Down below, Jack the milkman was busy with his deliveries from door to door, soon to be followed by that cheeky young boy Billy Thomas, on his newspaper round before going to school later in the morning. A few doors along, Rosie could hear her neighbour Gert Tagley's mongrel dog, Patch, barking at the milkman, and preparing another hostile reception for the impending arrival of poor old Nick the postman.

Once she had quietly unlocked the front door, Rosie took off her shoes, and, aware that her parents were not yet up, started to tiptoe up the stairs. Before she had got very far, however, she heard Christian calling to her from his bedroom on the ground floor, so she quickly retraced her steps, and, finding the door slightly open, went in to see him.

Christian was sitting in his wheelchair, peering up though the window to the tree outside.

'Chris!' called Rosie softly, closing the door quickly behind her. 'What are you doing up so early?'

'I'm waiting for the two sparrows,' he replied. 'They always come about this time. I've given them names. I call them Itsie and Bitsie. That's because they're always eating bits and pieces of bread I throw out to them.' He turned his wheelchair round to talk to her, but as it was only just getting light, he couldn't really see her too clearly. 'You've been out all night, Rosie,' he said quite casually. 'Were you with Joe?'

Rosie paused a moment before replying. Then she went across to him. 'Yes, Chris,' she replied. 'I was with Joe. How did you know that?'

'Oh, I heard Mother and Father talking about it. Actually they were having a terrible argument. I tried not to listen, but they were shouting, so I couldn't help it.'

'What were they arguing about, Chris?' Rosie asked.

'You,' replied Christian, still looking out for the sparrows. 'Mother said you were spending the night with Joe. Were you, Rosie?'

Rosie hesitated a moment. 'Yes, Chris.'

'Will you be spending more nights with him?'

Again, Rosie hesitated. 'Yes, Chris,' she replied. 'I will.'

'*Every* night?'

Rosie gently kneeled down beside him, and held one of his hands. 'Yes, Chris,' she said. 'I *will* be spending every single night with Joe. Will you mind that?'

'No,' he replied. He turned to look at her. His face in the gloomy early morning light seemed to be paler than ever. 'Not if you don't forget about *me*. Not if you come back and see me, and talk with me like we've always done.'

She squeezed his hand. It felt so cold, and yet his heart was so warm. Christian was not just her brother, he was her friend, and the very thought that she might never see him ever again brought a horrible empty feeling in her stomach. 'Chris,' she said softly, taking his hand and holding it tenderly against her cheek, 'I would never forget *you*. How could I? We've had so many good times together, haven't we?'

Christian nodded.

'Joe's your friend too,' said Rosie. 'He told me before I left him this morning that as soon as he can get over to see you, he's going to teach you some more bird sounds. Would you like that?'

The boy's eyes immediately lit up. 'Yes!' he replied, excitedly. 'And d'you know what? I'd like to go to the zoo. I read this book about a doctor who talked to the animals. I want to go and see if I can do the same. Especially crocodiles. D'you think *they* can talk too? I've never seen a crocodile – not for real, that is – but I'd like to watch one talking. Can you imagine it, with those great big jaws?'

'Joe and I will take you to the zoo, Chris,' said Rosie, fighting back tears.

'*Will* you?' The boy was moving his body up and down with excitement. 'Will you really?'

'Of course we will!' promised Rosie. 'Joe and I will make sure you get to talk to all the animals you want.'

Christian sighed with pleasure at the thought. 'That's wonderful!' he said. 'Father said he'd take me to the zoo one day, but he never has. He

325

always seems to be so busy.'

'Listen to me, Chris,' said Rosie. 'There's something I want you to do for me.' She drew closer, and lowered her voice. 'When I leave here, if ever there's a time when you're worried about something – anything at all – will you promise me that you'll tell Mrs Winnet? She'll know what to do. She'll get in touch with me, and I'll come over and see you right away. Will you promise me you'll do that?'

Christian nodded.

'You know, Chris,' continued Rosie, 'sometimes people think they're doing things for the best. But no matter how well intentioned they are, they can often do more harm than good. None the less, when they do the things they do, it's because they love you. I know it may be a strange way of showing love, but sometimes it's all they know. All I'm saying is that when you're feeling low, try not to blame those who love you more than you think.'

'What are you doing out of bed, Christian?'

Rosie looked up with a start to find her mother, in dressing gown, standing in the open doorway.

'How many times have I told you?' said Marian, coming across to them. 'You need your sleep, darling. It's far too early for you to get out of bed.' Ignoring Rosie, who was just getting to her feet, she wheeled Christian back to his bed.

'But, Mother,' protested Christian, as he was lifted out of his wheelchair, 'I've been waiting to see my two sparrows. I can talk to them.'

'Time for all that later in the day, my darling.' She helped him into bed and covered him with his bedclothes and eiderdown. 'Mother will come up later and read to you. Sleep well, Christian.' She stroked his hair. 'Close your eyes and sleep well.'

Rosie watched all this with absolute despair.

Marian waited for Christian to close his eyes, then left the room, ignoring Rosie's presence as she went.

'Mother!' called Rosie, as she followed her out.

Marian stopped and turned in the hall.

'We need to talk,' said Rosie.

'I can't think what about,' replied Marian coldly, going straight across the hall.

'I want to say sorry if I caused you any concern last night,' said Rosie, slowly following her to the drawing room. 'I should have let you know where I was going, but there just wasn't the time.'

'My dear,' replied Marian, 'it is immaterial to me where you were last night, or indeed who you were with. You've chosen your own life, so now you must live it.'

'My own life?' Before she could ask anything more, Marian disappeared into the drawing room. 'What d'you mean, my own life?' Rosie asked, following her in.

Richard was also in the room, also in his dressing gown, trying to stoke some life into the luke-warm embers from the previous evening.

'Where were you last night, Rose?' he asked curtly, without bothering to look up at her. 'You caused your mother and me a great deal of anxiety.'

'I'm sorry about that, Father,' replied Rosie. 'Joe and I went to look at – well, somewhere

where we might be able to live. It's some way from here, and we missed our last tram home.'

'So where did you spend the night?' asked Richard.

'Where d'you *think* she spent the night?' snapped Marian, who started to do her usual angry pacing up and down. 'With her canal dredger's son, of course!'

'Marian!' snapped Richard.

'Well, it's true, isn't it?' growled Marian, who had completely abandoned her earlier calm. 'What sort of daughter have we brought into this world? Her behaviour is no better than that of a street girl!'

'Marian!' shouted Richard.

Rosie was not prepared to take this; she turned and made for the door.

'No, Rose – wait!' pleaded her father. 'Your mother didn't mean what she said.'

'I *did* mean what I said!' insisted Marian. 'An eighteen-year-old girl spending the night out with a man is shame-making! What do you think people are going to say when they hear about this – our friends, relatives, neighbours...?'

'Frankly, I don't care a damn what *any* of those people think!' snapped Rosie, losing her own calm. 'I happen to love the man I spent the night with, and he loves me.'

Marian would listen no more. 'You disgust me!' was all she would say, as she stormed out of the room.

'How can she say such things to me, Father?' asked Rosie, flopping down in despair on to the sofa. '*Me* – her own daughter. I've always loved and respected her; I've always loved and respected you too. But to say a thing like that to me is more than anyone can take.'

'Rose,' said her father, sitting beside her, 'have you ever considered how much your mother loves you?'

'Loves me!' Rosie tossed her head back in disgust.

'Stop being so self-centred, Rosie!' snapped Richard.

Her father's outburst took Rosie completely by surprise. He was always mild-mannered, and certainly the most reasonable of her two parents. But when he spoke to her like that, Rosie felt guilt creeping into every part of her body. Unlike her mother, Richard was not outraged, but he *was* hurt.

'Yes, Rose,' said Richard, moderating his tone. 'You *are* being self-centred, yes – and deeply unfair. I know how difficult it is for you to accept your mother's outbursts – it's not easy for me either – but she's angry because you're doing something that is so completely out of tune with any known behaviour in this family, either past or present, and she finds it difficult to come to terms with it. In one sense, sleeping with a man...' for one moment he found it difficult to look her straight in the eyes, 'sleeping with a man at your age and before you are married is, for us, difficult enough to accept. But the fact that you cannot even contemplate how either your mother or I feel is, to be quite frank, most unfair of you.' He got up and walked to the other side of the room, where he sat down again at his card table.

'All right,' he continued, forehead resting on one hand, one elbow resting on the table, 'I agree that we may have tried to tie you down too much – after all, time marches on. But what *you* haven't taken into consideration is that your mother and I were brought up in one generation, and you in another. In today's society, Rose, a young couple living together without marriage is insensitive, uncaring and – in many ways – provocative. Now whatever your mother and I have been to you, we don't deserve that. We don't deserve the callous indifference you are showing us.'

'Father, I am not being callous,' pleaded Rosie. 'And I'm sorry if I'm in any way offending either you or Mother. But you have to understand that I'm in love with Joe Upton, and he's in love with me. It doesn't matter who he is, where he comes from, or what he's done, he's the one person I want to spend the rest of my life with, and if you won't give me your permission to marry him, then I can take no responsibility for hurting you.'

Richard looked across at her. There was a long silence between them, during which Richard could only think of the close bond he had always had with his daughter, only to be shattered now by her absolute defiance. 'Rose,' he said, his expression tinged with anguish, 'I love you now as I have always loved you. But if you will not accept my decision, then I fear there's nothing I can do about it.'

Rosie considered this deeply for a moment, her thoughts also bathed in the anguish of happy memories. 'Very well, Father,' she said, getting up slowly from the sofa. 'If that is your final decision, then you must also accept mine.' She turned, and quietly left the room.

Richard looked up and saw her go. He had known this would happen sooner or later, but now that it had, the pain he felt was almost unbearable.

Paul Upton arrived home from work to find Joe packing a small suitcase that had once belonged to their gran. Not that Joe had many possessions to put in there, but it would be enough for him to get started in the new home he was about to set up with Rosie.

'So yer've finally made up yer mind, 'ave yer?' said Paul, lighting a fag, perched on the edge of the old double bed he shared with his young brother in their tiny room at the top of the family house in Bethnal Green. 'Not that I blame yer. Rosie's worf it. Yer've got a real catch there, mate. Boaf Dad an' me fink the same.'

Joe paid no attention to what his brother was saying, and carried on with what he was doing. Ever since Paul had turned up to see Rosie at Charing Cross Station, he was afraid that if he started talking about her with him, there would be one hell of an argument, and that was the last thing he wanted just at the time that he was leaving home.

'Still, said Paul, regardless, 'at least I'll get a bit er room ter meself, *an'* a bit er kip. When I fink of all the years I've 'ad ter put up wiv your snorin'! Poor Rosie. I pity 'er!'

This did bring a smile to Joe's face. 'That's all right, Paul,' he said, folding up a pair of his long johns. 'At least *you'll* be able ter smoke yerself ter deff in 'ere now!'

This made them both laugh. 'That's not a nice fing ter say ter your big bruvver,' retorted Paul. For a few moments he continued to watch Joe packing. Despite what he had said, he was going to miss his young brother, not just because Joe had always been there, but because they had shared so much together over the years. Many a time they had lain awake in bed together, mulling over one bit of trouble or other, with Paul usually ending up threatening to go along and rough up someone who had upset his kid brother. Other times they had discussed their mum and dad, and the half-brothers they had never seen, and probably never would. Paul was always the one who wondered what they looked like, who they took after, and whether they had managed to make better lives for themselves than either he or Joe. Yes, Paul was going to find it odd not having to share their bedroom from now on; he was not looking forward to spending his first night alone.

'Can I take this?'

Paul snapped out of his thoughts to find Joe holding up something in his hand.

'What is it?' he asked.

'That snapshot we 'ad taken in Eppin' Forest tergevver,' said Joe. 'When Dad took us over there ter get the newts.'

'An' you fell in the pond,' said Paul, recalling the occasion vividly, 'an' Dad 'ad ter wade in and drag yer out by the scruff of yer neck! I tell yer, mate, yer was never much of a swimmer.'

'Can I take it then?' asked Joe again, holding up

332

the snapshot.

Paul avoided looking at the picture. 'It's yours, mate. Wot do *I* want it for?'

Joe placed the snapshot in the suitcase, then closed it. He then collected his coat and flat cap from behind the door. 'Be seein' yer then.'

''Ang on,' said Paul. 'Got somefin' for yer.'

Joe paused at the door whilst Paul got up from the bed, and went to the tatty old cupboard at the side of the window. After rummaging around inside there for a moment, he emerged holding out a crumpled ten-bob note. ''Ere!' he said.

Joe looked at the note with astonishment. 'Wot is it?' he asked.

'Wot d'yer fink it is, yer silly sod?' snapped Paul. 'Just take it!'

Bewildered, Joe took the note. 'You can't give me this, Paul,' he said. 'You can't afford it.'

'Who said I can't?' Paul replied indignantly. 'What's the point er me savin' fer a rainy day? I ain't got no gel ter keep. In any case,' he boasted, 'there's plenty more where that come from, I can tell yer!'

Joe stared at the note in his hand, and in that brief moment, his whole life together with Paul flashed before his eyes. He was too full to say more than, 'OK – fanks,' before picking up his case and rushing out of the room.

Downstairs, his mum, dad and gran were waiting for him in the back parlour. When Joe looked at them he thought it was more like a funeral than a family merely getting rid of someone who'd become a burden around the place. 'Right,' he said to them all, 'I'll be off then.'

'Take this,' said Annie, picking up a paper carrier bag from the table. 'It's a meat pie. I minced the left-overs from Sunday. It'll give you one good meal to start off wiv.'

Joe took the bag. 'Fanks, Ma,' he said, kissing her on the cheek. He then went to say goodbye to his grandmother, who had tears streaming down her face. 'It's all right, Gran,' he said. 'I ain't dyin' – not yet.'

Gran, shaking with tears, shook her head, and hugged him tight.

'You take it easy now,' said Joe. 'An' fanks fer the suitcase.'

She grabbed his hand and thrust something into it. A brief look showed him that it was a threepenny bit. He smiled his thanks at her, and she turned away.

'Give us yer case, lad,' said his dad, picking up Joe's suitcase.

Joe followed him down the dark narrow passage, and into the street outside.

'Now you listen ter me, my lad,' said Will, putting the suitcase down on the pavement. 'Don't forget to let the regiment know your change of address. If they come looking for you 'ere, I've told your mam to tell 'em you've gone away to t' seaside for a few days to get some fresh air into your lungs. If they decide to make contact wiv you, well – from there on it's up to you.'

Joe nodded that he understood.

'Keep your 'ead screwed on t' right way,' said Will, shaking hands with the boy. 'And make sure you keep an eye on that chest. Right?'

'Right,' replied Joe, trying to sound positive. He

didn't want to say any more. He *couldn't* say any more. He just picked up the suitcase, and walked off as briskly as he could.

As he went, he took a quick look over his shoulder. His dad was now joined by his mum, who put her arm around his waist. It was the first time he had ever seen them show any kind of affection, and it took him by surprise. Then he glanced up to his former bedroom window at the top of the house. Paul was there, peering down at him as he went. But once he had noticed that Joe had seen him, he quickly drew the curtains.

The seedy backstreet where Joe had lived for so many years of his young life was, at that moment, longer than he ever remembered, and it seemed to take for ever for him to turn the corner.

Rosie took far less time to pack her own suitcase, mainly because she wanted to get out of the house as quickly as she could. After the way her mother had talked to her earlier on, and the sad conversation she had had with her father, for her the parting from her parents was not going to be nearly as traumatic as she had expected. Once she had packed the few personal possessions and clothes that she needed, she closed the suitcase on her bed, and put it on the floor. Then she put on her hat and coat, took one check of herself in the dressing-table mirror, and picked up her suitcase. She stopped only briefly at the door to take one last look around at her bedroom. Then she left.

She had already taken her farewell of Christian, promising to visit him often, but when she reached the bottom of the stairs, Mrs Winnet, dabbing the tears in her eyes, was waiting for her.

'Don't worry, Winnie,' Rosie said reassuringly, 'I'll keep in touch. And don't forget, if you need to talk to me at any time, if Christian needs me, you know how to get in touch. All you have to do is to ask Monty. All right?'

Mrs Winnet couldn't speak. She just nodded her head. She had known Rosie since the day she was born. To her, she was still a child, *her* child, the child of her own that she had never had. This was one of the hardest moments of her life; things would never be the same for her in the Little household.

After Rosie had taken her leave of the tearful Mrs Winnet, she left the house. Neither of her parents was there to see her go, and even if they were, Rosie had already decided that she would not look back. In fact, as she made her way down Camden Road and struggled with her suitcase on to the omnibus, she hoped she would never *need* to look back. This was a time for the future, not the past.

Chapter 19

Cuthbert Jiggles had never had it so good – well, not since his wife, Gladys, died, and that was quite a long time ago. But now, he was living it up with a cup of tea in bed every morning, a hot freshly cooked meal every evening, and his house so transformed with daily cleaning that you could eat a fried egg off the floor, if, of course, you were so disposed. It had now been almost six weeks since Rosie and Joe had moved into the old railway carriage, and with Christmas now upon them they decided to break with tradition and not spend it with either of their families. This meant that old Cuthbert had struck lucky again, for when he gave his two tenants five shillings as a Christmas present, Rosie went straight to the market in Forest Gate and bought a chicken, which she cooked in Cuthbert's range oven for all three of them on Christmas Day. There was also a little of the money left over to buy the vegetables, and as Rosie had kept the savings from the monthly allowance her father had given her over the past few years, she was able to buy some mince pies and custard powder, which went down a treat when they all sat down at the portable table in the tiny kitchen just inside the carriage entrance. But the big surprise was when Rosie suddenly produced a bottle of Mrs Winnet's home-made blackcurrant wine, which brought a real sparkle to Cuthbert's eyes.

'Ladies an' gents,' announced Cuthbert, wiping the taste of mince pies and custard off his lips, 'I give you a toast!' He held up his almost empty glass, and looked towards Rosie. 'Ter the gel of my dreams, who not only makes the best cuppa Rosie of anyone I know since my Gladys, but cooks chicken so it melts in yer mouf!'

Rosie and Joe laughed.

'An' ter Joe,' continued Cuthbert, who was by now a bit tiddly, 'fer cuttin' up me firewood an' doin' all the fings round the place that I can't do meself any more. Oh, yes – an' 'ere's fankin' me ol' mate Monty fer sendin' yer to me. Gord bless yer one an' all!'

'You too, mate,' replied Joe. He and Rosie immediately stood up and raised their glasses to Cuthbert. 'Merry Christmas!' they said in unison. Then they turned to each other and kissed.

Cuthbert looked away, but to his surprise, Rosie gave him a kiss on his cheek too. 'Merry Christmas, Mr Jiggles,' she said. 'And thank you for all you've done for us.'

Rosie's kiss got Cuthbert all soppy and self-conscious, so he quickly sat up to pull himself together. 'I fink it's about time I went back 'ome fer me snooze,' he stuttered, easing himself up unsteadily from his chair.

Joe got up to help him. 'I'll come back wiv yer,' said Joe, taking hold of the old boy's arm.

'No!' snapped Cuthbert. 'I *know* the way. The fresh air'll do me good. Anyway, it's time you two 'ad a bit er Chris'mas day tergevver on yer own.'

Both Rosie and Joe knew there was no way to persuade Cuthbert otherwise. The one thing they had come to realise about the old boy since they moved into his railway carriage was that he was as obstinate as hell. So they let him go, and watched him from the kitchen door, leaning heavily on his walking stick as he made his way back through what had been just a light sprinkling of snow during the night. And as he went, they could hear his voice booming out 'Good King Wenceslas' until he went through the gate at the end of his yard.

Rosie sighed with great affection. 'I wonder if

God knew what He was doing when He made someone like that old man?' she asked, as she and Joe stood at the kitchen door, waiting to hear Cuthbert close the back door of his cottage.

'I dunno,' replied Joe, slipping his arm around her waist. 'But I reckon 'e knew wot 'e was doin' when 'e made *you*.'

Rosie looked up at him with a loving smile. 'You know something, Joe,' she said. 'This has been one of the happiest Christmas Days I've ever spent.'

'Yer mean ter tell me that yer don't miss bein' wiv yer family, big Christmas tree, roast turkey and Chris'mas pud, loads er presents...'

'I miss Christian,' Rosie said wistfully. 'He always loved waking up on Christmas morning and finding little presents tucked into a pillowcase hanging from the bottom of his bed. Actually, I think he was so excited he didn't sleep a wink; he just lay there waiting for the first signs of dawn.' She sighed. 'It was very cruel of Mother to stop me going to see him. She knows very well that Christian will think I don't care about him any more.'

'Why don't yer go down there one day?' suggested Joe. 'Yer know wot time Ma Winnet usually takes him out in his wheelchair.'

'I'm afraid Mother's got on to that,' replied Rose, sadly. 'She's told Mrs Winnet that if she finds out that either you or me has ever tried to approach Christian, she'll give her notice. Can you imagine it? Winnie's been with our family for years. I really don't know what Mother's so afraid of.'

'I do.'

Rosie gave him an inquisitive look.

'She's afraid of 'erself, Rosie,' replied Joe. 'Afraid that she's goin' ter be proved wrong – which she is. I reckon losin' you is the worst fing that's ever 'appened to 'er.'

'But how can she think like that?' Rosie asked. 'I'm her daughter. If only she would act responsibly, she wouldn't *have* to lose me. I'm so angry that she's driven me away from my own family.'

'Even so – yer still luv 'er.'

Joe's words took Rosie by surprise. Love for her mother wasn't something she had considered for a long time. Her father, yes, for he had a wonderful way of understanding two sides of every problem, but not so her mother. To her, everything was black and white; if you did something that she didn't approve of, you were from that moment on an outcast. And yet when Rosie was younger, Marian wasn't a bit like that. Rosie remembered her as her friend, someone she could go to when she was in trouble, a warm shoulder to cry on. But since the war started, all that had changed. She had set ideas about rules and regulations, and how her family should be expected to abide by them. In fact, Rosie thought of her mother as someone who was like an exile from the Victorian era, when children were brought up with strict codes of conduct. 'Yes,' she said. 'I suppose I do still love her. But for the life of me, I can't understand why.'

Paul Upton had had a lousy Christmas Day. For a start, his mum had burned the chicken in the range oven whilst she was out chinwagging with her next-door neighbour about the mass evacuation of British troops from the Dardanelles. And if that wasn't bad enough, there was no booze in the house, which for him was a disaster. A house without booze was, to both Paul and his father, a house of shame. The trouble was, his mum never drank, and as his gran could get tiddly on a thimbleful of shandy, no one had thought about stocking up, including himself. Of course, if his dad had been around, things would have been different. Before Will Upton joined up, he and Paul were habitual drinking partners, propping up the counter regularly on Friday and Saturday nights down at their local pub, the Pearly King. But as his dad had been back on active duty now for several weeks, spending Christmas Day with his mum and gran was, for Paul, hardly the way to enjoy the festive season.

His only solution was to go to his room, which he now had to himself, and spend the rest of the afternoon lying fully clothed on top of the bed, smoking himself silly in between dozing off and trying to shake off the nagging feelings that had been plaguing him ever since his young brother, Joe, had left home a few weeks before. The trouble was, he couldn't quite make out what those 'feelings' were; it was unlike anything he had known before, and it was driving him mad.

Soon after it got dark outside, he got up, put on his jacket, choker and cap, and went out. He had no idea where he was going, for there was never any public transport on Christmas Day, and even worse, the pubs were closed. He hadn't dressed properly for the ice-cold weather outside, so he pulled up the collar of his jacket, and lit another fag, which was his own bizarre way of keeping warm. After a while he found himself wandering along Roman Road, hands in trouser pockets, fag dangling recklessly from his lips. Although he had spent many a time strolling around the busy market stalls there, Paul found it an odd, unnatural sight to see the place looking so deserted, with only the moggies having the time of their lives rummaging around the dustbins to see if they could salvage something for their own Christmas meal. He dawdled along aimlessly, but those 'feelings' were still there, entrenched in his subconscious like a great lump that refused to budge. Fortunately, he was suddenly distracted by the sound of voices, voices loud and strong, men, women and children singing their hearts out to the accompaniment of some kind of organ, which seemed to be set up on the corner of nearby Grove Road. Paul quickened his pace, and when he drew closer, he saw a small crowd of people huddled around a dedicated group of Salvation Army singers, who were belting out a stirring rendition of 'Yes, Jesus Loves Me, the Bible Tells Me So', accompanied by a robust middle-aged lady in Salvation Army bonnet and uniform, whose feet were working madly on the pedals of a well-used wind organ, whilst behind her an elderly male Salvationist shuddered every time he clashed a pair of cymbals in time to the music.

Paul watched and listened from the back of the crowd, his focus wandering from the huge banner they had set up proclaiming 'WE ARE THE SOLDIERS OF OUR LORD' to the faces of the believers themselves, some young, some not so young, and one or two not so young at all. He couldn't help admire how, despite the evidence of their blood-red cheeks, they seemed to be quite oblivious to the cold, and with the only light coming from a few hand-held lamps, turned down low, for those who 'believed' it must all have been very inspiring. Unfortunately, however, Paul was not a believer in anything except how to keep himself going. Religion of any sort had never played a part in his life, mainly because he was never brought up that way. His mum had probably never been inside a church except to go to a funeral, and as for his dad, well, the only church *he* ever knew was the Pearly King pub just around the corner.

But when the hymn came to an end, Paul listened to the inspiring address given by a surprisingly young man in Salvation Army peaked cap and uniform, talking vigorously about the war, about forgiveness and about the opportunity to pick oneself up, and, with God's help, to start all over again. But when the believers started yelling out 'Hallelujah!' several times over, all Paul wanted to do was to get away. These people were no help to him. They were no help to *his* life. They couldn't even help him to get rid of the 'feeling' that was tearing him apart inside.

As he went, however, amongst the crowds dispersing to the call of 'Merry Christmas, brothers and sisters!' he did overhear one woman in the crowd say to her friend, 'Isn't it amazin' 'ow it was only this time last year young Jimmy got 'is lot down in those trenches out there?'

Paul swung a look at the fresh-faced young man who had just given the final address of the meeting. An empty uniform sleeve was pinned to his shoulder.

A short time later, the hustle and bustle of the enlightened believers behind him, Paul found himself once again ambling along empty streets. Despite the fact that food was scarce during these hard days of war, the smell of Christmas Day meals still floated enticingly from the windows of the little houses he passed. But he wasn't hungry. His mind was too preoccupied for that. But preoccupied about *what?* he asked himself. He still didn't know. And that's how it was until he turned into one backstreet that he had never seen before. It was here that the sound of Salvation Army hymns still in his head was almost by magic to have been transposed into another kind of singing. Paul came to a halt outside an old grubby-looking two-storey terraced house. Because of the blackout, there were no gaslamps to light up the street, but inside he could see the soft glow of candles, and what must have been a well-oiled collection of friends and relatives gathered around an old out-of-tune upright piano, where an elderly woman was accompanying herself to the words of 'Keep the Home Fires Burning'. The solo voice, immediate and poignant, singing a song that was so appropriate for the time, drifted out of the partly open front-room window, floating gracefully along the small backstreet on a tide of painful front-line memories. For Paul, however, it meant something quite different. The name of the song alone was enough to tell him why he couldn't explain the 'feelings' that had been plaguing him for so long. For him, it wasn't a song about the war. It was a song about something that Paul had never experienced before. It was about love.

Charing Cross Station was as busy as ever. It was Boxing Day, and most people were still enjoying their two-day Christmas festivities, but there was still a war on, and the troops had to be taken and fetched from the Front. Among them, of course, were the wounded and dying, and as usual, Rosie was there to greet them in her own inimitable way, with a cup of tea and a smile. For her, however, the job of nursing for which she volunteered earlier in the year had become a thing of the past, thanks to the intervention of her father, who had made the authorities at QAIMNS headquarters nervous about sending her out on active duty again.

But in many ways, her part-time duties at the station suited her better, for it gave her the opportunity to look after Joe, whose bronchial condition remained stubbornly out of control. She was now determined to spend as much time with him as she could, at least until he was well enough to regain his confidence, which was not easy after all he had been through.

Her one big problem, however, was the lack of money, for with Joe not earning, and her QAIMNS pay being only a pittance, it was only a question of time before her own savings would run out. She was no longer able to rely on the monthly allowance her father had given her over the years, and if anything should happen to old Cuthbert, she was concerned that a new owner of the old railway carriage would not be quite so charitable in regard to their free tenancy. None the less, Christmas with Joe had been like a dream come true, for apart from his disability, he showed her a love that was quite unlike anything her own parents had ever shown her.

Her one regret, however, was not being allowed to see Christian during the Christmas period; his health was also a lot for her to worry about, and if anything should happen to him because she was no longer around him any more, she would never forgive herself *or* her parents. The one saving grace was that, on Christmas Eve, Joe had managed to get Mrs Winnet to smuggle a rather special present in to him, a 'magic box' for viewing funny moving pictures. All this she dwelled upon wearily as she waited with her tea trolley at the end of the platform for the midday hospital train from Folkestone Harbour.

'You look all in, child.'

Rosie's daydreams were suddenly broken by the appearance of Sister Maisie from QAIMNS headquarters. 'Oh – good morning, Sister,' Rosie said.

'You could do with a good night's sleep, lassie,' said the rotund Scot, wrapped up well against the cold in her uniform cape. 'I've brought you some help.'

'Hello, Rosie,' said the smiling young girl at Sister Maisie's side.

'This is Judy,' said the sister, who seemed more solemn than usual. 'She joined us just last week. It'll give you a chance to cope when those boys get off the train. I'll see you both later.' She turned to go.

'Sister Maisie,' called Rosie.

Maisie stopped and turned.

'Forgive my asking,' said Rosie, 'but have you heard anything from Orlais? Are my three friends – are the girls safe?'

Maisie's expression changed. 'As far as *I* know,' she replied. 'You know as well as I do, lassie, communication isn't easy from the Front. Why d'you ask particularly?'

'Joe heard from one of his mates that there'd been some kind of a heavy offensive by the Germans at Orlais. Are the girls still out at the dressing station?'

Maisie hesitated a moment, then turned to the new girl. 'The train's not due for another twenty minutes or so,' she said. 'Can you hold the fort?'

'Of course, Sister,' replied Judy.

Maisie turned back to Rosie. 'Follow me,' she said.

Rosie dutifully obeyed, leaving the decidedly unconfident new girl to look after the trolley.

'Sit down, lassie,' said the Scot, patting a place at the side of her on a bench near the platform barrier. 'I've got something I want to tell you.'

Fearing the worst, Rosie sat beside her. 'Has anything happened to the girls?' she asked anxiously.

'I have no idea, lassie,' replied Maisie. 'All I know is that during the German attack at Orlais,

347

there *were* quite a lot of casualties – and not all of 'em were soldiers.'

Rosie clutched her forehead in despair.

'Now don't jump to conclusions,' said Maisie. 'The message we got was that, at the height of the attack, the advanced dressing station at Orlais had to be evacuated. Something happened there, but at the moment we don't know what.'

'But if any of our girls had been injured or – or anything else,' said Rosie, pressing her, 'surely you would have heard?'

'Those at the top might,' replied Maisie gloomily, 'but not the lower types, like me.' She watched Rosie's reaction and knew how she must be feeling. Even when they were doing their short period of training in England, The Terrible Four had proved to be quite a morale booster for the other girls. That was the main reason why Maisie was saying no more about what had happened out at Orlais, even though she knew. 'You know, lassie,' she said, 'in this war we can only live and hope. Unfortunately, with the way things are at the moment, it's easier for those of us safe at home to live than to hope.'

After Sister Maisie had gone, Rosie made her way back to the platform, where hordes of relatives and friends were waiting to meet the injured men off the hospital train. Their faces were a mixture of hope and foreboding.

Christian Little loved the Christmas present sent over to him by Joe and Rosie. The magic box was full of wondrously funny things, and he roared with laughter as he held it up to the light, turned a small handle at the side, and watched the crazy antics of people like Fred Mace, Fatty Arbuckle and Mabel Normand. He felt it must have been like going to the picture house, a place he had rarely been taken to, because, said his father, it had always been difficult to find a place in the auditorium for the boy's wheelchair. But this was just as good, Christian thought, even though he was watching it in full daylight down by the canal at Caledonian Road. He even allowed Mrs Winnet to take a look, and, like him, she laughed so loudly that a flotilla of swans took flight from the surface of the water and disappeared off towards Regent's Park as fast as their graceful wings could carry them.

Although it was a cold, crisp morning, Christian was enjoying his usual outing with Mrs Winnet, for she always took him to places that he wanted, and not to the boring old posh streets that his mother much preferred. Wrapped up warm, his legs covered with a tartan blanket, he loved watching the coal and timber barges ploughing their way along the calm waters of the canal, hoping that one day he would be able to actually visit the places they were heading for.

'You know, Mrs Winnet,' he said, quite out of the blue, 'I'd like to go and visit Rosie and Joe. Have *you* been to visit them yet?'

'Goodness no, Master Christian,' she replied. 'It's much too far to go all the way over to the East End.'

'But it must be wonderful to live in a railway carriage,' said Christian wistfully. 'I'd *love* to live in a railway carriage. I've seen so many pictures of them in my railway books.' He sighed, and watched some ducks drifting past on the water, their little tails wagging like dogs as they went. 'Mind you, where I'm going I doubt I'll have a chance to visit Rosie and Joe.'

Mrs Winnet looked up from the bench she was sitting on alongside Christian's wheelchair. 'Where you're going to?' she asked with some surprise.

'Mother says there'll come a time when she won't be able to look after me properly,' he replied. 'She said I shall need specialised medical attention, and the only place for that would be in some kind of a home.'

'What!' growled Mrs Winnet. 'I've never 'eard such nonsense! Your muvver never looks after you. *I'm* the one who does that, an' it's perfectly unnecessary fer you ter be placed in any old 'ome.' She was so distracted with anger she only just saved her feather hat from blowing off in the wind. 'What does yer farvver say about all this?' she asked.

'*He* doesn't think it's a good idea at all,' said the boy. 'Of course, they never said all this actually in front of me, but I can hear every word they say when they start raising their voices in the next room to mine. Father said they should be patient, that I was their son and that it was their duty to look after me until I get well.' He turned to look at her. 'I *am* going to get well one of these days, aren't I, Winnie?'

Mrs Winnet felt a great lump in her throat. It was the first time the boy had ever called her by her nickname. 'Of course you are!' she thundered.

350

'And don't you ever let anyone tell yer uvverwise!'

'Joe said I'm not going to die young,' said Christian. 'He said I'll probably live to a ripe old age, and get a telegram from the King on my hundredth birthday. I'd *love* to get a telegram from the King, Winnie.'

'And so you shall, my dear!' she assured him. 'And so you shall! Mind you, I won't be around when yer get it!'

They both laughed at that. But Mrs Winnet wasn't at all amused. In fact, she was red-faced with anger, appalled by the thought of Christian being put into some old home. Damn that woman, she thought to herself. Damn Marian Little for even thinking of such an idea. And she vowed there and then not to let it happen, even if she had to make that long trek all the way over to the East End to see Rosie.

Joe had a surprise waiting for Rosie when she got home. He had not only painted the bedroom of the railway carriage green with what was left over from a tin of paint that Cuthbert had had stored away in his shed, but he had also cleaned the place so much that it looked like new. On top of that, he had tried his hand at preparing a meal for them both. He peeled some spuds and carrots, and cut up some onions, which he partially cooked with two saveloys in a frying pan on the cooker. Once it was all ready, he had a shave at the kitchen sink, and went into the newly painted bedroom to admire his work.

The only trouble was, by this time he was feeling just a little breathless. It was his own fault

351

because even before he had left the military hospital at Stanmore Manor, he was warned by the doctor to be careful about inhaling anything that would aggravate his bronchial condition, and if he had to do any job that would endanger this, he should always wear some protective covering over his mouth. Although Joe dismissed all this from his mind, there was no doubt that he *was* feeling queasy. His first thought was to get out of the room for a few moments, and sit down at the kitchen table until the breathlessness passed. But before he could do so, he broke into a violent fit of coughing, which refused to abate, leaving him struggling to hold on with both hands to the wall.

'Sod it! Sod it! Sod it!' Despite his usual cry of frustration when this sort of attack came upon him, he felt worse and worse until he started to become dizzy, blacked out, and slumped with a crash unconscious to the floor.

At Charing Cross Station, the midday military hospital train arrived just a few minutes late. However, when it did eventually crawl its way along the track towards Platform 1, it was greeted with a great roar of approval, crowds laughing and crying with tension and relief.

The moment she saw the train approaching, Rosie's new assistant, Judy, started pouring tea into the cups that were lined up on the trolley and in trays alongside. Judy was a tough little soul, who had a practical attitude to everything she did, which meant that she was so efficient that Rosie reckoned that if she wanted to she could balance six cups of tea on top of her head at the same time. What Rosie hadn't learned at this stage, however, was that Judy was brought up in an orphanage, and had never known what it was like to have a family of her own.

'I reckon this lot would far sooner have a pint of bitter than a cuppa tea,' she shouted, above the sound of carriage doors opening while the train was still coming to a standstill. Within minutes the platform was a flood with tears, as the tide of casualties was taken off in stretches to the ambulances waiting outside. Rosie did her usual, handing out as many cups of tea as she could manage in as short a time as possible. To Judy's astonishment, practically every able-bodied soldier that got off the train seemed to know her for, as they passed, they all called: 'Wotcha, Rosie Lee!' or 'Good ol' Rosie!'

'Looks like every Tommy in the British army knows you!' yelled Judy above the noise on the platform, whilst in the background the resident military band pumped out as many current favourite songs as possible, including the one Joe had dedicated to Rosie, 'Little Dolly Daydream'.

It seemed to take for ever to clear the platform, and by the time the wounded and their groups had gone home or to the military hospitals, Judy was just about whacked.

'Don't know how you do it,' she said to Rosie, as they scurried up and down the platform, collecting the empty teacups. 'To work so hard and look so good is something I could never do!'

'Don't you believe it,' said Rosie. 'When you take over from me, you'll be so popular with the soldiers they won't even remember me.'

'When I take over?' asked Judy, pausing for a moment to look at her. 'What d'you mean?'

'Well,' replied Rosie, 'I shan't be doing this job for ever. I've got a sick man at home to look after. Even though he's getting better all the time, I've got to go out and get a job to earn some real money.'

Judy shook her head. The prospect of trying to take over from someone who seemed to have a reputation that stretched from Charing Cross to the battlefields of France terrified the daylights out of her.

Once they had cleared the platform, they started to wheel the tea trolley back to the kitchens, which were situated just behind the concourse. However, just as they were doing so, Rosie thought she heard someone calling her name, but when she turned round to look behind her, there was no one around she recognised, and as far as she could see, apart from the train driver and station staff, the platform they had come from was now completely deserted. But as they moved on, she definitely heard the voice again, distant at first, barely audible, but coming from somewhere.

'Rosie...!'

This time, Rosie stopped, straining to see who was calling her. Then, as she looked along the platform she and Judy had just come from, she saw in the distance two figures, one of them waving madly to her, both moving slowly. Rosie's eyes widened. As the realisation of who it was sank in, she suddenly broke into a trot and rushed straight past the ticket barrier. Waving and yelling, her trot turned into a wild dash.

'Eunice!' she yelled, over and over again.

'Rosie!' came the reply, with frantic waving from the far end of the platform.

When she finally reached her old friend, she found that she was walking heavily on crutches, aided by a nurse from the Red Cross. Regardless, Rosie threw her arms around her, and hugged her tight. 'Oh, Eunice, Eunice!' she gasped over and over again.

Both of them were sobbing uncontrollably, holding on to each other, refusing to let go. But when they did finally emerge, Rosie had to ask the question the answer to which she dreaded. 'Where are the others, Eunice? Where are they? Where are Binnie and Titch?'

Eunice broke down in a flood of tears. 'They're gone, Rosie,' she sobbed. 'They're boaf gone – dead. I can't bear it, Rosie! I just can't bear it!'

It took Rosie several moments to take in what Eunice had said. She was too stunned, too over-whelmed with disbelief to understand what had happened. There would be time for that later. For now, all she could do was to hold Eunice in her arms, and remember the faces of those two dear friends whom she could see when she closed her eyes, but whom she would never ever see in reality again.

Chapter 20

Rosie spent the night at Joe's bedside in the London Hospital in Whitechapel Road. Although he was recovering well from the bronchial spasm that had caused him to lose consciousness, finding him slumped on the floor of the bedroom at the railway carriage was one of the worst experiences Rosie had ever had. Fortunately, her short period of nurses' training had taught her not to panic, and by breathing into his mouth and massaging his back, she soon managed to bring him round. She didn't like waking poor old Cuthbert from his sleep, but as soon as he knew what had happened, he was out of bed in a flash, and on his way to the railway carriage to keep an eye on Joe whilst Rosie, with the help of a police constable, hurried off to fetch an ambulance.

However, at the hospital the doctor on night duty said that Joe was too weak to go home, and insisted that he spend a day or so in hospital.

'See wot yer've got lumbered wiv,' whispered Joe breathlessly, lying propped up in bed in the emergency ward. 'Ain't got a brain between me bleedin' ears. I should never've painted that bedroom.'

Rosie leaned closer and lowered her voice so as not to disturb the other patients, one or two of whom were also soldiers suffering from various front-line problems. 'I think the bedroom looks absolutely wonderful, Joe,' she replied. 'It was such a lovely surprise.'

'Yeah,' he said, 'especially findin' me on the floor like that. 'Ow long's this goin' ter go on, Rosie? 'Ow long?'

'You've got to be patient, my dear one,' said Rosie. 'Before you left Stanmore, the medical officer warned me it would take a long while to rid your lungs of that gas. All it means is that from now on, we've got to be on our guard – *both* of us. Now just try and get some sleep. Come on, calm down, close your eyes.'

Joe did as he was told; he was too exhausted and distressed to argue with her.

Rosie blew out the candle at his bedside, tucked him in, then sat with him for several minutes, hoping that he would soon nod off. All around her were the snores and smells of a night ward, which she recognised only too well from her time at Stanmore Manor, and her instinct was to go around each bed to keep a check on every patient there. However, the ward night nurse was there to take care of that, so Rosie just sat on her hard wooden chair in silence, closing her eyes, and thinking about all the ghastly events that had taken place during the course of the past twenty-four hours.

And what events they were! The sight of poor Eunice being helped along the platform from the midday hospital train at Charing Cross Station had shocked and distressed her. Binnie and Titch dead? She just couldn't take it in. But the battle at Orlais had been a savage one; no one had been spared, not the sick nor the dying, not even the

357

medical teams looking after them. The full horror of what had happened to the advanced dressing station would be made clear as soon as Rosie had the chance to go to see Eunice, who had been sent back to QAIMNS headquarters to recuperate from a shrapnel wound in her foot, shell shock and the trauma of what she had experienced over at Orlais. In the meantime, Rosie had to deal with the crisis of how she was going to look after Joe when he came out of hospital.

Monty Gubble hadn't been on either an omnibus or a tram for years. In fact, the last time he had done so was to go to a regimental reunion in Euston. That had turned out to be a very boozy affair, from which both he and Cuthbert Jiggles had had to be sent to their respective homes for drunken behaviour and disorderly conduct. For Monty, that was an evening he had done his best to forget, for he had always prided himself on what had become the unofficial motto of his old regiment, 'Fair play, good manners and not too much froth on the bitter.'

However, he was persuaded to desert his daily resting place on a coping stone in Camden Town by the worrying news Elsie Winnet had brought him from number 221 Camden Road, news that had to be passed on to Rosie as soon as possible. Unfortunately, by the time he had coped with the shock revelation that he was buying his tram ticket from a female conductor, he had almost forgotten the reason why he had travelled all the way from North to East London.

'The world's comin' to an end, mate,' he declared solemnly, the moment his old regimental pal had opened the door to him. 'Gels in the army's one fing, but sellin' tickets on the trams is takin' it too far! They'll be gettin' 'em ter drive the bleedin' fings next!'

'Don't worry, Mont,' said Cuthbert reassuringly. 'It's only a fad. It'll never catch on.'

The reunion of the two old codgers was really quite touching, but for the news Monty had brought. 'Rosie's folk are goin' ter put that poor boy into a home,' he said, as he downed a glass of bitter as fast as he could swallow it.

'Wot boy?' asked Cuthbert, as he and Monty warmed themselves in front of the fire in Cuthbert's kitchen.

'Rosie's young bruvver,' replied Monty. ''E's 'ad this consumption fing practically since the day 'e was born, an' now that Rosie's left 'ome, they say they can't cope, an' wanna lock 'im away. It's that woman, er course, that bleedin' muvver. If yer ask me *she's* a case fer the nut'ouse! Anyway, Elsie Winnet wants Rosie ter know as soon as possible.'

'I doubt the poor gel's goin' ter be able ter do much about it at the moment, Mont,' replied Cuthbert, taking a gulp of his bitter and shaking his head gloomily. 'Not after wot 'appened 'ere last night.'

'Wot d'yer mean?' asked Monty.

'When she come 'ome from work, she found Joe stretched right out on the floor. Seems 'e lost 'is breff an' passed right out. Rosie 'ad ter go get an ambulance. They took 'im ter the 'ospital in Whitechapel Road. As far as I know she's still there.'

'Blimey!' gasped Monty. 'That poor young feller.'

'It's the gas, er course,' lamented Cuthbert. 'Once yer get that stuff in yer lungs, there ain't a lot yer can do about it. Those bleedin' Huns've got a lot ter answer for.'

They both agreed with an angry grunt, and took simultaneous gulps of their own bitter.

'So wot can *we* do ter 'elp?' asked Monty. 'From wot Elsie tells me, the poor gel ain't been left wiv much cash. Apparently 'er ol' man cut orf 'er allowance the minute she left 'ome.'

'At the moment,' replied Cuthbert, 'it ain't the cash Rosie's got ter worry about. If yer want *my* opinion, 'er biggest problem's goin' ter be Joe 'imself. Yer should just 'ear the coughin' at night. I can 'ear 'im even from me own bedroom. Gord knows 'ow she's goin' ter cope wiv goin' ter work every day, an' lookin' after *'im* at the same time.'

'Oh, she'll cope all right,' Monty said confidently. 'You don't know our Rosie. Got a will of iron, an' an 'eart er gold. She won't go down, mate. She's got guts, that one.'

'Even so,' sighed Cuthbert, 'yer can't buy good 'ealth, mate. *I* should know.'

'Get orf it!' barked Monty, dismissively, dribbling bitter down on to his long white beard. 'Wiv all that spondulicks yer've got stashed away under yer floorboards, *you* can afford it!'

Cuthbert suddenly straightened up. 'Wot d'you know about my floorboards, Monty Gubble?' he asked indignantly.

Monty chuckled. 'I ain't no fool, mate,' he replied with a twinkle in his eye. 'I know wot yer

360

was like when we shared that tent wiv Charlie and Gus back in Balaclava. We all knew 'ow yer kept yer money in yer socks in case any of us nicked it. Tight as a drum, mate! An' while we're on the subject, that medal on your tunic – second from the left – you're wearin' that under false pretences.'

'Wot!' Cuthbert, outraged, got up from his chair.

'That's Sebastapol,' said Monty. 'You was never in Sebastapol. An' neivver was I.'

'Out!' growled Cuthbert, pointing to the door.

'Wot yer all worked up about, Cuff?' asked Monty, easing himself up from his chair. 'Yer know it's the trufe.'

'Out!' Cuthbert snatched the half-finished glass of bitter from Monty's hand. 'I've never bin so insulted in all me life!'

'Oh, yes you 'ave!' snapped Monty, grabbing back his glass. 'Lots 'er times! An' yer will plenty more times too. So stop gettin' on yer 'igh 'orse, Cuthbert Jiggles, an' let's see wot we're goin' ter do about Rosie and Joe!'

Paul Upton finished his early morning shift at the fish curing warehouse in Limehouse just in time to get down to the Pearly King for a quick pint. This being a weekday, he practically had the place to himself at lunchtime. But to his surprise and delight, his mate Mickey Manners was there. During the short time they were at school together, the two of them spent more time in the streets than in the classroom, usually conning the local tobacconist to sell them a penny Woodbine

361

fag, which they would share behind the public toilets in Bethnal Green Road. Mickey had bright red hair, and although younger than Paul, looked older than his years.

'So 'ow was Chris'mas then, mate?' Mickey asked, as he called for a pint of brown ale from Cyril, the pub's landlord.

'Bleedin' awful!' replied Paul, pulling on a fag, and gulping down his bitter.

'Me too,' said Mickey. ''Cept fer this gel I met in 'ere last night. She was wiv 'er mum 'n' dad, name's Gilda.'

'Gilda!' said Paul, pulling a face. 'Wot is she – a tart?'

'No, she's not a tart!' replied Mickey indignantly. 'As a matter of fact she's a very *nice* gel.'

'Then wot's she doin' wiv *you?*'

'Very funny!' replied Mickey, lighting up and quickly downing some of his drink. 'Nah, but seriously, Paul,' he continued, 'tell me somefin'. D'yer fink I look older?'

'Bleedin' 'orrible, more like!'

'Yes, I know all that,' retorted Mickey. 'But do I look *older?* The reason I ask is 'cos I fink I'm in love wiv this gel.'

'Wot!' spluttered Paul, nearly choking on his fag. ''Ow many times 'ave yer met 'er?'

'Only once,' replied Mickey. 'But I feel I've known 'er all me life. She 'as a way of lookin' at yer.' He lowered his voice, and leaned towards Paul. 'Got lovely tits.'

'That's not love, mate,' said Paul. 'That's lust!'

Mickey laughed, but immediately became serious again. 'Nah,' he said, 'I'm not kiddin', Paul.

I've really taken ter this gel. I was lyin' awake all night finkin' about 'er, tellin' meself it's about time I grew up an' settled down. I don't like this wanderin' the streets like we was still kids. I want some 'ome life an' a family of me own.'

'Yer call that love?' asked Paul cynically.

'I don't know *wot* yer call it,' replied Mickey. 'All I know is I'm changin'. I want ter move on. I mean, until ol' Kitchener catches up wiv me, I've got a good job down the coal yard. I could afford ter get 'itched an' rent a coupla rooms.'

'An' wot 'appens if Kitchener *does* catch up wiv yer?'

Mickey pulled a face, and thought about it. 'Well,' he said with a shrug, 'I should 'ope Gilda'd be waitin' fer me when I got 'ome. After all, when someone takes yer fancy in life, no matter wot gets in yer way, yer only 'ave one chance ter do somefin' about it. Don't yer fink?'

Rosie didn't leave the hospital until well after midday. By that time Joe was much improved, which left her confident enough to go off to see Eunice, who was being cared for by the staff at QAIMNS headquarters.

Sister Maisie was waiting there to meet Rosie. 'Don't worry about Eunice,' she said, as she and Rosie hurried up to the first floor. 'She's a strong-willed lassie. Once all this has sunk in, we'll soon get her back on her feet again. And don't you go worrying about your own problem either. Young Judy can hold the fort at Charing Cross till you can get back. Yer poor wee lassie. *What* a time you're having!'

Eunice was being looked after in one of the small bedrooms that was normally reserved for staff on night duty. When Rosie came in, her face lit up, and her first instinct was to get up from the armchair she was sitting in by the window.

'Oh, no, you don't, young lady!' said Maisie, opening the door for Rosie. 'Whilst you're here under *my* charge, you'll do what *I* say. And if she gives you any trouble, Rosie, just come downstairs and let me know!' She left the room abruptly without waiting for any response from either of the two girls.

'Oh, Eunice!' said Rosie, immediately going over to give her a warm hug. 'I've been so worried about you.'

'This is a fine bleedin' carry-on, in't it, mate?' replied Eunice, her face brighter, but drained of all the life it had had the last time she and Rosie were together.

Rosie pulled up a chair and sat in front of her. The curtains were drawn at the window, leaving a pattern of lacework shadows across Eunice's face. Rosie had no intention of talking about what had happened out at Orlais until Eunice was ready to tell her.

'Are they taking care of you?' she asked.

'Well,' replied Eunice with just a flash of her usual cheeky banter, 'I've only bin 'ere a few hours, but so far they ain't put any cyanide in me tea. Mind you, I'd sooner 'ave a cuppa *your* Rosie Lee any day er the week.'

Rosie gave her one of her special smiles, and took hold of her hand.

'In any case,' continued Eunice, 'I'm only

stayin' 'ere till me dad comes ter take me 'ome.' She laughed falsely. 'This lot can't wait ter get rid er me!'

'Something tells me that's not true,' said Rosie, more seriously. 'In fact, I *know* it isn't.'

Their eyes met. In a rapid change of mood, all the pretensions were dropped when Eunice's face suddenly crumpled up, and her eyes filled with tears. 'Jesus Christ, Rosie!' she sobbed.

Rosie immediately got up and threw her arms around her. 'It's all right, my dear,' she said softly, comfortingly. 'It's all right.' She waited for her to relax before saying anything else.

'It was so terrible, Rosie,' Eunice began. 'Every time I fink about it, every time I close me eyes, I can see 'em – Binnie, standing there firm as a rock, refusin' ter budge till the 'ole place caved in, an' Titch...' She buried her head against Rosie's stomach. 'Poor Titch ... I told 'er – we boaf told 'er, me *an'* Binnie – we *begged* 'er ter get out an' make a run fer it, then when she did...' She was now sobbing so much she could hardly speak. 'The last I saw of 'er,' she said, looking up at Rosie and dabbing her eyes, 'the last I saw of 'er was in this field. They shot Titch down ... the soddin' Boche shot 'er down like she was a bleedin' rabbit. I 'ate 'em, Rosie! Gord knows 'ow much I 'ate those filfy pigs!'

Rosie held on to her.

'So then wot d'yer fink they did?' Eunice said, looking up again, her cheeks streaming with tears. 'They shelled us. They shelled the farm'ouse, the cowshed, the 'ole bleedin' place. The first fing I did was ter throw meself fru the window. I was only just in time 'cos the roof caved in and ... and ... all the casualties, all those blokes, they din't stand a chance, Rosie. The medical officer who took over from Lieutenant Hillary, everyfin' came down on 'im, 'im an' everyone else – includin' Binnie.' She tried very hard to control her sobbing, but it was a great effort. 'D'yer know the last fing Binnie said ter me? D'yer know wot she said?'

In great anguish, Rosie slowly shook her head.

'She said, "Long live The Terrible Four!"'

Rosie felt as though her inside was being torn apart.

Eunice took another moment to recover, then slowly continued, 'I don't remember anyfin' after that,' she said. 'I must've blacked out or somefin' 'cos the next fing I knew was I woke up back in the village wiv the Lady and Gord knows who starin' down at me. Got a bit er shrapnel in me foot, though.' She grinned despite her tears. 'Just fer a souvenir.'

Rosie smiled at her. Suddenly Eunice was just like she always remembered her, that cheeky, mischievous twinkle in the eye. 'Tell me just one thing, Eunice,' she asked. 'Where did they take Binnie and Titch? Did they bring them back home?'

Eunice shook her head and sighed heavily. 'No,' she said. 'As far as I know, they buried 'em out there – don't ask me where. I wanted ter go an' see 'em, just once, just one last time, but the Lady said it wouldn't do no good, that the best I could do was ter be grateful ter God fer me 'avin' such good mates. In any case, I couldn't've done much, not wiv this foot the way it is. But one day, maybe one day, when this bleedin' war's over, you an' me could go out there, couldn't we – see where they've put 'em?'

'Yes, Eunice,' replied Rosie. 'I think we'll do that. In fact, I *know* we will.'

The door opened and Sister Maisie re-appeared. 'Someone to see you, Eunice.'

A grim-faced middle-aged man came into the room. When Eunice saw him, her face crumpled up again. 'Dad!' she sobbed as he rushed across to throw his arms around her.

The man hugged her tight. There were tears in his eyes. 'It's all right, gel,' he said, his face crumpled up with emotion. 'You're goin' ter be all right now. We're all waitin' for yer. You're comin' 'ome.'

It was raining heavily when Rosie finally got on her tram and headed back towards Forest Gate. On the way, she watched with fascination the way different people on the streets below coped with the weather. Some young girls laughed as they ran to find shelter, some put up brollies and didn't laugh. Others walked along briskly, but quite oblivious to the torrential downpour, accepting that it was, after all, December, and only to be expected. Resilience, thought Rosie. It had never really occurred to her before just how resilient people were, especially people at war. Despite the carnage and horror of the times, nothing seemed to deter them from going about their business in their own individual ways, whether it was coping with the weather, or burying loved ones. When the elderly conductor climbed the stairs to the top

367

deck and took Rosie's penny ha'penny for her ticket, he seemed keen, as good tram conductors always were, to engage her in a bit of casual conversation. Unfortunately, however, it was again about the war, which is something Rosie had just about had her stomach full of for one day. Apart from a mum and her small boy, there was no one on the top deck, so Rosie was virtually under siege by the old boy.

'They said it'd be all over by Chris'mas,' he said. 'But then, they said the same fing last year. The way it's goin' I won't be around ter see it come to an end.'

'I'm sure you will,' Rosie said encouragingly.

The old conductor shook his head. 'Yer know, I've bin on the omnibuses and trams fer the past firty-odd years. We used ter 'ave some fine young fellers workin' for us, not only sellin' tickets but drivers too. But I was just finkin' the uvver day, most of 'em've gone now, dragged off to a war they don't know nuffin' about. I probably won't see 'em again.' He started to go, but then changed his mind. 'Wot der *you* fink, young lady? Wot der *you* fink about all this?'

'What do *I* think?' Rosie repeated. Before she answered him, so much flashed through her mind: Joe struggling against the effects of poison gas; Eunice coming to terms with the savagery at Orlais; all those young and not so young people being carried on stretchers off the hospital train at Charing Cross every day ... the list was endless. 'I think,' she replied, 'that people in power should stop and think hard before they make decisions.'

"Ear, 'ear!' agreed the old conductor. 'That's exactly what I told my missus – well, more or less.'

They were suddenly distracted by the sound of the child in the front making ghastly sounds on a Jew's harp. 'No, Jimmy!' said his mother, trying to quieten the small boy. 'Not 'ere. Not till yer get 'ome.'

'Anyway, nice ter talk to yer, miss,' said the old conductor, moving off. And as he puffed his way down the tram's steep stairs again he called back: 'An' a 'appy New Year to yer!'

Rosie turned round to respond, but he had already disappeared.

Happy New Year? She could hardly believe what she had just heard. Was it really almost that time? And as the tram rumbled and clattered its way along the tracks to East London, her mind recalled the awful year they would shortly be getting rid of: the sinking in May of the *Lusitania*, a transatlantic passenger liner; the first gas attacks, at Ypres; the execution of Nurse Cavell in Brussels; and the bombing of London by German Zeppelin airships. How could anyone wish her a happy New Year after all that? As Rosie stepped off the tram at her stop, the rain had finally died away, and up above she could even see some substantial breaks in the thunderous grey clouds. At least, she thought, there was still *some* hope in this mad, mad world.

By the time Rosie got back to old Cuthbert's place, the ground on both sides of the railway track had been turned into a quagmire, so much so that she had to pull up her uniform dress to avoid the hemline being covered in mud. In a strange kind of way, however, she didn't mind the inconvenience too much, because at least she was breathing in some fresh air after being shut up all night in hospital, and again later in the day with poor Eunice. But she *was* exhausted, there was no doubt about that – absolutely drained to the core – and the one thing she was dying to do when she got into the carriage was to have a wash down, change into some clean clothes, and have a half-hour doze before heading off back to the hospital to see Joe. However, after she'd struggled ankle-deep through the mud, the moment she reached the door of the carriage on the other side of the track, she sensed that something was not quite right.

The first thing she noticed was that the curtains were drawn back, which was something neither she nor Joe ever did when they went out. This alone made her wary. Her inclination was to turn back to go and see old Cuthbert, but not only was the mud too much of a hazard, she also knew that the old codger always took a sleep about this time in the late afternoon. She felt uncomfortable, especially as it would be dark in just an hour or so, and being in an isolated position way out from the nearest houses, she didn't quite know what to do. But then she thought that if anyone had broken into the carriage whilst she was away, they would not have got away with very much. Life in the middle of a field wasn't exactly rich pickings for a dedicated burglar. With this in mind, she tried the door. To her horror, it was unlocked. She went in, to be submerged immediately by a thick cloud of cigarette smoke.

'Wotcha, Rosie Lee.'

The sight of Paul Upton stretched out on Joe's favourite kitchen chair sent a chill down Rosie's spine. 'Paul!' she growled. 'What the hell d'you think you're doing here?'

'I've come ter see where my favourite sister-in-law lives,' replied Paul mischievously, springing up from his chair to greet her. 'I asked the ol' bloke down the way. I told 'im who I am, an' 'e let me in – no problem at all. Surely there's no 'arm in that?'

'I am *not* your sister-in-law,' snapped Rosie angrily, 'and you have absolutely no right at all to be here! So please leave immediately.'

'Yer know,' he said, going slowly to her, 'fer the life er me, I don't know wot yer've got against me. I've not done anyfin' ter offend you, 'ave I?'

Rosie's back was against the open door, ready to make a quick getaway. 'No, Paul,' she replied tersely, 'you don't offend me. But you have no right to be here.'

'Then it's Joe, in't it?' he said. ''E's the one who's turned yer against me. That's the trouble wiv *'im*. 'E's always bin so jealous er me.'

'It may interest you to know, Paul,' said Rosie, watching like a hawk every little move he made, 'that Joe is lying seriously ill in the London Hospital.'

Paul did a double take. 'Wot's that?'

'When I came back here last night, I found him lying unconscious on the floor in the bedroom. He couldn't breathe, and I had to go and get an ambulance.'

'Blimey!' spluttered Paul. 'Poor ol' Joe.'

'Precisely,' said Rosie. 'And I'm going straight back to the hospital now to see the doctors, so I must ask you to leave.'

'I'll come wiv yer,' said Paul.

'It's not necessary,' replied Rosie. 'But if you want to go and see him on your own, I'll tell you which ward he's in. And I'd be grateful if you'd tell your mother as well.'

'Why do you 'ate me so much, Rosie Lee?' he asked, as though he hadn't even heard what she had just said.

'I don't hate you at all, Paul,' she replied. 'But there are certain standards, certain principles, that we all have to live by. You know how Joe feels about you. He was furious when he heard about you coming to see me at the station the other day.'

'I 'appen ter love my bruvver, Rosie,' he snapped back. ''E's my kid bruvver, an' I wouldn't want any 'arm ter come to 'im.'

'Then don't come to our home when he's not here,' replied Rosie, calmly but firmly.

For one moment Paul just stood there, staring straight at her. 'I like you, Rosie,' he said. 'I liked you the moment I set eyes on you down at Stanmore. You're not like most of the gels I've met in my time. You're different.'

Rosie stood aside from the doorway to let him pass. 'Please go, Paul. I'm asking you.'

He moved towards the door, and as he drew closer to her, he could smell her hair, her eyes, her skin, every part of her body. He anguished how he could get through to her, how he could let her understand that he was worth a million

372

times more than his brother, Joe.

For her part, Rosie was so tense she felt as though her back was glued to the wall. She avoided his eyes because she knew that if she looked directly into them, something might happen, something might give, and she would never want that.

Finally, Paul went past her and stepped down into the mud outside.

'If yer should need me any time,' he called, 'any time at all, yer know where ter find me – Rosie Lee. Oh – and by the way, it's a nice place yer've got 'ere. Really diff'rent. I must remember ter tell Joe when I see 'im.'

The moment he cleared the door, Rosie closed and locked it. For a moment she just stood there, her back pinned against the door, shaking from head to foot. She didn't quite know why. But when she briefly closed her eyes, she could still see Paul, standing there in front of her, looking more dazzling than she had ever seen him. For one split second, she regretted what she had done. After all, in many ways, he *was* very like his brother.

Chapter 21

Rosie didn't like the thought of going to see her father at the factory; to her, it seemed like taking a step back in time. That was the feeling she had the moment she went through the front door and smelled the brass and furniture polish in the reception office, everything spick and span, neat and tidy, nothing out of place. It was also the feeling when she was greeted, somewhat awkwardly, by Amy Desmond, the company's receptionist, who was clearly surprised to see her after all the rumours she had heard about a split in the Little family.

'He's upstairs, Miss Rose,' she said politely. 'Shall I tell him you're here?'

Rosie smiled. 'On this occasion, Amy,' she replied wryly, 'I think maybe you should.'

Amy came from behind the reception counter, and hurried upstairs.

Although it was in reality only a moment or so, it seemed an age to Rosie as she stood waiting for Amy to come back down. Through the interior factory window behind the counter, she could just get a glimpse of the great changes that had been made in the place since it had been converted into an assembly line for respirators, which were now in great demand because of the constant fear of gas attacks, not only on the battlefields but also back home. Somehow it all seemed so bizarre, so unreal; one day beautiful porcelain dinner sets, and then respirators.

'Will you come up, please, Miss Rose?'

Rosie looked up the stairs to see Amy calling to her from the landing outside her father's office. Rosie went straight up.

The moment she appeared at the door, Richard stood up at his desk. 'Rose,' he said, going to greet her with a light kiss on her cheek, 'it's good to see you, my dear.'

'Thank you, Father,' she replied coldly. 'I'm sorry to disturb you, but there's something important I *must* discuss with you.'

Little was concerned that she looked so pale and drawn. 'Come and sit down, Rose – please.'

She sat with him on the settee. 'It's about Christian,' she said. 'Is it true you and Mother are going to send him away to a sanatorium?'

'Who told you that?' he asked.

'It doesn't matter who told me,' she replied sternly. 'Is it true?'

Richard hesitated. 'I've taken no firm decision on the matter yet,' he replied. 'But when I do, it will be in Christian's interest and no one else's.'

'Is it really in his interest,' she asked, 'to be locked away for the rest of his life, with strange people around him, with no way to feel free, or to do the things he wants?'

'Don't you think that's a bit extreme, Rose?'

'No, Father,' she replied forcefully. 'I *don't* think that is a bit extreme. I'm so surprised at you. It would be cruel to do a thing like this.'

'Christian,' replied Richard, 'is at the stage where he needs expert medical attention.'

'It's not just medical attention he needs, Father,' replied Rosie. 'He needs *love*.'

Richard got up from the settee, and went to the arched window.

'Father,' said Rosie passionately, 'Christian can't get the kind of love you and me and Mother can give him at home in a place where he'll just be one more inmate.'

'Christian is going to die, Rose,' said Richard. 'We've all known that for a very long time. The doctors say there's absolutely no hope for him. The consumption is virtually eating away his lungs.'

'The doctors may be right, Father,' replied Rosie, 'but they may also be wrong. Joe is convinced that if Christian gets the right attention, he could at least have a good quality of life, so much so that he could possibly live much longer than everyone imagines.'

Richard turned to face her. He had always admired Rosie's ability to speak out, and this occasion was no exception. 'Rose,' he said, 'it may come as a surprise to you to know that I agree with Joe. But I can't be certain that we are right. As parents, it's our duty to—'

'As parents,' retorted Rosie, 'it's your duty to see beyond facts and reason. We may not be able to give Christian a long life, but whatever time he has should be rich with love and attention. If you shut him away in a home – whatever home you want to call it – do that, and you can take my word for it that he will not survive for more than a few months.'

Richard hesitated, then returned to his desk. 'I'm sorry, Rose,' he said with a sigh. 'I can't say anything more until I've had a chance to discuss it with your mother.'

'In other words,' said Rosie defiantly, 'it's Mother's decision.'

Richard refused to rise to her criticism. Although he knew only too well that what Rosie was saying was true, he could not and would not betray Marian's trust in him. From the factory floor down below, they heard the sound of Jim

Sayles ringing the hand bell for morning tea break.

Richard waited a few moments for the ringing to stop, then flicked his eyes up at Rosie. 'We've missed you, Rose,' he said suddenly, and with obvious affection.

Rosie lowered her eyes.

'The house hasn't been the same without you. Mrs Winnet goes around all day like someone who's in mourning, and Christian never stops asking when he can be brought across to see you.'

'Then why can't he?'

Her question caught Richard off guard. 'Why can't he what, Rose?' he asked, knowing what the answer would be.

'Why can't you or Mrs Winnet or *anyone* bring him over to see me and Joe? Forest Gate isn't a hundred miles away. There must be a way to get him on a tram. Oh, Father, it would be such a wonderful treat for him. He'd love it so much. You know how he loves anything to do with railway trains.'

'That is not an option, Rose,' said Richard. 'Getting him on and off an omnibus or a tram would be much too tiring for him.'

'Then why not pay for a taxi?' said Rosie, eagerly pressing him. 'For God's sake, Father, you can afford it.'

'I can't do that, Rose,' explained Richard in deep despair. 'You know very well that your mother would never forgive me.'

Rosie's face hardened. 'How extraordinary,' she said. 'You and she have always brought me up to believe that the head of the family is always the

377

one who makes the decisions. It seems that another of my illusions has been shattered.' She got up to go.

'Rose – wait!' Richard rose at the same time, and went to her. 'How are you managing for money?' he asked.

'Perfectly well, thank you, Father,' she said, trying to edge her way past him.

'If I can help,' he said gently, 'if I can do anything to help, you *will* call on me, won't you?'

Rosie waited a moment before she answered. 'No, Father,' she said, 'I won't. Goodbye.'

He tried to kiss her on the cheek, but she quickly turned away, and left the room, closing the door abruptly behind her. For a moment, Richard stared at the door as though she might change her mind and come back. When she didn't, he went back to his desk, and sat back despondently in his chair. He looked up at the wall, his eyes lingering on the family snapshot that had given him so much pleasure over the years. It was of him and Marian, together with Rose and Christian when they were small, sitting in this very same office, on the same settee where Rose had been just a few minutes before. In those few moments, his whole lifetime flashed before him, as though he was drowning, as though he was trying to look back and find out why he hadn't been a better father than he was. And then his eyes closed in on Marian in the group photograph. Marian, his wife, the woman he had married. Who was right and who was wrong? he asked himself. Out of her and their daughter, which one of them had the voice of reason, the voice of sanity? It was something that had haunted him so much over the years, and was now haunting him even more.

By the following day, Joe was well enough to be allowed home. During the short time he was in hospital, the chief medical officer from Stanmore Manor had visited there and assured both him and Rosie that as long as Joe followed all the medical advice he had been given, there was no reason at all why he shouldn't live to be a ripe old age. This news was a great morale booster for Rosie, who decided that the new year was going to be the start of much better things for her and Joe.

After ominous warnings in the German newspapers that London would have nothing to celebrate at the start of 1916, Rosie decided that the safest place for her and Joe to be at such a time would be at home in the old railway carriage. But once they were there, and on their own again, Joe expressed his fears for Rosie's safety.

'I want yer to give up the tea trolley at Charing Cross,' he said, as they lay in bed together that afternoon. 'They was sayin' up the 'ospital that Fritz is goin' ter make an all-out attempt ter bomb the daylights out er London. If you stay up West, yer'll be right in the fick of it. I don't like it, Rosie. I just don't like it.'

'I promise you there's nothing to worry about, dear,' replied Rosie, snuggling up to him. 'All the London railway stations are so heavily protected, a Zeppelin wouldn't have a chance to get near any one of them. In any case, believe me, I *do*

379

know how to look after myself.'

'That's wot we all say,' replied Joe. 'But just remember wot Fritz did to me, *and* ter your mates out at Orlais.'

'I know that, Joe,' Rosie sighed. 'God knows I do. I think about it all the time.'

He pulled her face close, and kissed her. 'If anyfin' was ter 'appen ter *you*,' he whispered, 'I'd 'ave nuffin' left ter live for.'

'Stuff and nonsense!' replied Rosie, tweaking his nose playfully with the tips of her fingers. 'You've got a lot to live for, Joe Upton. We *both* have.'

In the short silence that followed, all that could be heard was Joe's breathing and the wheeze that went with it. The bedclothes rustled as he gradually started to move on top of her.

Although she wanted him badly, and longed for this moment, she resisted.

'No, Joe,' she said softly. 'Not now.'

'Why not?' he asked, taken by surprise, suspended above her.

'You're just out of hospital, darling,' she replied. 'Get your strength back first.'

'I've got me strength back,' he replied, hurt by her response.

'It's too early, Joe,' she insisted. 'I wouldn't want the same thing to happen as the other night. I don't want to take any risks. We just couldn't cope if – well, if something should go wrong.'

Reluctantly, Joe rolled down on to his back. The idea of being rejected came new to him, and he didn't like it.

She immediately turned on her side to face

380

him. 'Don't take it to heart, Joe,' she pleaded, trying to cuddle up to him again. 'You know what I'm saying makes sense. I lay in this bed last night longing to have you by my side. But I also want you to get healthy and strong again.'

'So 'ow long do I 'ave ter wait?' he asked sourly. 'Till the war's over?'

'Do you love me, Joe?'

Her direct question took him by surprise; he was a bit flummoxed by it.

'Joe?' she repeated.

'Wot der *you* fink?' he grunted sulkily.

'I think you do,' she replied. 'And I love you too. Oh, God knows how I love you! But if we're going to spend the rest of our lives together, let's try and trust each other. Right?' As he didn't respond, she gently eased his face back towards her. 'Right?'

Gradually he warmed to her again, and smiled. 'Right,' he agreed grumpily.

They kissed, long and hard. But for the time being at least, that's as far as it went.

Charing Cross Station was in buoyant mood. With New Year's Eve only one day away, the families and friends who had gathered to meet their loved ones off the special hospital boat train that evening were being treated to a post-Christmas carol concert beneath the Christmas tree by the choristers of nearby St Martin-in-the-Fields. The combination of children's voices, the chatter of commuters rushing for their evening trains home, and the intermittent blast of engine whistles was quite a heady mixture, if not somewhat over-

381

whelming, but the overall effect was uplifting. Soon, everyone on the platforms and station concourse was joining in the words of 'Silent Night' and 'The First Noel', but it was not until the concert came to an end that something happened that turned all heads.

Drifting airily around the cold platforms and up into the elegant glass roof came the almost perfect tenor voice of a middle-aged bare-headed soldier in army uniform. Everyone stopped what they were doing and turned to listen to him, as he sang the poignant, popular song of the moment, 'When This Lousy War Is Over'. When he had finished, the sea of anguished faces who had been listening to him, including Rosie and Judy, remained silent, until, as if brought back from a deep sleep, they all suddenly sprang into life again, and continued what they had been doing.

'Yer know,' said Judy, dabbing the tears in her eyes, 'it's at times like this that I'm glad I don't 'ave no family of my own. If I 'ad a dad or a brother who 'ad to go off and fight, I don't think I'd sleep at nights.'

Judy's words lingered in Rosie's mind as she made her way through the crowds to the kitchen to collect a second tea trolley. When she got there, she found the room empty, but piled high with crockery being used by the other voluntary services as well as by QAIMNS. Once she had made the tea in the large urn she was taking back to the platform, she turned towards the door, where, to her horror, she found Joe's brother, Paul, waiting.

'Bit of a mad'ouse out there ternight,' he said. 'Wot time's the "special" due then?'

'Any minute now,' retorted Rosie, angrily. She quickly pushed her trolley towards the door. 'Will you please let me pass, Paul?'

Paul remained where he was, blocking her path. 'Can I 'ave a word wiv yer, Rosie?' he asked.

'No, Paul!' she replied sharply. 'I'm at work. I don't have time to chat.'

'Please,' he begged.

'What are you doing here, Paul?' she snapped. 'I do not want you following me around.'

'I've got a message for Joe,' he said quickly. 'From Mum.'

Rosie stared sceptically at him.

'She said she 'opes 'e's feelin' better, an' that if 'e needs anyfin', 'e's ter let 'er know.'

'Thank you, Paul,' replied Rosie curtly. 'I'll give Joe that message. Now will you please let me pass?'

Paul hesitated, then stood back. But as Rosie drew alongside him, he held up his hand to the doorframe to stop her from going. 'Yer know, Rosie,' he said softly, 'one of these days yer'll find I ain't so bad.' He slowly leaned forward to kiss her ear.

For one split second she felt the urge to let him do it, but then quickly pulled away. 'Keep away from me, Paul,' she said. 'I'm warning you for the last time. Keep away!'

'Oh – I'm sorry,' said Judy, who suddenly appeared at the door. 'I – I hope I'm not interruptin' anything?'

Paul smiled. 'Be seein' yer then, Rosie Lee.'

'Who's *that?*' gasped Judy, who couldn't take her eyes of him as he went. 'He's absolutely *gorgeous!* Who is he?'

Rosie pushed her trolley out through the door. 'Nobody,' she replied tersely. 'Absolutely nobody at all.'

Joe was having the time of his life. Whilst Rosie was away doing her evening tea duties at Charing Cross Station, he and Cuthbert were knocking the life out of a quart bottle of bitter, one of many that the old codger had hoarded in the cupboard in his front parlour for God knows how long. But the drink was not exactly conducive to playing the game of draughts set up on Cuthbert's kitchen table, and even when he wasn't topped up with bitter, the old codger was a notorious cheat at any game. But Joe enjoyed his company, for it helped to pass the hours until Rosie got home again. Being on his own wasn't something Joe enjoyed very much. Despite the fact that he loved every moment he was with Rosie, there were times recently when he had missed the companionship of his army mates, and the fact that he wasn't yet well enough to rejoin his regiment or get a job only made matters worse.

'Take it from me, young feller,' said Cuthbert, slurring his words, and craftily pushing one of the counters with his little finger, 'there's nuffin' like it in the 'ole wide world. If I was young enuff, I'd still be in the army terday. If it 'adn't bin fer my Gladys I'd've made it a career, instead er givin' it up an' workin' fer a bleedin' brewery.'

'Come off it, Cuff,' said Joe, fuzzily. 'You're not goin' ter tell me yer didn't like workin' fer a brewery. Yer probably drank all the profits!'

'Some 'ope!' sniffed Cuthbert, dismissively. 'Men who run breweries ain't got no 'earts. D'yer know I never got one single discount all the years I was workin' for 'em. I tell yer, I should've stayed in the army wiv ol' Monty. 'Im an' me was like bruvvers. We ate tergevver, drank tergevver...'

'An' lived it up wiv the gels tergevver!' laughed Joe, boozily.

'That's none er your business, young man!' snapped Cuthbert, haughtily. 'It may interest you ter know that we always treated the ladies we met with respect. Which is more than the fellers seem ter do terday.'

'Only kiddin', Cuff,' said Joe. 'Only kiddin'.'

Cuthbert immediately used his counter to jump over the last four of Joe's. 'One, two, free, four! My game, I believe?' he announced triumphantly.

Joe grinned. He knew what the old boy had been up to. 'Anyfin' yer say, Cuff. It's amazin' wot yer can do wiv that little finger!'

'Cheeky bugger!' Furious that he had been caught out, Cuthbert reached for the nearly empty bottle of bitter. 'Just like yer bruvver.'

''Ow would *you* know?' asked Joe, flopping back into his chair without really taking in what Cuthbert had just said. 'Yer don't even know 'im.'

'Who said I don't? Name's Paul – right?'

'So?'

'So I know 'im.'

'Since when?'

'Since the uvver night,' said Cuthbert, shakily draining the last of the bitter into both their glasses.

Joe's eyes suddenly darted up at him. 'What're yer talkin' about?' he asked, as though he had immediately sobered up.

''E was 'ere, I tell yer. Only fer a few minutes, though,' replied Cuthbert. ''E spent most of the time over in your carriage, waitin' fer Rosie ter come 'ome. It was when you was in 'ospital.'

Joe froze.

'Nice young feller,' continued Cuthbert, gulping down his booze. 'Good-lookin' too. Finks the world er you an' Rosie. That's why 'e come over – said 'e 'adn't 'eard from you an' Rosie since yer'd moved.'

At that moment a series of heavy artillery shots sounded in the distance.

'Jesus Christ!' yelled Cuthbert, leaping up from the table to go to look at the sky through his kitchen window. 'Turn off the gas, Joe! Quick! There's a bleedin' Zep on the way over.' When Joe remained static at the table, Cuthbert rushed to the gas mantle on the wall, and turned it off himself, plunging the room into pitch-black. 'Come an' look at it, mate!' he called, rushing outside.

From his back yard, Cuthbert could see the sky lit up by dozens of small explosions from a barrage of artillery fire. And in the midst of it all, slipping menacingly in and out of the dark night clouds, came the sinister shape of a Zeppelin airship, like a giant cigar, with engines droning behind its gondola to give it the maximum speed it needed to avoid being shot down.

'Buggers!' yelled Cuthbert at the top of his voice, shaking his fist up angrily at the eerie-looking monster as it gradually passed overhead. But his attention was suddenly distracted by a voice calling from the road leading to his cottage.

'Joe! Cuthbert!'

In the distance, Cuthbert could just see Rosie rushing towards the field from the tram stop at the end of the road.

'Rosie!' yelled Cuthbert as loud as he could, the giant airship now right overhead. 'Get inside! Fast as yer can!' Whilst she was doing so, he went to the kitchen door and yelled inside: 'Joe! Come quick! It's Rosie! Joe...'

Inside the kitchen, Joe sat alone in the dark, miles away from the threat of Zeppelins and the danger they were bringing. He was in another world. All he could think about was Rosie and Paul, and the intense feeling of betrayal that was tearing his guts apart.

'Take cover! Take cover!'

Although the giant enemy airship had not yet reached Islington, the air raid was already being signalled by a teenage boy racing from street to street on his pedal cycle, blasting out the warning on his bugle.

In number 221 Camden Road, Richard Little, in dressing gown and carpet slippers, hurried into young Christian's room, where he found the boy sitting up in the dark, rubbing his eyes.

'Hold on, son,' Richard said, as he pulled back the eiderdown, wrapped it around the boy, and gently lifted him up into his arms.

'Where are we going?' asked Christian, drowsily, completely disoriented.

'We're going down to the cellar, Christian,' replied his father. 'Don't worry now. Your mother's waiting for us. Hold on tight now!'

Christian did as he was told, but fell asleep again almost immediately.

Richard picked his way carefully down the stairs, but as he did so, he could hear the first whirring sound of the airship's engines approaching from the distance. Almost simultaneously, there was a loud explosion, quite a way off, but enough to make the place shudder. He waited a moment, then continued down to the ground floor. The cellar door was open, and once he'd managed to close it, the light from candles down below helped him to find his way down the stone steps. It was with great relief when he finally reached the emergency living area he had assembled for use during just such a raid.

'Let me take him,' said Marian, sitting in an armchair, stretching out her arms to take the boy from her husband.

'He's fast asleep,' replied Richard, perching on the end of the small trestle bed that had been provided for the boy. 'It's better I hang on to him whilst all this is going on.'

A touch hurt, Marian withdrew her hands, and folded them together on her lap. In the background, Mrs Winnet, in hairnet, curlers and dressing gown, was watching from her chair in the shadows.

'When he wakes,' said Marian, gallantly, 'the first person he's going to want to see is me. A child always needs his mother at a time like this.' She threw a quick glance over her shoulder.

'Don't you agree, Mrs Winnet?'

'Yes, madam,' replied Mrs Winnet, reluctantly.

As she spoke, there was a particularly heavy burst of gunfire from the street above. This disturbed Christian, who slowly woke up with a groan.

Marian immediately got up and went to the boy. 'It's all right, darling,' she said, leaning over him. 'Nothing to worry about. Mother's here.'

'Rosie?'

Marian did a double take.

'Is that you, Rosie?' murmured the boy, eyes shut tight.

Marian leaned closer. 'It's *me*, Christian,' she persisted, gently stroking his hair. 'It's Mother. You're quite safe with me.'

'Rosie?' the boy repeated, eyes still closed. 'I want Rosie.'

Marian's face stiffened, but she did her best to smile as she straightened up. However, when she turned to look at her husband, he said nothing, and merely wrapped the eiderdown more snugly around the boy, who went straight back to sleep again.

Chapter 22

Rosie couldn't believe what she was hearing. God knows, she thought, it was frightening enough to be caught in the street just as a Zeppelin was passing overhead, but then to be met by Joe in one of the most thunderous moods she had ever seen him in seemed to her to be utterly incomprehensible. Fortunately, he had held back his angry outburst until they had both left Cuthbert's cottage, but even as they made their way to the other side of the track, she found it impossible to make him believe that she had absolutely no feeling for his brother, Paul, whatsoever.

'Then why didn't yer tell me Paul'd bin 'ere?' he shouted over his shoulder as they sploshed through mud and dead grass all the way back to the railway carriage. 'Why din't yer tell me that yer couldn't wait ter get me into 'ospital and out er the way? Why did yer 'ave ter lie ter me, Rosie? Why?'

'I did *not* lie to you, Joe!' she called, keeping up with him with difficulty. 'Paul came here to see you, *not* me! He didn't even know you were in hospital.'

Joe came to an abrupt halt, and swung round to her. With the moon dipping in and out of dark night clouds again, he could only see her face for a few moments at a time. 'If yer wanted ter go wiv my bruvver,' he said, his voice showing signs of wheezing, 'then why din't yer tell me so? If that's the sort er person yer want, then that's fine by me.'

'Joe!' she shouted right at him. Now she was really angry. 'Don't say such absolutely stupid things like that to *me*. If your brother decides to visit you and you're not here, what exactly am I expected to do?'

'It depends, Rosie,' he replied despondently.

'On what?'

'On whevver 'e was invited.'

Rosie was at such a loss for words that she just stormed off across the old railway track to the carriage. This time it was Joe who followed behind.

The moment Rosie reached the carriage door, she went in, found the box of matches and lit a candle.

'Well, 'ow d'yer fink I feel, Rosie?' said Joe, as he followed her in. 'Knowin' my bruvver, knowin' wot 'e's like wiv every gel 'e comes across. 'Ow do I know that you're not carryin' on be'ind my back – especially when yer wouldn't even let me touch you yesterday?'

Rosie turned round to face him. She was shocked, and there were tears in her eyes. 'Oh, Joe,' she sobbed, 'how can you say such a thing to me? It's horrible, Joe! It's not only horrible, it's so unjustified.' Her face crumpled up, so she quickly turned away, went into the bedroom, and threw herself face down on to the bed.

Joe waited a moment, and sat down dejected on a chair at the kitchen table. He didn't know what had hit him. Rosie Lee was everything he had ever wanted, and here he was talking to her as though she was just the same as those village tarts his mates paid money to up front. And yet, Paul *had* come here, and she hadn't told him about it. Who or what should he believe? If Rosie *wasn't* telling the truth, if she *did* ask Paul to come to the carriage whilst he was away, how had she managed to contact him? After all, neither of them had been to visit his family since they left home more than six weeks ago, so it all seemed so unlikely. None the less, this *was* the second time Rosie and Paul had met, the first time being when he went to see her at Charing Cross Station. It was obvious Paul had taken a fancy to Rosie, so why blame *her?*

Gradually the guilt began to seep through. What had he done? What had he done to say such things to the girl who meant so much to him? He got up laboriously from his chair, and went into the bedroom. There was no light in there, but he could hear Rosie sobbing quietly to herself in the dark. He eased himself down gently on to the bed alongside her. 'I'm sorry, Rosie,' he whispered in her ear. 'I'm a dope, an' I'm really sorry.'

Rosie didn't respond.

He moved closer. 'Just try an' fink of it as the first time.'

She turned her face towards him. 'What d'you mean?' she asked, voice croaking.

'Let's face it,' he whispered, 'it's the first time we've *really* 'ad a barney. Chances are, it won't be the last. After all, it must 'appen ter all married people, don't yer fink?'

'We're not married,' she replied.

'No,' he replied, with a kiss on her forehead. 'But we will be – one day.'

They hugged each other tight.

''Ere, Rosie,' he whispered softly in her ear, 'can yer imagine wot this ol' carriage must've looked like in its time? All them people sittin' in different compartments, smokin' their pipes, readin' newspapers, feedin' the kids, snorin' their 'eads off. I reckon where we are now must've been first class, real posh.'

This brought the first smile to Rosie's face. 'How can you tell that?' she asked.

'Oh, I don't know,' said Joe. 'The smell, the feel of the place. Remember that bit of old seat we found when we moved in, you know – the fancy cushion wiv the tea cloff ter lean yer 'ead back on? That was class all right – not fer the likes of poor rumps like mine.'

This made Rosie laugh. This was the Joe she loved and cherished, not the mad creature who, just a few moments ago, had accused her of such horrible things. 'You're absurd, Joe,' she said, warming to him and snuggling up. 'I can't imagine them having much first class on a train to Southend.'

''Ere – just a minute!' he replied, with mock pretence. 'An' wot's wrong wiv 'avin' first class on a train ter Soufend as well as ter Brighton an' Bournemouth? I tell yer, this carriage was first class, an' no mistake!'

'Whatever you say, dear,' sighed Rosie, relieved that things between them were back to normal again. 'Whatever you say.'

'But, Rosie,' said Joe, sounding a quiet note of caution, 'the next time my bruvver comes near yer, I want ter 'ear about it – right?'

'All right, Joe,' she replied.

'Promise?'

'Promise,' said Rosie.

They kissed, hard and passionately. And then they made love.

In Trafalgar Square, even the pigeons felt cold. The bronze lions, however, always grim and unyielding, adapted well to the winter climate, their great lifelike figures resting imperiously on their plinths, guarding the monument of the great naval hero who kept a constant watch on the equally great city that surrounded him out and beyond. Although snow wasn't expected for a few more days, its arrival was certainly being heralded by a bitterly cold snap, which left a thin layer of early morning frost on Lord Nelson's head at the top of his column, but which was not visible to the small groups of visitors in the square down below. Amongst those visitors was a smartly dressed middle-aged man, pushing a young boy along slowly in a wheelchair, accompanied by a slightly older woman, who was wrapped up well in a black fox-fur boa, feather hat and warm woollen coat.

Christian Little was clearly having the time of his life. During the Zeppelin raid the night before, his father had given no indication that he would be bringing him and Mrs Winnet on such a treat. To be in Trafalgar Square on the morning of New Year's Eve was something he would never have even dreamed about, but now he was here. He was relishing every single moment, especially feeding the constantly hungry pigeons on scraps of bread provided by Mrs Winnet from the leftovers at breakfast, and trying to communicate with them through sounds taught to him by Joe. But he was also particularly excited to see the flurry of motorised traffic passing in and out of the square, the double-decker omnibuses, trams, taxis and trucks smugly overtaking the good old faithful horse and carts that had been the mainstay of industry for so many years. Every-where he looked, Christian found something new and fascinating to look at: army recruitment banners hanging from the foot of the column, posters urging women to do their bit for the war effort, a pacifist using one of the stone ledges to launch a scathing attack on the futility of war and a group of off-duty sailors doing an improvised shanty, to the delight of the visitors looking on. Christian laughed loudly at their antics, clapping in vigorous time to the elderly sailor accompanying them on his concertina.

To a young boy who had never been to such a place, despite the gloomy atmosphere of war, the hustle and bustle of Central London was infectious, and Richard loved watching his son enjoying it all. The idea of a trip out hadn't even occurred to him until Rosie had made him see how much the boy was missing in what might be such a tragically short life.

However, when they left home that morning, the real purpose of the outing was not revealed to Marian Little. Only Mrs Winnet knew their ultimate destination.

Over at Charing Cross Station, which was only a few minutes' walk up the Strand from Trafalgar Square, Rosie, preparing for the arrival of the final hospital train of the old year, was now in good spirits. This morning, Joe, still feeling guilty about the way he had behaved, had come along to the station to be with her for this, their first New Year's Eve together, which meant that he could give her a hand with the tea trolley, for Judy, who had been on night duty at the

QAIMNS headquarters, would not be coming in until later. Although the midday hospital train would not be arriving for another hour, the first relatives and friends were already streaming into the station concourse from the omnibuses outside. The anxious look on all their faces reflected what the mood would be, as the clock ticked relentlessly towards the new year.

Once the tea urns and trolleys were fully prepared, Rosie and Joe took the opportunity to slip away for a few minutes to stroll along the Strand. The place was positively jammed with last-minute shoppers and sightseers, crowds going in and out of the station, market sellers in the side streets and hectic stalls where the pungent smell of hot eel pies and mash mixed with the sweet aroma of roasting chestnuts.

''Ere, Rosie,' asked Joe, as they passed a stall where a young cockney boy with the gift of the gab was selling 'MIRACLE COLD CURES', ''as it occurred to you that I ain't coffed once all mornin'?'

'Yes, dear,' replied Rosie. 'I *have* noticed, and I just hope it stays that way. One of the important things in getting you well again is that you don't get too upset.'

'Point taken,' said Joe. 'But what I mean is, I fink it's time I reported back ter the regiment.'

Rosie, shocked, brought them to an abrupt halt. 'Joe!' she exclaimed. 'How can you say such a thing? It's only a few nights since you had that attack.'

'I know, I know,' replied Joe, restlessly. 'But I can't just sit around all day expectin' you ter wait on me 'and an' foot. I feel fine now, Rosie. I don't wanna get back inter uniform again, but I should at least go an' get a check-up at Stanmore. If *they* fink I'm on the mend, then I owe it ter me mates ter get back wiv 'em again.'

'And what about me, Joe?' Rosie asked. 'What do you owe to me?'

Joe turned to look straight at her. 'I owe *you* me life, Rosie Lee.'

'Then why d'you want to leave me?'

Joe shook his head. 'I don't ever want ter leave yer, Rosie,' he replied. 'I just want us ter get on wiv our lives.'

All the joy, all the renewed hope that Rosie had felt when she got up that morning had now gone. Although in some bizarre way she knew that what Joe was saying was probably true, in her heart of hearts she felt that he was trying to pretend to himself that suddenly he wasn't ill any more, that he could go about his life as though nothing had happened. She was at a loss for words, and could only say, 'It's up to you, Joe. I won't try to stop you doing what you want to do.'

'Not wot I *want* ter do, Rosie,' he replied. 'It's wot I *'ave* ter do.'

Rosie, looking up to his eyes, was quite suddenly distracted by something over his shoulder in the distance. 'Oh, my God!' she gasped.

'Rosie!' spluttered Joe, turning to see what she was looking at. 'Wot is it?'

'Father! Christian!' she yelled out, breaking away from him and rushing off back to the station.

Joe was stunned, for he eventually saw why

Rosie had gone. Slowly making their way into the station, he could see Richard Little, with Mrs Winnet, pushing Christian in his wheelchair. 'Blimey!' he gasped.

'Father! Christian!' yelled Rosie as she reached them. 'Oh, Christian!' she cried out, immediately throwing her arms around her brother and hugging him tight. 'Dear, dear Christian!'

'Rosie!' cried the boy, responding to her excitement. 'I've missed you so much. I wish you could have been with us. Father's given me the most wonderful treat. We came in a taxi!'

Rosie slowly looked up at her father. It was a look of silent gratitude.

'Blimey, mate!' said Joe to the boy, as he caught them up. 'This is a turn-up fer the books!'

'Good morning, Joe,' said Richard warmly, hand outstretched.

Joe, taken by surprise, shook hands with him. 'Mornin', sir.'

Quite impulsively, Rosie went to her father and silently pecked him on the cheek. Then she went to Mrs Winnet, who was moist-eyed. 'I'm so happy to see you, Winnie,' she said.

Mrs Winnet was too full to say anything, so she just smiled to show how happy she was.

A few minutes later, Joe and Mrs Winnet took Christian for an excited look at his great love, the train engines. Rosie and her father went into the station café, where they sat at a table for a quiet talk. As usual, the place was full and smoky, but, with the impending arrival of the hospital train, the mood there was anxious and subdued.

'All I can do, Father,' said Rosie, with difficulty,

'is to thank you. What you've done for Christian today is more than I ever dared hope.' Her eyes flicked up at him. 'But why?'

'I don't know, Rose,' sighed Richard, stirring his tea without actually putting the cup to his lips. 'I thought about it all the way here in the taxi, but I just don't know. I suppose it's because, in some ways, I understand what you were trying to say – about being able to see beyond fact or reason. We have no right to deny Christian a good quality of life, no matter how short that time may be.' He paused whilst he took a sip of tea. 'He does love you so much,' he continued. 'He wanted to come and visit you at – at the place where you live. I told him I'd have to talk to you first and, if you agreed, we'd have to see how we could arrange it.'

'How would Mother feel about that?' asked Rosie pointedly.

Richard considered this. 'You know, Rose,' he replied, 'I don't think you have ever fully appreciated how either your mother or I have felt about having a child who will not be able to live a full span of life. It's a complicated thing. Your mother feels guilty that she brought an imperfect child into this world. She feels as though she's let me down. I've always tried to tell her that it's not her fault – it's not anyone's fault. God made His judgement, and we have no choice but to abide by it. I know it isn't easy for *you* to accept, but it isn't easy for us either.'

Rosie hesitated before replying. 'Does that mean that you won't send Christian to a sanatorium?' she asked.

'I never had any intention of doing so,' he replied earnestly.

Rosie tried to disguise her immense relief.

'Your mother and I have also made another decision,' he said. 'It's about you.'

Rosie looked up, puzzled.

'I see no point in remaining an obstacle to your union with Joe.'

Rosie was genuinely shocked.

'If you are firmly convinced,' he said, 'that Joe is the man you want to spend the rest of your life with, then neither your mother nor I will continue to stand in your way.'

Rosie was so taken aback that she hardly knew what to say. 'Father!' she murmured quietly.

'But please remember, Rose,' he continued, putting on his bowler hat, 'don't think that our acceptance is unqualified. I have to admit that our decision is partly for our own benefit. It's not in our interest to have an unmarried daughter living with an unmarried man. However, hopefully, one day your mother and I will be proved wrong, and you will be proved right.' He got up from the table. 'In the meantime, for all our sakes, especially Christian's, let's end this strain between us.'

Rosie clasped her father's hand and they walked out of the café.

Once Richard and Mrs Winnet had taken Christian home in a taxi, Rosie and Joe mulled over the extraordinary implications of Richard's agreement to them getting married.

'We can't do it,' said Rosie, as they strolled to

the end of Platform 1 just prior to the arrival of the hospital train. 'Whatever Father says, we can't get married – not yet.'

Joe was baffled. 'Why not?'

'Because for one thing,' she replied, 'we can't afford it. There's no money left in the kitty, Joe, and I certainly don't intend to ask my father for any. What we're doing is *our* decision. It's up to us to cope with it. But in time.'

'Then there's only one fing ter do,' said Joe defiantly. 'I'll desert, and get a job.'

'Joe!' exclaimed Rosie. 'Don't say such things! You know what happens when a serviceman deserts. You'd be put before a firing squad.'

'I'd be willing to take that chance,' said Joe. 'You're worf it a 'undred times over, Rosie.'

'Not if I end up a widow before we're even married,' she replied ominously.

Joe brought them to a temporary halt halfway along the platform. 'Now you listen ter me, Rosie Lee,' he said, with people rushing back and forth around them. 'No wife er mine is goin' ter spend the rest of 'er life lookin' after me. The day I met yer – right 'ere on this very station – I said ter meself, there's only one gel I want in this world, an' that's *you*. Oh, not just 'cos of wot I saw on the outside, but 'cos of wot I *know* you 'ave *inside*. Rosie, 'ave yer any idea 'ow many men comin' back an' forf on these trains look out the window at you an' say, "That's fer me!"? Well, I beat 'em all to it, din't I, so there's no way I'm goin' ter let yer go now.' He glanced around to make sure no one could hear what he was saying. 'I love you, Rosie Lee,' he whispered. 'As long as there's a sun an' a moon, I'll always love yer.'

''Ello then!'

They both turned with a start to find Judy hurrying towards them.

'Sorry I'm late, Rosie,' Judy said, 'but Sister Maisie got me to sort out the medicine cupboard. I think the ol' bag's got it in for me!' Her eyes suddenly widened as she saw Joe. 'An' who's this?'

'Judy,' said Rosie, 'this is Joe.'

'Oh!' she cried. 'So *this* is 'im, is it, the one I keep 'earin' about all the time? Well,' she said, looking him up and down, 'you're all she said you was – *and* more!'

Rosie and Joe laughed.

'Except you're not as good-lookin' as your bruvver,' she added.

Rosie froze.

'Sorry to have to say it,' continued Judy, ignoring Rosie's signals to pipe down, 'but no two bruvvers can 'ave *everything*, now can they? Well, that's always been my experience.'

Joe's expression had turned to stone. 'Yer know my bruvver, do yer?'

'Well, I can't say I *know* him,' replied Judy innocently, 'but I'd like to! Yer'd better watch out, soldier. When he came here yesterday, the way he looked at Rosie I thought he was you.'

Joe swung an angry look at Rosie. Then without saying a word, he rushed off along the platform.

'Joe!' yelled Rosie, racing after him.

'What's up?' called an astonished Judy. 'Did I say something wrong?'

Just as Rosie caught up with Joe, the hospital

train sounded its whistle in the distance.

'Joe!' begged Rosie, grabbing hold of his arm, and bringing him to a halt. 'Listen to me! *Please* listen to me!'

'No, Rosie!' he growled. 'I reckon I've listened ter too much from *you*. But I tell yer this much, you ain't goin' ter make me look a chump any more. This is it! This is the end!' He pulled away and hurried off.

Rosie followed, but found it difficult to keep up with him. 'No, Joe!' she insisted frantically. 'It's not like that. It's not like you think...' She was going out of her mind trying to make sense of her stupid mistake. 'Yes, Paul *did* come here. I told him not to. I told him he was to keep away from me. But he wouldn't listen. He just wouldn't listen.'

Once again Joe stopped, and turned on her. 'Then why din't yer tell me? Why, Rosie, why?'

For one brief moment Rosie tried hard to think why. But she had no excuse. After all that Joe had said to her, after all he had made her promise. One word, that's all it would have taken to clear the air between them. 'I don't know what to say to you, Joe,' she replied, close to tears. 'I honestly don't know what to say, except that I was not trying to keep anything from you.'

'You promised, Rosie,' Joe reminded her. 'You promised!'

With those parting words, he stormed off. As he did so, the relatives and friends of the casualties arriving on the hospital train swarmed around her, and just as the train had rattled its way to a stop alongside the platform, the military

403

band on the station concourse struck up its usual medley of popular songs, starting with the perennial 'Little Dolly Daydream'.

Rosie, tears streaming down her cheeks, turned, and made her way back to the tea trolley.

New Year's Eve meant very little to Annie Upton. In all the years she had lived together with Will, she had always treated it as just any other day. In some ways it was even harder than many ordinary working days, for she often went out to do part-time jobs up at the posh houses in Grove Road in Mile End, such as silver and brass polishing, cleaning out porcelain lavatory pans and generally helping out in the kitchen as the rich folk prepared for their annual New Year's Eve feast. On one occasion the year before, owing to the shortage of manpower, she was even asked to do a bit of chimney sweeping, but as her enormous build made getting around on the roof a little precarious, she reluctantly had to preclude herself from that job. Although her employers thought that paying her between ninepence and a shilling for her services was highway robbery, to her it was a pittance. But at least it allowed her to put a couple of decent meals into her boys' stomachs. However, all that was no longer necessary, for, what with Paul earning a weekly wage up at the fish curing warehouse, and Joe now off her hands to fend for himself and his lady love, she felt she could take things a bit easier. But if money wasn't as big a problem as it used to be, having a son like Paul certainly was.

'So where're you off to tonight?' she asked him,

as he spruced himself up in front of the tiny mirror over the mantelpiece in the back parlour. 'Found yourself another 'eart to break, 'ave you?'

Paul grinned, and adjusted his tie. He liked what he saw in the mirror, and he knew the girls did too. But tonight was going to be special. There was one girl who was proving not so easy to win over, and he was determined to do something about her.

'Leave 'er alone, lad,' said Annie sternly.

Paul threw a passing glance at her reflection behind him in the mirror. 'Wot yer talkin' about?' he asked, assuming innocence.

'You *know* what I'm talking about,' replied his mum, reproachfully, continuing to darn a pair of his socks at the parlour table, 'Rosie's your brother's lass. Keep your 'ands off 'er, or you'll bring 'eartache to this family.'

Paul turned to face her. 'Don't know wot yer talkin' about, Mum,' he retorted. 'Me an' Mickey Manners are spendin' New Year's Eve down the Pearly King.'

Annie sniffed dismissively. 'Mickey Manners!' she growled in her severest Yorkshire brogue. 'That lad 'as got no more sense in 'is 'ead than 'is ol' man – an' we all know what 'appened to *'im!* Put 'is 'ead in t' gas oven 'cos of gamblin' on t' dogs!'

'That's not fair, Mum,' replied Paul, returning to his dog-end, which he'd left smouldering on the edge of the mantelpiece. 'Mickey's all right. 'E's got 'imself a girlfriend.'

''As 'e now?' returned Annie, unconvinced.

''E's finkin' about tyin' the knot.'

'Oh, aye?' asked Annie, with a sniff, tying her own knot on the woollen thread of Paul's sock, and biting off the end with her teeth. 'An' what's 'e using fer brass?'

''E earns enough,' replied Paul, putting on his best jacket. 'We boaf do. Only diff'rence between 'im an' me is that once this war's over, I'm goin' ter be a millionaire.'

'Fancy that,' replied his mum, with some irony. 'It's funny 'ow young folk always dream of being millionaires. They don't realise that life i'n't just about making money. It's about carin' for folk.'

Paul grinned, and went to her. 'I care fer people, Mum,' he said, without too much conviction. 'Specially *you*.' He leaned down and kissed her on her forehead. Then he put on his flat cap, and went to the door.

'Paul.'

He looked back at her.

'Remember what I said,' she warned. 'There's plenty more fish in the sea.'

Paul grinned. 'Don't wait up fer me, Mum,' he said. 'It could be a long night.'

Annie flopped back in her chair and sighed. She feared the worst. History was about to repeat itself – yet again.

Paul moved along the street with a spring in his step. He had already decided that this New Year's Eve was going to be the one that he would remember most, for despite the fact that he loved his kid brother, he knew that the time had come to put his cards on the table. He loved Rosie, and that's all there was to it. It was already getting dark, and in the distance he could hear the start of the last singsongs of the year filtering out from one of the neighbour's front rooms further down the street. As he went, he joined in the lilting strains of 'If Those Lips Could Only Speak', increasing his jaunty pace as he made his way to the tram stop just around the corner in Bethnal Green Road. But he had gone no more than a few yards when he suddenly felt a blow to his back, someone yanking him round roughly by his shoulder, followed by a thunderous blow to his face. The force of the blow sent him reeling to the ground, sending his best flat cap straight into a puddle of rainwater in the gutter.

'You sod! You bleedin' rotten sod!'

It took Paul a moment to clear his head and focus on his brother, Joe, who was standing over him. For the moment he said nothing, but dabbed at the trickle of blood dripping from his nose.

'Come on then, you sod!' barked Joe. 'If yer wanna fight, then fight! I ain't scared er you no more.'

Paul eased himself back on to his feet. 'Wos this all about then, Joe?' he asked quietly, rubbing his nose with the back of his hand.

'You *know* wot it's about!' Joe shouted. 'Yer just can't bear ter let anyone 'ave somefin' that *you* ain't got! Leave 'er alone, Paul, or I swear ter God I'll smash yer bleedin' brains ter bits!'

Joe's voice was so loud windows in the houses were flung open, and people came to their front doors to see what was going on. The few passers-by stopped at a distance to watch.

Under this sudden and unexpected provocation

from his brother, Paul did his best not to rise to Joe's anger. He knew only too well that if he wanted to, he could make mincemeat of Joe; his weekly visits to the boxing club in Roman Road made that an absolute certainty. But Joe was not well. His time in the trenches had left him weak of body, and, in Paul's opinion, weak of mind too. No, he would not rise to the bait. 'Let's talk about this, Joe,' he said calmly.

'There's nuffin' *to* bleedin' talk about!' yelled Joe, uncompromisingly. There was no stopping him now. He had made up his mind. The only way to deal with this situation was to face up to his brother, and play him at his own game. 'Yer can't leave 'er alone, can yer? Yer'll do anyfin' be'ind my back, anyfin' yer want. Well, I'm not goin' ter let yer. I love Rosie, an' as long as there's breff in my body, I'll *never* let yer 'ave 'er – never! D'yer understand that, Paul? Do yer?'

Joe's loud ranting was getting Paul down. 'No, Joe,' he replied quietly so as not to be heard by those watching them. 'It's fer *you* ter understand that you're not good enuff fer Rosie. Rosie's special. She's somefin' different. She don't deserve second-best.'

Joe took a swing at him, but Paul grabbed hold of his fist, and squeezed it. 'You're nuffin', Joe!' he growled softly. 'If by any chance you should live ter be an ol' man, yer'd never be able ter support a wife an' kids. Yer don't 'ave it in yer, Joe. I knew that even when we was kids.'

Joe suddenly summoned up enough strength to break loose. With a supreme effort, he lashed out at Paul again, this time landing a substantial blow on his brother's chin. Paul reeled back, but came charging back, striking Joe a heavy blow to his eye. Joe only just managed to retain his balance, but the two of them now fought like two mongrel dogs, puffing and panting and grunting and groaning. If the neighbours wanted something to look at, then they were now getting it. The shouts were loud, the struggle violent and bitter.

Finally they both fell to the ground, rolling around in the gutter, landing punch after punch on each other, squirming, cursing, a real fight to the death.

'Stop!'

Only the voice of their mother, booming out along the street, brought both brothers to a halt.

Leaning down, she grabbed hold of first Paul in one hand, then Joe in the other, each by the scruff of his neck. Annie Upton's weight had many disadvantages, but it certainly provided her with the strength to tackle her boys. 'You daft buggers!' she growled. 'I'm ashamed of you!'

The two boys stood before her, heads lowered, fighting for breath. Joe immediately started to wheeze, which suddenly turned into a violent fit of coughing.

'So,' snarled Annie, 'I 'ope you're both satisfied. Proved sommat, 'ave you? What? That being on top is all that counts? Well, I can tell you – it's not!' She turned quickly to Joe, who was doubled up with his coughing attack. Putting her arm around his waist to support him, she said one last thing to Paul before helping Joe back to the house. 'I told you, Paul,' she scowled. 'God knows, I told you!'

Rosie sat in the pitch-black of her kitchen in the railway carriage. It had been a terrible day. Since getting back from Charing Cross earlier in the evening to find that Joe had not returned home, she had spent much of the time crying. Most of this was frustration – frustration at her stupidity. She blamed herself for the way Joe had reacted when told that Paul had visited her at the station. Although it hadn't occurred to her that she needed to tell him, she now realised that trust, complete trust between couples, was absolutely imperative if their relationship was going to survive. She had learned a bitter lesson on this last day of an awful old year, and as she sat alone with her thoughts in the dark, she had no idea if she would ever be able to restore that relationship, or indeed, if Joe would ever come back to her.

From the top of the kitchen cupboard, Rosie's small alarm clock sounded the hour of eleven. With the minutes ticking by towards midnight, it was clear that 1915 was going to go out like a damp firework.

In the sitting room of number 221 Camden Road, Christian sat with his parents and Mrs Winnet, all warming themselves in front of a blazing coal fire, waiting for the final hour of the year to pass. It was the first time Christian had been allowed to see the New Year in, and the prospect excited him no end.

'Thank you for my lovely day, Father,' he said. 'And thank you for letting me see Rosie and Joe again.'

410

Richard swung a guilty, anxious look at his wife.

Marian's immediate response was anger at what she saw as her husband's betrayal. But there was something glimmering inside that made her feel that Richard had done the right thing. At the moment she couldn't understand why. Rose had chosen a path that was so alien to her that her instinct over the past weeks had been to forget that Rose even existed. But it wasn't as easy as that. Marian actually missed her daughter; the house, the family just weren't the same without her. For nights she had lain awake, deep in complicated thoughts about all that had gone on between them, and how in happier times things were so different, so down to earth, so compatible. So who was to blame? Marian had to struggle against her basic prejudice to work that one out, and it wasn't easy. All she knew was that there was a hole in her life, and it wasn't only Christian who missed Rose.

'Maybe next year?' asked Christian hopefully.

Marian snapped out of her thoughts to find the boy sitting up in his wheelchair, all bright and eager.

'Can we, Mother?' Christian persisted. 'Can we all be together again? Can we?'

For one stressful moment, Marian felt too emotional to answer. But fighting back tears, she finally managed to say, 'Let's wait and see, my darling. Let's wait and see.'

Richard stretched across from his armchair, took hold of his wife's hand, and held it.

Marian slowly looked up at him, and smiled.

At five minutes to midnight, Rosie decided to go to bed. There was no point in waiting, no point in thinking that Joe would ever forgive her enough to come home to her. After shaking out her hair with her fingers, she took the candle, went into the bedroom, put the candle down on the small cupboard, undressed, got into bed, and blew out the candle. With only moments to go now until that ridiculous hour when resolutions would be made – resolutions that would bring new life and hope in a troubled world – she closed her eyes, and thought of Joe, thought of the short but happy time they had spent together. In her mind's eye, she could see him, with the cheeks of that dear pale face caressing her own, warming it back to life on a cold night. But as the approaching New Year gathered momentum, she tried hard to block it all out of her mind. If she had to start a new chapter of life in the morning, then so be it.

In the distance, she heard the chimes of church bells all around the surrounding areas, sounding the triumphant arrival of yet another year. But before they had hardly started, she heard the bedroom door open quietly, and felt a cold figure climbing into bed beside her.

''Appy New Year, Rosie Lee,' came Joe's tender voice.

Rosie's eyes filled with tears as she was enfolded in a pair of loving arms.

'Yes, it is,' she wept, 'it *is* a happy New Year – my dearest one.'

Chapter 23

The new year had not started well for Paul Upton. After the stand-up fight with Joe in the street, and their mum's angry response, he had changed his mind about going to see Rosie, opting instead for a boozy New Year's Eve in the Pearly King with Mickey Manners. The licensing laws had been relaxed for this special annual occasion, but by the time midnight had struck, the two mates were absolutely paralytic, and had to be quite unceremoniously thrown out by the landlord.

Mickey somehow managed to crawl his way home, leaving Paul to pass out in a heap in a back yard behind the fruit and vegetable market. When he eventually came round, it was daylight, or at least he thought it must be because he could actually see the middle-aged police constable standing over him.

'Mornin' sir!' Paul said, sitting cross-legged on the cold paving stones, his wincing expression and partially closed eyes only emphasising the fact that he had such a hangover he didn't know where the hell he was.

'Time fer beddy-bies, young feller!' said the constable, with a grin. 'Anuvver day, anuvver year!'

For Paul, the voice seemed to boom out so loud that he had to cover his ears. However, he had enough sense to allow the bluebottle to help him

413

to his feet, and see him on his way. Just as well, for it was New Year's Day, and the market was just about to burst into life.

When he finally got home, he found his mum and gran having their usual slice of bread and jam and a cup of tea for breakfast. His appearance didn't surprise them one little bit. It wasn't the first time Annie had seen her elder son come home in such a state.

'Better get yourself into t'yard outside,' growled Annie. 'Looks like you could do with a decent wash down. You smell like t'gutter!'

Paul grunted, left the room and staggered upstairs.

'I don't know 'ow yer put up wiv that one,' sniffed Gran, her lips and false teeth covered in Annie's home-made strawberry jam. 'I'd've kicked 'im out years ago, along with that no-good husband of yours. Thank God he's gone back to France so he can't put his two penn'orth in.'

'You never 'ad any lads of your own, Mam,' snapped Annie, 'so you wouldn't know what you'd've done.' She wiped her mouth on the back of her hand, got up from the table, and left the room.

Gran snorted indignantly as she went.

Upstairs, Paul had collapsed face down on his bed. Annie came into the room, took one look at him, and shook her head in disgust. She'd seen it all before, many times. 'You drunken sot!' she growled, going to him. 'You'd better sober up or you'll be startin' the new year wivout a job.'

Paul grunted something, but as his mouth was pressed against the eiderdown, she couldn't hear what. 'Speak up!' she bellowed.

With great difficulty, Paul raised his head just enough to call, 'I said I ain't goin' in terday. It's an 'oliday.' He flopped down on to the eiderdown again.

'Oh, aye?' replied Annie acidly. 'Just for you, you mean?' With no response, she slipped her arms beneath his stomach, and turned him over. 'New Year's Day's not a 'oliday for *anyone*,' she shouted in her broadest Yorkshire accent. 'Now get yourself up, or I'll throw a bucket of bloody water over you!'

Paul groaned, sighed, and finally eased himself up. 'They don't need me in terday,' he grunted, finding it a major job to open his eyes. 'There ain't no fish comin' in till termorrer.'

'Good!' barked Annie. 'Then you can 'elp me and your gran to stuff a mattress.'

This brought Paul round immediately. 'I ain't stuffin' no mattress,' he growled. 'I've got fings ter do.'

'What things?'

'I don't 'ave ter tell you everyfin', Ma,' he replied irritably.

'Please yourself,' she replied tersely. 'But if you're thinking about visiting that lass again, I strongly advise you don't!'

'*Wot* lass?' he asked, trying to ease himself up from the bed. 'I dunno what yer talkin' about.'

'If that's so,' sniffed Annie, 'then just go and take a look at yourself in the glass over there. You look a right bloody wreck. Your brother may not be another Jim Corbett, but by t'look of your nose, 'e put *you* in your place!'

Paul went to the mirror and looked at himself. His nose was a bright blue, and twice its normal size.

'So if you've got any ideas about going after Joe's lass again,' she said with a wry grin, 'I'd forget it!' She started to leave the room, but stopped at the door. 'But I'll tell you this much, lad,' she added. 'That Rosie's worth 'er weight in gold to this family. If you break up those two, you'll 'ave me to deal with!' She left the room, and slammed the door behind her.

As she went, Paul did two fingers up at the door. But although his mum's words were not lost on him, that flame inside was still burning too bright to ignore.

Rosie had made up her mind. Unless she was reinstated as a nurse at QAIMNS, she was now ready to give up her voluntary tea-serving job and find work that would pay her a living wage.

Her sudden decision came as a shock to Joe, who told her that when the word got round that she was leaving, the wounded men arriving daily at Charing Cross Station would be deeply disappointed.

'They love yer, Rosie,' Joe said, as they trudged their way through the sludge on their way from the carriage to Cuthbert's cottage. 'I remember wot it was like comin' in ter that platform from Folkestone. I can still see yer standin' there, that great big smile, just like an angel, just like a saint.'

'You exaggerate, Joe,' Rosie replied dismissively. 'I'm just one of hundreds of girls doing exactly the same job. Judy can take over without any trouble at all.'

Once again Rosie felt that she had been given a new lease of life. When Joe slipped into bed with her just on the stroke of midnight, she thanked God that he had forgiven her for the stupid way she had behaved. If she had learned anything from what had happened between her and Joe during the past few days, it was that you can never take love for granted.

By the time they had reached Cuthbert's cottage, their feet were soaking wet, but they soon dried out once they were sitting in front of the old codger's oven grate.

Cuthbert himself was uncharacteristically pensive, which slightly worried Rosie, but when he told them why he wanted to have a little chat with them, they were curious.

'Raise yer glasses to me!' Cuthbert said, after pouring two small glasses of whisky for Joe and himself, and a sherry for Rosie. 'Yer'll be pleased ter know that yer won't 'ave ter look after me no more.'

Rosie and Joe swung each other startled looks. '*Wot?*' asked Joe.

'What d'you mean, Mr Jiggles?' asked Rosie, with an ominous feeling inside.

'They've accepted me, that's what,' replied Cuthbert, with a broad, smug grin. 'The ol' soldiers' 'ome in Stepney. They've accepted me application ter become a resident.'

Rosie was aghast. 'Mr Jiggles!' she gasped. 'What on earth are you going into a home for? You know very well Joe and I can carry on looking after you.'

417

'I know yer can, Rosie,' replied Cuthbert. 'But you and Joe've got lives of yer own ter live. Yer don't want an old fogey like me 'angin' on ter yer fer the rest of me days. As it is, yer've bin good ter me these past weeks. Yer've given me cups er tea in the mornin', and mince and mash fer me evenin' meal. I mean ter say, wot more could a man want?'

'A home of your own, Mr Jiggles,' said Rosie intensely. 'Somewhere that you can feel free to do all the things that you want to do.'

'Look, dearie,' Cuthbert replied, 'this don't mean I'm goin' ter be locked up in prison. This place I'm goin' to is mine by right. I'm an ol' soldier, an' ol' soldiers never die, they just go on an' on till they drop. I always told my Gladys that if anyfin' was ter 'appen to *'er*, I'd just pack up and sling me 'ook ter the ol' soldiers' 'ome. I don't know why I 'ung on so long. I should've done this years ago. The fing is, I've got some of me ol' mates there, not all that many, mind yer – not when you're *our* age. But at least I'll 'ave plenty er company, blokes like meself who can chinwag all day about what we did tergevver in the Crimea.' He suddenly noticed that Joe had put a comforting arm around Rosie's shoulder. 'Now come off it, you two,' he continued. 'There's no need ter look so down in the dumps. I shan't be kickin' yer out, yer know.'

Rosie was puzzled. 'But if you leave,' she asked, 'surely our next landlord will want to get us out of the railway carriage so that he can get a tenant who'll be willing to pay rent?'

'There won't be no next landlord,' replied

Cuthbert emphatically. ''Cos I'm givin' yer the carriage – *an*' this ol' cottage.'

Now both Rosie and Joe were truly shocked.

'Cuff!' spluttered Joe, completely taken aback. 'Wot're yer sayin'?'

'I'm sayin',' replied the old codger, 'that when I go, this place is yours. Let's face it, I won't 'ave no more need of it. Me army pension's enough ter keep me goin' in the 'ome, and since I ain't got no relatives of me own that I care one 'oot fer, I don't see why you two shouldn't 'ave a decent roof over yer 'eads. I talked it over wiv Monty, an' 'e reckoned it was a grand idea.' He looked with affection around the kitchen where they were sitting, years of memories reflected in his eyes. 'It's a good place, this. My Gladys loved it. She 'ardly ever moved out er this room. 'Er kitchen was 'er domain. I fink she would've slept 'ere if she'd had 'er way.'

Rosie and Joe were stunned into silence. 'Mr Jiggles,' said Rosie, quite overtaken by what he had said, 'I – I don't know what to say to you.'

Cuthbert leaned across and gently patted her hand. 'Wot's there *to* say, dearie?' he replied. 'Just remember that if yer decide to stay on 'ere, yer'll be makin' an ol' git very 'appy. Will yer do that fer me?'

Rosie slowly turned to look at Joe, then back to Cuthbert again. 'Mr Jiggles,' she said, 'nothing in the whole wide world would make us happier.'

When Rosie got to QAIMNS headquarters, she found the place alive with rumours about enemy activity in the English Channel that was affecting the troop ferry services. Until now, Zeppelin airships had been the main threat, but as the Germans had now increased the number of submarines patrolling along the Dover Straits and the coast of northern France, the twenty-mile or so Channel crossing was becoming increasingly hazardous.

This was very much at the forefront of everyone's mind when Rosie turned up to talk to Sister Maisie about wanting to return to nursing duties as soon as possible. However, she did not get the response she wanted.

'There's nothing we can do, lassie,' said Sister Maisie, as she and Rosie climbed the stairs up to her office on the first floor. 'Until your father has a change of mind, and we get fresh instructions from the War Office or whoever, we dare not let you go back to active duty nursing.'

'But surely I could be useful out at Stanmore?' Rosie asked. 'I hear you still need all the help you can get out there.'

'Aye, there's no doubt about that,' replied Maisie. 'No sooner do we get a new intake out there, than they're whisked off to France or Belgium. I tell you, it's getting frantic around here.'

'Then it seems madness that I'm not allowed to help out,' persisted Rosie. 'Oh, Sister Maisie, can't you put in a good word for me, please?'

Maisie sighed, and shook her head.

They reached her office, where, in the absence of Lady Braintree, two new young trainees were waiting to be interviewed.

'What I don't understand,' said Maisie, 'is why you should *want* to give up the tea trolley at

Charing Cross. A little bird told me that that the young man you're living with is still under the MO at Stanmore. I would have thought you'd want to stay as near to him as you possibly could.'

'I do,' replied Rosie. 'In fact, my life has never been more positive, especially now that we've just been given a permanent home to live in. But I don't want to go on being a tea girl until the end of the war. I feel so wasted. Sister Maisie, you must understand that I *have* to do something to help men like Joe, something more than serving cups of tea each day.'

Sister Maisie sat at her desk, and took off her spectacles. 'Shall I tell you something, child?' she began. 'I don't think you know what you've done for the morale of those boys coming in to Charing Cross every day. You're not just a tea girl, you're a symbol of what they've been fighting for, what they want to come home to.' She opened her desk drawer, and brought out a bundle of letters tied up with a piece of string. 'Here,' she said, putting them on the desk close to where Rosie was standing, 'these are for you.'

Rosie looked at the letters without picking them up. 'What are they?' she asked apprehensively.

'Appreciation,' replied Maisie, 'admiration, gratitude – not only from the boys being taken off those trains each day, but also from their relatives and friends. They don't talk about how well you serve tea, whether it's hot enough, or whether there's not enough sugar or milk. They talk about the way you've greeted them, the way you've comforted them, the way you've given them hope for the future. They all refer to you as "Rosie Lee", *their* Rosie Lee. It's so – heartwarming. To be able to do all that you're doing is more than a gift, lassie; it's an act of God. It seems you've made your mark down on that platform. I'd say that was something to be proud of.'

Rosie stared at the bundle of letters. 'I don't want to be proud, Sister,' she replied. 'I want to be a nurse.'

It took Paul Upton longer than he'd expected to get rid of his hangover. When he had gone to bed that morning, he thought he would never be able to get up again. But his mum had changed all that. After she had given him a piece of her mind about interfering in Joe's relationship with Rosie, he got up, went out into the back-yard scullery to shave and wash down, and get out of the house as quickly as possible. He took a motor bus to go to Charing Cross, because these days the horse-drawn ones were few and far between. Even so, he had to change at Liverpool Street on to a freezing-cold open-topped omnibus, so that by the time he arrived at the Aldwych, he actually relished the prospect of a short walk down the Strand to help get some warmth back into his veins.

As New Year's Day was a normal working day, the Strand was bustling with people going about their business, although there was a scattering of day-trippers who were using the end of the festive season to bring the kids into town for a treat. But even here, in the heart of the smart West End of

London, it was impossible to get away from the images of war, with soldiers sitting in cafés that offered cheap cups of tea for 'our brave fighting forces'. On the way, Paul passed an army recruitment centre, where he paused just long enough to look at the patriotic posters outside. Whilst he looked at them, he slipped his hand into his jacket pocket to feel the pair of metal spectacles that he was usually too vain to wear.

'Bleedin' stupid,' he said to himself. 'I could kill a Hun just like anyone else.'

To prove it, he peered across the other side of the road. Although he had to squint, he could see everything quite clearly – well, almost. He looked up at the clock high above the Savoy Theatre, where people were queuing at the box office to get tickets for a future Gilbert and Sullivan opera. It was almost eleven o'clock, so he knew that Rosie would already be at the station to prepare for the midday hospital train. But before he went to see her, there were a few things he needed to turn over in his mind, so he slipped into the nearest café to sober up a bit more on a strong cup of tea.

Once Rosie had left home that morning, Joe stayed behind with Cuthbert to help pack up the things that he wanted to take to the old soldiers' home in Stepney. What he hadn't told Rosie or Joe was that his application to become a resident at the home had been approved weeks before, and the date of his moving in was the following day.

"When the letter come,' said Cuthbert, as he

sat at the table and let Joe do most of the hard work, 'I felt really down in the dumps. But then I got ter finkin' wot a lucky ol' bugger I am, 'cos, let's face it, I'll be nice an' comfy fer the rest er me days. In any case, just like you, Joe, I miss army life. I bet yer'll be glad ter get back, won't yer, once you're in the pink again?'

Joe finished folding up the old codger's pyjamas, and put them in his suitcase. 'Don't fink that's likely no more, Cuff,' he replied. 'Looks like the army's the fing er the past fer me now.'

Cuthbert gave him a puzzled look. 'Wot d'yer mean?' he asked.

Joe came across and sat with him at the table. 'I 'aven't told Rosie yet,' he said, 'but a week ago I went over ter Stanmore ter see the MO. 'E give me a good look over, said I was gettin' better more an' more each day.'

'Well done, son!' said Cuthbert. 'That's a good bit er news, ain't it?'

'It is,' replied Joe, 'and it isn't. The MO said although I'm gettin' better, me lungs ain't in good shape, and certainly not good enough ter carry on in the army. They're going to discharge me.'

Cuthbert's expression changed. 'Oh,' he said gloomily.

'I ain't that worried, mind yer,' said Joe. 'As long as I take it easy I can live to a ripe ol' age, an' fer me that means the best – that means bein' wiv Rosie.'

'You're right, son,' replied Cuthbert. 'Always best ter look on the bright side. An' I tell yer, that's gel er yours is one in a million – ten million!'

'But listen ter me, Cuff,' continued Joe, lowering his voice as though Rosie was still in the room. 'I don't want yer ter mention any of this to 'er. I told 'er I wasn't goin' ter let 'er be the breadwinner in *our* family fer the rest of our lives. I told 'er that even though I'd prefer ter stay in the army till the end er the war, I'd sooner desert an' get a job, rarvver than let 'er look after a dead weight like me.'

'Don't ever talk about desertin', son,' warned Cuthbert. 'Some good young lads I've known 've bin shot down by their own mates up front, an' just 'cos the poor little sods were too bleedin' scared ter go over the top. The army's got a lot ter answer for fer that. Killin' the Boche is one fing, but killin' yer own side 'cos er rules and regulations is somefin' else. Don't even fink about it, son.'

'There won't be no need to now, Cuff,' said Joe. 'But I don't want Rosie ter ever know that I'll never really be a fit man again.'

Cuthbert winked, and gently tapped the side of his nose with one finger. 'Mum's the word!' he replied.

They were suddenly interrupted by the sound of explosions from the maroon air-raid warning signals from the town.

'Blimey!' yelled Cuthbert. ''Ere we go again!'

As the cottage shuddered with each explosion, they both rushed into the back yard. In the distance, they could hear the first barrage of ack-ack fire, which was greeting the arrival of a Zeppelin.

'Yes!' called Joe above the thunderous sounds.

'It's a Zep all right. Wot the 'ell does it fink it's doin' coming over in broad daylight? The papers said they was now only goin' ter be attackin' by night. I just 'ope fer Chrissake Rosie takes cover.'

The arrival of a Zeppelin over East London had not yet been signalled to the New Year's Day crowds milling around Central London. At Charing Cross, Rosie and Judy were too busy preparing for the imminent arrival of the midday hospital train even to think about the possibility of the first daylight raid in the area since the middle of December. In any case, relatives and friends of the casualties on the train had already paid for their penny platform tickets, and were swarming in vast numbers to reach the best positions along the platform. With just five minutes to go before the train was due, Judy brought up a second tea trolley, ready for the onslaught of a lot of very thirsty soldiers and their nurses.

'Blimey!' said Judy. ''Ow we goin' ter cope wiv this lot all over the place?'

'Tidy yourself up, Judy,' Rosie said, straightening her own cap and uniform.

Judy swung a look of total surprise at her. 'Do what?' she asked.

'Tidy yourself up,' repeated Rosie. 'You know very well the boys like to see us looking smart. It's the least we can do to greet them.' She chuckled when she saw Judy looking bewildered whilst doing what Rosie had asked. 'Remember,' said Rosie, 'you'll be taking over this job soon. You'll be the one they'll be looking for.'

426

In a small café just up the road from the station, Paul Upton sipped his tea on a stool by the counter. There were quite a lot of people there, mainly families out for the day on their way to see the sights in nearby Trafalgar Square and Piccadilly Circus. Paul thought the tea was lousy, more hot water than tea leaves, and not a patch on what he imagined Rosie was about to serve up to the blokes coming off the hospital train within the next few minutes or so. But tea wasn't the reason why he had come in out of the cold. What he wanted was a chance to mull over what had happened to him over the past twenty-four hours. Despite all his bravado, the angry brush he'd had with his young brother the previous evening had deeply disturbed him. It was the first time there had ever been a feud like that between them; he and Joe had always been the best of friends, even if they didn't share the same interests, and had different personalities. But who was to blame for that ugly incident in the street last night? No matter how hard he tried, he just couldn't get it into his head what Joe had yelled at him: '*Yer just can't bear ter let anyone 'ave somefin' that* you *ain't got!*' Was it true? Paul asked himself over and over again. Was it *really* true that he couldn't bear his kid brother to have a girlfriend that he, Paul, had fallen in love with? But – *love?* Was it love or something else that had drawn Paul to her, drawn him so much that he just couldn't leave her alone?

While he was pondering all this, his eye suddenly caught a glimpse of someone who was

427

sitting on another stool further along the counter, a girl, probably in her mid-twenties, a real good-looker, with blonde hair and blue eyes, and a beautiful clear, unblemished skin that, in Paul's opinion, would earn her a fortune if her face were to appear on a poster in Piccadilly Circus advertising Du Maurier or Craven A cigarettes. What was interesting, however, was that the girl was clearly looking at him, not directly, but at his reflection in the mirror behind the counter. But when he caught her eye, she quickly looked down at the cup of tea in front of her, started to stir it madly while talking to what were presumably her parents, sitting with her. But that one subliminal moment stirred something inside Paul. It was enough for him to know what he should now do about Rosie.

With the train whistle blowing, and the deafening sound of steam blasting out from the funnel, the midday hospital troop train slowly appeared at the end of Platform 1, grunting its laborious way towards the buffers. Rosie and Judy, trolleys at the ready, were waiting for it; so too was the enormous crowd of people who were now gathered on the platform. As usual, the two girls split up, Judy taking her trolley to the front carriages of the train, and Rosie to the rear. As the train gradually slowed right down, the excitement amongst the crowds was building, tinged with a mixture of elation, relief and anxiety.

The first doors along the train started to open, accompanied by the voice of the station guard with a loud hailer yelling: 'Stand back from the doors, please! Let 'em off the train!'

However, he had hardly finished his announcement when the air was pierced by the alien sound of bugle calls provided by two young boys, who then shouted out, 'Take cover! Take cover!' The crowd was shocked, even more so when the whole station was rocked to its very foundations by the maroon warning explosives from nearby St James's Park. The excitement amongst the relatives and friends of the previous few minutes was quickly replaced by bewilderment, consternation and fear.

Rosie immediately abandoned her tea trolley, and, together with her colleagues from the voluntary services, station staff and military personnel, started to direct people back towards the ticket barrier. Pandemonium followed as some of the crowd refused to budge until they had caught sight of their loved ones getting off the train, whilst others were pushing and shoving, eager to get off the platform and to safety as quickly as possible.

'There are shelters in the street outside!' yelled one of the station porters.

'Please move carefully!' called Rosie, fearing some kind of a stampede.

Then someone shouted out: 'Listen!'

The crowd continued to babble and call out for their loved ones on the train.

'Shut up!' yelled another person at the far end of the platform. 'Listen!'

The excitable crowd sounds began to lessen, until gradually, the great station fell into an eerie silence. Everyone stood around, nervously waiting to know what was going on, what to do, how to keep quite still without breaking the extraordinary mass of human bonding.

'Listen.'

Whoever spoke this time had no need to shout, for, out of the distant skies came the now familiar sound of engines, only this time supplemented by the unfamiliar sound of engines of another sort.

'Zep!'

The soldier bandsman who called out from half-way along the platform was pointing up towards the sky, directly above the railway track leading into the station platform. All eyes widened as the giant cigar-shaped shadow appeared, flanked on either side by two German fighter aircraft escorts, machine guns blazing as they strafed from the air the railway track and open part of the platforms below.

'Oh my God!' gasped Judy, at the ticket-barrier end of the platform.

As the bullets got closer and closer to the roof over the station, a woman screamed. This led to complete pandemonium, as everyone made a wild dash to escape from the platform. Simultaneously, the glass roof above the platforms was shattered as the entire station shuddered beneath a volley of ack-ack gunfire from Hyde Park, St James's Park and two floating gun carriage barges moored at the Victoria Embankment on the River Thames.

'Stay on the train!' yelled Rosie, as she rushed along from carriage to carriage urging the soldier casualties to take cover there, and not to come out

430

into the open where they could be shot down.

A tremendous explosion rocked the station from the first bomb dropped by the giant airship. By now there was white-hot shrapnel raining down on the railway track from the massive barrage of guns lined up against the Zeppelin and its two protective aircraft. By this time, however, most of the crowd had cleared the platform, thanks in part to Rosie getting a lot of them organised in an orderly way, and also to the discipline of both the station staff and the military. But with the deadly sound of the Zeppelin's engines whirring almost directly above them from its gondola suspended beneath the giant silver frame, a tragic catastrophe was in the making as two young injured soldiers suddenly leaped off the train on to the platform, and made a dash for it.

'Get back on the train!' yelled Rosie, racing after them, knowing that they stood more chance of survival in the protection of the carriage. 'Get back! Get back!' she yelled over and over again. But even as she reached them, a massive explosion brought masonry tumbling down from the roof on to the platform below. Without a moment's thought for her own safety, Rosie flung herself at the two young soldiers, bringing them to the ground, and shielding them both with her own body.

From the other end of the platform, Judy screamed out: 'Rosie!'

A few moments later, the Zeppelin and its two escort fighter aircraft had cleared the air space above the station, only to be shot down later on

431

the eastern outskirts of London.

When it was all over, there was a mad rush by the emergency services to reach the wounded soldiers, who had been trapped, without harm, on the hospital train. By the time they had reached the fallen debris, glass and shrapnel halfway down the platform, there was great relief to find that the two young soldiers had survived. But as they were pulled clear, there was deep consternation from the crowd who had rushed to help. Among them was Joe's brother, Paul Upton, who used his bare hands to help claw away at the fallen masonry.

'Jesus Christ!' he gasped in horror, as he eventually uncovered the unconscious figure of Rosie, lying beneath the huge pile of rubble...

Chapter 24

Charing Cross Station had escaped relatively unscathed after the daring Zeppelin attack. It was little short of a miracle that no one had been killed, or even seriously injured – no one, that is, except Rosie. Almost twenty-four hours later, she was still lying unconscious in the Great Northern Hospital in Holloway Road, watched over night and day by Joe and by her father, her life hanging by a thread. In fact, her injuries had been so great that the consultant treating her constantly referred to her condition as 'poorly'. Being realistic, he thought her chance of survival was very little indeed. That condition included multiple fractures to her arms and legs, severe concussion, which had left her unconscious, and a spinal injury that, even if she did survive, would mean that she would more than likely never be able to walk again.

Joe was heartbroken. He hadn't slept for one single moment since a police constable came tapping at the door of the railway carriage to tell him what had happened. The shock was immense. He felt as though nothing was left in the world for him to live for. But when he reached the hospital, his shock was compounded by the sight of Paul, smoking fag after fag, sitting on a bench outside the emergency wing where Rosie had been taken.

'I went to see her, Joe,' said Paul, with deep anguish, before Joe had the chance to go for him again. 'It wasn't what yer fink, Joe,' he pleaded. 'I only went ter tel 'er that I was a chump, an' that I'd never give 'er *or* you any more trouble. Yer've got ter believe me, Joe. On my way to the station, I fawt about wot I'd done. I fawt about it an awful lot. I realised that the way *I* loved Rosie wasn't the way *you* did. I only wanted ter ask 'er ter fergive me. Now I'm askin' you, Joe.' His voice was cracking from the horror he had witnessed. 'Don't let's get at each uvver again. I'm sorry. That's all I can say. I'm so bleedin' sorry...'

Joe was astonished as his brother just fell against him, hugged him tight, and sobbed his heart out. Then tears streamed down Joe's face too.

The two brothers just stayed like that for several minutes, until a ward sister came out with all the information she could pass on from the doctor about Rosie's condition.

When Joe was shown in to Rosie's bedside, he found his own anguish unbearable. There she was, his own Rosie Lee, covered in bandages from head to foot, fast asleep, oxygen mask covering those lips that he had never wanted to stop kissing. Maybe she would never wake up again, leaving him without the chance ever to say goodbye. It was more than he could take. He sat on a stool silently at her side, holding her hand, gently stroking it with his fingers, whispering over and over again, 'Come on, Rosie. Come on, Rosie Lee, you can do it. Wake up. Got a lot of fings ter get on wiv, you an' me.'

'Joe.'

The voice of Rosie's father, calling softly from his side, a hand on his shoulder, gradually brought Joe back to reality.

'How is she?'

Joe slowly shook his head, and rubbed his eyes with the back of his hand.

There were, of course, other patients in the overcrowded ward, casualties from previous Zeppelin attacks around London, and those of them who were well enough were trying to im-agine what was going on behind the screens around Rosie's bed, knowing only too well the heartache and distress they were having to endure.

Richard Little remained standing, looking down at his almost motionless daughter. 'I'm so proud of her, Joe,' he said softly. 'When I heard what she did on that platform today, it made me feel so very humble. I could never be like her –

never. I've known it all these years, but never had the courage to believe in her. I just wish Marian... I just wish my wife could...' Clearly distressed, he leaned down and placed his hand over Rosie's. 'But now, it's too late.'

Joe shook his head. 'No,' he said firmly, staring at her as though she could hear him. 'You're not goin' ter leave me, are yer, Rosie? *You'd* never do that. I won't let yer!'

Richard straightened up again. 'I'll be outside,' he said. 'If you want to go home to get some rest, Joe, I'll be here.'

'I'm not goin' 'ome, sir,' said Joe. 'This is my gel 'ere.'

Richard, not an emotional man at the best of times, put a comforting hand on Joe's shoulder and squeezed it. He was close to tears. Then he left.

Joe sat with Rosie for the best part of an hour. By then it was getting dark outside, and the ward nurses came round to draw the curtains. Even after that was done, however, the last throes of the sun filtered through and lit up Rosie's face with a deep golden glow. Joe waited for the nurses to leave, then moved closer to her, lowering his voice to whisper the poem he had tried to write for her:

'Rosie Lee, Rosie Lee,
Oh, how I love you,
Saviour of life, weaver of dreams,
Oh, how I love you...'

He got no further, because the ward sister came

435

in. 'I'm sorry, young man,' she said, 'but I'm afraid you'll have to leave for a few minutes. The doctor's coming in.'

Joe nodded, got up and, with one last look at Rosie, made his way along the ward. When he got outside, however, he was shocked to find his mum sitting there with Paul.

''Ow is she?' asked Annie, grave-faced, and wearing the only decent coat and hat she had in the world. 'Is she still asleep?'

Joe nodded.

Annie sighed. 'So we'd better do sommat about it,' she said, with the old Annie Upton resolve.

'Don't be daft, Ma,' said Paul. 'Rosie's – pretty bad.'

'I know that,' replied Annie in her determined Yorkshire way. 'But she's going to get better.'

'Oh, yes?' asked Paul. 'An 'ow d'yer reckon on *that?*'

Annie eyed him. ''Cos just before I came 'ere,' she replied haughtily, 'I said me prayers.'

'Prayers!' gasped Paul. *'You?* You don't believe in religion.'

'I may not believe in religion,' she countered, 'but I believe in God. As a matter of fact, from time to time, 'Im and me 'ave quite an 'eart-to-'eart chat.'

Paul tried to exchange a mocking look with his brother, but Joe was suddenly struck by what his mum was saying. It took him back to when he and Paul were kids, when he walked into her bedroom one night and found her on her knees, arguing with someone who seemed to him to be in the ceiling. All he could remember now was

436

that it was something to do with her not knowing where to find enough money to put food in her kids' stomachs the next day, and how the mutton bones she'd been boiling up for soup for the past three days were now so bare they had nothing left on them. The funny thing was, though, that a couple of days later, his dad found a job on the canals, and by the end of the week, they were all eating a good stew again.

'The point is,' said Annie, popping a pepper-mint into her mouth whilst she was still talking, 'you don't just give up, 'cos if you do, it only means you're feeling sorry for yourself. From what I've seen of Rosie, she's a fighter. *She* won't give up.' She threw a quick look up at Joe. 'She's got far too much to live for.'

Some time later, Joe returned to the ward, and, taking turns with Rosie's father, sat with Rosie through the night. There were several false alarms, one of which came when Rosie's heart seemed to have stopped beating. With both Joe and Richard quickly dispatched outside into the corridor again, the emergency medical team worked frantically on Rosie, using cardiac mass-age and emergency drugs until they were eventually able to restore her vital signs. Every attack she had seemed to indicate that she was losing her battle to survive, but, as Annie had said just a few hours before, neither Joe nor Rosie herself gave up.

For just a short time during the night, Joe curled up on the floor beside Rosie's bed. Although he dozed intermittently, he had dreams about what

437

he would do if he lost her. He woke up in a sweat, unable to think clearly, his back aching from the cold lino floor. But then something strange happened. As he placed his hand gently on the edge of the bed to ease himself up, he felt one of Rosie's fingers moving slightly so that it touched the tip of one of his own fingers. Sitting up with a jolt, he tried to see what was happening in the dark.

'Rosie?' he whispered close to her ear. 'Rosie? Can yer 'ear me?'

At this moment, a nurse came in with a candle. 'What is it?' she whispered.

'She moved 'er finger!' replied Joe, his voice low but quivering with hope. 'She touched me. I'm sure she touched me!'

The nurse held the candle over Rosie's face, but there was no sign of movement. 'No, Mr Upton,' she said, 'it's probably just the nerves that are–'

As she spoke, Rosie groaned softly.

'Rosie!' called Joe, his voice now not quite under so much control. 'Rosie Lee, can yer 'ear me? Oh, *please,* Rosie,' he called over and over. 'Please say yer can 'ear me – *please!*'

Rosie again groaned, this time a little stronger.

'I'll get Sister!' said the nurse, rushing off.

Joe drew closer so that his face was almost touching Rosie's. 'Come back ter me, Rosie,' he said, doing his best to avoid her oxygen mask. 'Please come back ter me...'

As he spoke, her lips moved slightly, and she tried to murmur something.

'Yes, Rosie!' he said, urging her on. 'Tell me,

dear one. What is it? What d'yer want ter tell me?'

Rosie's eyes gradually opened. They tried to focus, but without success, so they closed again. But this time, her lips managed to slowly form words: '"Ro-sie..." she mumbled. '"Ro-sie Lee..."'

'That's right!' gasped Joe, half laughing, half crying. 'Say it, Rosie! Say it!'

'"Oh ... how ... love you..."'

Joe was ecstatic to hear Rosie trying to form the words of his stupid boy's own poem. 'That's it, Rosie,' he said softly, gently leaning his head against hers. 'You know the words. Yer know 'em better than me,'

'Rosie Lee, Rosie Lee,
Oh, how I love you...'

He stopped reciting the poem, and held on to her. 'Dear Jesus Christ, fank you!' was all he could say. 'From the bottom of me 'eart, fank you!'

After a week or so, Rosie had gathered enough strength to sit propped up in bed. Although her injuries were still very painful, she took great comfort in seeing Joe at her bedside every day, and as soon as she was able to take in what everyone was saying, her father told her about Christian, and how distressed the boy had been when he heard what had happened to his sister. However, Richard promised her that the moment she was a little stronger, he would bring Christian in to see her, and this cheered Rosie up no end. None the less, her one great sadness was that her mother hadn't been in to visit her.

'Does she *really* hate me so much?' she asked, when her mother's name was mentioned.

Richard stood over her bedside, fumbling for an adequate reply. 'You mustn't ever say such a thing, Rosie,' he said softly. 'Your mother has always loved you; she will never stop loving you. But you must know that she can't bear the thought of seeing you the way you are. I know she feels guilty about it, but she just can't help herself. Just before I came here, she made a point of asking me to tell you this. You *will* see her, Rosie, that I can promise you. But not now, not until you are out of this place.'

Rosie didn't know whether her father was telling the truth, or merely trying to cover up for her mother's unkind behaviour.

After Richard had gone, Rosie lay in bed for hours, wondering if her mother would ever forgive her for all the things she had done. In many ways, she felt sorry for her. After all, everything Marian had tried to do to keep her daughter under control had failed. Marian Little had been brought up to observe convention, but the kind of convention that was so rigid there was no room for compromise. As long as her children were young and under her control she was happy. She couldn't cope when they grew up and wanted to live life their own way. As she lay there, struggling against pain and discomfort, Rosie couldn't help wondering what it would be like in the future, when the war was finally over, and young people sought a different way of life from everything they had known in the past. What part would parents play in the destiny of their children? Would love be allowed to be expressed in ways that a mother or father might not fully understand? But most of all, she worried about her *own* future, a future in which it was likely she would be incapacitated for the rest of her life. As she tossed and turned in bed at night, she repeatedly asked herself how she could expect Joe to cope with an invalid who, like her young brother, would have to be confined to a wheelchair. As she got stronger and stronger, the future seemed a great blur to her. It was not something to look forward to, only something to fear.

What Rosie hadn't anticipated was the outpouring of love and gratitude that arrived throughout each day she was in hospital. Her remarkable act of bravery by saving the lives of those two young soldiers had not been overlooked, for it had even been the subject of glowing articles in the national newspapers. Most rewarding of all for Rosie, however, was the stream of visitors who were calling on her – nurses and friends from QAIMNS, such as Eunice, who, despite the traumatic experience of her time in France, was a wonderful support to Rosie, making her laugh with her own special brand of cockney repartee. But perhaps the most touching visitor of all had been Binnie's husband, Harold Osborne, a quiet-spoken, cultured man, still a serving officer in the army, struggling to come to terms with the loss of his wife whom he had adored.

Some of Rosie's neighbours from Camden

Road also popped in to see her, bringing gifts of home-made biscuits and treacle toffee, flowers and get-well cards. Even old Monty Gubble had turned up, carrying a pot of chrysanthemums from himself and Cuthbert, who was now comfortably set up in the old soldiers' home. In fact, there were so many bunches of flowers that one of Rosie's fellow patients in the ward complained that the place looked more like a funeral parlour. None the less, Rosie was uplifted by all the wonderful messages of support.

One card, however, did bring tears to her eyes. It was from Clara and Emile Harrington, who, despite the mindless attitude of some of Richard's employees at the factory, were now embarked on raising funds and collecting clothes for the Red Cross emergency aid appeals. Their message was warm and from the heart: 'There is, and never will be, anyone quite like you. You are the daughter we wish we could have had.'

Last, but not least, there were the soldier boys themselves; so many turned up at the hospital to see Rosie that they were told to take their turn and wait in the hall downstairs. They all wanted to thank Rosie Lee – *their* Rosie Lee, the girl in a million, who, to quote from the many letters of appreciation that Sister Maisie was still receiving, gave them comfort, hope, a great big smile and the best cuppa tea since they left home. Despite her protests – but to the intense pride and love of Joe, her father and everyone who knew her – Rosie had become an institution, and this was made even more apparent when, to her astonishment, she was paid a visit by the Lady herself.

'QAIMNS is proud of you, Rosie,' said Lady Braintree, a wonderfully serene figure in her supremely smart cap and uniform, looking so different from the pale and drawn figure Rosie had last seen in that freezing-cold room in Orlais. 'It's amazing how someone who has only really presented the face of the nursing service by serving cups of tea has managed to capture the hearts of everyone who knows you.'

Rosie moved around uncomfortably in bed. She had never been able to accept praise or compliments easily, and the Lady's comments caused her a great deal of embarrassment.

'But what you did out on that station platform,' the Lady said, both hands resting on the top of her cane, propped up in front of her, 'was beyond the call of duty, of tea cups, and anything else. It showed sacrifice of the highest order, a complete disregard for your own safety. You've survived death, Rosie, while doing what you knew you had to do, no time to think first, no time to think of the consequences. That's the stuff of *real* courage, the type of courage you also displayed at Orlais, when you walked a great distance to get help for Lieutenant Hillary.' She stopped briefly, to reach into her handbag, from which she produced an envelope. 'Here,' she said. 'When you feel up to it, I'd like you to read this. It's from Lieutenant Hillary himself. He's at home now with his wife and children, and grateful to be alive, thanks to you.'

Rosie was now feeling so out of her depth that she moved around in bed, pretending to feel discomfort. But the Lady was not to be deterred.

Once a ward nurse had been summoned to make Rosie more comfortable, the Lady began to reveal the particular reason why she had come to see her. 'I think you should know, my dear,' she said, 'that I wrote to the Prime Minister today recommending you for a British Empire Medal.'

Rosie was thunderstruck, and had to look away.

'My recommendation,' continued the Lady, 'was accompanied by a petition, signed by many hundreds of ordinary servicemen, all of them wanting you to be recognised in the way that *they* want you to be recognised. I can only hope that their wishes – and ours – will not fall on deaf ears.'

It was some weeks before Rosie left hospital. Only then were her wounds healed enough so that she could be helped into her wheelchair, which she had now been told would be her constant companion for the rest of her life. Her right leg was still pitted with tiny fragments of shrapnel, and embedded in her shoulder on the same side were splinters of glass from the roof above Platform 1 at Charing Cross Station, all of which would have to be removed over a period of time. On the day Joe came to collect her from hospital, a small group of people were waiting outside to see her off, including hospital nursing staff and several young soldiers who were there to present her with yet another bouquet of flowers as a mark of gratitude from themselves and their mates. The only people missing, however, were her own parents, and in particular her mother, who had not shown up at the hospital since Rosie had been admitted.

In the ambulance provided by QAIMNS to take Rosie back home to Forest Gate, she and Joe sat hand in hand for the entire journey. It was an emotional time for both of them, with an indeterminate future, and a lot of decisions to be made as to how they were going to cope for money once Joe had been officially discharged from the army. It was whilst they were discussing all this that Rosie decided to tell Joe what she now felt about their relationship.

'Joe,' she said, trying to put a brave face on something that she had been churning over in her mind ever since she had regained consciousness several weeks before, 'I think it's time for us to go our own separate ways. Everything's different now. When we first met, we were two young people with a lifetime of opportunity ahead of us. But now, I shall be stuck in this wheelchair, relying on you to do everything for me. I don't want that to happen, Joe. I *won't* let it happen. You're a young man. You're getting stronger each day. You have a whole life ahead of you.'

'That's my gel,' replied Joe, squeezing her hand and teasing her. 'Practical as ever. Well, fanks fer the speech, but yer're stuck wiv me, so that's all there is to it.'

'Listen to me, Joe,' she replied earnestly. 'I asked Sister Maisie if there was any way QAIMNS could help me find a place in some kind of a nursing home. I know for a fact they've got places, and it would be the most practical thing for someone with my kind of disabilities.'

'Is that so?' replied Joe, eyeing her with a look

bordering ridicule. 'An' what did the ol' gel say?'

Rosie sighed. 'She didn't really say anything, just that she'd have to talk it over with Lady Braintree – and you. Has she?'

''As she wot?'

'Talked this over with you?'

'Oh,' replied Joe, casually. 'Yes, as a matter er fact, she 'as. I told 'er that I'd sooner put me 'ead in a gas oven than let yer go in a place like that.'

'Joe!' she protested.

'Come off it, Rosie!' said Joe. 'Wot d'yer take me for? I love yer fer wot you are, fer wot yer've always bin and always will be. I love you 'cos there's somefin' between us I can't explain 'cos I ain't bright enough ter be able ter work out such fings.'

'Oh, Joe,' replied Rosie, 'that's rubbish! Your mind is as good as the best of them.'

Joe shook his head. 'OK,' he replied, 'so I've got savvy, but just enough ter know that wotever 'appens, I'll never allow anyone ter look after you 'cept me.'

'But how, Joe, how?' asked Rosie, pressing him. 'How are you going to be able to cope with all the practical things, washing and cleaning, and all the terrible chores involved with looking after someone who's housebound? My life is over, Joe. Yours is just beginning.'

Joe immediately pulled his hand away from hers. 'Stop feelin' sorry fer yerself, Rosie,' he said sternly. 'Fings may not be the same as when we first met, but yer're still the same person, Rosie, still the same gel I first saw at the end of that platform.'

446

Rosie's face crumpled, so he gently put his hand under her chin, and smiled. 'Don't yer understand, Rosie Lee?' he said, remembering what his mum had told him in the hospital. 'Once yer give up, there's nuffin' left. An' no matter *wot* you say, I don't intend ter give you up – ever.'

By the time the ambulance reached old Cuthbert's cottage, dark grey clouds had gathered, and there was a prospect of some fine, bitterly cold rain. Once the female driver and Joe had between them lifted Rosie's wheelchair out of the ambulance, he was able to get her inside the cottage with very little trouble at all. After the ambulance had left, Rosie looked around Cuthbert's tiny front parlour, and remembered all the exciting plans she and Joe had made on the day the old codger had told them he was giving them the cottage and the railway carriage. The memory of those few moments gave her a strange feeling inside – a feeling of hopelessness and despair.

'This is never going to work, Joe,' she said, watching him with great affection as he bustled around lighting a paraffin heater to get some warmth into the place. 'For a few days maybe, but not for a whole lifetime.'

Joe stopped what he was doing. 'Yer're only sayin' that 'cos yer're 'omesick.'

'Homesick!' she gasped. 'For Camden Road?'

'For the ol' carriage.'

Rosie sighed despondently. 'Oh – yes,' she replied, wistfully. 'On the other side of the track.'

'So – come on then,' Joe said eagerly, grabbing hold of the wheelchair. 'Let's get over there!'

447

'Don't be silly, Joe!' she said, astonished when he started to push her wheelchair into Cuthbert's kitchen. 'You'll never be able to get the chair over through all that mud. It's impossible!'

'Who said anything about the chair?' replied Joe, as he opened the back door.

To her astonishment, he carefully placed his arms around her back and beneath her thighs, and gently lifted her.

'No, Joe!' she protested, cringing in some pain. 'You can't do it! It's impossible!'

Impossible or not, he slowly carried her out into the back yard, where the door to the rear field was already open. Within a few minutes, he was struggling through the muddy weeds and dead Michaelmas daisies that led to the old railway track.

'Oh, Joe,' groaned Rosie, 'this is madness. Turn back. *Please* turn back.'

Holding her firmly in his arms, Joe picked his way up the grassy slope to the track itself. Once he was on the other side, the path to the old railway carriage was much easier to walk on, for during the past weeks he had covered it with shingle he had taken from an abandoned heap further down the track. 'Nearly there,' he said, as they gradually drew nearer and nearer to the carriage.

When they did finally get there, Rosie was surprised to see the door being held open for them from inside. Treading carefully, raising one foot up slowly, and then the other, Joe eased them both up into the kitchen. 'Welcome 'ome, Rosie Lee.'

There was suddenly wild applause from someone inside. To Rosie's astonishment, it was Christian, in his own wheelchair. At his side was their father, who beamed at her, and came forward.

'Rosie, my dear,' he said quietly, affectionately, kissing her gently on her cheek.

Then Mrs Winnet appeared, tears streaming down her face. 'You get around, Miss Rosie,' she said, also kissing her on the cheek. 'That's fer sure!'

Rosie, still held in Joe's arms, then stretched out to Christian, who took her hand with both his own hands, which she held lovingly against his cheeks.

'Oh, Rosie,' the boy said, 'I love your home. I wish *I* could live here too!'

Finally, Joe was able to set Rosie down on a comfortable, soft chair that had been brought in for her. Once she was seated, she looked around the tiny kitchen, overjoyed to find the people she cared for most gathered there to welcome her. Even so, something, *someone*, was missing.

'How's Mother?' she asked.

All eyes turned towards the curtains that led to the bedroom. Standing there was Marian Little, watching and waiting, slowly coming forward.

'Hello, darling,' she said, with the sort of affection that Rosie had not seen from her for many a year. Then she leaned down and kissed her warmly on the cheek. 'You've been in my thoughts – *and* prayers,' she said, gently caressing Rosie's cheek with the back of her fingers. 'Please forgive me. I've missed you – so much.'

449

That night, Rosie and Joe slept in the bed where they had made love before the events of the past few weeks had changed their lives so dramatically. The curtains of the small window had been pulled back to reveal a massive expanse of clear night sky, nothing like the dreary cloudy weather that had promised rain earlier in the evening. It seemed that every star, every planet, all the galaxies had come out to give Rosie the welcome home she had at one time thought would never be possible.

'You know something, Joe,' she said, reaching for his hand beneath the bedclothes. 'I feel as though we're on the night train to Southend – our old railway carriage, our home. Can you feel the movement? Can you feel the wheels turning?'

'First class, I 'ope?'

'What's wrong with third class?' she asked. 'As long as it gets us there, that's all I care about. I'm dying to have bangers and mash there, and one of those famous ice-cream cornets you keep telling me about.' She turned her face to look at him. A shaft of moonlight just picked out his features, stronger features than she had ever seen before, and handsome, more handsome than anyone she had ever seen. 'The thing is, though,' she added, 'with me as I am, how will we get around?'

'We'll get around all right,' he promised. 'Yer can count on that.'

Outside, it was so quiet they could hear the night owl hooting to his lady love on a distant tree on the other side of the track. He was glad things were back to normal – because that's the way he liked it.

Epilogue

Summer had come early to the wide open fields of northern France. Everywhere you looked there were signs that it could be a bumper harvest this year, for the wheat and corn were shooting up faster than anyone could remember, mainly because there had been plenty of the right kind of rain during the winter months, which gave the young roots the chance to appear on time and embrace the warmth of the dazzling spring sunshine. Late May was always popular with the tourists, most of whom flocked to see these very same fields, where two major wars had wrought havoc and destruction, and taken the lives of thousands of brave young men. There were, however, no signs now of the dugouts and trenches used by the Allied troops and their German enemy during the First and Second World Wars, nor of a terrain that had been fractured by shells and land mines. And how fresh the air was, scented with the sweet smell of spring flowers where once the choking man-made killer gas had devastated every living thing in its path. But sweetest of all were the fields of red, once of blood, now of poppies, swaying majestically in the cool breeze of an early summer day, hardly the stuff of memories for Rosie and her old friend Eunice Huggins, who had kept their promise to each other to return one day to the countryside around Orlais, to pay tribute to those they had left behind.

'Funny, in't it,' said Eunice, now an eighty-one-year-old whose bright ginger hair had turned to a soft white. 'It don't look nuffin' like it was in those days. There was so much mud around. I never felt clean again till I got 'ome.'

'Hardly surprising, Eunice dear,' replied Rosie, who after so many years still hardly had a line on her face. 'Don't forget it *was* winter.'

Both of them were now widows of less than ten years. Eunice's husband, Reg, whom she had first met at a policemen's ball in the 1920s, was, after more than forty years of marriage, first to go. Soon after that it was Rosie's Joe, who, until then, had lived a full and reasonably healthy life, despite the trials and tribulations bequeathed him by the German poison-gas attack. For both Rosie and Eunice, it was a journey of remembrance, staring out at a vast unrecognisable landscape from the window of the British Legion bus that had brought them all the way from a very different Blighty to the one they had helped the soldiers to fight for so many years before. But it was something that both women wanted to do, *had* to do. Rosie had always promised herself that if she ever reached her eightieth birthday, she would return to Orlais and the site of the advanced dressing station where tragedy had struck a cruel blow on that winter's day in 1915.

'Ladies and gentlemen,' came the pleasant voice of the elderly British ex-serviceman tour guide, who, from the start of the journey at Boulogne, had been using the bus's microphone and Tannoy system to give graphic accounts of the battles that had taken place at endless former battlefields en route, 'we shall shortly be arriving at the village of Orlais, temporary headquarters of the advanced field artillery of the Seventh Middlesex Regiment during a decisive phase of the First World War. Here, many good young Tommies lost their lives, and only a few kilometres away, an army medical team, including young nurses from Queen Alexandra's Imperial Military Nursing Service became victims of a particularly brutal enemy attack.'

Eunice pressed against the bus window to look out, but not Rosie. She could see all she wanted to see in her mind's eye.

When the bus stopped at Orlais for a lunch break, Rosie and Eunice were the last to get off. This was mainly because Rosie now relied heavily on her walking stick to get around. However, she never complained. Sixty-odd years ago she was told that she would spend the rest of her days in a wheelchair, but with Joe's help and encouragement, within a couple of years she was on her feet again. No, she would never ever complain about having to use a walking stick; she only ever thought of it as her 'old faithful'.

The village of Orlais was so changed that it was barely recognisable. What had once been a hard-working little community, with its own baker and butcher and even undertaker, was now spreading its wings, with housing developments and apartment blocks springing up all over the place. There were also souvenir shops that were doing a roaring trade, selling postcards and cheap trinkets to the pilgrims who were keen to get their hands on anything they could take back that would prove that they had visited the old battlegrounds where their loved ones had fallen. And yet, for Rosie, there was still something about the old village high street that brought back memories, for as she and Eunice walked along they came across what had once been the mayor's house before its empty shell of a building had been requisitioned by the Allied forces command, only to be battered constantly by the Boche long-range field artillery.

She and Eunice ventured inside the building. It was not at all how Rosie remembered it, for it was now a mass of marble crazy paving, and aluminium-framed windows, and used as some kind of administrative local council offices. But Rosie knew enough French to be able to translate the brass plate over the entrance hall, which paid tribute to the brave men and women of the Allied forces who, during the First *and* Second World Wars, had held on to the village of Orlais against all odds.

A little later, the group were taken to the site of the advanced dressing station, where The Terrible Four served on active duty during the height of enemy bombardments. For both women, it was a daunting experience to be even in the same area where they had lost two of their dearest friends, Binnie and Titch, and in particular for Eunice, who had been injured there and only just escaped with her life. Once the group had cleared, they stayed behind for a few minutes, looking at what were now no more than a few lumps of bricks, mortar and timber, which was all that remained of the old farmhouse and cattle shed.

'Yer know,' said Eunice, who still had her cheeky expression from the old days, 'I should be cryin' me eyes out, but I don't fink I can. I mean, it's such a long time ago, in't it? Everyfin's so diff'rent now. Sometimes I 'ave ter pinch meself an' ask if it really did all 'appen, if Binnie an' Titch *did* stay be'ind.'

Rosie slipped a comforting arm around her friend's waist. 'Oh, it happened, all right, Eunice,' she said. 'It happened. You were such a brave soul.'

'Not 'alf as brave as wot you done,' replied Eunice. 'Settin' off ter the village like that, all alone, in the dark. And wot about all that at Charin' Cross? No wonder they gave yer that medal. My God, if anyone deserved that, *you* did.'

As they walked back to the coach, both of them were silent, mulling over the strange and terrible memories of those days in the old cattle shed.

'Yer know,' said Eunice, once they were back in their seats on the coach, 'yer never did tell me wot the King said to yer when 'e give yer that.' She nodded towards the single medal that Rosie had pinned to the lapel of her cardigan.

Rosie smiled to herself. 'Oh, he just said, "I hear you make a wonderful cup of tea. You must come and make one for the Queen and myself some time."'

They both chuckled. The coach moved on.

The final stop of the day was the regional British War Cemetery just outside Orlais. When they got there, the sun was drowning the whole area in a welcoming red glow, which gave the hundreds of simple headstones grace and dignity.

With the help of a British Legion guide, arm in arm, Rosie and Eunice slowly found their way to the two graves they had promised to come and see. Once they got there, the guide left them alone for a few minutes to respond in their own individual ways.

'Hello, Binnie,' said Rosie, standing with Eunice at the foot of Binnie's grave, where a simple white headstone was engraved merely with her name, her dates of birth and death, and the nursing service with whom she had served so briefly, but so proudly. 'You knew we'd come back, didn't you?'

Both women then dipped into their handbags to produce their own tributes that they had brought with them from England. Eunice's contribution was a small bag of soil from her back garden in Shoreditch, which she distributed amongst both graves, first for Binnie, and then for Titch, who had been interred next to her. 'A bit of ol' England for yer, gels,' said Eunice. 'Just ter let yer know that we don't ferget yer.'

For Rosie, the tribute was simpler: two red artificial poppies, which she had saved from the Service of Remembrance in Whitehall the previous November. It was too difficult for her to crouch down to put them on the graves herself, and so Eunice did it for her.

For several minutes, both women stood there looking down at those two names on the headstones, awash with memories of the short time they actually knew each other. 'Here we are then,' said Rosie. 'The Terrible Four are all together again.' It seemed an eternity that they stood there in silence, heads bowed, memories flowing, two old ladies arm in arm, their lovely summer dresses and cardigans turning a deep red in the gradually approaching sunset. The silence was finally broken by the distant wailing of a solitary bugle call sounding 'The Last Post', a nightly tribute from the local village, who never forgot to be grateful.

As they made their way back to the coach, Rosie couldn't help turning to look at an elderly woman who had been watching her from a distance all the time she and Eunice had been at the grave-sides. It worried Rosie immensely, because the woman's attention was so obviously directed at her, so she came to a halt, leaving Eunice to get back on to the coach, and stared back at the woman until she came across to talk to her.

''Allo, Rosie,' said the woman, in heavily accented English.

For one brief moment, Rosie was muddled and confused. 'I'm sorry...' she said.

'You don't remember me?' asked the woman. 'We met together in the dark one night, out there behind us, in the field just outside the village.'

'Oh my God!' gasped Rosie, who suddenly knew. 'Antoinette! Is it – is it *you* – Antoinette?'

The elderly woman chuckled. *'Oui, ma chère,'* she replied. *'C'est moi.* It's me.'

Shaking with emotion, Rosie opened her arms, and they embraced.

'A long time, dear lady,' said the woman who had once saved Rosie's life. 'A very long time.'

Rosie couldn't take her eyes off her. 'But – how did you know?' she spluttered. 'How did you know I'd be here?'

'It's no problem,' said Antoinette. 'My son works for the British Legion over here in Orlais. He checks the lists of visitors each day. I knew you were coming.'

'I simply can't believe it,' said Rosie breathlessly. She just couldn't take it in that the two of them could meet again like this after so many years. 'You look so – wonderful, so elegant.'

Antoinette chuckled. 'Not bad for an old lady of eighty-two, eh!' she replied. 'But what about you? The last I heard of you was soon after that terrible thing that happened to you on the railway station in London. Lady Braintree told me that you'd been so badly injured you would have to spend the rest of your life in a wheelchair. But just look at you! A spring lamb!'

Now it was Rosie's turn to laugh. 'I cheated the doctors!' she said. 'It was all to do with Joe. He made me do exercises, he made me get out of the wheelchair for a few minutes a day, he made me walk a few steps, he gave me massages on my back – oh, I can't tell you what else he did, Antoinette. He just wouldn't let me give up.'

Antoinette hardly dared ask the question: 'Joe?' she asked. '*Your* Joe? Is he still with us?'

Rosie shook her head, but without sorrow. 'No,' she replied. 'I lost him ten years ago. But, despite suffering from the effects of that wicked gas for all those years, he had a good, long life. Once my father allowed us to get married, Joe and I *both* had a wonderful life.'

458

'And your young brother you told me about? The one who had consumption?'

'Christian?' Again Rosie's face lit up. 'Oh, he had a good life too. He went on until he was fifty-one, still not a ripe old age, but, thanks to Joe – and eventually my mother and father – he had a good quality of life. He even got up and walked, walked a great deal, again thanks to Joe. The girls were quite taken with him.'

'And now?' asked Antoinette. 'What does the future hold for you?'

'The future!' Rosie tossed her head back and laughed. 'At my age?'

'There's always a future, Rosie,' Antoinette reminded her. 'No matter what age we are.'

'Rosie! We're just going!'

Both Rosie and Antoinette turned to see Eunice calling from the coach window.

'Coming!' Rosie called, before turning back to Antoinette. 'I'm afraid I have to go.'

'Go well, Rosie,' said Antoinette, leaning forward and giving her a gentle kiss on each cheek. 'It's been wonderful. Just a few moments in time – but wonderful!'

'Maybe we'll meet again one day?' asked Rosie, eagerly. 'Maybe you'll come to England, to London. I have a spare room. It would be so nice if you could–'

'Thank you, Rosie,' replied Antoinette, her English gradually becoming exhausted. 'We can never tell – can we?'

The last Rosie saw of her was from the coach window. As the vehicle joined the queue of other pilgrims' coaches leaving the cemetery, Rosie stared hard for as long as she could at that tall, elegant figure, in a long summer dress of black and white, and large cartwheel hat to match, waving her hand with such little movement, such little effort. But then, that's how Rosie remembered Antoinette, the partisan from so many years before, during that dark night in a field outside Orlais – unflustered, still and unyielding. That's what made her so special.

In the middle of a long queue of vehicles, the British Legion coach slowly moved on board the cross-Channel ferry to Folkestone. Together with all the other passengers, Rosie and Eunice took the lift up from the car deck to the lounges on the upper deck. Fortunately, a teenage boy and a girl with backpacks, who had grabbed the best seats by the window the moment they rushed on, immediately gave them up when Rosie and Eunice appeared. 'I love puttin' on an act at times like this,' whispered Eunice, after the youngsters had gone. 'Limp a bit, an' it does wonders!'

It wasn't long before the ship's engines started to roar and the vessel set sail. It also wasn't long before Eunice fell fast asleep. Retracing her steps along a journey of so many memories had proved very tiring for her. But not for Rosie. She had far too much to mull over, to share with Joe, as she always did, in her mind. 'I'm glad we did that, Joe,' she said, as she stared out at the ship's departure from Boulogne Harbour. 'Memories are all very well, but if you don't clear the shadows, you can never be sure that they're real.'

A short while later, the ship was gliding along

on waters so calm that it reminded Rosie of the Serpentine lake that day she and Joe strolled down at the water's edge, and the bird population were so snooty about not getting any titbits from them. It was very different when The Terrible Four first travelled on this same route across to France on their way up front. Rosie remembered the wind and the rain and the heavy swell, and she remembered standing on the deck with everyone being sick, whilst thick black smoke billowed back at them from the ship's funnel. But that wasn't all she thought about. She thought about the two sons and the daughter she and Joe had brought into the world, and the pride and joy they had felt at having an extended family of children that were now all grown up. She felt a surge of warmth flooding through her veins as she looked back at her long life, and remembered the man who had given her so many years of happiness. 'Well, we've done our bit, Joe,' she told him in her mind. 'We can't do any more now. Now it's up to the kids. All I hope is that they don't forget. It's too easy to do that, isn't it? Too easy to forget what we all had to go through. I mean, none of them would be around if it wasn't for the likes of you, and all those boys in the next war, of course. *And* us girls too, I hasten to add!' She chuckled to herself. 'But *I* won't forget, Joe. *I* won't forget what a wonderful life we had together, all the laughs – yes, and the tears too. It's all part of it, isn't it, Joe? I mean, it's just like what you and your mum said: "There's no use just giving up, 'cos if you do, there's nowt left."'

A few minutes later, Rosie, like Eunice, was

also fast asleep. She had a lot to dream about – her mum and dad and Christian, Antoinette, The Terrible Four, cups of tea on Platform 1 and especially that silly old poem of Joe's that he probably copied from a book, but which she would love to the end of her days:

Rosie Lee, Rosie Lee,
Oh, how I love you,
Saviour of life, weaver of dreams,
Oh, how I love you.

Dark of night, cold outside
War, bombs and danger.
But warm and tender is your touch,
A glow of light, a ray of hope,
Oh, Rosie Lee, how I love you.

The publishers hope that this book has given you enjoyable reading. Large Print Books are especially designed to be as easy to see and hold as possible. If you wish a complete list of our books please ask at your local library or write directly to:

Magna Large Print Books
Magna House, Long Preston,
Skipton, North Yorkshire.
BD23 4ND

This Large Print Book for the partially sighted, who cannot read normal print, is published under the auspices of

THE ULVERSCROFT FOUNDATION

LP FIC Pembe

Pemberton, V.
The other side of the track.

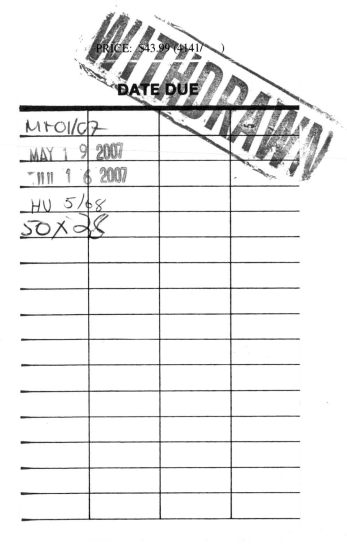

PRICE: $43.99 (4141/   )

DATE DUE

Mr01/07		
MAY 1 9 2007		
JUN 1 6 2007		
HU 5/08		
SOX 28		